PRAISE FOR
THE HOUSE OF SHATTERED WINGS

"*The House of Shattered Wings* exists in a rich, evocative Paris that is thick with magical history. Pathos and beauty intertwine in a novel filled with longing."

—Mary Robinette Kowal, multiple-Hugo-Award-winning author of the Glamourist Histories

"De Bodard aptly mixes moral conflicts and the desperate need to survive in a fantastical spy thriller that reads like a hybrid of le Carré and Milton, all tinged with the melancholy of golden ages lost." —*Publishers Weekly*

"Fantastic! De Bodard's tale of a post-everything Paris, struggling toward an uncertain future beneath the burden of its imperial sins, burns with vengeful magic and subtle, shining prose."

—Max Gladstone, author of the Craft Sequence

"There's an intelligence—and, yes, an elegance—to *The House of Shattered Wings* that is as rare and precious as angel essence. It's a wonder, in a word, and I for one want more." —Tor.com

"An intense, beautiful, brutal journey written with an eye for the stunning, vivid detail and the cruel demands of duty, loyalty, and leadership. Its portrait of a ruined Paris ruled by fallen angels is one I won't soon forget."

—Kate Elliott, author of *Court of Fives*

"A few times in a lifetime, a book comes along that wraps you completely in its world and its characters. . . . *The House of Shattered Wings* is one of those books, convincing, gripping, and filled with wonders."

—Kari Sperring, author of *The Grass King's Concubine*

ued . . .

D0830322

ALIETTE DE BODARD

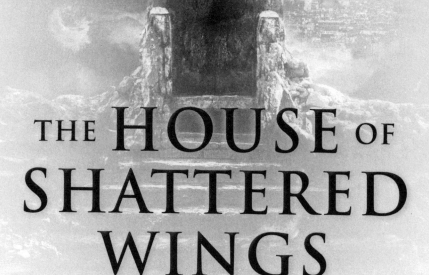

THE HOUSE OF SHATTERED WINGS

A DOMINION OF THE FALLEN NOVEL

A ROC BOOK

ROC

Published by New American Library,
an imprint of Penguin Random House LLC
375 Hudson Street, New York, New York 10014

This book is a publication of New American Library. Previously published in a Roc hardcover edition.

First Roc Trade Paperback Printing, August 2016

For more information about Penguin Random House, visit penguin.com.

ROC TRADE PAPERBACK ISBN 978-0-451-47764-4

THE LIBRARY OF CONGRESS HAS CATALOGED THE HARDCOVER EDITION OF THIS TITLE AS FOLLOWS:
Bodard, Aliette de
The house of shattered wings/Aliette de Bodard.
p. cm.
ISBN 978-0-451-47738-5 (hardcover)
1. Magic—Fiction. 2. Angels—Fiction. 3. Paris (France)—Fiction. I. Title.
PR6102.O33H68 2015
823'.92—dc23 2015013751

Printed in the United States of America
10 9 8 7 6 5 4 3 2 1

Designed by Spring Hoteling

Penguin
Random
House

To my son, the snakelet, for showing me magic and wonder

THE HOUSE OF SHATTERED WINGS

ONE
THE FALLING STAR

IT is almost pleasant, at first, to be Falling.

The harsh, unwavering light of the City recedes, leaving you in shadow, leaving only memories of relief, of a blessed coolness seizing your limbs. Nothing has turned yet into longing, into bitterness, into the cold that will never cease, not even in the heat of summer.

The wind, at first, is pleasant, too—softly whistling past you, so that you almost don't notice when its cold fingers tear at your wings. Feathers drift off, blinking like forgotten jewels, catching fire and burning like a thousand falling stars in the atmosphere. Some part of you knows you should be experiencing pain; that the flow of crimson blood, the lancing pain in your back, the fiery sensation that seems to have hold of your whole body—they're all yours, they're all irreversible and deadly. But you feel nothing: no exhilaration, no relief, not the searing agony of your wounds. Nothing but that sense of unnamed relief, that knowledge you won't have to face the judges in the City again.

Nothing, until the ground comes up to meet you, and you land in a jumble of pain and shattered bones; and the scream you didn't think you had in you scrapes your throat raw as you let it out—like the first, shocked breath of a baby newly born into a universe of suffering.

*   *   *

IT was Ninon who first saw her. Philippe had felt her presence first, but hadn't said anything. It wasn't a wish to protect the young Fallen so much as to protect himself—his status in the Red Mambas Gang was precarious as it was, and he had no desire to remind them how great a commodity he could become, given enough cruelty on their part. And Heaven knew, of course, that those days it didn't take much for cruelty or despair to get the better of them all, when life hung on a razor's edge, even for a former Immortal.

They'd been scavenging in the Grands Magasins—desperate and hungry, as Ninon had put it, because no one was foolish enough to go down there among the ruins of the Great Houses War, with spells that no one had had time to clean up primed and ready to explode in your face, with the ghosts and the hauntings and the odor of death that still hung like fog over the wrecks of counters and the faded posters for garments and perfumes from another, more innocent age.

No one, that is, but the gangs: the losers in the great hierarchy, the bottom-feeders surviving on the carrion the Houses left them. Gangs could be huge, could number dozens of people, but they were fractured and powerless, deprived of the magic that made the Houses the true movers of Paris. And as far as gangs went, the Red Mambas were small; twenty or so members under Bloody Jeanne's leadership; and Philippe, on the bottom tier of the bottom tiers, just doing his best to survive—as always.

He and Ninon had been under the dome of the Galeries Lafayette, crossing over the rubble in the center—what had once been the accessories department. On the walls were fragments of advertisement posters, colored scraps; bits and pieces of idealized human beings, of products that had long since ceased to be manufactured; and a fragment promising that the 1914 fashion season would be the headiest the city had ever seen: a season that, of course, had never been, swallowed up by the beginning of the war. Ahead were the stairs, blocked by debris; the faces of broken mannequins stared back at them, uncannily pale and expressionless, their eyes shining like cats' in the dim light.

Philippe hated the Grands Magasins—not that he was as superstitious as Ninon, but he could *feel* the pall of death hanging over the place, could almost hear the screams of the dying when the petrification spells had struck. Like any Immortal—even a diminished one, far from his home and his people—he could feel the *khi* currents, could sense their broken edges rubbing against him, as sharp as serrated knives.

"Ninon—"

Ahead, on the stairs, she'd turned back at him, her face flushed with the excitement of it all, that incomprehensible desire to flirt with danger until it killed you. A wholly human thing, of course; and he was meant to be human again, now that he had been cast out of the Heavens; but even as a mortal in Annam he'd just never had that kind of reckless death wish. "We should go—" he'd started, and then he'd felt it.

It was pure and incandescent, a wave of stillness that seemed to start somewhere in his belly and spread to his entire body—a split second when wind ran on his arms and face, and darkness stole across his field of vision, as if night had unexpectedly fallen in the world beyond the dome; and a raw sense of pain rose in him, a scream building in his lungs, on the verge of forcing its way out . . .

And then it was gone, leaving him wrung out, panting on the staircase as if he'd just run for his life across Paris. The pain was still at the back of his mind—a faint, watered-down memory that he would recognize anywhere—just as he would unerringly be able to find its source.

A Fallen. A young one, barely manifested in the world, lying in pain, somewhere close; somewhere *vulnerable* in a city where young Fallen were merchandise, creatures to be taken apart and killed before they became too powerful and did the taking apart and the killing.

"You okay?" Ninon asked. She was watching him, eyes narrowed. "Not going to go all mystical on me, are you?"

Philippe shook his head, struggling for breath—couldn't show weakness, couldn't show ignorance, not if he wanted to survive . . . At last he managed, in something like his usual flippant tones, "No way, sis. This is about the worst place in the world to get an attack of the mystical."

"Doesn't mean you idiots wouldn't get one," Ninon said, darkly. "Come on. Alex said there was good booty on the third floor, perfumes and alchemical reserves."

The last thing Philippe wanted to do was go upstairs, or hang around the place any longer than he had to. "And they've remained miraculously untouched for sixty years? Either Alex is misinformed or there's some pretty heavy defenses. . . ."

Ninon grinned with the abandon of youth. "That's why we have you, don't we? To make short work of anything."

"Sure," Philippe said. He could cast some spells; call on some small remnants of who he had been, drawing from the *khi* fields around him. He would, however, have to be seriously insane to do it here. But he daren't protest too much, or too loudly; he was, as Ninon had reminded him, only useful as long as he could provide magic—the conscious, mastered kind, one cut above the lures of angel essence and other adjuncts. When that ceased . . .

He forced himself not to think about it as he followed her upstairs—past landing after deserted landing, under the vacant eyes of models in burned posters, past the tarnished mirrors and the shards of chandeliers. As he had feared, the pain at the back of his mind grew steadily, a sign they were approaching the Fallen's birth site. Ninon herself wasn't a witch—the magical practitioners had long since been snapped up by the Houses—but for all that, she was uncannily, unerringly headed toward the newly manifested Fallen. "Ninon—" he said, as they rounded a ruined display promising exotic scents from Annam and the Far East, a memory of a home that was no longer his.

Too late.

She'd stopped, one hand going to her mouth. He couldn't tell what her expression was, from behind, if it was horror or fascination or something else. As Philippe got closer, he saw what she saw: a jumble of crimson-stained feathers, a tangled mass that seemed to be all broken limbs and bleeding wounds; and, over it all, a gentle sloshing radiance like sunlight seen through water, a light that promised the soft warmth of live coals, the comfort of wintertime meals heated on the stove, the sheer relief just after the breaking of a thunderstorm, when the air was cleansed of all heaviness.

Philippe recovered faster than Ninon. While she still stood, gaping at the vision, he cautiously approached, circling the body with care, just in case the Fallen turned out vicious. But Philippe didn't think it would.

Close up, the body was a mess: bones broken in several places, not always cleanly; the hands splayed out in abandon, loosely resting above dislocated wrists; the torso covered with blood and unidentifiable fluids. There was no smell, though; no stench of blood or ruptured guts; just a tang to the air, an acridity like a remnant of burning wood. Young Fallen never smelled like much of anything, not until the light vanished. Not until they joined the mortal plane like the rest of their kind.

The face . . . the face was intact, and that was almost the most gruesome thing about the Fallen. Eyes frozen in shock stared at him. The gaze was somehow ageless, that of a being that had endured beyond time, in a City that had nothing human or fragile about it. The cheekbones were high, and something in the cast of the face was . . . familiar, somehow. Philippe glanced back at the mess of the torso, noting the geometry of the chest: this particular Fallen manifested as female.

He hadn't expected to be so . . . detached about things. He'd thought of a thousand ways she could have reminded him of the Great War, of the bloodied bodies by his side; but in some indefinable way she seemed beyond it all, a splayed doll rather than a broken body—he shouldn't think that, he really shouldn't, but it was all too easy to remember that it was her kind that had torn him from his home in Annam and sent him to slaughter, that had gloried in each of the dead, that had laughed to see his unit come back short so many soldiers, covered in the blood of their comrades—her kind, that ruled over the ruins of the city. . . .

"Awesome," Ninon said. She knelt, her hands and arms bathed in the radiance, breathing in the light, the magic that hung coiled in the air around them. Fallen were magic: raw power descended to Earth, the younger the more powerful. "Come on, help me."

"Help . . . ?"

Ninon's hand flicked up; it came up with a serrated knife, the wickedly sharp blade catching the light.

"Can't carry her. Too much work, and there's only two of us. But we can take stuff."

Stuff. Flesh and bone and blood, all that carried the essence of a Fallen, all that could be inhaled, put into artifacts, used to pass on magic and the ability to cast spells to others. He put his hand in the blood, lifted it to his mouth. The air seemed to tremble around his fingers as if in a heat wave, and the blood down his throat was as sweet as honey, warming his entire body, reminding him how it had been when he'd been an Immortal; and a flick of his hands could have transported him from end to end of Indochina, turned peach trees into magical swords, turned bullets aside as easily as wisps of vapor.

But that time was past. Had been past for more than sixty years, turned to dust as surely and as enduringly as his mortal family.

Ninon's face was bathed in radiance as she knelt by the body—she was going for a hand or a limb, something that would have power, that would be worth something, enough to sustain them all . . . It— The thought of her sawing through flesh and bone and sinew shouldn't have made him sick, but it was one thing to hate Fallen, quite another to cold-bloodedly do *this*.

"We could take the blood," he said, forcing his voice to come back from the distant past. "Use the old perfume bottles to mix our own elixirs."

Ninon didn't look up, but he heard her snort. "Blood's piffle," she said, lifting a limp, torn hand and eyeing it speculatively. "You know it's not where the money is."

"Yes, but—"

"What's the matter? You feeling some kind of loyalty for your own kind?"

She didn't need to make the threat, didn't need to point out he was as good a source of magic as the Fallen by her side.

"Come on, help me," she said; and as she lifted the knife, her eyes aglow with greed, Philippe gave in and pulled his own from his jacket; and braced himself for the inevitable grinding of metal against bone, and for the Fallen's pain to paralyze his mind.

SELENE was coming home to Silverspires when she felt it. It was faint at first, a chord struck somewhere in the vastness of the city, but then she tasted pain like a sharp tang against her palate.

She raised a hand, surprised to find she'd bitten her tongue; probed at a tooth, trying to see if the feeling would vanish. But it didn't; rather, it grew in intensity, became a tingling in the soles of her feet, in her fingertips—a burning in her belly, a faint echo of what must have been unbearable.

"Stop," she said.

There were four of them in the car that night: two of her usual guards, Luc and Imadan, and Javier, the Jesuit, the latest of several incongruous additions to the House. He had volunteered when Selene's chauffeur fell ill. She'd found him in the great hall, stubbornly waiting for her, his olive skin standing out against the darkness of his clothes; and had simply gestured him into the car. They'd hardly spoken a word since, and Selene hadn't probed. Like the rest of the motley band that constituted the House, Javier would open in his own time; there was little sense in trying to nudge or break him open—God knew Selene had had enough experience, by now, of what it meant to break people. Morningstar had taught her well, from beginning to end.

"What is it?" Javier asked.

Selene raised a hand to silence him, seeking the origin of the magic. Young, and desperate; she'd almost forgotten how that tasted, how bittersweet it all was, that mixture of bewilderment and pain that came just after the Fall.

West, in the ruined blocks that had been the great department stores and the great hotels before the war, their names like a litany of what had been lost: the Printemps, the Galeries Lafayette, the Hôtel Scribe, the Grand Hôtel . . . West, where the House of Lazarus still stood. And if she could feel it, so could every other Fallen in the vicinity; and perhaps their pet mages, too, if they had the right artifacts or were pumped up on essence.

Needless to say, Selene did not approve of essence.

"We don't have much time," she said to Javier. "It's an infant Fallen, and it's in trouble."

Javier's face was pale, but set. "Tell me where."

"Right," Selene said. "Left at the next intersection."

The car moved smoothly under Javier's hands—though of course there was nothing smooth about it, and the battered and old metal carcass ran as much on magic as it did on expensive fuel.

Left, straight ahead, right, left. It was in her bones now, a dull vibration, a vague hint of something red-hot and searing, something that would overwhelm her, given half a chance.

Ahead was the dark mass of the Galeries Lafayette: the dome had miraculously survived the war and everything thrown at it, but the insouciant crowds that had once filled the shops at the beginning of the twentieth century, marveling at hats and brocade robes, sitting in droves in the tearoom and reading rooms, were all gone. It had been sixty years, and none but the insane would enter the Galeries now.

The insane, or the powerful.

"Park here," Selene said, pointing to a somewhat clear space among the rubble. She glanced at the shadows; there were people there, the lost and the Houseless, but they wouldn't move unless Selene showed weakness of some kind. Which wouldn't happen. She was old enough by now to know the rules of the city, and not foolish enough to leave her car unprotected. Anyone who attempted to open it after they were gone would get a nasty shock as a warning, and incineration if they persisted.

"Here?" Javier asked, slowing.

"Yes. Come on, there isn't much time." She could feel the pain and the fear, the way they were building up, faster and harder than they should have.

Which meant only one thing.

Someone was trying to hurt the Fallen. In her city, within her reach.

She didn't think. Without pausing to check if Javier was following, she strode under the dome and onto the vast stairs, vaguely feeling rubble shift and crumble under her feet. The pain and the need were within her, rising—a sharp, short stab followed by agony that would have doubled her over in pain, but her wards took the brunt of it, leaving only anger, only fear. . . .

Magic was building within her—drawn from the House, from the city and its river blackened by ashes, from the devastated countryside that surrounded them all beyond the wastelands at the foot of the city's surrounding walls, layer after layer of gossamer-thin spells, not as powerful as they had once been. But she was old and canny, and forged into a weapon by her master, Morningstar, and what she'd lost in power she more than amply made up in skill. The pain in her mind receded, to be replaced by white-hot anger; so that, by the time she reached the third floor and saw, among its shattered counters, the two people crouching in the unbearable radiance of a newly manifested Fallen, her thoughts were as clear and as sharp as glass blades.

"You will stop," she said in the silence.

They looked up, both of them: a girl no older than fifteen or sixteen, her face coated with grime, her malnourished frame making her seem even younger; and a boy of perhaps twenty, dark-skinned, narrow-eyed—an Annamite, by the looks of him—and then she saw the blood splayed on their hands and on their clothes; and the blades they'd been using to saw two fingers loose from the Fallen's shattered hand.

That was the fear she had felt—waking up, fuzzy and disorientated after the Fall, still struggling to adjust to a bewildering world; and finding only pain and the slow, excruciating sawing of a knife against her hand. . . .

"You will stop," Selene said again, coldly. "Now."

The girl laughed. Her lips were stained with blood and her high-pitched voice was all too familiar, the voice of someone drunk on strange and unaccustomed power. "Or what? You'll make me? I don't think you can. You're old and scarred and the magic doesn't sing to you anymore."

"Ninon—" the boy said—no, not a boy. Selene had been mistaken; he must have been older, twenty-five or thirty. He was breathing heavily, his pupils dilated; but apart from the blood, nothing about him indicated he'd consumed the flesh of the Fallen. Or perhaps he was merely more experienced. Either way, she was the real danger: the leader, the hothead.

Selene threw a thread of magic, intending to pick up the girl and fling her aside from the prone Fallen—but Ninon laughed, and the power buried itself among the shards of glass from perfume bottles.

"Told you," she said. "My turn."

What she sent snaking toward Selene was brutal, undiluted, with the potency of a wildfire, its heat as scorching as the naked sun—and somewhere in its heart was the pain and hurt and betrayal of being cast out from the City, as raw as open wounds. Selene had to take a step back while she wove and rewove furiously, knitting her wards so that the magic, instead of shattering them, was guided until it buried itself into the floors of the Galeries.

Fallen blood. Fallen magic. Stolen magic, hacked away in a rush of pain, the same pain that was now at the back of her mind like a coiled snake.

That upstart girl would never steal again.

The young man was tugging at Ninon's sleeve now, his face twisted in panic, though Selene could still hear his exhausted panting. "Please. You can't go up against her. Not for long. She's *House*, Ninon."

Ninon turned and threw him a withering glance, opening her mouth for some scathing retort. Selene didn't wait. She gathered all that she could, pulling in from the ghosts of the Grands Magasins, from Silverspires and the throne where Morningstar had once sat, from the mirrors and water basins where witches strove to re-create glimpses of the City—and sent it, not toward Ninon, but toward the floor. It left her hands, a barely distinguishable tremor, a pinpoint that became a raised line, and then a rift across the faded ceramic tiles that would tear the girl apart.

She had no pity. Not tonight, and certainly not for people who fought for the right to dismember Fallen as if they were cattle.

Too late, Ninon saw it. She turned away from the young man and, raising her hands, tried to absorb the magic as Selene had done. But she was untrained; and the light of the magic left her face, the little flesh and blood she'd consumed burning like wastepaper in a hearth—her face twisted as she realized that she didn't have power anymore, that she didn't have time to find more, that it was going to hit whatever she did. . . .

"Get out!" Ninon screamed to the young man, in the split second before the rift was upon her.

There was no time left. None at all, and the young man was still there by her side as the rift hit, and the light flared so brightly that even Selene had to avert her eyes. She braced herself for the impact, for the wet sound of bodies twisted past endurance, for the gouts of blood to join the Fallen's on the floor.

Instead . . .

It was like nothing she'd ever felt: a stillness, a quiet like the eye in a storm, a slow, delicate weaving that drew, not on the ghosts, not on the City, but on something else entirely. The rift stopped, inches from the young man, who stood with his hands open and sweat glistening on his face, his hair raised on his scalp. For a moment—a brief, sharp moment that etched itself indelibly in Selene's mind—he seemed to hold the weight of her spell in his hands, the whole of her fury and her anger—and then he opened his hands and it was gone, harmlessly snuffed out.

A witch, here? Why hadn't he—?

She had little time for introspection. Time seemed to resume its normal flow; the young man crumpled like a puppet with cut strings, lying bathed in the Fallen's radiance. The girl, Ninon, stood for a moment, looking at him, looking at Selene; and then she spun on her heels and ran.

Selene made no movement to stop her. Ninon was hardly worth the trouble, and in any case it was all she could do to stand.

"You're a fool," Javier said gruffly, coming up behind her.

"You felt it?"

Javier shook his head as he moved to survey the wreckage. "Credit me with a little perception. You can't draw on this much power and hope it'll suffice to end fights. You usually don't get a second chance of casting that kind of spell."

"With amateurs, it usually suffices," Selene said absentmindedly. She looked at the young man again. There was nothing special about him, no tremor of recognition racing up her arms. He was clearly no Fallen. But no witch—even high on angel essence, even with the most powerful artifacts of a House at her disposal—should have been able to do anything like this.

Her gaze moved, at last, to the Fallen. A young girl, black-haired, olive-skinned, sharp-featured, looking for all the world as if she'd just come from Marseilles or Montpellier. In the brief interval, her innate magic had had time to start healing the worst of her broken bones, though neither her wings nor the two fingers she'd lost would ever regrow. There were rules and boundaries set on the Fallen: the bitter cage of their existence on Earth that they all learned to live in.

"I heard from Madeleine," Javier said. "She's on her way with a couple helpers. Should be there in a couple minutes."

"Good," Selene said. "Go and prepare the car, will you?" She looked again at the young man, at the foreign features of his face. Annamites were a familiar sight in the city: they were citizens of France, after all, albeit, like all colonial subjects, second-rate ones. Emmanuelle, Selene's lover, manifested as African; but Emmanuelle was a Fallen who had never left Paris in her life. Whatever the young man was, he was not and had never been a Fallen.

"As you wish," Javier said. "I'll send you the helpers to pick her up."

Selene shook her head. "Not just her. We'll have two passengers this time, Javier."

She didn't know what the young man was, but she most definitely intended to find out.

TWO
ESSENCE OF LOSS

MADELEINE d'Aubin, alchemist of House Silverspires, had seen more than her share of prone bodies brought in at the dead of the night: she slept little these days, in any case, spending her nights in her laboratory, remembering the past and what it had cost her.

She arrived in one of the largest rooms of the admissions wing of Hôtel-Dieu, the House's hospital: row after row of metal beds, all unoccupied save two. Two doctors in white blouses hovered by the new arrivals' side, and her assistant, Oris, was waiting for her, leaning against the wall and trying to appear casual; though his face was sallow in the dim light.

She nodded at Oris and went to his side, pulling a chair so she could sit. Madeleine dropped her heavy shoulder bag onto the floor, and settled down to wait in silence.

The room was dusty and the air dry, and her wasted lungs wouldn't take it: a cough welled up. She desperately tried to quench the trickle that was going to become a cough, but it was never enough. The bout that followed racked her from head to toe—she was going to choke to death, never finding fresh, wholesome air again.

At last she sat back, wrung out, enjoying the sweetness of uninterrupted breath. One of the doctors—Aragon, surely—was looking straight at her with disapproval. Madeleine waved a hand, letting him know it was nothing. She'd lied about it; told him it was too much breathing the Paris air, of the areas around the blackened flow of the Seine—he'd seen so many combatants with the same problems that he'd been all too ready to believe her. She was not proud, but she was safe. The last thing that'd occur to him, prim and proper as he was, would be to question her; to realize how wasted her lungs were, and the true cause of such extensive and fast-progressing damage.

At length, the doctors peeled away from the beds, and one of them removed his mask. Madeleine found herself staring at Aragon's sharp features. The Fallen doctor looked, like Oris, on the verge of exhaustion, his skin pale and beaded with sweat, his graying hair slick against his temples.

"Shouldn't you be asleep?" Madeleine asked, after the brief pleasantries were over. Unlike her, Aragon was paid for his work, not a dependent of the House, or bound in Selene's service.

Aragon shook his head. His colleague had left the room already, no doubt heading for the comfort of his own bed. "For something like this? You know she wouldn't let me sleep." He shook his head, amused. "In any case"—he spread his hands—"I don't have much to say. Both healthy, neither carrying horrible contagious diseases or hair-trigger spells. You can collect your toll from them." There was something—some hint of anger in his poised demeanor?—some feeling she couldn't quite place. But she knew enough not to ask him; he would just shake his head with infuriating politeness and assure her that nothing was wrong.

"I see," Madeleine said. "Thank you."

Aragon made his way toward the door. He paused as he crossed the threshold, looking back at the bodies on the beds, as if he were about to say something more, but then shook his head and moved on.

Now it was just her and Oris. Madeleine glanced at the beds: a girl shining with the residual light of newborn Fallen, and . . .

"Who's the young man?" she asked. He didn't look Fallen, but why would Selene ask her to take care of a human? There was no entry toll for humans, or at least none that an alchemist could collect.

"I don't know," Oris said. "But Lady Selene was quite clear that you had to take care of both of them."

"We," Madeleine said, absentmindedly. "You're an alchemist as well, you know." She still held hopes that, one day, Oris was going to outgrow his maddening shyness. For God's sake, the boy was Fallen, with enough magic to start his own House if he had to, yet he crept through life as if he didn't quite belong anywhere.

She moved to the Fallen first. At least she was used to dealing with those, though it had been many, many years since she saw one so young, just hours from her first manifestation, with the scars of her Fall still visible: the ribs that were slowly knitting themselves back together, the limbs that didn't quite seem to be at the proper angles yet, the face with its high cheekbones and features that seemed to be subtly, slowly shifting even as she looked at it. Madeleine gently turned her over. The telltale signs were there: the large V-shaped scar spread across the back, where Aragon had cleanly cut off the mangled, irretrievable wings— the scar would fade a little in time, but never completely heal—the hint of ribs below the translucent skin; and the weight, much, much lighter than a human body of the same size, with fluted bones that would take much less effort to shatter.

By the Fallen's side was a small tray, in which someone had set out three vials of blood that shone with the characteristic rippling, soft light; and two severed fingers, obviously hacked away by someone who hadn't the time for finesse.

"Lady Selene wasn't the first on the scene," Oris said, apologetically. "I've taken the liberty of setting the blood aside; I don't know what you want done with the fingers."

The same thing they always did with any detached body parts. Madeleine sighed, but made no comment. "Will you see to the young man, please?"

She had no illusions; she'd be required to point out precisely what needed to be done to Oris in a moment or two, but at least it got him out of the way. Madeleine went back to her shoulder bag and withdrew her equipment: a handful of treated mirrors, a set of sterilized scalpels, a series of containers with primed preservation spells, and one last thing: a small black box, which, at a casual glance, seemed nothing more than a woman's private vanity, a container for some small item of jewelry like a ring or a brooch. This last she hid under the mirrors, after throwing a glance to make sure Oris wasn't looking at her.

Time to perform her role, then.

She went back to the Fallen's side and set the mirrors, one by one, by the nose and mouth, waiting until the breath had misted them over—and the glass seemed to shine with reflected light. She closed them after she was done, muttering a brief incantation to seal them, ensuring that the magic would remain trapped in them without decaying. Then she trimmed, one by one, the long, clawlike nails on the fine hands, and similarly collected the trimmings in a box which she sealed. Any stray hairs she also took, and dealt with in the same fashion.

Madeleine worked almost without thinking; she'd done it for so many years it had become routine. The younger the Fallen, the more potent their magic—the closer their link to the City they had Fallen from and the grace of God. And this Fallen was an infant, hours from her manifestation in the mortal world. House Silverspires, like all Houses, knew the value of preserving some of their earliest leavings. Not everything; that would have been tantamount to what the gangs did, taking Fallen bodies apart before they grew strong enough to retaliate—though there were also rumors of spells strong enough to negate Fallen magic, and places where they were kept in cages or in chains like sheep or dairy cows. Silverspires was not one of those places, thank God.

Madeleine reached for the fingers next, and for her scalpels. She carefully scraped the flesh free from the delicate bones underneath. So far, she'd done what was expected of her: preserve magic where it could be preserved.

And, as expected of her, she sealed the flesh in one of the containers set aside for this purpose.

That only left the bones.

Selene's instructions on this had been clear. Bones should be burned, nothing of them preserved. Bones could be used, with a little chemical expertise, to manufacture angel essence; and angel essence was forbidden in the House. Not because it was more refined and powerful than preserving Fallen's leavings; but because—as Madeleine knew all too well—it was highly addictive, and Selene wouldn't support junkies in Silverspires.

Bones should be burned. Always.

Madeleine's hands were shaking. She thought of the heady rush of power spreading from her lungs to her entire body, a sweet, sweet sensation that made her feel that she, too, was in the City, that she was the equal of a Fallen: what did it matter that the stuff was eating away at her lungs? She hadn't come to Silverspires for a long life.

Madeleine threw a glance at Oris. He was still busy cleaning the young man up for her inspection, and unlikely to look up from his task.

Good.

Casually, in one practiced movement, Madeleine removed one of the bones from the tray and slipped it in the small box. There was enough there to last her a few months, if she was careful, if the need didn't come on her too often. . . .

She said aloud, keeping her voice even, "I'll go and burn the bones in the incinerators."

Oris nodded. He trusted her. He shouldn't have, but he always did.

All the way to the incinerator and back, Madeleine kept expecting something to happen: some orderly jumping from one of the other deserted rooms, some nurse taking a break in the ruined cloisters, inquiring what she was doing. But nothing happened. There was only the silence of the night; and her own conscience.

Ah well. She'd never had much of one in the first place. Silverspires wasn't her refuge; it was the place where she would die, and she'd known as much since the night Morningstar carried her into the House.

If she was caught, though . . . Selene wasn't merciful. It'd be back on the streets of a city that had grown alien to her, with no easy means of sustenance—another kind of death by inches, far more unpleasant and painful than the one she'd chosen for herself.

But she wouldn't be caught. Not if she was careful, and she always was. Selene need never know what she did; Aragon would likely figure it out at some point, but she would deal with that then.

Good.

In the admissions room, Oris was fussing around the young man. He raised his gaze when she arrived. "Madeleine? May I use your mirrors?"

Madeleine nodded. She wished she could muster some anger at his lack of initiative, but she had none, too relieved he hadn't questioned her further. She turned back to her patient, and to the last thing that needed to be done.

She reached for the scalpels; and, carefully picking one out from the row of blades, made a small nick in the palm of the Fallen's left hand, where the heart line would have been. Blood leaked out, red and lazy, sinking into the beaten earth of Silverspires. She braced herself for saying the binding words; but before her mouth could curve around them, the young man sat bolt upright in bed, clutching at his own left hand. "No," he said. "Don't—I may not be bound to the earth of this land, of any land—"

Oris, in shock, had taken a step backward, leaving Madeleine to say aloud, "What do you mean?"

The young man's narrow eyes turned toward her, though it was clear he wasn't seeing anything in this world. "I know what you want to do, *alchemist*," he said, and there was a touch of malice in his voice. "Bound to the earth, bound to the House. Do you truly think you can have this one?"

"This one?" Madeleine said. "The young man, or the girl?" Either term, of course, was relative, since Fallen didn't really have gender; or much that was human about them.

But the young man had fallen back on the bed, unconscious.

"Don't move," Madeleine said to Oris. Someone had to keep a level head, and it would definitely not be her assistant.

She spoke the words of binding over the girl first, finishing what she had started. Blood and magic and earth, the oldest things, as the young man had said: a spell-oath to bind her to the House, to its welfare, though how had he known, and who was speaking through him? "By this, I bid you welcome into Silverspires; I give the House leave—"

She never got to the end. As she spoke each word, the resistance in the air grew, an expanding weight that pressed against her throat; and when she reached "leave" it was all she could do to force syllables between clenched teeth. There was . . . something vast, something infinitely larger than either of them—larger than the House, larger than the City—and it was somehow tied to those two, to either or both of them. She broke off then. "Oris, can you do the binding for me?"

She'd hoped that, since Oris was Fallen, he would have more power to draw on; but as he stumbled his way through the binding, he, too, met the same obstacle. She rose, and touched the young man's hands; they were wet and clammy to the touch, and his complexion was paler than it should have been, for all that he was Annamite. "You're doing this," she said aloud. "Aren't you?"

"Doing what?"

Madeleine whirled around, her heart hammering against her chest. Selene stood behind her.

The mistress of House Silverspires wore practical, no-nonsense clothing—even though the fashion she favored was that of fifty, sixty years ago, before the war, at the height of the Belle Epoque: a black swallow-tailed coat over black trousers, a white bow tie, and a simple sash of indigo crossing the white shirt. She had no hat, and her short, masculine bob of auburn hair shone in the light. Behind her was a crowd: Father Javier, the archivist, Raoul, Dr. Lesbros and two orderlies, and a dozen other people who worked in the kitchens and in the libraries and in the classrooms of the House: a sea of gazes unerringly trained on Madeleine.

Selene's gray eyes were mildly curious, but as always with her,

Madeleine was . . . awkward, gangly. Selene might not have been the oldest Fallen in the city, but her master, Morningstar, had been, before he had vanished; and as his favorite student she had picked up many of his mannerisms and sharpened them until it seemed nothing of Morningstar's occasional, amused mercy remained.

Madeleine swallowed, feeling embarrassed and ill at ease. "It's . . . not working well," she said.

SELENE received the new arrivals for a private audience, as had always been the custom of the House: alone in her office, with her bodyguards standing at attention outside the room. She received them both at the same time—not what custom dictated—because, as Madeleine d'Aubin's report had made clear, they would not be so easily parted.

The young man, Philippe, was stiff and prim. Madeleine's exam had confirmed he was no Fallen, that he bore no scars on his back, nor possessed any characteristics that could be of use. His breath, sealed in Madeleine's containers, had no magical properties; to all intents and purposes, he was what he appeared to be: a young man adrift in Paris joining a gang as his only way to survive.

His behavior, though, was nothing like a young man's; but spoke of customs and manners from another culture, from another age. "Lady Selene," he said. "I understand we both owe you our lives." His face was calm, expressionless, nothing of anger or of shame in it. What was he, truly? Like nothing she had ever seen or heard of—and there was potential in that. Morningstar might have considered him a threat, but she wasn't Morningstar; and, especially, she didn't have the magic he had used to effortlessly keep the House safe.

"You are here because I was curious. Don't mistake it for mercy on my part. I know exactly what you were doing." Blood and flesh and severed fingers; no better than the gang thugs in the streets, a handsome face covering the mind of a savage.

Philippe gazed back at her, quite unfazed. "So, if not mercy . . . what can I expect of you?"

A sharp eye on him, for a start. An education, if it was not too late to bring him back to decency; to unravel who and what he was, and how he had come to be in Paris. And ultimately, how he could be of use to the House, to guard it against its rivals and make it flourish in the lean, famished times after the war. "From this House? A chance to mend your ways, I should say."

Something was in his eyes: amusement, anger? He was oddly hard to read, closed off like no human or Fallen she'd ever met. "And why should I take up this offer?"

What pointless arrogance. "I think you misunderstand," Selene said, and let a fraction of power brush against him; a cold touch to remind him of who he was facing. "You don't have a choice. But if you did have one, I would point out that living in a House is much better than scavenging in the streets."

"Being fed and fattened while you seek to untangle my deepest secrets?"

"You could always save me time and tell me what you are," Selene said.

He shook his head. "As you said, your curiosity is all that's keeping me alive at the moment, and I'm not foolish enough to sate it."

She wanted to open him like a nut: here, in her House, at the center of her power, she could burst through his thoughts, drain every drop of blood from his body if she had to. Except, of course, that he was probably more than capable of defending himself against her. With difficulty, she controlled herself. What was it about the young man that made it so hard to keep her temper in check? "Have it your way, then. I'll certainly have mine in the end."

"Perhaps." Philippe's voice was shaking, and this time the anger was unmistakable. "So I am to be your prisoner?"

Selene had little use for his anger; and no pity for the riffraff of the streets. "For what you did—for the fingers you severed from her—the punishment would be death. You should count yourself lucky."

Philippe's lips quirked in what might have been amusement; but then his gaze turned to the young Fallen by his side; and much to Selene's surprise he said, gravely, "I'm sorry. I didn't intend things to turn out this way, but that doesn't excuse me."

It didn't, Selene wanted to say; but she wasn't the one with the grievance. The young Fallen gazed back at Philippe levelly, her hands in her lap, the left hand with its two missing fingers quite visible in the sunlight. She said nothing, until at length Philippe lowered his gaze, and fell silent.

Good. She might be innocent, but she was not altogether defenseless.

Selene said, a fraction calmer now, "I have set a spell on you that will prevent you from . . . wandering too far away from the House. I'd advise you not to tinker with it, or you'll regret it."

He looked as though he might laugh, then; and then shook his head, casting a glance in the Fallen's direction. "Security and a bed; and a golden cage. I guess it will have to do, for the moment."

She was no fool. Of course he would not submit, and would attempt to escape the moment her back was turned. But it was the best she could do. Her spell had taken long to set in: as with the binding to the House, it was as if something within him was resisting the very notion of magic. But with luck, she'd hold him long enough.

"Wait outside, will you?" she asked; and watched him leave, casual and at ease. One certainly wouldn't think he was the prisoner here, and she the jailer.

She turned to the young Fallen, who stood, watching her warily, and said, in a much kinder voice, "None of this applies to you."

"Then why am I here?" The young Fallen was quite recovered now, the unearthly light of her first hours gone. She appeared almost human, almost whole, except for the two fingers missing on her left hand. Her face in repose would never be called beautiful, but an innocence hung about her, a guilelessness that made Selene's heart ache. She had been like this once, but such things never lasted for long; not in Paris.

"Because you're one of us," Selene said; and before the Fallen could voice a question, she added, "What do you remember?"

The Fallen's face shifted then, became for a moment wreathed with soft light. "The City," she whispered, and looked up into Selene's eyes. "You remember, too."

It was not a question. "Not as much as I once did," Selene said. All she had were grainy, fuzzy images like old photographs; faces and voices that all seemed to merge together. "You have to be young to remember."

Young, and innocent, and brimming with raw power. She envied that child, in that moment; who did not yet know bitterness, or how much the abandonment of God lay heavy on one's shoulders.

What had her sin been, the one that had cast her out of the City? She'd wondered over the years—at what could be so grave that a God of forgiveness and love would condemn them all to this slow, agonizing path on Earth, with the wound of His absence lancing like salted knives—and known, in the darkness of her own room, that there would never be any answer.

"I Fell," the girl said. And, bringing both hands up to stare at them: "I don't remember why."

"We never do," Selene said, which wasn't quite true. Morningstar had remembered; but Morningstar had been the first to Fall, the ringleader of the revolt in Heaven. "You'll find out much of what you need to know over the coming months. We all do. You'll—" She took a deep breath. "You'll have to work out your own answers to what it means, to be Fallen. We have a priest here, Father Javier, if you think religion would help. And a library where you can find histories and books." Emmanuelle would be glad to take her in hand, to show her everything that she needed to see. "As for me . . . there are three things I can give you, if you will have them. The first is help to come into your powers. The second is the protection of this House. Paris, as you will have gathered, is a dangerous place to be."

The girl swallowed. "Madeleine told me . . . that I didn't have that protection."

"Not all of it," Selene said, mildly. If the binding had taken, any attempt to put her in danger would have sent alarms rippling through the House; would have been as loud as a clarion call to anyone bound to Silverspires; but it hadn't happened. Which meant they would need to keep an eye on her. "Be careful, will you? And we'll find out why."

At least, she dearly hoped so, because she'd lose patience with Philippe very soon; and she doubted anyone in the House, save perhaps Aragon, had the forbearance to deal with him.

"You said three things," the girl said, her large eyes on Selene's face. "What's the third one?"

Selene rose, feeling the weight of the earth against her bones: that odd, awful sensation that everything should have been lighter, easier on her. *"Angels but touch the earth,"* Morningstar had said, but his smile had been bitter as he said it—he who had felt the weight of age and loss more keenly than most, who had watched so many centuries pass by, patiently gathering his kin to him—as Paris grew from a small town to the bloated capital of an empire; and from this arrogant, conceited city to the devastated wreck huddled around the dark waters of the Seine. At least he'd disappeared before he could see how far the damage ran; how far the House he'd founded had tumbled.

Though, damn him, she still missed him: she'd wake up in the morning and remember that the House was hers, that he was not there to offer biting comments or advice; that he had walked out of the House twenty years ago and never come back. They'd searched for him, of course—turned the House upside down, gone into every nook and cranny, and never found anything, a body or a hint of where he might have gone—Selene didn't even know if he was still alive or not, or if he was truly lost, truly beyond any meeting she might have dreamed of.

"Fallen have no parents," Selene said, extending a hand toward the girl. "And no kin, beyond those that are willing to claim us. I will give you what my mentor once gave me: a name of your own."

Morningstar had liked old-fashioned names, drawn straight from the pages of some of the obscure books he'd favored: Selene, Nightfall, Oris, Aragon; even Emmanuelle had been called Indigo before she changed her name.

Selene chose something far simpler. "Isabelle," she said. "It was the name of a queen once. Wear it well."

"Isabelle." The young Fallen sat very still, repeating the name to herself as if testing it for suitability. Her gaze, for a moment, was disturbingly adult, as if Philippe had contaminated her. "It is a good name. Thank you."

Selene nodded. "You have the run of the House. Use it well."

She watched Isabelle leave the room. She heard voices outside, guessing that she'd be talking to Philippe. The link between those two concerned her; but if it was Isabelle's choice, what right did Selene have to interfere?

"She's strong, this one," Emmanuelle said behind her.

Selene turned, only half-surprised. Emmanuelle had thrown open the curtain that lay between her office and her private quarters, and stood wreathed in the light of the lamps. "You should rest," she said.

Emmanuelle walked into the room, and laid a hand on Selene's cheek, briefly, affectionately. "I've rested enough for a lifetime. Or several of them. Have you given thought to the young man?"

"He's no Fallen," Selene said.

"He said he was born abroad." Emmanuelle's face was thoughtful. "Who knows what this might mean? There were other creatures in Annam, and other rules of magic—before the French came over and brought the word of God to those benighted shores." Her voice was lightly ironic. Emmanuelle manifested as an African woman. Most people mistook her for a Senegalese, though they couldn't place her in a precise ethnic group.

"I don't know anything about Annam," Selene said. They had people there, of course; got the occasional shipment of silk and rubber, but she hadn't had any reason to focus her attention on the colonies. Travel after the war was slow, expensive—boats to Asia almost inexistent, and communications difficult and infrequent. Heavens, it had taken them ten years and an armed battalion to get back Calixta, and she'd only been stuck in London. Asia might have been another world entirely.

"Indochina," Emmanuelle said, distractedly. "Once called Viet Nam. Annam is just one of the five regions, but everyone calls them Annamites anyway. Not that most French can make a difference between an Annamite and a Cochinchinese. He might just be one of the witches trained by French schools, you know."

Witches, even Annamite ones, shouldn't have been able to stop her magic. Perhaps younger, more remote areas retained a vitality that old, bloated cities like Paris never could recapture. Selene sighed. Either way, she would find out more about Philippe and his magic; and how best to use him for the good of the House.

THREE
BURIED DARKNESS

IT was a hard spell to untangle.

Back in his rooms, Philippe had sought traces of what Selene had done to him. He found, without too much trouble—Fallen magic was never subtle or hidden, especially not House magic—the magic that Selene had woven.

It stretched around his neck, an invisible collar that trailed around his entire body before earthing itself into the floor of the House—a tangled labyrinth of ten thousand threads, each of which burned like living fire when he tried to touch them. When at long last he managed to get hold of one of them, heedless of the pain it caused him, it was only to discover that it went straight into the heart of the tangle, where he lost it.

He tried severing the threads closer to the ground, to burn them with the little fire in the House, to dry them out with metal. Each time, he felt the pain of his own spell reflected back at him; until, shaking, he had to stop and suck in burning breaths, waiting for the agony to pass him by; and the threads merely re-formed, seconds after he had burned them.

Demons take Selene, she was thorough, and powerful. But then again, what had he expected of a Fallen; of one of the ruling elite of the city?

He lay on the bed, shaking, and stared at the ceiling until the wooden carvings seemed to dissolve into blurry water. He might not escape this time. He was her prisoner until her goodwill ran out; her victim after that. She had made it clear she would kill him for what he'd done in the Galeries Lafayette. It was . . . frightening, a prospect for which he had no name; as if he were back in the regiment during the war, prodded and poked until he ran with the rest under mortar fire, under a hail of bullets, in the midst of spells that could drain the breath out of him.

He'd survived *that*; but it had been sheer luck, and nothing else. Heaven no longer looked upon him with favor, as he knew all too well. He was not Fallen, but he might as well be; exiled from the Imperial Court of Immortals, and unable to speak with his own kind; his kin long since dead, the only remnants of his blood descendants who worshipped at a distant altar.

He might not survive this. But did it matter? There was no way forward, no return to the Imperial Court. He was trapped in Paris, all the paths back to Annam closed to him—and now worse than this, trapped in a House as a prisoner.

Sometimes, on the edge of sleep, he would dream of when he had first ascended, and turned from mortal to Immortal. He was back in the cave where he had fasted, a thousand years ago—shivering with hunger, hanging on the knife's edge of unconsciousness as he meditated—and there was a sound like the bell toll of a pagoda resonating in his bones; and the shadow of cloud-encrusted buildings and of a vast courtyard, materializing a hand span away from him; and the Jade Emperor awaiting him on the throne, congratulating him for overcoming his banishment . . .

Such a wishful, childish dream. There was no truth in it, not a single gram. He was stuck in France, in Silverspires; and no amount of meditation would make the Imperial Court's power stretch to foreign shores.

The door opened. Philippe was on his feet, drawing on the few scattered hints of *khi* currents in the room, before he saw that it was Isabelle.

"Oh," he said. "Hello." After the interview with Selene, he'd walked away, back to the room he'd been assigned. The last thing he'd wanted was to talk to her—his brief apology was all he felt like extending to her. He fully intended to stay away from Selene's prize; and he didn't want to be reminded of what he'd done to her. But it was a small room, and there was only one exit, in front of which she stood.

She looked at him for a while, speculatively. Her brown eyes were still halfway translucent, the irises dilated and washed out, as if some of the light he'd seen resided still in her. "I thought I would find you here. We need to talk."

"I'm not sure we do."

Isabelle smiled. There was something primal and innocent about the look, something that seemed to set the whole room alight—but then again, she knew the power of that smile, and she was using it. Fallen all over, that curious mixture of naïveté and guile. She raised her hand; the one that was missing the two fingers, the ones he and Ninon had cut off. Demons take him, he wasn't one to shirk away from responsibilities.

"I owe you that: apology for inflicting that wound," Philippe said. "But nothing else. Can we leave it at that?" He sat on the bed; which wasn't much, but was the farthest he could get from her.

"Do you think I can? Breath and blood and bone"—she sounded as though she was quoting an old children's rhyme—"all linked in the same circle. Can't you feel it?" To Philippe's horror, she bent her hand toward the parquet floor in a graceful gesture, letting him see the two threads of luminous magic that started from the stumps of her fingers and stretched through the air, straight toward his face—no, straight toward his mouth, which was suddenly filled with the same sweet, electrifying taste of Fallen blood, a memory from his nightmares.

"I can't do more than apologize." Philippe swallowed, trying to banish the taste in his mouth. Never get tangled with Fallen—a lesson he'd learned, over and over. Why hadn't he listened to it? "I'll apologize again, if that's what you want to hear, but it won't change anything. . . ."

"Can't you feel it?" Isabelle asked, again; and suddenly she was no longer ageless or terrifying, but merely a young, scared girl.

"The—" Philippe swallowed, trying to banish the taste of blood from his mouth. "The link? Of course I can. I'm assuming it's not a usual thing." He meant to be flippant, and regretted it when he saw her face. "I'm sorry." It seemed all he could do to her was apologize.

Plenty of people drank Fallen blood without any side effects; but then again, plenty of people weren't former Immortals. Blood was the body's embodiment of *khi*, of the vital breath that saturated the universe—the source of long life and stability. He closed his eyes—could still feel her, a tenuous presence at the back of his mind, like a distant pain.

"I don't know what to do," Isabelle said.

"And you think I do?" Philippe shook his head, unsure of where the conversation was going. He doubted the link could be broken, and with Selene's spell on him he wasn't about to attempt experiments.

"You have more experience," she said, slowly.

"I'm no Fallen," Philippe said. "And not experienced in magic, either." He'd never made use of magic that wasn't his, or consumed the more refined magical drug of angel essence, save for that one moment of weakness—why did such a small thing always have such large consequences? But of course he understood about discipline, and how the smallest lapse could lead to the largest failures. "I can't tell you what to do."

"Selene says no one can," Isabelle said. She came into the room; and sat on the bed, by his side. He held himself rigid—trying to be polite; to not frighten her, even though everything within him screamed at him to move away as far as he could, as fast as he could. He couldn't help breathing in her smell—musty, like old books falling into dust—couldn't help feeling the raw magic in her, a temptation forever beckoning to him. No wonder mortals went mad over Fallen, one way or another; hungering for essence, for breath, or even for a simple touch. "But I'm not Selene. I need—"

"Advice?" Philippe said. It wasn't much, but he could give her that, at least. "Look, it's not a bad place, as Houses go." It was the House keeping him prisoner, but that wasn't her problem. "You have people to talk to, inside and outside it. I can't give you guidance or wisdom; I'm not qualified."

"What about company?"

Startled, he looked up at her; at the dark eyes that seemed to have no expression. "You're among your kind here."

"They're old," Isabelle said. Her hands, he saw suddenly, were shaking; the threads between them contracting and expanding on a rhythm that seemed to echo a heartbeat. "They talk about things they barely remember. I can't—"

"Neither can I," Philippe said, more gently this time.

"No, but you can help me. Can't you?" There *was* something in her eyes, a reflection of the fear and emptiness the City had left behind. What would it be like, to remember snatches of what you'd lost; to know that you were in the mortal world, away from the communion of angels or whatever else had fulfilled her in Heaven?

Not far from how he'd felt, when he was first cast out of the company of Immortals: the bleak despair that had sent him roaming from end to end of Indochina; the black veil descending over the forests and the rivers, turning the chatter of town markets into small, petty tripe, and the beauty of mountain retreats into aimless desolation.

There was a gulf between them—in age, in nature, in magic. But . . .

They were not so different, after all—isolated and new to the House, trying to learn its rules fast enough to survive—and linked, by blood and magic—thrown into similar circumstances. No wonder she would see a kindred spirit in him, no matter how incongruous the thought was.

"You heard Selene. I'm not House; and I shouldn't be here. I won't stay," he said.

"I know," Isabelle said. "But while you're here . . ."

"You realize what you're asking?" Philippe asked. "I cut your fingers. I tasted your blood."

Her face was turned toward his, her need bare—for the familiar; for anything that wasn't the House and its ageless, unwelcoming rituals. "Yes," she said. "You did. I haven't forgotten that. But—because of it— you'll understand."

He raised his hand: the invisible collar Selene had woven around him rested like a yoke on his shoulders; tying him to the House, to its unbearably arrogant mistress and her will. "Fine. I'll help you. Inasmuch as I can."

And when she smiled, the entire room seemed to become bright with the same soft, low-key glow she'd had in the Grands Magasins— when she was young and barely manifested; before everything had changed.

THE House creeped Philippe out.

It was a big, sprawling place—not a single edifice, as he had assumed, but a series of buildings joined by a maze of corridors and courtyards, stretching across the entire Ile de la Cité. Most of it was derelict: the western part of the island seemed to be entirely deserted, with not even the lowest in Silverspires' hierarchy daring to venture there, though it was not so much fear as a disinclination to go into empty rooms where every piece of furniture was covered in soot or dust or both.

His first communal dinner had been a nightmare. He had sat at one of numerous trestle tables in the great hall, surrounded by what seemed to be the entire House: hundreds of people pressed together in a suffocating mass—turning, from time to time, to stare at him, the only Viet in the room, and then turning back to their discussion of subjects and House concerns that seemed utterly alien to him.

He had fled then, back to the safety of his room, and begged until Emmanuelle agreed to let him dine alone. But even that didn't make him feel better.

It had been weeks since that first dinner; and he hadn't stayed that long in a House since the fall of House Draken—in fact, he'd rather have swum in a river at monsoon time than go anywhere near the fastnesses of the Fallen. And to do so while under a spell of imprisonment . . .

His only comfort was Isabelle. He never thought he'd say that of a Fallen, but she was fresh and young and naive—pulling warm bread from the oven and tearing into it with relish, while the cook, Laure, frowned affectionately at her—skipping stones in the courtyard with the children—and keeping a stash of biscuits and tea in the drawer of her room, which she shared with him around a card or a dice game—she was a terrible gambler, but then, so was he, so it all balanced out.

Those were the bright spots—the few, desperately few. In between, there was the House.

Philippe had a continuous feeling of ants crawling on his skin; an itch that never went away, that woke him up at night; an elusive, ghostly pain somewhere near his heart and liver, as if his organs had been subtly changed while he'd been unconscious. Perhaps it was the House; perhaps it was the spell; but he couldn't seem to be rid of either, much to his annoyance. He'd been on a French leash sixty years before, in the war: taken from his home in Thu Dau Mot and conveyed to foreign shores under duress; abandoned in Paris to fend for himself when, against all odds, he'd survived the war. Never again, he'd sworn, but fate made fools of all men, it seemed.

Isabelle found him in Laure's kitchens, kneading dough. Laure, who had little time for anyone, had taken pity on him and allowed him a table corner—there was something infinitely relaxing about feeling the dough coming together between his fingers; the stretching and turning and pulling until it all came together smooth and silky, effortlessly detaching from his fingers. When he was done, Laure would find something else for him to do: chopping up meat or vegetables or keeping an eye on soup stock. He wasn't sure she ever served what he'd touched—though she did present him with his baked loaf of bread every morning—but it was a way to pass time.

"Still here?" Isabelle asked.

Philippe shrugged. "As good a place as any."

Isabelle slid in next to him, dislodging a kitchen boy—who smiled at her, though she didn't acknowledge him. "Want help?"

He held out the dough to her. She took it in both hands, and started kneading in turn. "No, not like this. Here." He moved, placed her hands, showed her how to do one stretch and one fold. "You turn, and then you do it again."

Isabelle frowned. Her hands moved, slowly, carefully.

"Feeling it take shape yet?"

"No. I feel dough sticking to everything. You make it sound much simpler than it is."

"Of course." He'd learned back in Annam, baking rice cakes he'd later steam in bamboo baskets—the dough, made with a mix of wheat flour and rice flour, had been sticky and translucent—but the kneading was the same. "Try again. You did volunteer."

Isabelle smiled, but didn't speak. For a while there was nothing but her hands, folding and stretching and turning, again and again. Philippe watched the dough. "Almost," he said. "See how it's coming loose?"

"Mmm," Isabelle said. "Emmanuelle's been teaching me more about the history of the House. It's the oldest one in Paris."

And they'd never let her forget it. "You're done," Philippe said, taking the dough from her.

"How do I know?"

He took a piece of dough the size of a ball; stretched it, gently, until they could both see daylight through it. "It holds," he said. He divided it in half and carefully shaped his half into a round, laying it in the floured basket by his side. "Try it." And, to answer her, "The oldest House. That's good. Old is safe."

Isabelle shivered. "You don't really believe that, do you?"

Philippe shrugged. "It's . . . not my world."

"No." Isabelle paused, gently prodded at her piece of dough—which refused to tighten up into a ball. "I don't even know what it's like, where you come from."

He started to say, "Different," another platitude, and then changed his mind. "It functions on different rules. We . . . don't have Fallen in Annam. Didn't used to."

"But they're there now."

"They were," Philippe said. Who knew what was happening in Annam and the other colonies, after the war? Had the Fallen's arrogant, brash magic finally faltered? Had the Jade Emperor finally decided to end the court's isolation and interfere in the affairs of mortals once more? "And the Fallen carried their magic with them. It's . . ." He paused then, wondering how much he would reveal to her. No more, he guessed, than what Selene would find in books. "The Fallen were powerful," he said at last. "More powerful than any magical beings we might have had. It was . . . not pretty." The guardian spirits of the villages had been slaughtered; the dragons, the spirits of the rain, had withdrawn to the depths of the sea, to the safety of their coral and nacre palaces; the mountain spirits had retreated to their most isolated peaks, licking their wounds; and the Jade Emperor had sealed the court, forbidding Immortals to approach mortals.

And Philippe, of course, had had no refuge.

"Emmanuelle said it was because Fallen magic was innately stronger. That it had been our destiny to conquer." Isabelle shrugged. "She didn't sound convinced."

She might not be, but there were plenty of others who would. Philippe said nothing. He stared at the dough, trying to ignore the memories; the powerlessness he'd felt then, watching the Fallen come and take anything they wanted—and destroy what was of no use to them. "I didn't come here by choice," he said at last. "And it's not choice that keeps me here, either. I don't know how much you'll believe of what they teach you. But—if you can, remember that."

Isabelle looked at him, uncannily serious for once. "I didn't come here by choice, either," she said, dropping her piece of dough into another basket. "And I'll try to remember."

She meant it—he could tell from the sense of stubbornness he got from their link—and yet she probably wouldn't remember. He was guessing that even Selene had started out this young, this earnest, this naive—and look at what she was now.

"Philippe?"

"Yes?" He peered at the dough, drew a cloth over both baskets. It was the kitchen's slack hour. The kitchen boys and girls had scattered, some of them playing cards in a corner, some of them listening to Laure telling a fairy tale about a Fallen who was unable to pay the price for summoning a manticore—the kitchen staff was rapt, listening to Laure's elaborate descriptions of blood, gore, and disembowelment as if their lives hung on it. Isabelle and he were alone around the large table, surrounded only by the preparations for this night's dinner.

"You're not mortal, are you?"

He'd had some inkling she was going to ask an awkward question—it was the only reason he didn't drop the cloth. His first instinct was to lie, to deny as he'd denied Selene. She was Fallen; he couldn't trust her.

But then again . . . he felt her presence at the back of his mind; her curiosity, tinged by no afterthought of greed or thirst for knowledge she could use against him.

Such a child, and the thought was like a fist of ice closing around his heart. "I was mortal once," he said, exhaling. Now he was . . . not Immortal anymore, and not mortal, either; he hadn't aged since being thrown out of the Jade Emperor's court—some remnant of what he'd achieved still clinging to him, as did the magic he'd mastered. It probably didn't make any difference. Selene knew, or suspected, that he was no young man. "Before I ascended."

"There are others like you?"

"In Paris?" There were other former Immortals in Annam—it wasn't as though the Jade Emperor had been particularly tolerant or compassionate. "I'm not sure, but I don't think so." During the war, he'd caught glimpses of other creatures from French books, sphinxes and golems and chimeras—made with magic, his sergeant had said, curtly and in a tone of voice that discouraged further questions—and he'd fought colonials who weren't Fallen or witches, and yet moved a little too fast, a little too smoothly out of the path of danger.

There *were* others; from other countries, other magics that weren't Fallen. But he would have known, or suspected, had he crossed another former Immortal from Annam—it was something in the way they moved, in the way they held themselves, the imprint of the Jade Emperor's Court that persisted long after they'd been cast out. "You don't have to worry about an invasion of us, if that's the question."

Isabelle snorted. "Very funny." She pushed the baskets aside. "We're done, aren't we?"

"I guess?" They both had lessons with Emmanuelle—and not Choérine and the children, because they were too old. But their next lesson wasn't for a few hours yet. "You can come back later and ask Laure about the ovens, if you want the bread."

Isabelle shrugged. "Maybe. Let's explore the House."

"I—" The last thing he wanted was to get more of this feeling of ants on his skin. "I'm not sure that's a good idea."

"Are you frightened?" Isabelle's smile was mischievous, irresistible. "Come on."

And he followed, because he'd promised.

The House was huge, and most of it was deserted, or ruined. Like most buildings in Paris, it was covered with soot, the blackened streaks characteristic of spell residue. Once, it must have sheltered thousands—a natural refuge, an island only connected to the rest of the city by seven bridges, but now it lay empty and dark, and the river that had once been its first line of defense had turned wild, become a power that snapped and killed anything that came near its shores.

"Come on," Isabelle said, pushing a small stone door in an unremarkable corridor; and Philippe, with a sigh, followed.

To stop, awestruck, at what lay inside.

It had been a church, once. You could still see the columns and the beginning of the vaulted ceiling, a first row of arches gracefully bending toward one another; and the remnants of wooden benches, burned where they had stood. The stained-glass windows were broken, or absent; but the gaze was still drawn, unerringly, down the nave and to the altar at the other end—or where the altar would have been, if it hadn't been turned to rubble long ago, and the only things remaining were the wrecks of three statues—the central one was least damaged, and had probably been a Virgin Mary carrying the corpse of Jesus.

No, not a church. A cathedral, like the pink-hued edifice the French had built in Saigon. It was . . . like a knife blade slowly drawn across his heart: he could almost have been back home, except that it was the wrong architecture, the wrong atmosphere, the wrong setting. He could still feel the fervor of its builders, of its worshippers, swirling in the air: a bare shadow of what it had once been, but so potent, so strong, so *huge*.

"Notre-Dame," Philippe whispered.

Isabelle hadn't moved; her eyes were on the sky, and on the smattering of stars visible against the dark background of the night. "It's . . . like the City," she whispered. "So much . . . intensity."

"Faith," Philippe said, though her faith wasn't his, and would never be his. "That's what built this up."

The *khi* elements there were quiescent—almost too weak for him to pick them out, though. . . .

There was—a flash of something familiar: the magical equivalent of the smell of jasmine rice, a touch of something on the nape of his neck that brought him, instantly, back to the banks of the Red River, staring at the swollen mass of the river at monsoon time—breathing in the wet smell of rain and churned mud. Had some other Annamite been there?

No, it was impossible. Merely nostalgia—he was going mad, cooped up inside this House, inside this city, that was all. He needed a way out, before he lost himself.

Isabelle slowly moved, picking her way through the ruins of the benches. Throughout, her gaze remained staring upward. Was she praying; did she even remember how to pray—or perhaps it was like breathing, something that took hold of you when you had no other choice, when you were lost and cut off from your god?

She stopped long before the altar, in the raised space before it, which, like the rest, was covered in debris: the black-and-white lozenge tiles riven from end to end until their pattern had altogether gone. There was a chair left there; a stone one, battered and cracked, that nevertheless exuded a quiet power, something different from the remnants of fervor Philippe could taste in the air.

"He sat there," Isabelle said, in the silence, her voice echoing under the broken vault. "Morningstar."

"Emmanuelle told you this?"

"I don't need to be told. Can't you feel it?"

And he could; there was no point denying it. Not when the urge to abase himself was so strong he barely dared to move; afraid that anything he did would be the beginning of a bow.

"The oldest of us," Isabelle said. Hesitantly she reached out, touched the chair with her three-fingered hand; and withdrew as if burned. "He must have known . . ."

"The answers to your questions?" Philippe shook his head. "He would have been wise, yes, versed in everything. But if he had no memories of before his Fall . . ."

"You're not Fallen," Isabelle said, turning back to him. "How come you know all this?"

"I've traveled. And kept my ears open." He crept closer to the chair. It was like approaching an ancestral altar, the air thick with reverence and the coiled, deep power of old age; and the itching, of course, getting worse and worse, as if the ants had suddenly decided to become stinging wasps. "Oldest and most powerful among you, wasn't he?"

"When he was there," Isabelle said. "Now he's dead, for all they know."

Or merely gone; how to tell, without a body, without any messages? Not that it mattered much to him. Morningstar probably wouldn't have much to say to him—though it was hard to ignore the voice in his mind that whispered that age should be respected, that the oldest Fallen in existence had to be wise, had to be knowledgeable, as his grandparents had once been—in a time so far away that even the bamboo bindings of its books had rotted through.

There was something . . . He paused before the throne, though every instinct he had was telling him to step back, to let the magic cool down to levels he could bear. But within the pinpricks of pain, there was . . . a note that shouldn't have been there, a wrong tone in a poem, a slip of the paintbrush in a painstakingly calligraphied text.

"Philippe?"

He shook his head. "Not now, Isabelle." The wrongness was coming from the throne, but not close to him. His fingers, fumbling, lingered along the delicate carvings, descended to the chair itself, the place Morningstar had been (and the power on his skin was worse, like a winter wind, like a crucible where swords were born)—probed into niches and hollows, but it wasn't that, either. Where—?

It was below the throne, in the slight hollow between the four squat feet that carried it—once glued to it, but now it came easily undone under his touch. It was all wrong, anger and bitterness emanating from it like the howls of the souls in the Hell of Hunger.

"It hurts." Isabelle's voice was a thin thread of sound.

"It's meant to hurt," Philippe said, recovering his voice from where it seemed to have fled. In his hand, it looked like a heavy object wrapped in paper; carefully, he spread the paper flat on the ground, tipping out its contents. The paper was thin parchment, translucent and covered with spiky black handwriting; and the same feeling of darkness, of hatred, arose from it. The language wasn't French, or Viet, or anything he could read.

"All you hold dear will be shattered; all that you built will fall into dust; all that you gathered will be borne away by the storm. . . ." Isabelle's voice was a whisper, but there was an echo, deep within: a hint of someone else speaking the words and imbuing them with the weight of cold iron.

"You understand it? How?"

"I don't know," Isabelle said, carefully. She laid her hand on the paper, following the curve of the words on the page. "I think it's a Fallen thing. The language of the City, maybe . . ."

"I thought that was meant to be love," Philippe said, attempting to summon some remnant of sarcasm, though it was hard, with the cloud of anger and hatred hanging thick around them.

"The love that drowned the Earth underwater and caused Noah to build the ark?" Isabelle asked, her voice flat. "That sent us tumbling down to Earth?"

"I don't have answers," Philippe said dryly. "A priest would probably tell you about atonement and forgiveness, but that's your religion, not mine." Not quite true: the Buddha also preached forgiveness, but Philippe couldn't forgive. Not those who had torn him from Annam.

"I don't even know what your religion is," Isabelle pointed out, carefully folding the paper. Philippe searched her face, but there was no hint of reproach or sarcasm, merely a statement of fact. Her calm was uncanny: how could she not feel the magic roiling in the air, the pressure against their lungs, the irrepressible urge to pick a weapon and—? No. He was stronger than that.

"What was inside?" Isabelle asked.

It was a black stone disk, polished until he could see his distorted reflection in it; and it shimmered with the same power that was all around them. "Angel breath," he said. "Trapped in a stone mirror." And before he could think, he had reached out and touched the cold, shining surface—Isabelle cried out a warning, and then everything went dark.

He was in the House, but not in its ruins. Rich paintings and tapestries hung in the corridors, and the cathedral was whole, the graceful Gothic ribs arching into the vault; majestic and overwhelming, as it had always meant to be. Someone sat in the throne: a Fallen with pale blond hair that seemed to catch all the light streaming through the stained-glass windows. Unlike all the Fallen Philippe had seen before, this one had wings—not his real ones, but a metal armature that supported sharp, golden feathers, spreading out behind him like a headdress. Across his lap was a double-handed sword, his hand loosely wrapped around its handle; the sense of coiled power was almost unbearable, a pressure to abase himself, to bow down to age and power. . . .

Morningstar. Lucifer. The Light Bringer, the Shining One, the First Fallen.

By his side were other Fallen, other humans. He caught a glimpse of Lady Selene, though her face was smoother, more childish than the one she'd shown to him. Younger, he thought; but the words seemed very far away, moving as if through tar through his mind. And other, younger faces: Emmanuelle the archivist; Aragon—who alone of everyone appeared unchanged, prim and unsmiling—two human warlocks holding breath-charged mirrors and watches; and a stern older woman wearing the mortar-and-pestle insignia of the alchemists, whose bag bulged with bottles of elixirs and boxes of charged artifacts.

And then Morningstar's gaze, which had been trained on one of the stained-glass windows, turned; and fell on him.

The pale eyes transfixed him like a thrown spear—it wasn't so much the power contained within, as the rising interest; the slow focusing of a monstrous magic exclusively on him; on who he was; on who he could become, given enough time in which to utterly reshape him; and who wouldn't want to be reshaped by Morningstar, to be forged into one of his beloved weapons?

"Come here," Morningstar said; and, like a puppet propelled by his maker, he walked up the stairs and stood in the shadow of the throne, shivering as the gaze unraveled him, picked apart his body until not even the bones remained. . . .

"Philippe!"

He was back in the ruined cathedral, and Isabelle was shaking him. His hand had left the mirror; hung, limp, bloodless, by his side.

"Philippe!"

He breathed in air—burning, painful air, but he had never been so glad for the irritation of the House on his skin. Everything seemed lighter, limned in starlight; and the oppressive anger and hatred seemed to have gone, as if the night wind had blown it away. What—what happened?

"Philippe?" Isabelle asked.

"I'm fine," he said, the lie small and unconvincing to him. He could still feel the weight of Morningstar's gaze; could still feel the magic turning, slowly focusing on him: the gaze of a gigantic cobra, annihilating his will, turning his own desires into dust.

And something else, too, something darker, quieter—that had lain biding its time away from the light, and that now stretched and turned, sniffing the air like a predator searching for prey . . .

A summoning. Of what?

"I don't know what happened. But it's gone now. There is nothing to worry about."

His gaze, roaming, found the stone mirror: the luster had gone from it, leaving only a bleak darkness. "It's gone now," he repeated; but he knew that, whatever had been contained within the mirror, it was within him now; and that whatever had been summoned with its magic was outside—within the House.

IT was late at night, and Madeleine couldn't sleep.

By no means unusual. Nights like these, with the lambent starlight hanging over the House, brought back memories—of how she'd first come to it; of Elphon's death, and his shimmering blood on her hands as she crawled away from the House of Hawthorn; as she prayed so very hard to a God she no longer believed benevolent to spare her, to let her go just a bit farther, to reach safety before Asmodeus's thugs found her.

On nights like these she took angel essence; breathed it in, and let the rush of power sweep everything from her mind; let herself believe that she was safe, that nothing like Asmodeus's coup would ever take place in Silverspires; that even if it did, she would have the power to protect herself, to protect Oris. That what had happened in Hawthorn would never happen to her again.

It was a good lie, while it lasted.

An insistent knocking at the door of her laboratory drew her from her trance. Slowly, carefully, she rose, fighting a feeling of weightlessness that promised she only had to wish to take flight; the rush of power slowly settling into her limbs. In that moment, she was the equal of any Fallen, had she wished to cast spells—but of course that wasn't why she took angel essence. It never had been.

"What is it?"

She'd expected many things, chief among them either Selene or Isabelle; but the one on her doorstep, his face pale with fear, was her assistant, Oris.

"What are you doing here?"

"There's . . . there's something in the House," Oris said. "It's after me."

"Don't be ridiculous," Madeleine said, but then she took a closer look at him. His hands were shaking; and if she focused the magic within her she could see through his skin, could feel the panicked rhythm of his heart. Whatever he'd seen had badly frightened him. "Fine. Calm down. Tell me about it."

"It's . . . I don't know. It's dark and angry and if I turn my head to look at it, it's gone. But it's following me. It's . . ." He stopped then. "You think I'm lying." His voice was flat.

"No," Madeleine said. "But Silverspires has strong protections, so unless someone within the House is working magic on you, I can't see why . . ."

Oris drew himself to his full height. "I don't have enemies in the House."

"I didn't think you had." And even if that had been the case, personal vendettas were outlawed by order of Selene. "Where did you see it?"

"First? In my rooms," Oris said. "But it has been moving around—"

"Then let's start with your rooms," Madeleine said, gently.

The House at night was different; expectant, as if poised on the edge of something that Madeleine could not name. It wasn't the first time she'd been out at night—a few weeks ago she'd gone to Hôtel-Dieu to examine Philippe and Isabelle—but surely things had been different?

Or perhaps she was just overreacting. Oris was frightened, yes, but that didn't mean his fear was of something real.

His room was on the side of a cloister courtyard, in an architectural complex that must have dated back to the Middle Ages. The ceiling of the room was low and skewed, and wooden beams crossed the white-washed walls—each of the two floors was actually larger than the previous one, creating an unnerving impression, from outside, that the entire building was going to collapse. Climbing the narrow stairs, Madeleine gazed left and right; but even with the essence in her, she couldn't see or feel anything out of place. A few wards were set, here and there, and they were a little singed, but that happened, especially so close to the Seine and its magical outbursts.

Inside, the room seemed almost claustrophobic, overrun with bookshelves. On a low table was a book held open by means of another, heavier one; and a small book stand that held a sheet of paper covered with a spiky handwriting: presumably what Oris had been working on. The bedsheets were rumpled, and a simple icon of the Virgin Mary lay on the bedside table.

"Still at your research?" Madeleine asked.

Oris forced a smile. "Of course. I found a rather interesting passage, which argued that the proper translation of 'adelphos' was 'brothers,' not 'cousins.'. . ." Bible studies were Oris's hobby: he begged Father Javier for lessons, and had borrowed an astonishing number of religious books from the library. Together with Emmanuelle, he was one of the few Fallen in the House who was quite confident in his faith. "We're not here to talk about books, Madeleine—"

Madeleine nodded, keeping a wary eye on the room. "I know. But I see nothing." The room was bathed in gentle magic residue, the inevitable traces of a Fallen; and only in a few places could she feel the tug of a deeper, sharper fear. "I can't see anything," she said.

"It was here." Oris pointed to the book stand. "I was working on a translation, and all of a sudden it went dark, and—" He swallowed, and fell silent.

Madeleine moved, touched the paper on the book stand. It was warm, but there was nothing wrong with it, other than that the paper seemed curiously brittle.

She withdrew and focused her essence-fueled magic on the paper, willing it to show what it had shown Oris—what had fed the fear she could feel traces of in the room. Nothing changed, or moved.

"I don't think—" she said; and then the surface of the paper went dark—as if something huge and black had passed in front of it, spreading its wings as it moved—a moment only, and then it was gone, but she could imagine what it would have been like, to be staring at printed paper only to see *that* show up.

"That was it," Oris said. "But it was everywhere. Every time I turned my head, it was a shadow in the corridors; every time I looked at something, it would seem to lie across it. I've never seen anything like it."

Madeleine sent a small, fading burst of magic into the paper; watched the darkness cross its surface, once again. Definitely something large, and she wasn't quite sure where the suggestion of wings came from, but it was . . . unpleasant. Stomach-clenchingly frightening—a hint that it would spread, and forever engulf her, take her apart until not a trace of her was left, nothing but her screams . . .

The last of the essence vanished from her system, leaving her drained, her lungs reddened and hoarse—while she was on it, it was so easy to forget what the drug was doing to her, but she wasn't fool enough to lie to herself. She was dying; but she'd been dying for twenty years, ever since Hawthorn ceased to be a haven—ever since Elphon died. "I've never seen anything like this, either," she said. Her voice rasped against her throat; she brought it under control with an effort. "But it's gone now, right?"

Oris nodded. "It could come back."

"Mmm," Madeleine said. She considered her options. He seemed worried, but not as bone-deep frightened as she'd been—was what she'd seen a hallucination induced by angel essence?

On the one hand, she emphatically didn't want to be there when it came back; but on the other . . . with it gone, she couldn't investigate further. She could take it up with Selene, but then there was a risk—a not insignificant one—that Selene would see she was on essence. "It won't come back."

Oris grimaced. "I don't want it coming back, Madeleine. You saw it."

"I did," Madeleine said, doing her best to keep her voice level. "I'm sure it's nothing."

"Nothing? Are you . . ." Oris hesitated. "Are you sure?"

Madeleine said, with a glibness she didn't feel, "It's an old House. Not everything in it is entirely savory. You should know." God knew Morningstar had had his share of darkness.

"I . . ." Oris frowned. "I guess I do?"

"You'll be fine," Madeleine said. "It's gone. And if it does come back, you can call me. Anytime. I'll come. Promise."

She could feel Oris wavering—he trusted her and her opinions, and she seemed confident enough to sway him. She wished she felt as confident as she appeared to him.

"Look. Why don't I stay here awhile tonight, and we'll see what happens?"

It was a mark of how desperate Oris was that he readily acquiesced to this, without even a show of protesting.

But at the end of the night, there was no trace of whatever had frightened him out of his wits, nor could any of Madeleine's spells detect any trace of an intruder. "Let me know if it comes back," she said, as she left the room and went back to her own quarters for some much-needed rest.

Oris didn't see anything the next day, or the next night, or for the next week. By then, Madeleine had lulled herself into thinking they'd just had a hallucination; or seen the last of a stray spell from the war, which had finally spent itself in manifesting to Oris. She went through the routine of her days at Silverspires: collecting breath and nail clippings from Fallen and making artifacts out of them; teaching the children in the House's school the bases of alchemy—and through the routines of her nights, too, inhaling angel essence and glorying in its futile rush of power.

FOUR
MARKET OF BETRAYALS

PHILIPPE found Aragon in his office, reading a file yellowed by age. How old was Aragon, really? All he had told Philippe was that he owed Morningstar a debt, and this was the reason why he gave part of his time to Silverspires, taking away from his valuable practice—it had no small value, to be an independent doctor in a polarized city.

Aragon's office was a small room that looked like a cross between church stalls and hospital: the lower half of the walls was covered with wooden panels, while the upper half bore a thick layer of white paint, over which Aragon had aligned pictures and paintings. The room had a faint, unpleasant smell—a remnant of bleach or some other chemical, mingling with the heady one of wood varnish.

Beside Aragon was Emmanuelle, who gave him an embarrassed smile. "Selene told me to report on the exam." She, too, had a file in her hands. She didn't sound altogether happy, or approving.

Aragon nodded, curtly, at Philippe. They'd been observing each other warily in the weeks that had preceded, and had had a few desultory exchanges, nothing particularly deep or meaningful.

"Sit here," Aragon said, pointing to an examination table covered with a white sheet. "I will come in a moment."

Emmanuelle pulled her chair away into the farthest corner, staring at the images of human bodies on the wall—there was a cross section of lungs, accompanied by information on magical rot and on the nonexistent ways to prevent it; a detailed anatomy of a Fallen, compared point by point to a human, with peculiar emphasis on the muscles of the back—paying particular attention to the muscle pairs that had been used for lifting and pulling down wings; and a detailed map of Paris, charting the points of greatest magical pollution.

After a while, Aragon closed the file. "So," he said. "A complete exam. Selene seems to think I have time to waste."

"You certainly took your time humoring her," Emmanuelle said, with a tight smile. "It's been weeks."

"I had other things to do," Aragon said, stiffly.

Emmanuelle shrugged. "I'd be careful, if I were you."

Aragon didn't deign to answer.

"She doesn't like insolence. Or mysteries."

That last was clearly directed at Philippe. Mysteries. As if he were a thing, to be prodded and analyzed; and then he realized that, to Selene, he might well be.

The arrogance of her . . .

No. No anger. He couldn't afford that. Not here, not now. He had been in a House army once; had kept his face a blank through the orders that sent him into the fray to buy a plot of land with blood and death. He could do it again here; it wasn't so hard.

The Jade Emperor had said it was vital to maintain dignity in all things; what advice would he have had, if he'd seen Philippe in Silverspires, imprisoned by Fallen magic? Perhaps he would have been glad; after all, he was ruler of Heaven; he had exiled Philippe from the company of Immortals—so he could learn humility and decorum. He'd probably never dreamed that foreigners would sweep in with Fallen magic, seizing Philippe when he was still weakened from his exile; sending him to a land where his status meant almost nothing. Perhaps he'd have viewed it as a fitting punishment.

Humility and decorum. What a joke.

Aragon unhooked his stethoscope from the wall, and came closer to Philippe. "Open your mouth, please."

After a while, Philippe found it easier to tune out and let his body take over the simple exercises—Heaven knew what Aragon had been asked, or how he'd chosen to interpret it, but he was performing a simple medical exam.

The *khi* currents in the room—as elsewhere in the House—were slow and lazy, as if everything had been severely depleted. Water was the strongest one, because of the proximity of the Seine and the general stagnation of the place; wood was the weakest one, because nothing had grown fast and vigorous in the House for years now. They swirled around Aragon's feet—metal, for harvest, for collecting—around Emmanuelle's still face—water, for stillness, for withdrawal into one's self—but of course all of it had deeper meanings, insights he couldn't read or draw on anymore.

And there was darkness, too; but there always was—ever since he had touched the mirror. It lay like a shadow across everything he looked at; and sometimes in his dreams he would meet Morningstar's pale gaze, and stand transfixed, like a deer before a hound or a hunter—and he'd wake up drenched in sweat, both terribly afraid and terribly awed. There was . . . something infinitely seductive about Morningstar, the promise that he'd be welcomed as a Fallen, reshaped until he was part of Silverspires—tied to the House in ten thousand ways, each stronger and more durable than the ties of families—until he finally became worthy of Morningstar's regard . . .

But Morningstar was dead; or gone; or beyond communication. Surely that was just an illusion; a side effect of whatever curse had been laid on the House—of the summoning that he'd felt when touching the mirror, but could no longer trace?

All you hold dear will be shattered; all that you built will fall into dust; all that you gathered will be borne away by the storm. . . .

"Does the House have enemies?" he asked; and was startled to see Emmanuelle's pleasant expression darken.

"Anything powerful and old always has enemies," Emmanuelle

said—her eyes on the posters on the walls. "And Silverspires is oldest of the Houses. Much diminished, to be sure; but that is when the wolves and carrion birds see their opportunity."

"I see," Philippe said.

"You'll want to know what you've gotten into," Emmanuelle said, not unkindly. "The other Houses are our enemies, mostly. The gang lords are numerous and weak; and the Houses make sure they stay that way."

"I know," Philippe said, curtly, as Aragon fussed around him with a stethoscope. "I was a gang member." He was surprised how easily the past tense came to him; but truly there had been no future for him with the Red Mambas. "What about the Houses?"

Emmanuelle shrugged. "Lazarus is our ally for the time being. Harrier is . . . neutral." She rattled off, effortlessly, a dozen other names that meant less to Philippe; presumably on the other end of the city, where he'd never set foot. "And, of course, there's Hawthorn."

"Hawthorn?" The word meant nothing to him, but the way Emmanuelle said it . . .

"In the southwest," Emmanuelle said, pursing her lips. "Surely you've heard of them? If Silverspires is on the wane, they're on the rise." There was almost . . . venom in her voice, which, coming from the quiet and good-natured archivist, was as disturbing as being savaged by a fawn. "They protect their own, and have no scruples beyond that— they grow rich on selling angel essence, and angel breath, and God knows what else they can get their hands on."

And Silverspires was no doubt a model of morality—he held on to the thought, did not voice it, because he knew that it would not please his captors—because Emmanuelle was on Selene's side, in the end, and it would do him good not to forget.

"I see," he said. But none of those enemies, surely, could have reached that deep inside the cathedral and planted the curse? "And the House is . . . united?" he asked.

Emmanuelle's face closed. "Of course it is. We're not Hawthorn, as I said. Selene rules as Morningstar's heir, and there is neither question of her legitimacy, nor attempts to unseat her."

He felt more than saw Aragon wince in the middle of prodding at his shoulder blades. There was more to it than that; but the time to ask was not now.

"And now," Aragon said, "let us see some magic."

"No," Philippe said, recoiling instinctively from the suggestion. Magic was not cheap, to be thrown around like fireworks; or wasted on pointless demonstrations of might; or, worse, shown to Selene, whose sentence of death was only held in abeyance until she understood everything that made and moved him.

"You will find," Aragon said, with a tight smile, "that you have no choice in the matter." His face was as severe as ever, but he raised his gaze; and Philippe saw the hint of a smile in the dark eyes. Aragon was right: he might breathe fire, summon dragons from the depths of the Seine, transport himself to the other end of Paris—and still, neither Emmanuelle nor Selene would even begin to understand what he was and what he drew on—because his magic was as alien to them as his customs; because he was far from home, an exile in the midst of this broken, decadent city; a foreigner even among his own people, trapped in the ruins of a wrecked city.

No anger. No sorrow. He couldn't afford them.

He'd already observed where the *khi* currents in the room were; it was but a simple matter to call up fire, even as diminished and as weak as it was, here in Silverspires; to cradle the living flame in the palm of his hand, feeling the warmth of it travel through his veins—through his shoulder and straight into his heart.

Through the light of the flame, he saw Emmanuelle's shocked face—the dilated pupils, the dark features frozen in shock, the gaze trained on him, frantically trying to see a trace of magic and finding none.

Good. Not everything in the world was subject to the Fallen.

Gently, slowly, he closed his hand around the flame; let the magic dissolve in the midst of the *khi* currents and of his body until no trace of it was left. As he did so, for a bare moment, something else connected to the *khi* currents: water, but not the stale water within the

House—something bubbling and simmering, almost youthful in its enthusiasm. Something he'd felt once before in Annam; but no, this was impossible. There were no dragon kingdoms here—no spirits of the rain and rivers, not under the polluted clouds that rained acid; not in the blackened waters of the Seine; not in the wells that had long since run dry.

But he'd felt this, once before—in the ruined cathedral—much fainter, almost spent, but still . . .

Impossible. Nostalgia and the fancies of a prisoner, that was all it was.

"Satisfied?" he asked, shaking his head to dismiss the odd feeling.

Emmanuelle grimaced, but she nodded. "As much as one can be, I guess."

Aragon returned to his desk, put down his stethoscope with an audible thump. "I trust that is the end of the examination." His face was severe; his opinion of the entire affair all too clear—a waste of time.

Philippe said nothing. At length, Emmanuelle got up, closing the file she held in her hands. "I will report this to Selene," she said; and left the room.

Aragon waited until her footsteps vanished from hearing; and they were well and truly alone. "You surprise me."

Philippe raised an eyebrow. "Why?"

Aragon's smile was terrible to behold. "You are still here."

"Not by choice," Philippe said, stiffly. He tried, every night, to untangle Selene's spell on him; stood on the border of the House, feeling the resistance in the air and wondering if he dared test himself against it. But that spell was a vast maw; something larger than anything he had seen. "Believe me, if I could undo Selene's spell—"

"Yes? Do tell me." Aragon put down the paper he was holding. "What would you do? Go back to your games with the gangs and the misery of the streets?"

"Careful, old man," Philippe said.

But Aragon went on, relentless. "Or will you go home instead? Surely you have to realize it's a dream you can't go back to?"

The rest of Europe was ashes as well: the Great War had spilled outward from Paris, engulfing every region and every department—and reaching across borders through the alliances struck between Houses, a network of mutual support that had turned into tinder for a continent-wide conflagration—English Houses against French Houses; and then, as governments collapsed and the circle of conflicts tightened, each House for itself. Outside Paris, ruins dotted the landscape—the minor, provincial Houses in other cities shattered, their Fallen and human dependents dead in their hundreds, and the manors of the countryside fastnesses in the midst of wastelands. The travelers from Madrid or London arrived with delegations as large and as armed as a battalion, after a grueling journey that had taken them months to complete. And the boats for Annam and the colonies were few, the exclusive province of the favored of Houses: an impossibility for such as him. He'd tried, numerous times, to sneak into convoys bound for Marseilles and Saigon; but the security was too tight, the spells too powerful. He'd have to be a dependent to get on board; and he wasn't ever going to sell himself into servitude to a House—his return wasn't worth the degradation.

Aragon was right: he would never see Annam again—he would never smell the green papayas, freshly cut open; or the garlic and the fish sauce; never climb into the mountains of the west and see them shrouded in bluish clouds; never hear the chants of worshippers at the ancestral altars . . . "I know," Philippe said, in a whisper.

Aragon's gaze was piercing. "If you'll forgive me for meddling where I shouldn't—it's long past the time where you should make a life for yourself here."

"As a pampered captive on reprieve from a death sentence? No." Philippe clenched his fists. "And you are meddling, aren't you?"

Aragon smiled; this time more gently. "Because I believe in helping my own kin. All Fallen, not just those of the House you belong to."

"I'm not Fallen," Philippe pointed out—he wasn't sure he'd ever understand Aragon. Bodhisattva ethics, perhaps; saving everyone whether they'd asked for it or not; sacrificing himself and his good reputation by helping wounded and sick Fallen, whatever their House. Or his Hippocratic oath, perhaps, though Philippe laid no claim to understanding that peculiarity.

"You're not Fallen," Aragon said, at last. "But you still should be free to choose. It's not right, what Selene did to you. I already asked her, but she won't lift the spell; and she holds it together with the entire strength of the House. It's not right."

Neither was what he had done to Isabelle, but Philippe clamped his mouth shut on that response before it could doom him.

Aragon drummed his fingers on his desk. "I don't meddle," he said, more to himself than to Philippe. "I don't take sides—that was the bargain I struck. But they have to keep their side of it; and they're not." He looked up; as if genuinely surprised to still see Philippe there. "There is someone who could help you, but it will not come cheap."

"Do I look like I have money?" Philippe said.

"No," Aragon said. "It's what they'll ask for that preoccupies me, in fact." He drummed his fingers on the desk again, staring at Philippe as if he could dissect him. "You're a decent being, underneath. Can you promise you'll follow your own heart in this?"

"I can promise," Philippe said, "but—"

"Then do so."

"Fine, fine," Philippe said. It didn't seem to be much, in any case. "I promise."

Aragon sighed. "The next Great Market is in two days. Wait in the courtyard near the Préfecture's former entrance—you know where that is? I'll show you on a map. Midday, I suspect, is the time he'll prefer, but I'll confirm with you. Oh, and naturally do keep my name out of this."

"I don't understand—" Philippe started, but he did understand— that somewhere, somehow, there was a person who could effortlessly shatter Selene's spell; who could make him free.

And wasn't that all that mattered, ultimately? That, and not the bleak maw of the future that Aragon had described so well; the closed doors to an Annam he couldn't return to, to a pale, bloodless life with

Ninon and Baptiste and the rest of the Red Mambas; or to the cessa-
tion of life itself, the supreme attainment of the Buddhists, the thought
of which scared him sick in his belly?

PHILIPPE went to see Isabelle, afterward—to check up on her, en-
sure that she was still around. He wasn't sure why, but the interview—
and Aragon's promise—had left him shaken, no longer sure of what he
ought to do.

He found her in the kitchens, stubbornly trying to handle a wet,
sticky dough under the amused gaze of Laure. "She's getting better at
this," Laure said to Philippe when he arrived. Her husband, Gauthier,
was nearby, showing two junior cooks how to prepare flaky pastry for
bouchées à la *reine*. "Though still a bit of a disaster, if you ask me."

Philippe forced a smile he didn't feel. Laure was kind, and he
couldn't fault her; but right now he couldn't handle another House
dependent—except for Isabelle.

Isabelle was kneading the dough as if it had personally offended
her—bits and pieces of it were clinging to her fingers, the work surface—
and even her hair.

"I take it the lesson with Choérine didn't go well," Philippe said.
He didn't really need to see the state of the dough; this close, he could
feel her frustration through the link—strong enough that it drowned
everything.

Isabelle snorted. "Just tiring," she said. "She wanted me to hold a
spell for a long time—and it's hard."

"You'll get it, eventually." The small things were always harder—
especially for a Fallen whose raw power was too strong, too uncon-
trolled.

"Of course. Choérine said it could take time, with . . . young
Fallen. How did the exam with Aragon go?"

Philippe shrugged, with a nonchalance he didn't feel. "Not as bad
as it could have gone."

She looked at him for a while. "Performing like a circus animal?
Did that make you happy?"

Again, that odd mixture of naïveté and shrewdness—thrown around with the subtlety of a club. "I suppose not."

Isabelle tore the dough back from the wooden table, stared at it for a while. "Laure says there'll be financiers for dessert tonight. With real almonds. I can beg some if you want."

Philippe suppressed a smile. "Trying to distract me with food?"

"Trying to distract both of us," Isabelle said, sharply—clearly still unhappy about the lesson with Choérine. "What do you think?"

"Of course," Philippe said. He was never quite sure of what to tell her—already, she moved in a world different from his—a world of magic lessons and etiquette courses, while he got taken apart by Aragon and Emmanuelle—observed, to see what he could do; what his value as a weapon was.

But it wasn't going to last, not if Aragon kept his word.

"Do you miss home?" Isabelle asked.

He shrugged again. From her—from her face, and the faint link between them—only concern. "It was a long time ago."

"Liar."

He couldn't put it into words. "I can't return," he said, at last, and that was true.

"Because of the Fallen?" Isabelle asked.

Because . . . "Because of the Houses, yes. Because there are no boats left, except for dependents. Because, even if I did get on board one, the Jade Emperor—you would call him God, I suppose, if God was in Annam—wouldn't accept me back." He left it at that; didn't mention offenses that were never forgiven—what was the point? It was, as he had told her, a long time ago in another land.

"The Jade Emperor." She rolled the name on her tongue, as if it were some foreign, exotic ingredient. "Does he rule over Annam?"

"No, of course not," Philippe said, bitterly. "That would be the Fallen."

"I mean, before the Fallen."

"He . . . is the guardian of Heaven," Philippe said. "The keeper of Heaven's will and its closest personification. But no, he doesn't rule over mortals. Just over spirits. The mountain spirits, the dragons, the village protectors . . . they all bow down to him."

"But you're not a spirit," Isabelle said. "So you could come back. Just not in his court."

"I wanted to," Philippe said. "Even if I didn't really know what kind of life I'd have, back there." He hadn't really had time to get adjusted to his exile from court before the Fallen swooped in—but he'd had a life as a mortal, once—had tasted rice and fish sauce and all the sweetness of banquets; had once known contentment as he'd rounded the bluff and seen his home, with the smell of jasmine wafting from the door. He was still Immortal enough that his body didn't age, that his powers didn't fade; but . . . "I suppose I could," he said, finally. "Do something else, be different from what I was—before." It was an absurd, childish idea, but Isabelle's matter-of-fact tone made it all seem real.

Isabelle watched him for a while. "You should," she said fiercely. "There will be boats. Maybe not today, but tomorrow or in five years, or in a decade, and you'll find one you can board."

"There—" Philippe opened his mouth, and then shut it. It was hard to argue, in the face of her faith—as pure and as incandescent as a falling star. "I'm sure you're right," he said, slowly. It was a lie, a mad dream; but it was in his belly like warm rice; like a comfort he'd forgotten, years and years ago.

Isabelle said, as if utterly oblivious of the struggle within him, "I asked Selene."

"About what?"

"Lifting the spell."

"You—" He was going to say she was insane, and then measured the import of what she'd said. "You shouldn't have done that."

Isabelle shrugged. "She wouldn't listen. She smiled and patted me on the head, as if I were a child."

You are a child, Philippe thought—but he could feel her in his mind; could feel her anger—that pure, sharp rage of the young at injustice. His heart twinged, in his chest, and for a moment he wasn't sure what he could tell her.

"That's not what I meant." And, because he owed her something, anything, in return, even if it was worthless fancies, he added, "I get those flashes, sometimes. Those traces of something familiar, almost as if I only had to turn a corner to be home. It's . . . not a pleasant feeling." The cathedral; Aragon's office—impossible dreams that he should be adult enough to set aside.

Isabelle's gaze was disturbingly shrewd. "Sometimes, dreams are true things."

"Not these ones," Philippe said; and thought of the other ones; the suffocating nightmares about the darkness; his waking drenched in sweat, breathing hard, as if he'd run ahead of a tiger in its own territory.

These ones, too, had to be false—*please, Heaven, let them be false.*

"SELENE?"

Emmanuelle came into Selene's office, carrying a stack of books— one that was so large it threatened to dwarf her.

"Oh dear," Selene said. "What are those?" She got up from behind her desk, helped Emmanuelle divest herself of some of the books, before the whole precariously balanced pile fell down.

"Lady Selene?"

"Oh." Behind Emmanuelle—equally dwarfed by a pile of books, although in this case it was a much shorter one—was Caroline, the six-year-old daughter of two dependents of the House. "Here, let me help."

Caroline shook her head. "I can do it," she said, walking slowly but with determination to the desk—where she attempted to put the entire pile of books in one go, with predictable results.

The noise the books made when they tumbled onto the parquet must have woken up the entire House. "Sorry." Caroline shook her head and picked up the books, one by one—standing on tiptoe to reach the desk and lining them all up one by one.

Emmanuelle watched her, trying very hard to suppress a smile. "She insisted on helping."

"I see." Selene considered the books while Caroline continued her ever-widening invasion of her desk. "*My Three Years in Annam* by

Gabrielle Vasseur, *Annamite Myths and Legends* by Antony Landes. You've been busy, I see."

"I thought I'd keep you busy," Emmanuelle said. "Since the examination was unsuccessful . . ." She didn't sound altogether grieved about that. Selene wasn't sure why she gave so much leeway to Philippe—had she forgotten what the young man had done, so readily?

She was right, however: Aragon's examination had been singularly unsuccessful. Philippe's blood, examined under Aragon's microscopes, appeared nothing more than human. His lungs were quite free of the rot she associated with angel essence (she hadn't thought he was an essence addict, but one never knew); in fact, they were surprisingly healthy, even for a young man—Aragon's face had been creased into something almost like surprise when he gave her the results. All that remained was this strong, unexplained magic that he seemed to wield as easily as he breathed.

"All done!" Caroline stood, proudly. Behind her, the desk was covered in books—she'd been too small to make piles of more than two or three, and had had to expand to either side—a good thing Selene hadn't yet sorted out the paperwork on her desk, because Caroline had pushed things left and right to fit the books where she could, heedless of whether that disturbed anything.

"Very good," Emmanuelle said, while Selene made a deliberate effort not to step forward and pile everything properly. "Now go find Choérine, will you?"

"Thank you," Selene said gravely to the little girl.

Caroline nodded. "I'll tell all my friends I helped you with House business, Lady Selene!"

To which Selene had no answer; except watching the little girl rush away while Emmanuelle struggled not to laugh. "She means well."

"I know." Selene smiled, then gathered all the books into a pile, which she slid onto one corner of her desk, atop the older reports, the ones she always put off reading. "I presume you didn't come just to deliver books."

"Of course not," Emmanuelle said. "Knowing you . . ." She pulled a chair, and sat down. "Consider they come with a reading guide. You asked about Annam, and what it was like."

"Yes," Selene said. If Philippe wouldn't talk, and if she couldn't analyze his magic, she'd find another way to discover what he was. "Tell me."

Emmanuelle closed her eyes—gathering her thoughts for a recitation. When she opened them again, she spoke without hesitation. "What do you know of the beings who ruled the world before the Fallen?"

Beyond Europe, before the mad rush to colonize other countries and bring their wealth back to the motherland, there had been—other beings, other Houses: the *nahual* shape-shifters of Mexico, the *jinn* of Arab countries, the Jewish *shedim* and *nephilim*—and once, a long time ago, the demigods and heroes of ancient Greece and ancient Rome— long since vanished and crushed by newer magics, their creatures cannibalized to form the constructs of the war, or buried so deeply in the earth they required a painstaking and dangerous summoning that no Fallen would dare undertake. The other beings in other lands, too, had either yielded to Fallen rule, or been killed. "Much. But not about Annam."

"Annam . . . is a land of spirits," Emmanuelle said. "Magic is tied to the land—there's a spirit for each village, for each household—for mountains and rivers and rain."

"Rain," Selene said. "Really."

"Don't laugh," Emmanuelle said. She held up one of the books, where an engraving of a huge, serpentine animal circled text—all the way to the maw, which was huge and fanged, like that of tigers. It had a mane, too; like a lion's, and deerlike antlers—and it looked . . . wrong, as if bits and pieces of animals had been jumbled together by a creator with little common sense. "They call them *rong*. Dragons. They live in clouds, or at the bottom of rivers and seas."

Not the dragons of Western lore, then—not that anyone had summoned one in centuries, too dangerous. . . . Even the one on House Draken's arms had been a fiction; a mere statement of power without substance. "I take it they're not friendly."

"No." Emmanuelle laid the book back on the desk. "But they've withdrawn now. According to the books, they haven't been seen in several decades."

"Mmm," Selene said. "And you think . . . Philippe is a dragon?"

Emmanuelle laughed. "No, of course not. They can take human form, but they always have scales somewhere—or a pearl below their chin, in some of the more . . . dramatic drawings."

"I see," Selene said. She didn't; or, more accurately, she felt she knew more, but not enough to help her. "Was there anything else?"

"There are other spirits," Emmanuelle said. "Flower fairies"—she raised a hand to forestall Selene's objections—"they're not cute and small, trust me. Also, fox spirits, in Tonkin; and Immortals, though no one has ever seen these. Apparently they all live in something called the Court of the Jade Emperor—who rules over all the other spirits—and they never come down to Earth."

That didn't sound very promising, either. And she had other preoccupations, too—with the market coming to Silverspires, there were things she needed to go over with Javier and Diane, the head of security for the House. . . .

She was about to dismiss Emmanuelle and go back to her reports, when something else happened. At the back of her mind—where the dependents of the House were all lined up like lit candles—a light flickered, and went out.

"Selene?"

Selene closed her eyes; felt for the shape and heft of the missing dependent. Théodore Ganimard; one of the informants who kept her apprised of what was happening in other Houses, and in the rest of the city. "Someone just died."

"Oh." Emmanuelle said. "Is it . . . bad?"

Selene shook her head. Being an informant was a dangerous business; and in a bad year she would lose half a dozen men and women. But still . . . it was odd, that she'd never even felt that Théodore Ganimard was in danger—as if he'd died so quickly and brutally that it had never had time to register with the House's protections. Like many dependents of Silverspires, he had a tracker disk; but all it told her was that he had been out in the south of Paris, near the ruins of Hell's Toll.

The market was arriving the next day, and there were other things requiring her attention; but she wasn't about to let the death of one of her dependents slide past.

"I don't know how bad it is. Can you get me Javier? I'll ask him to look into this."

A month after Philippe and Isabelle's arrival, the Great Market came to Silverspires—or rather, just outside the House, in the vast square that had once been the parvis of Notre-Dame. During the Belle Epoque, it had been held in the same place week after week—Les Halles, the belly of the city, the exuberant display of abundance of an empire that had believed itself immortal against all the evidence of history. But the squat, majestic pavilions of glass and iron had been destroyed in the war; and the fragile magical balance that had followed led to an arrangement where the Great Market rotated between the major Houses.

Madeleine took Oris, Philippe, and Isabelle with her while she went shopping for magical supplies; keeping a wary eye on Philippe as Selene had instructed. But, other than his being moody and brooding, there seemed to be nothing extraordinary about the young man.

Isabelle, on the other hand, looked at everything and everyone— fascinated by the bright, colored jewelry on a stall; by the vast array of cheeses and hams in the food section, from blue-veined Roquefort to the large, heavy whole rounds of Emmental, their interior peppered with holes like a thousand bubbles; from the glass bottles and mirrors that alchemists used to trap Fallen magic, to trinkets that shone with nothing more than glitter and cheap crystal.

Madeleine watched Isabelle, not sure whether to be amused or af- fected. She was so young; so careless—like Madeleine in another life- time, when she'd still been a child in Hawthorn, running wild in the market under the indulgent gaze of her teachers. Back then, she'd never even dreamed of Silverspires or of another House: her duty had been to her family and to Hawthorn, and to nothing or no one else. And now, of course, she was older—she wished she could say wiser, but her wasted lungs and life on the knife's edge of fear told her otherwise. Her parents were a distant memory—she had been barely talking to them before Asmodeus's coup; and, of course, after the coup, even the thought of sending a message back had made her sick—that roiling fear that Asmodeus would intercept it—that he would remember her existence, remember that she was still worth claiming; and come to Silverspires with his mocking smile, to kill her as he had killed Elphon . . .

With an effort, she shook off the past, and focused on the present.

The crowd was colorful and variegated: delegations from other Houses; gang lords in leather, swaggering through the market with their entourages; and a host of grimier, poorer people who congregated in the food sections, haggling for basic necessities. There was not much danger in the crowd, as long as they remained together: the Great Market was a place of truce (which, of course, didn't mean their purses were safe from opportunistic thieves). Children chased one another, laughing, under the wary eyes of their parents or their minders.

As they stood before one of the stalls, waiting for Oris to complete a purchase of a small mother-of-pearl container, Philippe spoke up.

"It was bigger during the war," he said.

"Wasn't everything?" Madeleine said. She hadn't been born when the city was devastated; those days, you pretty much had to be Fallen to have survived. Sixty years was long in human lifetimes, and most of those who had breathed in the air of Paris in the aftermath had not recovered well. But he wasn't Fallen, and still he remembered. Odd.

"They had entire stalls like these," Philippe said, fingering a lacquered box with a pattern of flowers. "Exotic woods from the Orient, and incense, and all the rubber you could ever want, for manufacturing car tires for the front." His voice was lightly ironic.

"We still have those. But they're mostly from our existing stock. More expensive," Madeleine said, unsure of what to answer. He was a native, of course; he would disapprove of the empire, if there was still such a thing after the war—with communications and travel so difficult, the colonies had all but become independent kingdoms by now, with the French colonists still in charge. She . . . she didn't like the idea of invading countries, but she was no fool: the empire had made them rich and powerful, and even its bare, pathetic remnants after the war brought them riches and standards of living far above those of the street gangs or other Houseless. Sometimes, you did what you had to, in order to survive.

He gave no sign of noticing her hesitation: he nodded, gravely. "It was another age."

"And yet you're still here," Madeleine said.

His face closed, as if a cloud had darkened it. "Through no fault of my own," he said, bitterly, and wouldn't speak up again.

"Madeleine!" A voice made her look up as they approached the eastern area of the parvis.

It was Claire, the head of House Lazarus; surrounded, as usual, by a gaggle of unruly children. Lazarus, among all the Houses, was the only one ruled by a human; Claire had been its head for thirty years, and Madeleine had known her for about half of that. She was small and plump, the image of a gray-haired, kindly grandmother; though of course one did not get to be the head of a House through kindness alone. Claire was ruthless, and many of her tactics would have put a Fallen to shame.

"I see you've grown an entourage of your own," Claire said, wryly. Her gaze took in Isabelle and Oris, and stopped at Philippe.

"They belong to the House," Madeleine said, acutely embarrassed.

"You surprise me." Claire smiled. "I never thought you would get Philippe to join a House of his own free will."

She knew him? Madeleine waited for him to protest; or to acknowledge the fact that he was bound to the House by far less than his free will, but he merely scowled at Claire. "There is a time to try everything, I guess," he said, darkly. "How have you been, Lady Claire?"

"Well enough," Claire said. Without missing a beat, she caught a boy's hand and held it away from the bracelet he was trying to grasp. "No touching, I said."

Madeleine made a mental note to talk to Claire away from Philippe, or to tell Selene to do so. There was even more to the young man they didn't know, it seemed. "We had Philippe for a while," Claire said. "A long time ago, though, and we couldn't hold him."

Philippe wasn't meeting her gaze; though now that Madeleine thought of it, he seldom met anyone's gaze but Isabelle's. "None of your fault," he said at last, inclining his head in a practiced gesture. "You know that."

"Of course." Claire shook her head, as if to clear away a persistent thought; and her gaze focused on Isabelle. "You haven't been here long," she said.

Isabelle hesitated, clearly reluctant to say much of anything. Madeleine stepped in. "She's too young for the advanced inquisition, Claire. Or for your power plays with Silverspires."

"Power plays?" Claire smiled again. "I don't play them much, as you well know."

No, Madeleine thought. *But when you do play them, you leave us all in the dust.* She did not relish the idea that Silverspires was bound to find itself on the opposite camp of House Lazarus one day. Claire might be human, but that merely meant she was ten times the strategist that most Fallen were; and ten times as ruthless when it came to downing her enemies. "If I were playing such games, though . . ." Claire's face was thoughtful. "If I were playing, I would congratulate you on sheltering so young a Fallen, who will do honor to her House."

"A weapon, you mean." Philippe's hiss of anger was all too audible, even in the din of merchants offering their wares.

"I see you haven't changed," Claire said. "Ideals will betray you in the end. You should know this."

Philippe said nothing—perhaps he'd finally understood that all Claire did was to goad him, in the hopes of getting information. "You didn't stop me simply to exchange pleasantries," Madeleine said, going for the blunt approach.

Claire's pale blue eyes focused on her. "Did I?" But in the end, as Madeleine had known all along, she couldn't resist. "If you see Selene, you might want to suggest she show an interest in doings outside the House."

"What things do you think she would not have seen?" Madeleine said, keeping her voice low and pleasant.

Claire's face darkened, and she hesitated for a while. "As I said, I don't play your little power games. I'm not Harrier or Hawthorn, or Silverspires, indeed. But there is word, in the city, of something abroad."

"Something?" Madeleine couldn't help the bark of laughter. "There's always something abroad in Paris. It's not like it's a safe place." She couldn't help remembering the shadow; the touch on her thoughts, the fist tightening in her innards as the wings unfolded, always just out of sight, always just out of reach—until they weren't.

"Something that kills," Claire said darkly. "Something that leaves multiple bite marks on its victims and takes their blood."

"Fallen blood is power," Philippe said. He kept his gaze away from Isabelle, but Madeleine saw the way the young Fallen flinched. "But not much power."

"Did I say the victims were Fallen?" Claire shook her head.

Oh, of course. Word would have spread much faster, if there had been Fallen dead. "What are you suggesting?" Madeleine asked.

"I don't know. I never said I had the answer. But I would suggest you tread even more carefully than usual at night." Claire's face was utterly serious; and there was a hint of something in her eyes—fear?

Claire went on, with a tight smile. "The victims are human. Five of them, none who would be missed—low in gang hierarchies, grimy and ill-fed, too insignificant to be worth a House's regard." There was no mistaking the anger in her voice. Among other things, Lazarus ran charity kitchens, hospitals, and hostels, where, regardless of your allegiance or your past, you would be made welcome for a few nights.

"Which gangs?" Philippe asked sharply.

Claire gave him an appraising look. "None of the Red Mambas, though I would guess your . . . friends will be worried as well."

"Those deaths don't really concern the House," Madeleine said, though she didn't know, not really. It was dark out there, in the devastated streets of the city; and if one crazy person had got into his head to play serial killer, she wasn't really sure what Silverspires could have to do with it. "I'll tell Selene, but you know I can't guarantee anything."

"No, of course not." Claire inclined her head. "But it'll be something. Good-bye."

It was only after she and her entourage had gone, when Isabelle looked up and asked, "But surely she could tell Lady Selene herself?" that Madeleine thought back on what Claire had said. "I don't know," she said. "I don't like it. There's a sting in here somewhere for Silverspires, but I don't know what it is yet."

"She wanted something out of us," Philippe said. "And I'm not sure if she didn't get it."

"How do you know her?" Madeleine asked.

Philippe looked straight at her; and suddenly she understood why he rarely met people's gazes, because there was something disturbingly intense about him, a coiled strength that made her feel as though her ribs were being compressed against her lungs, as though some icy hand were squeezing her heart. "I was in one of her hospitals for a while," Philippe said at last. "Not for long, and not with an entirely satisfactory resolution, but that's another story."

And that seemed to be the end of it; his gaze, boring into her, dared her to question him further; she had no desire to do so.

They were all uncannily silent as they walked through the rest of the market; even though Oris, who hadn't said anything in Claire's presence, attempted to maintain a one-sided patter, oblivious to the yawning maw of heavy silence that his words fell into. Isabelle was the only one seemingly unaffected by it, staring wide-eyed at the bead necklaces and crystal bracelets on the stalls they walked by.

What had Claire wanted? Information? She'd sounded as though she believed Selene would have information on the dead humans—but surely that was a trivial affair, some madman in a mad city; unfortunate, but surely not worth mentioning?

Except that Claire seldom mentioned things just for the pleasure of it; and she certainly wouldn't have bothered to lean so much on it if she'd thought it insignificant. Madeleine would have to find someone in Lazarus; perhaps Aragon had contacts there who'd know what was going on.

Lost in her thoughts, she almost bumped into Philippe—who had come to a dead stop at an intersection on the edge of the market, mere meters from the ruined entrance of Notre-Dame. "What—" she asked; and then saw the procession.

It was coming up Pont-au-Double, the small cast-iron bridge that stopped at the edge of the parvis. There were a good twenty people with the gray-and-silver uniform of House Hawthorn, the same one Madeleine had once worn. They walked slowly, leisurely, as though they had all the time in the world, as though they weren't standing close to the river, close enough for a spinning arm of water to snatch them over the parapet, or for a toothy creature to rise and attack them. Few people in Paris were mad enough to linger near the Seine, nowadays; only God knew what kind of power the accretion of war magic had released in the blackened waters.

Madeleine's gaze, sweeping over the procession, caught a glimpse of familiar faces: Sare the alchemist; Samariel, ever as achingly young and innocent; Pierre-François, older and grayer but still every bit the consummate bodyguard—she remembered that night, when the noise had erupted, and he had simply reached for a knife and a gun, and rushed out of the room without any further words.

And, at their head . . .

He hadn't changed, not one bit; but of course Fallen seldom did. He was tall and thin, with horn-rimmed, rectangular glasses—his particular affectation, since all Fallen had perfect eyesight—his hair dark, save for a touch of gray at the temples; his hands with the thin, long fingers of a pianist, even though the instruments he played on did not make music—unless one counted cries of pain and ecstasy as music, as Madeleine knew he did.

"Who is he?" Isabelle asked in a whisper, and it was Oris who answered her, with the barest hint of pity in his voice.

"Asmodeus. Head of House Hawthorn."

He hadn't changed. He still leaned on the same ivory cane with the ease of a gentleman who had no need for it; still had the same sharp, pointed smile of predators, the one he'd worn in the House—how could Uphir not see it, not feel the naked ambition burning that would one day depose him? How could Elphon not have seen it—not suspected anything, until the thugs' swords slid home into his chest and blood spouted over her—a split second before they sent Madeleine to her knees, struggling to breathe through the pain of shattered ribs?

Asmodeus's entourage had almost cleared the bridge: they had finished negotiating with the guards at the booth that guarded Pont-au-Double. He saw her then, bowed gravely, without a trace of irony, and turned right into the heart of the food market. Madeleine was surprised to realize her fingers had clenched into fists.

Breathe. She had to breathe. He had seen her, and turned away. She had nothing to fear from him: it was just her memories of that time that wouldn't be banished. He had no interest in her, no grudge: she had been among the lowliest of the low in Hawthorn, and he must have been barely aware that she existed. And then, with a feeling of dread that pulled her bowels into knots, she remembered that he did know who she was. Else why would he have bowed to her?

Surely he—

Her gaze, roaming through the market—somewhere, anywhere she wouldn't have to look at him again—fell on the rear of the procession, where three of the escort had stopped for a moment while one of them readjusted the straps on a large basket; which, judging from the movements from inside, probably contained some large, live animal. The first two were the kind of pale, faded women Asmodeus enjoyed having around; the third one, head bent over the basket, was a brown-haired man. . . .

No.

There was something—something in the tilt of his head, something in the bearing of his body . . .

And, having finished with his work, he raised his head, and she saw.

He, too, hadn't changed much: he was perhaps younger, less hardened, with the particular mix of innocence and agelessness of newly
manifested Fallen. But the face—she would have known that anywhere.

Elphon. *Oh God, Elphon.*

It was impossible. Elphon was dead. She had seen him die; had felt
his heart stutter and stop, seen the radiance fade from his translucent
skin until there was nothing left but dead meat. Then, weeping, she
had started the long crawl that would lead her to Silverspires and
Morningstar's arms.

Surely it was another Fallen; surely . . .

He rose, precariously balancing the basket against his waist, and
smiled at his two companions, in a way that was engraved into her
memory.

No. That wasn't possible. The dead did not walk the earth again;
not even dead Fallen.

"Wait here," she said to the others, and elbowed her way through
the crowd of Pont-au-Double, struggling to reach the little group before they moved away from her. By the time she caught up with them
in front of a fowler's stall, her ruined lungs were protesting; and, at the
worst possible moment—when she stood in front of them—a bout of
coughing racked her body and left her, wrung, to stand in their path.

"Excuse me," she said.

They looked at her, puzzled. The older woman pinched her lips as
if noting the unkempt state of Madeleine's dress, or her hoarse voice, or
both. "You're the alchemist for Silverspires?" the woman said at last.
"What can we do for you?"

"Can I speak to your friend?" Madeleine asked, pointing to the
Fallen who looked like Elphon.

The woman shrugged. "If you want. Elphon?"

Madeleine's heart skipped a beat; seemed to remain suspended in
her chest in an agony of stillness. But when Elphon looked up, there
was nothing but mild interest in his eyes. "Good morning," Elphon
said, looking at her with puzzlement. "What can I do for you?"

Show some hint of recognition. Something, anything that would explain why he was there—why he still bore the same name, still behaved the same, but he didn't recognize her. "How long have you been in Hawthorn?"

Elphon shrugged; and even that gesture was heartbreakingly familiar, a dim but treasured memory from the depths of the past. "A few months," he said. "Lord Asmodeus found me near Les Halles."

A few months? That was impossible. "Are you sure?"

"Of course." Elphon's voice was mild, but it was clear he was wondering about her sanity. So was Madeleine. This conversation could in no way be described as sane. "Are you trying to recruit me to Silverspires? I assure you I'm already spoken for."

"No, of course not," Madeleine said, feeling the blush start somewhere in her cheeks and climb, burning, to her forehead. "I wouldn't dare. It's just . . . I knew someone very much like you, once."

"Some Fallen look very much alike to mortals," Elphon said, with a tight smile. He hefted his basket, and made to rejoin his companions. "Now, if you'll excuse me . . . Lord Asmodeus will be expecting us, and he has little patience for tardiness."

"I have no doubt." Asmodeus had little patience for anything. He'd chafed enough, in what he viewed as an inferior position in Hawthorn; had waited just long enough to be certain of his coup. "I'm sorry for disturbing you," Madeleine said. "It seems I was mistaken."

Elphon bowed—low, old-fashioned, the same bow he'd used to make to her, all those years ago, half in mockery, half in earnest. "There's no harm in it. Good-bye, my lady."

She watched him retreat, the basket shifting with each movement of his body. Whatever he said, it *was* him. It had to be him; another Fallen, especially a young one, could have mimicked his appearance for a while, but not the gestures. Not the expressions.

But, if it was him, if he had somehow been resurrected by some mystery she could not comprehend—then why did he not remember her? Was it something Asmodeus had done? Surely he had to know that the "young" Fallen he had rescued was one of the loyalists who'd opposed his coup twenty years ago?

Surely—

Lost as she was in her thoughts, it was a while before she realized that, in the place where she'd left the others, there was no trace of them whatsoever.

At first, she wasn't unduly worried; they were adults, and the market was as safe a place as there could be in Paris. She looked for them, desultorily, amid the brightly colored stalls, sure that she would meet them at the House if she couldn't find them.

A scream—terror and agony, rising through her mind—no, not hers, someone bound to House Silverspires was in mortal danger.

She ran, but she knew even before she started to run that she would be too late.

FIVE
THE HOUSE OF HAWTHORN

PHILIPPE had used Madeleine's departure to slip away from the group, mumbling something about looking at primed lacquered boxes. Oris had made a face, but Isabelle also expressed a desire to do some shopping of her own. So they split up, each going in a separate direction—after all, what could happen to them in the middle of the busy crowd, in a place where the old alliances still held?

It was after midday, and the crowds of the market were thinning away, leaving Philippe free to leisurely walk to his destination.

On the edge of the market, he ducked into the Old Wing, the barely used buildings that had once been the Police Préfecture and the Commerce Tribunal. There was a side street there, which widened into a makeshift courtyard between the two derelict buildings.

There was a man there, waiting for him, sitting under the wide arch of the entrance to the Préfecture.

Philippe recognized him as one of House Hawthorn's members, still wearing the gray-and-silver uniform with the ease of a soldier; and the eyes, too, were those of a soldier, wide and blue and naive, until one truly looked into them, and saw the darkness lurking within.

"Ah, Aragon's little friend," the man said. He rose, impossibly lithe, scarecrow thin, dancing to music only he could hear: he was Fallen, though his face was as round and as smooth as a baby's, without any of the edge Philippe would expect from a former angel. But the eyes . . . the eyes gave him away. "My name is Samariel."

"Philippe." He felt awkward, gangly, out of place—even though he was quite probably older than Samariel. Arrogant bastard, like the rest of them.

"'Lover of Horses,'" Samariel said, gravely. "Was that the name Lady Selene gave you?"

Philippe flushed. "That is the name I gave myself. I owe nothing to Selene." Nothing except the chains she'd wrapped around him.

"I see." Samariel's gaze was mocking. "Aragon tells me you need help. I assume he also told you—"

"That it would come at a price? I'm no fool."

Samariel looked him up and down, as if weighing his options. "No," he said. "Perhaps you're not."

"What makes you think you can remove Selene's spell?"

Samariel smiled. "May I?" He reached out, and stroked Philippe's neck—a careless gesture that made Philippe shiver. His skin was cold to the touch, as cold as the high reaches of Heaven; but soon it grew warmer. Philippe saw the tangle of threads around his neck, plunging deep into the earth—linking him to the House, Aragon had said, shaking his head. Samariel reached out, thoughtfully plucking two of the brightest strands and raising them to his eyes. He pursed his lips and spread out his fingers like a conjurer doing his best trick; and, just like that, the threads were gone.

Illusion. It had to be. The casualness with which Samariel had acted, the frightful ease with which he'd undone a spell that had had Philippe stumped for weeks, that Aragon had said only Selene could raise . . .

"You can't—" Philippe started, but when he shifted he felt it; the slight yield in the bonds that tied him to Silverspires; the lessening of the weight around his neck; and it wasn't an illusion.

"A nasty piece of work," Samariel said. His face was still impassive;

his hand still casually rested on Philippe's neck, once more as cold as carved marble. He made no move to withdraw. "Untangling the entire thing, of course, would be another matter. Each thread is harder to smooth out than the previous ones." He smiled—this close, Philippe could see the sharp, white teeth under the lips as red as blood, the smile of a predator in the instant before it struck. "I don't know what you did to Lady Selene, but she must value you very highly."

Philippe had no desire to go there. Samariel was no fool; and if told about his little tricks in the Grands Magasins, he would no doubt wish to take Philippe for Hawthorn, just as Selene had taken him for Silverspires. "I did something foolish," he said.

"Indeed?"

"I tasted a Fallen's blood." He gambled that Selene's aversion to hurting Fallen would be a known thing; and that it was close enough to the truth to satisfy Samariel.

At length, Samariel nodded. "I see." He withdrew his hand; but remained standing close, uncomfortably so. "You should have known better, but never mind."

Philippe bristled, controlled the angry retort that came to him with an effort. "You said you could take it away, for a price. What's the price?"

"Tsk. Manners." Samariel shook his head. "A few years in Silverspires would have corrected that, at least." He smiled, waiting for Philippe to rise to the bait. Philippe said nothing, and thought back to the almost alien serenity that had once been his, as an Immortal—to the misty landscape of mountains stretching into infinity until the entire world seemed to blur away and dissolve; the boats scattered on the expanse of the river at dawn, and the hypnotic songs of the fishermen as they cast their nets into the liquid mirror of Heaven.

"Your price," Philippe said, again, shaping his lips into the smile that Ninon called "inscrutable."

Samariel's eyes drifted toward the clouds in the skies. "My price. Tempting as it is to charge nothing—I imagine it would be quite a setback for Selene to lose you—I still should not undervalue my time.

We both agree on this, don't we?" He didn't wait for Philippe's answer, but went on. "You know that House Hawthorn and House Silverspires are . . . at odds."

"To say the least." Philippe didn't care much, one way or another. Let them destroy each other, and they'd have got nothing but their just deserts.

"At the moment, Silverspires is . . . strong." Samariel made a grimace. "Morningstar's legacy is not to be trifled with."

"So?" Philippe shook his head. "I have no hold over it."

"That would be where you are wrong, my little friend," Samariel said. "The greatest cracks in a building come from within—that's what I want from you. A way for Hawthorn to gain the ascendant."

"I don't play House politics," Philippe said. "And how would I know what you're looking for?"

"A weakness." The sky had gone dark, and the few birds had fled. In the dim light, Samariel's teeth shone as white as bleached bones. "A hold on Silverspires. Bring me that, and Asmodeus will do the rest."

Weaknesses. Aragon had feared the price Samariel would ask for. He had known, or had suspected. "You want to destroy the House."

"Don't be a fool." Samariel shook his head. "It's not the war anymore; just a game that we play among ourselves. Yes, we'll bloody Selene's nose, and humiliate her. Neither I nor Asmodeus have the least interest in destroying anything or anyone."

A game. In a way, it would have felt cleaner, if Samariel had outright asked for destruction; but then, what had Philippe expected, from a House-bound? They were all the same; replete with the casual arrogance that had brought over Annamites and other colonials to fight their senseless war; the ones who had risen to power on rivers of blood; on deaths and suffering and the wreck of lives such as his.

He should have walked away. He'd meddled enough with Fallen, and it had cost him enough—he should have shaken his head and gone back to Silverspires, to his unbreakable captivity, to a future that he could no longer envision.

But there was a darkness, at the heart of the House, a curse within him, and that was Morningstar's legacy, not the House Selene was so proud of that she'd sacrifice anything, imprison anyone for it. It was nebulous and unclear; and not something he could give Samariel, not yet; but it was a start, all the same.

"A weakness. And when I bring you this, you'll lift Selene's spell?"

Samariel pursed his lips. "You don't trust me? Perhaps you're right. You should trust no one. But I'll swear it on the City, if that makes you feel better. Bring me a weakness of House Silverspires, and a way to exploit it; and I'll lift the spell that keeps you here."

On the City. "That's binding," Philippe said.

"Close enough. Will you do it, then?"

It was no light request; it was a risky one—it could be more damaging, more far-reaching than he thought, burning like embers kindled back to life. But . . . but, if he did this, he would be free. He would walk away from the House, from Selene and all her power games, and the uncertain future when she owned him and his powers; when he was, once more, pressed into servitude as a weapon.

Free.

He could—no, demons take Isabelle—for a moment he'd had this mad dream she'd given him, that he could, somehow, go back to Annam, make a life for himself again, away from the pomp and decorum of the Jade Emperor's court—again, that warm feeling in his belly, the beginnings of a hope he'd started to cling to but shouldn't afford; of a dream he should lose faith in.

Samariel lifted his head again, to stare at the sky—his nostrils flared, though not a muscle of his face moved. Something. He'd smelled something?

Philippe looked up. The air was tight, as heavy as before a storm; the few birds overhead moved sluggishly, dwarfed by the dark clouds that covered the horizon.

Something was wrong. "Yes," he said. "I'll do it."

"That's a bargain, then," Samariel said. "Until we meet again." He bowed, as dapper and as lithe as ever, and withdrew, but not before Philippe had caught a glimpse of his hands—and the slight tightening of his fingers that marked wariness, or anger, or both.

He was alone in the courtyard, staring at the storm clouds gathering in the sky; and there was a pounding against his head, a slow dimming of the light as if something large and winged had flown across the sun; but the sun was already hidden, so it couldn't be that.

With difficulty, he tore himself from the contemplation of the sky—and saw Isabelle, who stood at the entrance of the courtyard, a half smile on her lips.

"You—" How much had she seen? "Why are you here?"

"Because I felt what you were doing. Through the link."

She smiled, her face smooth and innocent, and as deceptive as Samariel's. "You could have trusted me. We had a bargain."

"I don't know what you mean." The pounding was getting worse; that feeling of standing at the edge of an abyss.

"Liar," Isabelle said. "I saw him leave. I caught some of what you were thinking."

The link again—why was it much stronger in her—why could she read his mind sometimes, while he could only feel her in moments of calm and silence; or when they were physically close to each other?

"It's no business of yours," Philippe forced through clenched lips. "And nothing that need concern you." She was part of the House; but how loyal was she? How much would she report to Selene?

She was there at the back of his mind; angry, scared for the House—and scared for him.

He'd have been afraid, too; if he didn't feel so sick.

"Philippe? Is something wrong?"

But he wasn't with her anymore; he stood in the courtyard, and the buildings around him had the warm golden color of limestone. The courtyard was packed with people: with the old-fashioned clothing he'd seen pictures of in Indochinese schools—the top hats, the swallowtails, the voluminous dresses and corsets.

He knew, even without turning around, that Morningstar would be by his side. The other's presence had an intensity that seemed to distort the very air around him. He wore a top hat, too; and the wings were folded; though he still had the sword, which he leant on as if it were a gentleman's cane.

"Beautiful, isn't it? We stand at the pinnacle." He smiled; and Philippe's entire being was suffused with warmth. "This," Morningstar said, pointing to the crowds and the buildings and the blue sky above, "this will last forever."

No, it won't, Philippe tried to say, but the words were stuck against his palate. *You have a few decades, at the most, and then comes the war; and then comes the decline; and then you vanish, you become nothing, a figure in the history books. You become . . . lost.*

And the darkness was within the blue sky, too—the flocks of white seagulls would soon drop dead from exhaustion, the storm clouds were gathering; the House itself was built on cracked foundations, on secrets and guilt and buried pain; the mirror was below the throne in the cathedral, and one day it would release its nightmares into the streets. . . .

"Philippe!"

Isabelle was shaking him. "What is wrong with you?"

Ash and blood on his lips: a memory of her blood, except it was dry and tasteless, and instead of giving him power it had drained him of all his strength. "I—" He struggled to breathe through parched lips. "We have to go."

Isabelle did not question him as to why. "Where?" She pulled him upright with surprising strength in a body so slight. "Show me where."

Philippe closed his eyes for a moment. When he opened them again, the world was still whirling around him, and the darkness was still rising from within him—as if he were the mirror, cracking from end to end. But it wasn't a pall over everything—rather, it was intensely focused, as sharp and as heavy as a thrown spear.

"This way," he said.

AFTER Isabelle and Philippe had left to go shopping, Oris headed back, slowly, to Pont-au-Double. Isabelle and Philippe would be fine:

it was a market, and the worst that could happen to them was getting fleeced by traders, or pickpocketed by children. Oris, meanwhile, wanted to catch Madeleine at Pont-au-Double when she was done with whatever mysterious errand had brought her back into the arms of House Hawthorn—he didn't know, not exactly, what the circumstances of her leaving had been, but he'd caught enough glimpses of her face darkening whenever Hawthorn was mentioned—and, of course, of the scars on her ribs and hip, which told their own story.

People dismissed Oris as a wallflower, but it wasn't because he never spoke up that he didn't *see* things. He'd seen, for instance, the light in Madeleine's eyes at night, which made them seem almost insectile; the way her long, graying hair had grown dull and lusterless, her round, pleasant face sharp and hollow. He had heard her cough; listened to the way her voice had grown subtly hoarser over the past few months. Aragon should have seen it, if he wasn't too busy with too many patients—Oris wasn't Aragon, but he could still make his own predictions. She had a year, perhaps; a little less, a little more.

And the thought of that was a cold, cold emptiness in the pit of his stomach, more disturbing than the thought of his own end or the end of the House. He shouldn't have cared so much; but she cared, too. She tried to do her best by him, even though he couldn't rise to her expectations.

He'd prayed, of course; but her face had continued to subtly grow thinner, her skin sallower; and the bouts of coughing came stronger and more often. Perhaps God didn't acknowledge the prayers of Fallen; having cast them from His presence, perhaps He'd forgotten all about them. Perhaps the more extreme priests were right, and redemption was a gift reserved for humans. He didn't know. He'd continued to go to Father Javier's masses, because he couldn't bring himself to believe in that kind of angry, hate-filled God—because his faith was all he had left, and he clung to it as if to a raft in a stormy sea.

He was halfway back to Pont-au-Double when the light dimmed. Puzzled, he looked up, but the sky was the same light gray overcast as it had been a moment ago. Surely . . .

And then, on one of the stalls in front of him—which sold boxes and large, flat mirrors for imprisoning Fallen breath—he saw a flash of the darkness, of something huge and winged crossing the glass for a heartbeat.

No.

That first time, that horrible night of turning left and right and seeing *it*—always barely out of reach, always oozing in some corner of his field of vision—that had been an illusion. Madeleine had found nothing in the House; and nothing more had happened. It was . . .

Across the polished surface of the largest lacquered box, the darkness passed again, and this time there was no mistaking it.

No one else seemed to have seen it. The crowd was slowly dispersing, except for a few hangers-on haggling for a bargain as the market came to a close and merchants had to unload their stock. They met his eyes with idle curiosity, and then turned back to what they were doing.

Oris turned, but there was nothing behind him. But, as he turned back, there was a flash of movement; something barely perceptible against the colored background.

There.

He ran.

He made for the safety of the House, his heart hammering against his chest—and, in every stall that he passed, the darkness flashed, and lingered for a moment, spreading huge black wings; and he could hear a persistent hiss—he'd thought it was some kind of gas spreading, but after a while he realized it was the hiss of dozens of snakes, which he couldn't see anywhere.

He didn't look behind him. He didn't dare to. But there was a shadow at his back, growing as he ran, dimming the light around him; and the hiss grew stronger and stronger.

At the ruined entrance of Notre-Dame, he took the steps two by two, and staggered into the nave—for a moment he stood, breathing hard, voicing the words of a familiar prayer, praying that consecrated ground would be enough to stop them—but he was Fallen, and already knew the answer to his prayers.

Light played on the ruins of benches, of statues, of arches; and the darkness slithered across them all, and this time he could see the full span of the wings as they unfolded—as black and as huge as the ones folklore lent to his kind. They were behind him; close enough to touch; close enough for him to feel the wind of their passage, if he dared to look back. . . .

He turned, and looked; and was lost.

SIX
REQUIEM FOR A FALLEN

MADELEINE took a deep breath and forced herself to look at Oris's corpse.

He lay in the abandonment of Aragon's hospital room, opened up from neck to pubis to the searching of scalpels and scrapers; the inner organs taken out, labeled and weighed by the nurses; the face bloodless and staring upward, with a faint tinge of blue under the eyes.

There was something . . . utterly final about Fallen corpses, some irretrievable loss of lightness, of grace—the skin going blotchier, the hair losing its luster, everything suddenly becoming squatter, heavier— the mortal world's final act of catching up, its final embrace and good-bye, a Fall more definite and eternal than their original one. What lay on the cold metal table, under the ceiling of the Hôtel-Dieu, was Oris, but Oris stripped of everything that had made him such a joy to behold; and only God knew if there was a soul, or where it had gone.

She would never again reprove him for not knowing what to do; or discuss his latest translation from ancient Greek, and argue with him over whether Fallen were exempt of the original sin—half-amused, half-angry, discussing a theology she only had scant time for. She'd always had scant time for Oris—had always fought her annoyance at him, wishing he would stop asking her questions and just get on with things.

She had always had scant time for him, and now there was no time left. None at all; and he was forever gone; forever out of reach—not until the Resurrection and its breaking open of tombs, a thought that was as much dread as it was comfort, for what would God think of Fallen, there at the end of time?

Watch over him, she thought, to her uncaring, cruel God—the one whose existence she couldn't deny, but in whom she had no faith. *Please, watch over him.*

Her fault. Her own fault, for not believing him, for reassuring him that his nighttime experience had been an illusion, that he need not worry about anything; for concealing his fears from Selene because she'd been afraid of being exposed as an angel-essence user.

Coward.

Selene was standing by her side, staring at the corpse; as usual, effortlessly elegant, effortlessly arrogant. Behind her, her bodyguards leaned against the wall of the room; and the nurses were folding used sheets and clearing a table; laying on a tray the scalpels Aragon had used, and everything that had touched Oris. One of them—Pauline, the big woman with the gentle touch—smiled at Madeleine apologetically.

Of course. Of course, the tray was for her, the alchemist of Silverspires. Not one drop of blood would be wasted; the way of life in all Houses, the only one she had ever known. Madeleine took a deep breath, trying to still the trembling of her hands—trying to make the blurred world swim back into focus.

Without warning, Pauline was by her side, laying a callused hand on her shoulder. "You all right?" she asked.

Madeleine shook her head, trying to swallow the salty taste in her mouth. "I'll—be fine," she said, and Pauline shook her head.

"Of course you won't." Pauline squeezed again—a little painfully, but not unkindly. "Come by the office later, if you want. We have strong stuff." Alcohol, of course; Cointreau or chartreuse or pastis: a pleasant way to pass the time, but not what she wanted or needed. The ache for angel essence was enough to make her hands shake—she couldn't afford that, not now. She took a deep breath, and stilled their trembling.

"Thanks," Madeleine said.

Pauline smiled, and withdrew.

Behind her, Selene and Aragon were getting on; of course there was no time for something so trivial, so insignificant as grief. "He was found in the cathedral?" Selene asked Aragon.

"Arms spread, clothes torn," Aragon said, curtly. He removed his gloves and surgical mask; the magic that had been surging through him flickered and died, leaving the room a little less warm, a little less oppressive.

It was a small audience for an autopsy: Emmanuelle and Selene were there; and Madeleine, of course. Oris had been her apprentice, her responsibility.

"What did he die of?" Madeleine asked.

Aragon stood ramrod straight, putting her, incongruously, in mind of a soldier reporting to his commander. "Difficult to say. There's nothing wrong with him, per se. The major organs are intact—everything is clean, or at least as clean as it can be for a Fallen of his age."

"But he's dead," Emmanuelle said, from her place by the door. Her face was set in stone; her skin pale; her hands clenched in front of her, so tight blood had fled her fingertips. It was her, years ago, who had welcomed Oris into the House; who had seen him grow from a naive Fallen into an infuriating apprentice alchemist.

"Yes," Aragon said. "He is dead."

"And the pinpricks?" Selene asked. There were dozens on his arms, spaced in some frenzied, obscene pattern, dizzying in its complexity. Needle pinpricks? Except that they were too large for that—each a small, perfect circle of blood that had barely had time to smudge.

"They didn't kill him," Aragon said. "They're too small, and the blood is clean."

"What are they?" Selene asked.

"They look like snakebites," Aragon said. "That is, if there were a venomless snake that could reach to man height to strike repeatedly. It's certainly not a behavior I've seen in animals. It could also be a weapon of near that shape, though that raises the question of why it'd be used."

Snakebites. Bite marks. Claire's warning. The five deaths.

"Animals can be controlled by spells," Madeleine said, softly; still struggling with the fact that this was happening. That Claire had been right. She should have passed Claire's warning on to Selene, but there had been no time; no time at all before Oris died.

"No doubt," Aragon said. "There is no trace of magic on the wounds whatsoever, though. And, in any case, that's not the culprit. It's almost as if . . ." He paused, shaking his head.

"Go on," Selene said.

"Fallen are an impossibility," Aragon said. "Bones that fragile can't support the body, even if we weigh less than humans. And no back muscle, no matter how strong, would have powered wings; and yet Morningstar wielded his metal wings like a weapon. But—"

"But we have magic." Emmanuelle's voice had the sharp intensity of a dagger slipping between ribs.

"Precisely. Magic, in a very real sense, is what keeps us alive. It's never been proved, of course, but I suspect that lack of magic is what eventually kills us, the Fallen equivalent to dying of old age."

"And?" Madeleine asked.

"It's as if he ran out of magic all of a sudden—and his body went into deadly shock," Aragon said.

"Anaphylactic shock?" Emmanuelle asked.

"Something like that, yes, except that something was taken away rather than added." Aragon made a grimace; he hated using layman approximations. "And the magic is back now—it's a perfectly normal Fallen corpse. So it makes no sense."

"Why not?" Selene asked. "I trust you. If you think that's the explanation . . ."

"Yes, yes," Aragon said. "But there is no spell that has this effect. By their very nature, spells bring magic. They don't cut it off."

"Perhaps we don't know everything about magic yet," Emmanuelle said, gently.

Or perhaps they weren't asking the right person. Claire's dead had been humans, not Fallen, but the similarities were enough to be more than a coincidence.

"He's not the first," Madeleine said.

"The first?" Selene's smooth face creased in puzzlement.

"Claire said—" Madeleine started, swallowed the bitter taste in her mouth—"Claire said there had been other victims."

"Claire of Lazarus?" Selene's voice was harsh. "You didn't tell me you had met her."

Madeleine shrank back from the cold anger, scrambling for excuses that seemed to have disintegrated. "There was no time—"

"There is always time." Selene pursed her lips, as if deliberating punishment. "You should have—"

"Selene." Emmanuelle's voice was gentle. "You can't change what's past."

By Selene's sharp gaze, she clearly wished she could. Madeleine had never set herself against her, had never been overly concerned with the future of the House; but standing by Oris's corpse, she became aware, uncomfortably so, of how little she and Selene had in common. She'd loved—no, "love" wasn't the word; one couldn't love that kind of person—she'd *respected* Morningstar, who could be kind; who had carried her all the way into the House when she lay wounded and dying. But to Selene he had passed nothing of his random bouts of gentleness; of his amused humor. Merely the arrogance, the overweening pride of all Fallen.

"You will tell me everything Claire told you." Selene's voice was clipped, precise.

When Madeleine was done with her halting tale, Selene remained staring at the corpse; though her gaze was distant, and Madeleine doubted she saw Oris at all, except as one of her possessions. "They weren't Fallen," she said. "So that can hardly be the explanation. Nevertheless, it is something that should be explored." She pursed her lips. "Javier is busy with something else, but I'll ask Alcestis—"

"Alcestis isn't concerned with this," Madeleine said, sharply.

"Alcestis doesn't need to be personally concerned with this to be efficient," Selene said.

"I could do it," Madeleine said. "Oris was my apprentice."

"Indeed," Selene said. She didn't need to speak up; her gaze said, all too clearly, that she wouldn't trust Madeleine. "But you'll be busy training your new apprentice."

"Who?" Madeleine asked.

"I don't know yet," Selene said. "Possibly young Isabelle."

She hadn't bothered to ask for Madeleine's opinion; or for anything from her but thoughtless obedience.

Emmanuelle spoke up. "Madeleine could—"

"No," Selene said. "Madeleine will act as this House's alchemist, and strip the corpse, and wait for further orders. There is no way"—her eyes were cold—"I will let a witch untrained in House politics walk into Lazarus. The potential for diplomatic incidents is too high."

"You could have some trust," Madeleine said, stiffly, but it was pointless. Selene had already made her decision; and it probably meant Madeleine would be stuck with Isabelle, too. Not that she had anything against Isabelle, but it was the imposition of her that galled.

Madeleine bowed her head. "Fine. I'll strip the corpse." She'd known this was coming, of course. First and foremost, she was House Silverspires' alchemist, and it was the duty of an alchemist to see that no fragment of Fallen magic was lost. "And I will await further orders."

Selene appeared not to notice the terrible irony in her words; she was apparently deep in thought, possibly planning the next step in her relations with House Lazarus. "Come," she said to Emmanuelle. "There is no time to be wasted."

Aragon and the nurses followed them out of the room—Pauline lingering for a moment, making a gesture that reminded Madeleine the drinks were still waiting for her in the nurses' office, cold comfort for after she was done.

And now, she was alone with Oris.

Strip the corpse. Such casual words, for such a routine thing, for part of her trade—she thought of knives taking flesh apart, of hair saved in small boxes, of bones scraped clean and burned in the incinerator—of her work, now so sickeningly empty of meaning. Later, she'd go back to her room and get high on angel essence; feel the surge of power within her, strong enough to obliterate grief.

But for now, there was only the cold: the merciless clarity rising from her wrung-out lungs; the sharp, biting awareness that she could trust no one but herself.

It had been her fault, from end to end. And she might be dying, she might be weak and incompetent in House politics, as Selene had said; but she knew exactly where her responsibility lay.

She would go to see Claire at House Lazarus, and get what she needed to make sure that Oris was avenged.

IN the end, as he'd known he'd have to, Philippe crept back into the cathedral—because it was the only way he would understand what was going on in the House, and fulfill his deal with Samariel.

The place was as bad as ever; the magic swirling within strong enough to make him itch all over. If anything, it seemed to have gotten worse since Oris's death, though that was absurd. There'd been nothing but the usual Fallen magic on Oris's corpse, and that would have been recovered; the body scraped clean by Madeleine until hardly a trace remained. Unlike former Immortals—who lived long but died, in the end, the same as any mortals, rejoining the eternal cycle of rebirths and reincarnations—Fallen never left much of anything on Earth.

Nevertheless, Philippe gave the blood-spattered stone floor at the entrance a wide berth, before walking closer to the throne.

It stood limned in sunlight, its edges the warm, golden color fit for an emperor; and somehow, even timeworn, even broken, it loomed over the entire cathedral, made his breath catch in his throat—as if, for a moment, a moment only, he had stepped back in time and stood in the cathedral of his visions, and Morningstar still sat in the throne with the easy arrogance of one to whom everything had been given—power, magic, the rule of a House that was the first and largest in the city, destined to stand forever tall and unbroken.

He crept rather than walked, fighting a desire to abase himself; to crawl on the floor as if he were in the presence of Buddha or the Jade Emperor; and when he reached the throne, and touched it, the warmth leaped up his arm like an electric shock, leaving a tingling like that of blood flowing back into emptied veins.

The mirror and the parchment were still where he'd left them, tucked under the throne. He took them out, and laid them in the sunlight.

What could he make of them?

The mirror was a simple affair, engraved with the crest of House Silverspires. He'd seen the same in Madeleine's bag, and a dozen others like it on the stalls of the marketplace. Reaching out, cautiously, to the *khi* currents in the area, Philippe found them only the thinnest thread of water curled around the glass: a confirmation that whatever was inside now lay dormant or dead. There was the hint of another thread, too; a bare trace of wood and its attendant anger: a shadow of something that had once been much stronger, a watered-down image of a flame with none of its heat or vibrancy.

He didn't practice Fallen magic, but he'd learned enough about it; because he had to, because it was a matter of his survival. It had been a powerful spell, held together by a trigger, and it had completely disappeared—drained, all of it, straight into him when he'd touched the mirror; and perhaps elsewhere, if he'd only been the conduit for it.

It had summoned something, something that was loose in the House. He couldn't take the spell apart or intuit what it might do, but he could try to trace it back to its source.

He reached out, and cautiously traced the threads. They might be small and innocuous, but the shards of something this powerful could still be potent. There was . . . sorrow, and the roiling anger of a just cause. . . .

Revenge, then. Someone, somewhere, had had a grudge against Morningstar, or against the House.

Philippe touched the mirror again, following the *khi* currents. They had decayed so much he'd have been hard-pressed to put an age to them, but such decay was the work of years, decades, which meant an old spell. A Fallen, perhaps—to whom the years would be as nothing—or a human who was old by now, with the satisfaction that his vengeance would come to pass. They had left the mirror here, hidden away—never thinking that Morningstar would never come back, that the throne would gather dust and never be touched, and that their spell would only be triggered years and years after it had been put together.

He tugged at the thread of wood, gently unspooling it from around the mirror: loop after loop of thin, shimmering green light that hung on his hands, with a sharp touch like a spring breeze. Then, breathing slowly, carefully—inhale, exhale, inhale, whispering a mantra from bygone times—he withdrew his awareness from his body, and let the thread carry him where it willed.

For a while, he hung suspended in time and space; back to a serenity he'd thought lost, doing nothing but letting the world wash over him, every sensation diminishing until he was once more in that quiet, timeless place where his enlightenment took root.

Gradually—and he wasn't sure why, or how, or when—it all went away, a slow slide from featureless bliss into something stronger, darker; shadows lengthening over the House, until he stood in a room lined with bookshelves, the only furniture of which was a red plush armchair.

Morningstar sat in the chair. Or rather, lounged in it like a sated tiger, his wings shadowing the sharpness of his face. His pale eyes raking Philippe from top to bottom. "So good of you to come. Shall we start, then?" He inclined his head, and between his spread hands magic whirled and danced, a storm of power that pressed against the bookshelves, stifled the air of the room—cut off Philippe's breath until it was all he could do to stand.

"I can't—" he started, and Morningstar shook his head.

"This is power. Embrace it, or others will do it, and leave you gasping in the dust."

Philippe shook his head, or tried to. He couldn't seem to move, and Morningstar's presence was as suffocating as ever—lead pressing on his chest, on his fingers—until it seemed that his nails would lengthen and sharpen, becoming the claws of Morningstar's own hands. . . .

"Come," Morningstar said, smiling. "There isn't much time."

And he found his feet moving of their own accord, his hands reaching for the magic Morningstar was offering; he took one faltering step into the room, even though his skin was being peeled away from muscle and fat, from bones and glistening veins: one step, then another, straight into the growing maelstrom. . . .

Philippe came to with a gasp. He was standing in a room he had never been to, though he recognized it instantly. It was the same room as in his vision, except that it had badly aged. He had vague memories of exiting the cathedral through a side door, following corridor after corridor; gradually leaving behind the more crowded areas until the House became entombed with dust, gray and bowed with the weight of its true age.

A thread of wood; a thread of water and fire, all curled up and dormant: a vision from the past. Memories. Someone else's memories. He hadn't been really interacting with Morningstar; merely seeing someone else do so, in some faraway past.

The same person who had laid that mirror under the throne, in all likelihood—someone who had admired, and feared, and hated Morningstar. Was Philippe's reaction to Morningstar memories, too, or would he have felt the same in the actual presence of the Fallen? There was no way to know.

The bookshelves hadn't been maintained, and the dry smell of brittle paper rose all around him. The flowers of the wallpaper were speckled with rot, and the oaken parquet bore only the imprint of his own footsteps. The armchair was still there, its colors faded and worn; and there was a smaller chair in front of it, carved from rich mahogany, the only thing in the room that didn't seem to have deteriorated. He could sit in here; in fact, he had sat on it, sometime in the distant past—no, that couldn't be. That wasn't him. He had never been in this room, and his memories stretched back centuries.

Across the threshold was a very faint line of magic, which itself came from two small vials on either side of the frame. A few Fallen tears, sealed in glass and used for a spell, and he didn't have to touch them to know who they'd have come from: the same suffocating presence that haunted his dreams.

Morningstar.

He crossed the line; a faint resistance held him, but not for long. When he looked at the room from the outside, it would waver and wriggle, trying to squirm its way out of his field of vision, out of his memory. The spell, then, was still there; obscuring the room from sight, though it had been much stronger, once.

The *khi* currents in the room were stronger: roiling wood; and a burst of metal, subsuming the other three. Metal. Tears, sadness; the act of contracting, of looking backward—the past. And wood. Wood was for anger; wood was the wind, the vegetation bursting through the ice of graveyards. It wasn't visions that he was having; no prophecies, no cryptic dreams requiring him to swear allegiance to Morningstar. They were memories. Someone's memories, encased in so much anger they'd been preserved with the force of a storm.

Revenge, then.

That didn't help much. Philippe stood in the room, staring at the stool; wondering who had sat on it, and why they had hated Morningstar so much. He'd taught them, hadn't he—who wouldn't be glad to have such a teacher?

But, then, this was the West, and they'd never had the proper respect for their elders.

Whoever it was, they had lived for a long time: he'd caught enough glimpses of enough time periods that they spanned centuries. A Fallen, then, whom the years barely touched—humans could have used magic to lengthen their life spans, but not by this much. A Fallen student of Morningstar; with a grudge.

Was this of use to Samariel? Possibly, if he had more information—on whom it was, and what the curse was. He would only have one chance to give this information, one moment of the other's time, so that the spell on him could be removed. He wasn't fool enough to believe that Samariel would care for him beyond that.

He needed more information, and he knew exactly where to find it.

PHILIPPE went to see Emmanuelle early in the day. He knew from experience that she'd get up at dawn and head straight to Father Javier's Mass in the small chapel of the North Wing, before setting to work. He went, therefore, to the library, and found it already buzzing with activity. The archivists—Raoul and others he couldn't name—were busy, carrying piles of leather-bound books from one shelf to the next and arguing about proper placement, the location of a lost volume, or the latest finds on the history of the House.

He found Emmanuelle behind her desk, staring dubiously at a wobbling pile of books from which arose a strong smell of rot. Two children—they couldn't have been more than six or seven years old—were kneeling on the floor, setting books aside and having an argument about which books fit where. "Emmanuelle, Emmanuelle," the youngest—a girl with dark hair and brown eyes the color of autumn leaves—"Pierre-Alain says this one isn't interesting—"

The boy—Pierre-Alain, who looked enough like her he had to be her brother or cousin—scowled. "It's too badly damaged. We should throw it away."

"We can fix it," the girl said, holding the book against her as though it were beyond worth. "I'm sure we can, Emmanuelle. Please?"

Emmanuelle knelt and gently pried the book from the girl's fingers—carefully turning the pages in a rising smell of mold. "Mmm. It's pretty wet. Can you get some absorbent paper from the back shelf? And put a sheet of it between every wet page?"

"Of course! Come on, Pierre-Alain!"

When the children were gone, Emmanuelle rose. "Market finds," she said, with a shrug. "I'm pretty sure there's not much worth salvaging in there, but one never knows—and Caroline loves feeling useful. Did you want something?"

Philippe pulled a chair, and sat next to her. "You said to come to you if we had any questions—"

"Oh, yes." Emmanuelle pulled the topmost book from the stack—it had a stylized, naturalistic design reminiscent of the art nouveau buildings in the city—and blew on it absentmindedly.

"I wanted to know more about Morningstar," Philippe said. "You knew him when he was . . . here, didn't you?"

"You could say that," Emmanuelle said, cautiously. "I wasn't there for very long, though: a century, at most, and he never paid attention to me, not the way he did to others."

"Like Selene?"

"Yes." Emmanuelle set the book aside. "Selene was his student; the last among many. He was . . . different. Most Fallen don't exude more than a trace amount of power, but with Morningstar you felt as though you stood in the presence of a furnace."

I know, Philippe wanted to say, and bit his tongue, lest he betray himself. "So he taught many students in the House?"

Emmanuelle shook her head. "He taught them for the House, yes, but—" She bit her lip, uncomfortable. "The war came."

The war. Philippe thought of the clamor of explosions; of huddling in the doorways of ruined buildings, peering at the sky to judge the best moment to rush out; of his lieutenant in House colors, urging them to lay down their lives for the good of the city; of his squad mates buried in nameless graves, on the edge of Place de la République. Ai Linh, who had a laugh like a donkey, and always shared her biscuits with everyone else; Hoang, who liked to gamble too much; Phuong, who told hair-raising stories in the barracks after all lights had been turned off. "I don't know what the war was like, inside the Houses," he said, and it was almost the truth.

Emmanuelle stared at him for a while, her pleasant face almost hard. Did she suspect how he'd come to be here; what the war had been like for him? "Our magicians turned into soldiers," she said at last.

"Our students into thoughtless killers, and our best men into corpses. When the war ended, most of Morningstar's students were dead, as were so many in the House."

Philippe remembered the fall of House Draken; remembered retreating down corridor after corridor, as armed mortals and Fallen overwhelmed every inch of available space, and the lieutenant breathed down their necks, screaming at them to resist, to show that House Draken died with honor; he remembered thinking that he was the House's possession, not its cherished member, that he had no honor and no desire to acquire any.

There had been so many corpses, by the time the House had succumbed; so many corpses in the abandonment of death; and he had not wept for a single one of them.

"But Morningstar—"

"Morningstar wasn't on the front lines. He was always more comfortable manipulating people, after all. Not that it was unpleasant; people *loved* following his orders: who wouldn't? It was such . . . terrible bliss, from what I have heard." Her voice was resentful; it wasn't clear whether she was angry at Morningstar's behavior, or jealous that she hadn't been singled out for that bitter honor. "Selene was lucky; he was teaching her at the time and didn't want his efforts to go to waste before she was ready."

So he'd sent students to their deaths. "So they died. And were happy. And those who survived?" Philippe said cautiously.

Emmanuelle frowned. "There were two, I think? Leander and Oris, and Selene, of course."

"He taught Oris?" Philippe asked. That he'd seen something in Oris—of all people—

Emmanuelle shrugged. "Did you think Oris was always that way?" She smiled, but the look never reached her eyes. "Morningstar was . . . like living fire," she said at last. "It can fill you up and make you shine harder than you ever did, or it can seep through every crack and burn you from the inside out." She closed the book. "Selene . . . took it well, I think, and Leander . . ." She thought about it for a while. "Leander was always a bit odd, and it never changed him, though from time to time he'd look up and there'd be this odd light in his eyes. Cracks."

Were there cracks, too, in Selene's mind? What must it be like to succeed that kind of Fallen, and forever try to live up to their image? Living fire, Emmanuelle had said.

"I've not met a Leander," Philippe said.

"You wouldn't," Emmanuelle said. "He's been dead for decades."

"An accident?"

"Old age," Emmanuelle said.

A mortal, then. An odd choice for Morningstar, but then again, who was he to judge? What had the Fallen looked for, in his students—and what had he found? What had made someone burn with that twisted, dark anger he'd felt, when touching the mirror?

Leander was dead, which ruled him out. And, of course, Selene was out, because she'd been in the vision.

"You're sure there were no other students of his who survived the war?" Taking students like commodities; bewitching them and sending them to slaughter: it was powerful and plausible motivation for someone to *hate* Morningstar, perhaps enough to doom his entire House in the process. But if everyone was dead or ruled out, then it left only Oris.

Who was also dead.

A terribly convenient coincidence, if it was a coincidence at all.

"That's an awful lot of questions," Emmanuelle said. Her eyes narrowed. "Why the curiosity?"

Demons take him; he'd pushed her too far. He couldn't let her press further; she was perceptive enough to realize that he was hardly asking about Morningstar for the good of the House. "I guess I'm trying to understand Selene," he said, falling back on the first excuse that came to mind.

Emmanuelle stared at him for a while, but he'd had lots of practice staring Ninon and Baptiste down. "I see," she said. "Don't get any ideas, Philippe. I'm not the pathway into her mind."

"No," he said, glibly, and left her staring at her book—going back to his biography of Morningstar.

*   *   *

ISABELLE found him, hours later, halfway through the book and not much more advanced. The names of Morningstar's students were in there, all blurring together like glass on a windowpane: Hyacinth, Seraphina, Nightingale, Leander, Oris. . . .

Hyacinth had been a minor mortal of the House, a laundry servant vaguely dissatisfied with his life but not overly power-hungry: after Morningstar was done with him, he'd risen to be the personal valet of a high-rank Fallen, and, insofar as Philippe could see, had remained in that position all his life. Seraphina had been found by Morningstar himself, on a night when he was prowling the city—lying weak and helpless in the wreck of the Arc de Triomphe, and taken in tow like a child until he had grown bored with her. Nightingale had been mortal: one of the House's minor witches, noted for her wild theories about spells and her unorthodox way of doing magic—probably what had drawn Morningstar's eye in the first place. Leander was mortal, too, and ambitious—unlike Nightingale, he had been steadily rising through the ranks, becoming one of the House's foremost magicians, powerful enough to rival Fallen. And Oris . . . Oris had already been an alchemist's assistant, and after Morningstar gave up on him, he'd simply gone back to his beloved artifacts and charged mirrors.

Without preamble, Isabelle pulled a wooden chair toward her, and sat facing him across the low table. "You owe me a few explanations."

"I'm listening," he said.

Isabelle shook her head. She wore pale clothes, which only emphasized the cast of her olive skin, and the mortar-and-pestle insignia of alchemists sat uneasily on her breast—skewed, showing large swaths of the adhesive patch that was meant to keep it in place. "*I* came here to listen," she said. "Like what you were doing with House Hawthorn."

Philippe set the book aside, and looked up. They were alone in this section of the library—where the bookshelves were half-empty; the books torn and stained, not painstakingly put back together by Emmanuelle's hands; and the smell of rotten, wet things rather than comforting mustiness.

"That's my own business," he said at last.

Isabelle smiled, but the expression didn't reach her eyes. "I thought I could trust you."

He hadn't seen her since the market—he'd have said she was avoiding him, but he was, too—not sure of what he could tell her.

"You've changed," he said, slowly. "What has Madeleine done to you?"

She sat straight-backed—her skin a pale golden rather than the shade he was used to, but her bearing regal. "Madeleine? Nothing."

"Oris—"

Her gaze remained steady. "I had to take Oris apart. Madeleine was trying not to cry the entire time. It wasn't so bad for me—I didn't really know him, after all." She worried at the hole on her left hand; the two missing fingers—how did you scrape flesh and muscle from bone, with half a hand? Badly, he guessed.

"But it wasn't easy. I'm sorry." It was rote, and thoughtless, and it was the absolute wrong thing he could have said.

"You're not. And don't change the subject, please."

What could he tell her? He ought to lie; ought to make life easier for himself; but staring into those wide, shining eyes that still reflected the light of the City, Philippe found himself unable to twist the truth. "I'm not House, Isabelle. I'm only here under duress. You know that."

"So you want to escape." There was no condemnation on her face; only an odd kind of thoughtfulness, as if she'd found a behavior she couldn't quite explain. In a way, that was worse. "Into another House."

"No," Philippe said. Anywhere but Houses. Back on the streets, or into Annam—waiting, as she herself had said, for a boat, for regular traffic to resume, or security on maritime commerce to grow slack. "But I can't stay here, not on Selene's terms. You have to see that."

"I do." Isabelle's voice was still thoughtful. "I do understand. But this can't be the right way to go about it."

"Then give me another one."

Isabelle flinched; but did not draw back, or apologize, as she might have done once. She *had* changed; carbon pressed together until it became the first inklings of a diamond.

"I can't—I don't know enough, Philippe."

"I know," he said, wearily. "But I need a way forward, Isabelle." He needed—freedom? The same sense of weightlessness he'd once enjoyed in Annam, in the court of the Jade Emperor; when he moved among bejeweled ladies and haughty lords, drinking pale tea in celadon cups as fragile as eggshells—a feeling that was now lost forever. In that desperate longing he wasn't so different from Fallen, after all: a frightening thought.

She sat still for a while, staring at him; biting her lip, young and bewildered and lost. "I—I know. But you're playing with fire, and I can't. I need the House, Philippe, or I won't survive. I can't allow you to damage it, even if I understand why you're doing it. I have to tell Selene."

"No. Please."

He *was* hurting the House, or planning to—it wasn't a bad place to be, insofar as Houses went, and the people—Laure, Emmanuelle, the kitchen staff—had been kind to him. But it was a House—built on arrogance and blood and the hoarding of magic—and its master held the keys to his chains. He had . . . He had to be free.

"I won't tell her it's you," Isabelle said. "But she needs to know what Hawthorn is doing."

As if Selene wouldn't guess which of her new arrivals was being unfaithful. "She'll flay me," Philippe said, reflexively; but something within him, something older and prouder, whispered, *Let her try*—and the voice was Morningstar's.

What? No. That wasn't—that wasn't possible.

Isabelle shook her head. "She's not like that. You don't know her—"

Of course he knew her. She'd do anything to preserve her chosen Fallen and mortals, and let everyone else rot—and he couldn't tell, anymore, if the thoughts were his or Morningstar's. He teetered on the edge of the abyss where he would lose himself in a way utterly alien to him, subsumed in the unpalatable memories of a Fallen. . . .

"Give me time," he said through clenched lips. "Please, Isabelle. You know—"

"That you don't mean harm?" She was silent for a while.

"That's not what I mean. I don't wish the House harm." And it was a lie, and they both knew it. "But you have to see I'm a prisoner here." As she was not. She was Fallen, with all the privileges this afforded her; and Silverspires was her home. It could never be his, even if it had been as welcoming as his own mother's hearth. He was . . . Annamite. Other. "Please."

Her eyes shone in the paleness of her face. "I can guess what you feel. I can—" She took in a deep, shaking breath. "I feel some of it."

Philippe looked away, trying to avoid her gaze, or her three-fingered hand. What was it for her, the same as for him: an odd twisting in his belly; a nagging sense of always knowing where she was, a faint echo of what she felt? Affection, embarrassment? It was too weak an emotion, whatever was in her mind; and he wouldn't understand her so easily. They moved in wholly different worlds.

"Then—" He hardly dared to breathe.

She didn't move for a while. "Three days. That's all I can give you, Philippe."

After she'd left, he sat in his chair, staring at the book in front of him—the past that should have had no bearing on him—breathing hard.

Three days. He had three days before Selene was informed of what he was up to, and his life got a lot more difficult, and possibly a lot shorter. Three days to find something; that was if the memories didn't kill him first.

He had to find out what was going on in the House, and not entirely so he could get rid of his chains.

No, he had to know, because it looked as though the curse wasn't going to be content with the occasional vision from the past. If he didn't understand it, he was going to find himself swept along in whatever twisted revenge the unknown Fallen had dreamed of, and utterly lose himself in the process.

SEVEN
A Darkness Within the House

HOUSE Lazarus stood a few hundred meters west of the Grands Magasins, though the contrast could not have been greater. The House had cleared its own surroundings. The streets were grime-splattered, the buildings stained with the black of magical residue, but everything was clear of debris: the railings freshly painted a shade of dark green, the clock on the frontispiece on time and chiming the quarter hours, and every window of the building decorated with elegant baize curtains. There were even a few cars parked in the large plaza in front of the House—though, judging by their worn-out appearance, they were more likely to belong to minor Houses or wealthy independents. Then again, Madeleine wasn't sure how she'd have reacted, if she'd seen one of House Hawthorn's big limousines parked in front of the House.

She'd taken one of the city's large omnibuses; clutching the bag with the tools of her trade against her, enduring the suspicious gazes of her neighbors as they wondered why a House-bound would bother to take a horse-drawn, communal vehicle.

There were no guards at the main entrance; or, to be more accurate, no one who challenged her as she made her way under the wide arches of the House's central building. House Lazarus prided itself on welcoming anyone in need, though that didn't mean anyone could go wherever they wanted within the House. The relaxed attitude hid powerful defenses. Every House was a fortress guarded by spells and men. They had to be; otherwise they wouldn't last long in the city.

The lower floor of House Lazarus was a wide, airy hall. The founder, Eugénie, had wished for it to be a place of sharing where the entire House could congregate, Fallen and mortals alike. In design it somewhat resembled the nearby Saint-Lazare station: a series of metal arches supporting a low roof, and long trestle tables where the rails would have been—each table divided in several segments where people dispensed anything from food to medical help. It was the heart of House Lazarus's network of safe houses, the place everyone received their supplies or their attribution of beds or rooms, according to their needs. Philippe, apparently, had gone through there, too, which was unexpected; and even more unexpected was that he knew Claire. What was their relationship, exactly?

The queues were as busy as ever—watched over by what seemed like an army of guards. As Madeleine made her way to the right—where stairs led to the more private part of the building—there was a commotion—a scuffle, a burst of magic, and a brief scream, soon cut off. Someone had tried to cut ahead, or to steal something; and now lay dead on the floor. Claire ran a tight House, where there was no place for disorder.

Madeleine approached the guards leaning casually against the metal pillars—they tensed, slightly, when they saw her. "I'm from House Silverspires, and I need to see Lady Claire," Madeleine said, without preamble. Diplomacy had never been her forte, and she wasn't about to try it now.

The left-hand guard looked her up and down. He had opened his mouth for a dismissal, when his neighbor nudged him. "She's their alchemist, Eric. Don't you think—"

Eric bit back an obvious swearword, and gestured her toward the foot of the staircase. "Wait here," he said. "I'll send someone for Lady Claire. But she's busy, mind you—and I'm sure she has no time for the likes of you, alchemist or no alchemist."

Madeleine sat down on the first step, clutching her bag. It was silly, but the weight of familiar tools reassured her. Going to another House was very much entering enemy territory, even if House Lazarus was friendly by House standards.

She tried not to think of Oris—of his face, shrunken and distorted in death; of her hands, saving flesh and nails and blood; parting skin to reveal red, glistening muscles underneath, peeling back everything that had made him—and nowhere could she see his smile, or his infuriating habit of hovering nearby, or the way he'd had of taking tea in the laboratory, drinking the dust-covered liquid as if nothing were amiss. . . .

She would not cry. She had spent all her tears on Elphon, a long time ago; had crawled away from Hawthorn, her wounds weeping blood. All her grieving was done, a thing of the past—or should have been of the past.

Oh, Oris . . .

Now, when Madeleine looked up in her laboratory, she saw Isabelle; reaching for a bowl or a mirror with a frown on her face; carrying a precariously balanced pile of books from one end of the room to the other—trying to put order in Madeleine's things, she'd said with a smile.

She meant well, and yet Madeleine wanted to scream at her; to shake her until she understood whose place she was taking, whose memories she was driving out. It was unfair and unkind, but she couldn't help it.

The walls of the staircase had been painted with a long frieze, which seemed to depict the history of the House from its founding. It was a short history, as Lazarus was barely older than the Great War, and a painful one—Eugénie had died in one of the first skirmishes, almost causing the House to vanish before it could even find its place in the hierarchy of the city. But Claire and her predecessor had worked miracles.

"Miss d'Aubin?"

Madeleine got up, staring at a young girl dressed in the brown and green of the House. "Lady Claire will see you now."

She'd expected Claire to receive her in her salon; in rooms that would show her exquisite taste, making it clear that she might be younger than Fallen, but that she still knew exactly how to impress her visitors.

But instead, her guide took her downward, into the bowels of the House, into a maze of unadorned, identical concrete corridors, their walls shining with moisture; the weight of the entire House seemed to be pressing down on her. Damn it, she hated enclosed spaces, and modern enclosed spaces even more.

The corridors narrowed; the doors became thicker and thicker—and the noises that filtered from within became moans and cries and screams—petering out into utter silence. The cells, where those who had displeased Claire awaited her pleasure—and she doubted Claire was ever pleased. It was easy, in the light of day, to forget that Claire was ruthless; that it took ten, fifteen times the cruelty of a Fallen to run one of the greatest Houses in Paris when one was mortal.

Madeleine kept her bag against her, trying not to show the emotions on her face—by her side, the young girl did her the courtesy of not saying anything; though she had little doubt everything would be reported to Claire, eventually.

The silence grew and grew—and there was a faint smell of blood, like a charnel house, filtering through the doors—and then nothing, which was scarier than anything she'd seen or heard before. Finally they reached a door of rusted metal, and her guide gestured for her to enter. "Are you sure?" Madeleine asked, and the girl nodded.

Inside, it was dark; the only illumination coming from an exposed bulb in the center of the room, which cast wavering shadows on the walls. The back wall was occupied by a series of square drawers; and, suddenly, Madeleine knew exactly what she was staring at. "The morgue?" she asked, aloud.

"Good." Claire's voice came from behind her—she hadn't expected that, and almost jumped out of her skin when the other woman spoke up. "You're fast on the uptake. But then, you always were."

"What the blazes was that for?" Madeleine asked. "Love of drama?"

"Partly." Claire came into view. She wore a grubby lab overall, over a knitted woolen jacket. Behind her was a Fallen in the same kind of overall, carrying a clipboard. "I wasn't expecting you here, Madeleine."

Madeleine shivered. She shouldn't even be there; Selene's warning was all too present in her mind. "When we last met, you dropped some cryptic warnings."

Claire smiled, though the look didn't reach her eyes. "Cryptic? I thought I was being very clear."

"You wanted us to tell Selene about your murders," Madeleine said, remembering what Philippe had said. "Why?"

"Why? Why are you here, Madeleine?"

"Because I need to know more about your corpses."

"Someone died at Silverspires," Claire said. She put both hands on the wooden table in the center of the room, leaning on it as if she could drive it into the floor. "A Fallen, by all accounts." Her face darkened, slightly. "I'm sorry for your loss. I genuinely am. But I hoped someone would follow through on my warnings. I didn't think it was going to take a death before that happened."

"Oris died a handful of minutes after you gave your warning," Madeleine said. "Even if we'd heeded your warning, there was no time."

Claire's face darkened; she looked genuinely angry. "I am not responsible for his death. I couldn't possibly have known when it would occur, or even that it was going to occur at all. Can you believe me?"

She wasn't sorry. Madeleine didn't think Claire would grieve for anything or anyone that didn't concern her. But her anger seemed genuine.

"You know something," Madeleine said.

"No more than what I pick up." Claire smiled. "But sometimes, it's enough. Come here, Madeleine. Let me show you what we gather on the streets."

The box at the end of the morgue opened up with barely a noise, sliding on oiled rails; showing the face of the corpse inside, his eyes staring listlessly at the ceiling. For some incongruous reason, Madeleine found herself thinking of dead fish at the market: he had been kept on ice, but for so long that decay had settled in, bloating the shapes before her until he hardly seemed human anymore. Not that it would have mattered: she was used to corpses, so much that they were now like old friends, and she flirted close enough to death that it held no fear anymore—save that of the Resurrection, when she would have to face God and number her many sins. Pride. Despair. The vanity of second-guessing God's plans for the Fallen, raging at their unfair abandonment.

The face . . . The face, bloated and decayed almost past recognition.

She knew that face. She'd seen that man—she foundered, for a moment, struggling to recall his name. Théodore. Théodore Ganimard. She'd seen him in passing, going in and out of Selene's office at odd hours—part of the network of spies and informants that kept Selene apprised of what was going on in the city: Madeleine knew most of them—a side effect of being up at odd hours herself.

Claire laid something by the body's side, negligently. "He had this on him."

It was a heavy, polished disk of wood: a minor artifact, used for tracking down whoever bore it; except that on the wood's surface were engraved the arms of Silverspires: the sword of Morningstar against the silhouetted spires of Notre-Dame. Madeleine had one exactly like it in her trouser pocket. "A tracker disk," she said numbly. Once, it would have pulsed to the rhythm of magic, but the wood was blackened and charred; and the magic quite gone from it.

"They are given to dependents of Silverspires." Claire's face hadn't moved.

"He . . ." He was dead with the disk on him, and it didn't matter anymore whether Claire knew. "He was one of our informants."

Claire nodded. "I thought so." Behind her, the assistant made a note on the clipboard—his broad face creased in thought.

On the marbled skin of the corpse were the same marks she'd seen on Oris's forearms: the perfect circle with a sharper wound in the center. They'd have been smudged with blood once, but now that everything had been cleaned, nothing was left but the imprint of the wound. Fangs, Aragon had said. Snakebites. But no snake had just one fang— and why strike someone repeatedly?

She foraged in her bag by touch; found a sealed mirror, and undid the clasp while keeping her eyes on the corpse's face. The angel breath was like fire in her nostrils; descending into her wasted lungs and wringing them from the inside out—she was bent over, gagging and coughing with the strength of it, already longing for something else the mirror couldn't provide, for the sheer potency of angel essence. . . .

She looked up through eyes streaming with tears. The corpse in front of her was shining. There was no other word. Every wound was outlined in a thin, scattered radiance: not the furious blaze of infant Fallen, or even the stately glow of mature ones like Selene and Emmanuelle, but faint and faded like glow worms. "Magic?" she asked. "This was done by a spell?"

Claire, who had been watching her in silence, shook her head. In Madeleine's new sight, she shone, or rather, the space between her breasts did. An artifact within a locket, hidden under her clothes; not a surprise, for the mortal head of a House.

Madeleine whispered the words of a spell, willing the magic to show her how they had died. Nothing happened. For a moment she feared she'd cast the wrong thing; and then the corpse lit up like a bonfire, washing the entire room in radiance. Claire cried out, and then there was darkness again, shot through with painful afterimages.

"Magic killed him," she said, slowly, hoarsely, forcing the words through what felt like a mouthful of burning sand. "Like being burned. A blast of Fallen power so strong it stripped him bare." And blasted the tracker disk, too, rendering it unusable. The human body wasn't meant to hold Fallen magic; in the long run, people who absorbed too much angel—or too much angel essence, or both—died.

Claire said nothing.

"The Fallen who died in Silverspires—" Madeleine said, the words torn out of her mouth before she could think them through. "—he died when his magic was taken away from him."

Claire nodded. She didn't seem surprised. She reached out, and gently folded the sheet back over the corpse. "You'll want to see the others, too," she said.

She opened another drawer: a woman, with the same dead eyes staring upward at Madeleine, filmed over by the haze of death; the same mysterious circle wounds.

Madeleine knew her, too. Hortense Archignat, another of Selene's informants.

Gritting her teeth, Madeleine whispered the words of the spell again, bracing herself—and felt the same blaze of magic spreading from the wounds, incinerating the internal organs and then dying down to that sickly glow.

"Something . . ." She breathed in, willing her heart to stop hammering against her chest. "Something that kills. Humans, by overwhelming them with magic until their bodies shut down. Fallen—"

"With the reverse," Claire said. She threw something on the body, negligently—but of course she never did anything negligently. "She had this on her."

Another tracker disk—Madeleine reached out, expecting to see the arms of Silverspires, but the engraving on it was a hawthorn tree circled with a crown. "Hawthorn," she said. Some informants made ends meet by working for several Houses, and Hortense Archignat must have been one of them. The heads of Houses might not like this state of affairs—or trust them with their secrets—but they were pragmatic enough to make use of what tools they had. "I don't understand—" she said, hoping to hide her confusion.

Claire looked at her, her gaze as sharp as spears, but said nothing. Instead, she gestured, and her assistant opened another drawer.

"He was homeless," she said, as the third body slid into view. "Slept in the ruins of Saint-Eustache. He died in the wreck of Les Halles."

Jean-Philippe d'Hergemont—his family, minor nobility, had been ruined during the Great War. Madeleine remembered chatting with him; giving him a charged mirror on Selene's orders. He'd carried one of the loaves from the kitchens, awkwardly balancing it in arms full of the old clothes Choérine had pressed onto him.

Another of Selene's informants.

"He didn't have a tracker disk," Claire said. She was still watching Madeleine, and Madeleine struggled not to show her rising anxiety. Someone was killing Silverspires informants. Someone was . . .

She couldn't afford to show weakness. She couldn't afford to reveal said weakness to Claire—Selene would have her head, not to mention the disastrous effect this would have on the House.

She took a deep, trembling breath; hiding her confusion beneath a forced cough. One good thing about having wrecked lungs was that she could fake one quite easily. "He died like the others, didn't he?"

"Of course," Claire said. She smiled, like a grandmother amused by one of her grandchildren's tricks; except there was no warmth in the look whatsoever. "Look at the next one, will you?"

Madeleine braced herself—tried to prevent her hands from clenching, aware all the while that Claire probably read her like an open book. But she had to try. If there was a chance, any chance, she could hide how flustered she was—what she knew, the secrets she couldn't afford to share . . .

The next corpse was a man again, much younger and with an arm missing—and she knew him, too. Jacques Rossigny, one of the ravagers on the banks of the Seine, living off what he scavenged from the angry river; and on his work as informant to Silverspires.

By now Claire's smile was as sharp as that of a tiger sighting its prey—filling Madeleine's entire field of view, quenching the breath in her lungs.

"I don't know him," she said, forcing the words out between clenched lips.

Claire's gaze didn't waver; but she didn't produce a tracker disk, or anything that looked as though it might bite. Her smile abated a fraction, but it didn't make her less worrisome. What was she up to? How much did she know?

"Here's the last one," Claire said, as her assistant opened the last drawer.

And the last . . . the last was an older woman; a Senegalese-French, Marie-Céleste Ndiaye, the owner of a bookshop in the southwest, near Hawthorn—who usually came in toward the end of the night, carrying one or two tattered books as if they were treasures.

Claire didn't bother to throw the tracker disk this time; she merely handed it to Madeleine. "Harrier. Infused with Guy's rather distinctive brand of magic," she said, casually. "Do you see, now?"

"No," Madeleine said, reflexively. Five dead. Five of Selene's informants, their identities unknown to anyone but the Houses who employed them. It couldn't be a coincidence; but only someone from Silverspires should have known the identity of all five.

Claire's voice was thoughtful. "One of these is a dependent of yours. I assume Selene knows he's dead by now, but not the circumstances in which he died."

"The others belong to other Houses," Madeleine said; the words a reflex, driven out of her before she could think. Of course House Silverspires was the target. Of course the corpses were all theirs—from the five in Claire's morgue to poor Oris. "And you could have sent a message."

"Perhaps I should have." Claire was silent for a while. At length, she picked up the tracker disks, one by one. "It's a fragile city. A careful balance of magic, to protect all against a resurgence of the Great Houses War, and all of us seeking to change it, to grasp what advantage we can. We wouldn't fight the war again, of course; but if we can have a chance, even a small chance, of making others tumble down—if we can humble down our rivals, even our allies . . . we would seize this opportunity in a heartbeat, and never even look back."

"I'm not interested in your games."

"I know. What a pity. You'll find, I think, that you need to play to survive, Madeleine; that you can't go through life enamored of your artifacts and mirrors and scraping of bones." Her voice was sharp, mocking—Madeleine froze at the reference to bones, but Claire couldn't possibly know about the essence—couldn't . . . No, she was going on, not touching on it again. . . . She couldn't possibly know.

"If you don't take control of your own life, other people will do it for you—with far less kindness and far less compassion than you would expect or deserve. The Houses shape Paris, and there is very little that isn't caught in their nets. To attack them all . . . would be sheer folly." A clink of wood against wood, as Claire played with the charred tracker disk; and the noise of the drawer as she closed it, gently leaning against it.

Madeleine struggled to see things the way Claire did—dead informants belonging to different Houses, killed by a spell no one had seen the like of. "Someone has found a way to power," she said, slowly, lightly. The room felt too small, the air tightening around her as if it were going to crush her against the floor.

"Of course," Claire said. "They always do, in this city. As I said—we all hunger for power; for what we grasp to haul ourselves to the top of the hierarchy, even if it's just to crow over the ruins."

"Silverspires doesn't crave power at all costs."

Claire smiled. Something was wrong. Something . . . "You don't know much about what Silverspires does and does not do, do you? I imagine Selene finds it wiser to keep you in the dark."

As she'd done, insisting Madeleine shouldn't come here, but she'd been right—Madeleine shouldn't have left all her protections behind—shouldn't be here, trying to spar with Claire, who had so many more years of experience at this than she. Was Claire trying to rile her up? Madeleine didn't have much pride to speak of. "Do you think I'm unhappy being kept away from the limelight? I'm not. To each her role."

"Oh, Madeleine." Claire's voice was almost sad. "To each his or her place, and let no one question it? You are worth more than this."

Something was wrong. Claire would never give her compliments unless there was something she needed from her. Something . . .

And then, with a lurch in her belly that seemed to turn the entire world upside down, Madeleine realized that there were only the two of them in the room. The assistant was gone—when had he left? She hadn't paid much attention, engrossed by the corpses and what Claire was saying. A mistake. It could all have been innocent—a minor Fallen, gone because Claire had no more need of him.

Except . . . Except Claire had been stalling for time, hadn't she— that rambling, lengthy tirade on power within the city, making small talk in a place where there should have been no need of it?

The assistant was gone, and no doubt he had carried a message—to whom, and what for?

She—she needed to get back to Silverspires. She needed to warn Selene; and she needed to warn her *now*.

"I need to go," she said. "Thank you for showing me your dead. I'll tell Selene to keep an eye out; I'm sure she'll appreciate the attention." She was babbling by now; utterly incoherent, her fear and worry all too visible, broadcast like a foghorn on a calm sea.

"So soon?" Claire hadn't moved from where she stood, with her arms crossed on her chest, and that same satisfied smile on her face.

Keep calm. She needed to keep calm. She needed to . . . breathe, but the breath wouldn't come to her clogged, wasted lungs. "You wanted me to warn Selene."

"Perhaps I did." Claire smiled. "Or perhaps I didn't."

No. Madeleine saw, suddenly, with painful clarity, that it had never been the point. Claire had wanted something from her; and she'd had it.

"If I were unable to read people, I wouldn't have got to where I was," Claire said, softly—with that same smile that Madeleine suddenly wanted to smash from her face. "And you're so easy to read, Madeleine. Like a child."

"You—" Madeleine shook her head. Nausea in her throat, sharp and acrid; the room seeming to compress around her—all the thoughts she was desperately trying to keep from showing on her face, in her voice. "You can't—"

"Thank you. It was a pleasure to entertain you here, Madeleine," Claire said; and her face seemed to fill the entire room, her voice like knives driven, again and again, into Madeleine's ears until it was all she could do to keep upright.

She ran, then—tottering straight for the door of the cell with the memory of Claire's thoughtful, smiling face indelibly etched in her mind—through the maze of corridors with barely any idea of where she was going, struggling to remember the way they had come—turning back once, twice, with the moans from the cells in her ear—panic rising, the breath rattling in her lungs, every false start, every wrong turn keeping her away from going back to the House in time; from warning Selene from whatever was going to happen. . . .

Too late. Too late.

SELENE was in her office, trying to sort out her paperwork. She was worried, though she'd said little to anyone but Emmanuelle: something was happening with her informants.

Like every House, Silverspires had a loose network of spies and informants, ranging from dependents to more punctual services. They reported infrequently to Selene; sometimes a week elapsed before she heard from them.

One day before the Great Market, she'd lost Théodore Ganimard. She'd sent Javier to investigate, but the body was gone and the tracker disk unresponsive. It hadn't been a surprise, per se—bodies and enspelled artifacts were valuable commodities in a wasted city—frustrating that she should be unable to take better care of her dependents, but business as usual in a dangerous environment.

Now, though, in the wake of Oris's death . . .

The previous night, Hortense Archignat and Jean-Philippe d'Hergemont had failed to report in. Neither had been proper dependents, and Hortense had worked for Hawthorn in addition to Silverspires. There had been no warning from either of them, but Selene hadn't expected one.

Being an informant was dangerous, and not an occupation for a long, happy life. But three in three days was too many. Something was up.

Selene finished tidying up her paperwork, and was considering sending for Javier—when a knock at the door made her look up.

It was him. "That was quick," Selene said; but then she saw Javier looked pale and ill at ease in his clerical clothes. "What is going on?"

"Selene, there are people here—"

And she had other things on her mind. "I said I didn't want to be disturbed," Selene snapped. "Tell them to come back later."

"I don't think it's going to be possible," a voice said behind Javier.

It was low, and cultured; and its owner leaned against the door-jamb with the ease of someone checking out a home for purchase, his arms crossed over the gray and silver of his elegant jacket. Selene's heart sank in her chest.

"Asmodeus. This is an unexpected surprise." Unexpected, and wholly unpleasant.

The head of House Hawthorn bowed to her, his top hat in his hand; though there was nothing of submission or respect in that gesture.

"Did you come here alone?" she asked.

"Hardly. My delegation is waiting in the antechamber. I thought it best our business remained private."

"I didn't know we had business," Selene said. And she had little wish to stay with him any longer than she should have. Asmodeus was a thug; he'd had the ruthlessness to cut himself a bloody path to the supreme position in his House, but that hardly made him respectable material.

"We do." Asmodeus turned to Javier, who was still standing, petrified, in the doorframe. "Run along, little man. This is business for the powerful."

Javier went pale. He glanced to Selene, who shook her head. Thankfully, Javier got the message and left, though he looked as though he'd swallowed rotten meat.

Selene said, "Now that you've finished being unpleasant . . ."

Asmodeus gently closed the door. Now it was just the two of them, and he made her uncomfortable in a way she couldn't quite pinpoint. He had the smooth, ageless beauty of Fallen: bright eyes behind his horn-rimmed glasses; and thin, long fingers that seemed to belong to some kind of insect rather than a former angel. "There are rumors, Selene."

"Rumors?"

"About deaths." Asmodeus smiled. He came forward to lean on her desk with both hands, entirely too close to her; his perfume of orange blossom and bergamot thrust into her nostrils like the tip of a blunt knife—acrid and suffocating.

Oris. Théodore Ganimard, perhaps. Selene kept her face smooth, expressionless. How she ached to throw him out of her rooms, but he was too important for her to afford this misstep. "Deaths are nothing unusual."

"Six deaths," Asmodeus said. "Five humans, one Fallen."

"And?" She was primed by Claire's message, as relayed by Madeleine at the autopsy—but Madeleine, disastrously untrained in House politics, had probably not paid enough attention to every nuance of Claire's words. Now Selene felt like a fish out of water, but she wasn't about to reveal that to Asmodeus. "This is hardly a city without casualties, especially considering what we're reduced to today."

"The rumors, Selene, are that Silverspires is linked to those deaths."

"I fail to see—"

"Théodore Ganimard," Asmodeus said. "Jacques Rossigny. Yours, weren't they?"

Théodore was dead. Jacques wasn't due to report for another four days.

Selene kept her face perfectly still; her hands remained open on the desk, her entire body at rest. "I fail to see what you're talking about."

"Then you should get better informants." Asmodeus's smile was sharp, wounding. "They're both dead. And before you ask—no. I didn't kill them."

"You said five human dead," Selene said, slowly, carefully. "You didn't name the others."

Asmodeus smiled. "I didn't, did I?" He raised a hand to forestall her when she opened her mouth. "You will ask why this matters. One of the other six—Hortense Archignat—was my dependent." His smile opened yet wider. "And one does not casually hurt that which belongs to Hawthorn."

No, one didn't. She had to grant him that; he might be utterly ruthless, but anyone who pledged and kept fealty with him knew that Asmodeus was behind them, no matter what happened—he would fight tooth and claw for their well-being. It was the others—those in Hawthorn's path—who feared him. "I haven't committed any murders. Or ordered any committed. I've lost people, among them a Fallen." Oris. Scatterbrained, gentle Oris, who had been meant for other times, for other places than postwar Paris. "What makes you think Silverspires is behind this? And where do these rumors come from?"

She didn't expect him to answer that one; so she was surprised when he said, "I came alone, but I'm not on my own. I have Harrier and Lazarus behind me."

Lazarus, untrustworthy and slippery as always. "Claire put you up to this?"

Asmodeus shook his head. "She was very . . . convincing, shall we say?"

She was going to have Claire's head before the week was over. "Convincing about what?" These were dependents. Murders that would require an accounting. Houses vied with one another for power, but there had always been an unspoken truce between them: private feuds were acceptable, and so were murders, if they couldn't be traced back to a House. If they could, though . . . "What do you want, Asmodeus? Compensation for them? I already told you: I'm not responsible."

"I want your assurance that this will cease. Let me give you the other names, Selene. Jean-Philippe d'Hergemont, Marie-Céleste Ndiaye." He watched her; watched her face. Selene wasn't about to give him any hint of her shock.

They were all hers. Shared with other Houses, sometimes, but all linked to Silverspires. She weighed the cost of admitting to that, against that of being thought guilty of the murder of dependents by three different Houses. It wasn't a hard decision to make.

"Fine," Selene said. "You want to hear me admit it, don't you?

They're all mine. They all report to me. Or reported, since they appear to be quite dead. If anyone is owed compensation, I am."

"That doesn't prove anything," Asmodeus said. "You could have—"

"Decided to clean house among my own informants? Be serious, Asmodeus." She was—in deadly earnest, even if he was not. Someone knew exactly who her informants were, and had been killing them over the space of days. This was no joke.

Asmodeus smiled. "There are precedents, as you well know. Your House . . . has cleansed its own informers before. Those insufficiently loyal for your master's taste."

"Don't be an idiot," Selene said, sharply. "We wouldn't do this in our current situation." They were small and diminished, and not about to turn on one another just for amusement.

Asmodeus looked at her for a while. "Perhaps *you* wouldn't," he said, and it was like a slap in the face.

"If you're not behind this, you appear singularly inefficient at dealing with it. Again, you forget. You might be the common link, but other Houses are involved. I'm not losing another informant or a dependent because you can't keep track of what is yours, and neither are Harrier and Lazarus."

That stung. "We're not powerless."

"No, but you're hardly . . . powerful." His arms spread out, encompassing her office: the faded wallpaper; the mold on the stones, the single, flickering magical light above her. "You were once at the top of the hierarchy of power, weren't you?"

As if she needed more reminders of what they'd lost.

"Why are you here, Asmodeus? To insult me?" He had two other Houses behind him, and that made him dangerous.

"Of course I'm not." Asmodeus bent over her, blowing the pungent, sickening smell of flowers into her mouth. "You say you're not responsible. You say you want it to stop. Fine. Then let us come here and help you investigate."

"You want a conclave? You're insane." There had been one conclave of the major Houses, in days gone by. By the end of it, five people had

died; every House had retreated, licking its wounds and vowing revenge on every other House; and the Great War had begun, swallowing
everyone and everything in its maw.

"No," Asmodeus said. "Pragmatic. It has to be one of the other
Houses. With us all gathered in the same place, we'll find out who is
behind this."

"It could be a rogue. Someone unaffiliated with anyone," Selene
said. Why did she think of Philippe, suddenly? It was absurd; the
young man couldn't be responsible for six deaths, and he hadn't been
there at Oris's death. And yet . . . and yet, so much untapped power . . .

"No rogue has the power to do this," Asmodeus said. "But fine; let
us say it's a rogue. Then every House will need to ally with each other
to put him down."

As if that would ever happen. "You mistake your desires for reali-
ties."

"Desires?" Asmodeus shrugged. "I have no desire to ally with any
other House. In an ideal world, Hawthorn would reign supreme, and
every House would be our vassal."

"You didn't used to be that ambitious."

"Don't presume to know me." He put his hand, almost gently, over
hers; touched her on each finger as if playing some secret instrument.
Bile rose in her throat.

"You go too far," she said, withdrawing her hand.

"Or not far enough." He moved away from her desk, and leaned
against the wall, watching her: a predator through and through, a shark
or a tiger or something more unpleasant still, lurking in the murk and
fog, oozing out only to destroy others. "What do you say, Selene? Shall
we have a conclave in Silverspires?"

She had little choice. She could have said no; which was the equivalent of admitting guilt; or worse, weakness—that the House wasn't
strong enough, not protected enough to welcome other Houses on its
grounds, and to withstand their scrutiny. "It can't end well," she said.
"You know this, Asmodeus."

His smile was all sharp, pointed teeth. "You mistake me. Who says I want this to end well?"

WHEN Madeleine, out of breath after running from the omnibus stop, finally reached Selene's office, she found Father Javier in the antechamber, his face dark. "You might not want to come in—" he said, but she'd already pushed past him.

Selene rose from behind her desk when she saw Madeleine. "I have other worries at the moment," she said, and then she must have seen Madeleine's face. "What is it?"

"We're under attack," Madeleine said; and in the cold, unfriendly silence that followed, told the entire tale of her expedition to Lazarus, and what she had learned.

When she was done, she looked up. Selene hadn't moved, and her face had not changed expressions. If anything, it was even colder. "You're late," she said. "And you disobeyed my express orders that you weren't to go to Lazarus."

That was all—all she had to say? After the information that Madeleine had brought her? After she'd ventured into enemy territory on her own with only trinkets for protection—after she'd spent ages examining corpses in a dark, dank basement with the head of a rival House— all Selene could think of was whether she'd followed orders? The arrogance of it, the casual anger . . .

"I don't understand—" she said, because the other words would have damned her.

"You don't have to understand," Selene said. She pulled her chair, and sat, staring at the papers on her desk—looking, for a bare moment, disoriented and panicked, an odd, disturbing expression Madeleine had never seen on her face. Then she looked up again; and the familiar cool, arrogant mask was back on. "You missed Asmodeus."

Madeleine took a deep, burning breath. So that was why Javier had been so agitated, and with reason. The thought of him so close to her . . . She willed her heart to stop beating madly against her chest.

She was safe here in Silverspires. She would be protected against him and anything he could think of. "What did he want?"

Selene's lips contracted; a rictus rather than a smile. "A conclave," she said. "Considering that the six deaths are linked to us, he thinks he can help us find out who did it. Or help us fall farther. Or both."

A conclave. Every child in the city knew what a conclave meant, and how the previous one had ended—too many people with magical powers, too much pent-up rage and too many grievances. The Houses hadn't meant to start a war; they'd just thought to use the opportunity to weaken a few rivals—except that the wrong people had died, compensation had been judged inadequate; and the fragile peace of the city had fractured into magical duels and assassinations that soon escalated into ranged battles and large-scale destruction spells.

A conclave wasn't safe, by any stretch of the imagination. "How—" Madeleine stilled the trembling of her hands. "How bad is it?"

"As you said—we're under attack." Selene's smile was mirthless. "By another House."

"But you'll have all the other Houses coming here. . . ."

"Among which might well be the culprit. Yes. We're invaded, and quite possibly compromised." Selene didn't move.

"Do you . . ." Madeleine hesitated. Selene's wrath appeared to have abated, or to not be directed at her any longer. "Do you know who is behind it?"

Selene pushed her chair away from the desk. "No. The Houses forcing my hand for the conclave are Harrier, Hawthorn, and Lazarus, and it's obvious that Claire is working in concert with Asmodeus. She got you where she wanted: to confirm that the bodies were all linked to us."

Madeleine flushed. "I didn't mean—"

"That's why you weren't to go into Lazarus," Selene said, but without anger. In a way, that made it worse. "You're an open book, and you know many of the secrets of the House. Dealing with Claire requires diplomacy and politics, neither of which you have mastered."

Madeleine was silent for a while, and then thought of the shadow that had stalked Oris. It could have been a hallucination; it could have been induced by the angel essence—but the situation was desperate. On the off chance that it turned out to be of use, she owed it to Oris, if nothing else, to mention it. "There's something else I haven't told you," she said.

Selene didn't even blink. "Out with it."

"Oris . . . saw something, sometime before he died. Two weeks, three weeks maybe? He came to me one night and said—there was a shadow in his room."

"A shadow." Selene clearly didn't seem impressed. "Silverspires is full of them."

Madeleine shivered; remembering what it had felt like to see it; to be touched by it. "It was . . . like wings unfolding where you can't see them, but still blotting out the light."

"And you think it killed him?"

"I don't know," Madeleine said. "I tried to look for it, but it didn't come back, and Oris never mentioned it again. It might be unrelated. We might have been . . . imagining things."

"Mmm." Selene shook her head. "I don't see how it helps us now." She rose and came to stand by the window, staring at the spread of the plaza below them. "Anything else?"

Madeleine thought of Elphon, and then clamped the thought before it could show on her face. This could not have any connection to the matter at hand. "No," she said.

"Good," Selene said. "Talk about it with Javier, will you? He'll set up security for the conclave, and it will be good if he can keep an eye out for your shadow."

She didn't reproach Madeleine, or consider that the hallucination might have been induced by drugs—she didn't even ask how Madeleine had tracked the shadow. Probably she assumed Madeleine had used a potent artifact, but she didn't even reprimand her for the unauthorized use of that.

She *was* worried. And if Selene was worried, then Madeleine was scared out of her wits.

EIGHT
THE CONCLAVE

TWO days after Asmodeus's visit, the Houses arrived at the conclave much as Madeleine had expected: in full force, with delegations of twenty or more people resplendent in their uniforms, wearing their insignia like a badge of honor. Selene welcomed them all, standing on the parvis of Notre-Dame: bowing gravely to the stiff countenance of Guy from House Harrier, and the freezing gaze of his wife, Andrea; the arrogant smile of Asmodeus from House Hawthorn; the expressionless face of Claire from House Lazarus—and the minor Houses, Stormgate, Minimes, and Shellac and a host of other obscure names, living on the scraps the other, bigger Houses left them.

The presence of the House's alchemist was not required—so Madeleine found herself a place from which to watch the proceedings, in a disused room on the second floor of the Hôtel-Dieu. She took Isabelle with her, though the young Fallen's attention was half on a compact mirror she was infusing: she'd been trying to trap her breath into it for the past half hour, without much success so far.

Good. Madeleine had no need to take part in the proceedings of that nest of wasps—at least, not yet, not so soon. Though of course she was lapping it all up—pathetic, really, to want to be part of the game that had undone her already. She was no Fallen or great magician, and her competence as an alchemist did not make up for her lack of raw power.

Among the delegation from House Hawthorn was the face Madeleine had been seeking: Elphon walked next to the young woman Madeleine had already seen. He showed only the curiosity she'd expect of an infant Fallen; no spark of recognition or any indication that he had been to Silverspires before, in another life, when he still knew and cared for Madeleine. He was dead. She was sure of it—his blood warm and sticky on her hands, her holding him as the life drained out of him. And the dead didn't come back to life. They couldn't.

"They look like they're from another time," Isabelle said. She'd closed the compact mirror, and was looking at the courtyard, where the Hawthorn delegation had finished the welcome formalities. Asmodeus led his lover, Samariel, by the hand, to stand on the steps—his face turned upward to look at the sun; and, for a moment, Madeleine could have sworn that his gaze found her, impaling her like a gutted fish on a spear. Impossible. He couldn't know, or care, that they were up there. She was safe. She was safe in Silverspires. But, at the back of her mind, there was always the same unspoken fear; that he would come back for her one day, to finish what he had started when he'd killed Elphon.

"They're all dressed like the pictures before the war," Isabelle said. Top hats and swallowtails and shirts pressed so earnestly they were as stiff as planks.

"You'll find many of them are still living in a world before the war," Madeleine said, more angrily than she'd intended. "Believing nothing is wrong with the city."

"Emmanuelle showed me the pictures," Isabelle said. "She said it was a golden age."

"I'd say the gilding was rather thoroughly shattered," Madeleine said, more forcefully than she'd meant to.

"I suppose so." Isabelle unfolded her mirror again, and went back to her ritual of trapping her breath within. "I can't do it," she said after a while.

"I'll show you again," Madeleine said. She rose, and set both hands on either side of Isabelle's, feeling the lambent coolness of the Fallen's flesh, the trapped magic shimmering within. "Like this," she added, drawing on small scraps of magic. She wasn't on angel essence; too dangerous, with Selene on the prowl for any offense she could use—and she missed its fire; missed the ease of casting spells.

It should have been a small spell; but, senses dulled, she overreached. Something cold and vast squeezed her entire body, leaving her drained of energy. Her hands fell back limp, and it was all she could do not to fall to her knees. Instead of being dulled, the compact mirror's surface went the black of tarnished silver, flipping fully open in Isabelle's hands. "Oh," she said.

"Sorry," Madeleine said, fighting back a fit of coughing. "I—didn't—"

The mirror was—no, not quite black, but shot through with slowly moving patterns, like magma in a live volcano—which was probably the feeling it'd leave any magician who attempted to use this much trapped power.

Isabelle closed the clasp, and then opened it again. All the blackness fled upward, straight into her nostrils. For a brief moment she was outlined in the same darkness as the mirror's surface, and then the magic was back within her. "I see," she said. She closed both hands around the mirror, and *breathed*; and this time the mirror's surface lightly frosted over. "I see."

She didn't even appear out of breath. The world was unfair. Magicians and witches could only cast small spells on their own magic, or run the risk of being exhausted into a comatose state by their own workings; and here was this child with more power in her left fingertip than anyone in the whole of Paris. "Well-done," Madeleine said, quashing the twinge of jealousy before it could overwhelm her. She had enough to do without that to bother her. "We'll move on to nail trimmings next time."

Isabelle closed the mirror. "Madeleine?"

"Yes?"

"You hate me, don't you?"

What—? "Where did that come from?"

"I'm not a fool," Isabelle said, gently. She handed the mirror to Madeleine. "It's easy for me, but not so much for you—and I don't age, whereas—"

Whereas Madeleine was, to say the least, far from the days of her youth. "You've been talking to Emmanuelle? She means well, but long life isn't why I envy you." She was too busy drugging herself into an early grave anyway.

"But magic?" Isabelle asked, with Selene's knack of putting her finger on what hurt. "You envy me that."

"No," Madeleine said. "At least, not that way. When I see you—I do envy you, because things come so easily to you, because you're never tired. But it's not easy, being a Fallen. I can leave this House and wander the streets, and no one will pay me a second glance. You—"

Isabelle grimaced, worrying at the hollow of her crippled hand with the fingers of her intact one. "I wouldn't do such a thing."

"Not unless you had enough magic to defend yourself. And even then." Most Fallen didn't really go beyond the boundaries of their Houses. The fortresses ran both ways.

"And you have God's grace," Isabelle said.

That would have implied faith in God, which Madeleine had lost. Her God was impersonal, uncaring, sometimes outright cruel. "I guess. Shouldn't you be asking Javier about this?"

Isabelle snorted. "Javier lost his faith. And he doesn't like Fallen."

Javier was . . . probably not the best help Isabelle could have found—as she said, he could be rather abrasive and snobbish. "Rather a contradictory position," Madeleine said. "There must be other people, nevertheless—"

"Yes," Isabelle said. "But I'm asking you."

Oh dear. In Isabelle's eyes was the same admiration Oris had once had for her; the same devotion that had ignored everything she was, everything she was capable of doing. She couldn't—couldn't be any kind of role model or giver of wisdom. Not again. And yet . . . "I don't have answers."

"I know," Isabelle said. "But it's enough that you try to give them, when you can."

She shouldn't. She couldn't afford another apprentice to mother, another potential wound on the fabric of her heart. Oris had been bad enough; but Oris had been old, and canny enough to learn the basics of survival, even if he had never learned to think for himself as an alchemist. Isabelle was a child, that odd Fallen mixture of shrewd and naive and reckless; and who knew if she would learn the lessons she needed before it all killed her?

She shouldn't.

"I'll do my best," she said, and let her hand stray over to Isabelle, to cover the hollow place where the two fingers were missing.

Below, the interminable welcoming ceremony looked to be over, all the Houses aligned on the steps in a blur of uniforms: an image from the past, Isabelle had said, but they reminded Madeleine of nothing so much as Asmodeus's picked men and the orange scarf they had worn, on the longest night Hawthorn had ever known. She shivered.

"Madeleine? I know you're up there." Aragon's voice, coming from the stairs. "Selene wants us all for the banquet, and that includes both of you."

Selene probably didn't want to see Madeleine right now; but the presence of a House alchemist at a formal banquet was, sadly, not negotiable. Every asset of the House had to be put on display: an alchemist, a young Fallen, a doctor—though Aragon would probably find a way to wriggle out of the banquet before long.

"We're coming down," she said.

"Selene has been very busy," Isabelle said as they rose to leave.

"Yes," Madeleine said. She looked up, intrigued. Isabelle had sounded . . . disappointed. "You wanted to see her?"

"I'd hoped—" Isabelle shook her head. "Never mind. It can wait until after the conclave."

Assuming they survived the conclave. Well, it wasn't her business to pry, and she had other things on her mind. Someone was out there, killing people connected with Silverspires—like Oris. It was probably too much luck to hope they would kill Asmodeus; but what better location to strike than at a banquet, where everyone would be gathered in the same room?

MADELEINE caught up with Aragon after she'd changed into evening clothes. "Well, my lady," he said with a gruff smile. "You look radiant."

Madeleine hated the dress. It was an overcomplicated thing with a strapless bustier, which meant it kept sliding up at the top; the waist was positively unnaturally tightened; and the train was too long, which meant she kept tripping over it. She'd drawn the line at wearing high heels; she'd have broken an ankle for sure. Let Selene complain it was inappropriate if she wished. "You don't look bad, either," she said.

Aragon looked about as uncomfortable as she felt; the swallowtail hung awkwardly on his large frame, and his shoes made ominous squeaking noises as he walked. "I didn't see Isabelle," Madeleine said.

"She's with Emmanuelle," Aragon said, pointing ahead. "Shall we?"

Selene had opened the great ballroom of Silverspires for the occasion, though even the scented candles couldn't quite disguise the smell of humidity. People in evening wear moved past in a blur of colorful clothes. Madeleine caught a glimpse of Laure and her husband, Gauthier; Alcestis and his lover, Pierre; Asmodeus and Samariel standing together; Claire and her usual escort of children, though for once they seemed to be behaving—and, as Aragon maneuvered to reach the buffet, she saw Elphon, laughing politely at something Father Javier said; and she felt as though someone had dug nails into her heart.

"Can I ask you something?" she said to Aragon.

Aragon turned, proffering two canapés. "Of course," he said.

"Can the dead come back to life?"

"You're asking this of a doctor?" His face was grave. "I've seen enough corpses on slabs to know that they won't get up and walk, except perhaps at the Resurrection we're all promised." He believed in God; though his belief was—like that of many Fallen—more doubts and questions than confident, careless faith. "Is this about Oris? I'm sorry he's dead, but—"

"No, it's not that," Madeleine said. "I've seen—I've seen someone, Aragon. Someone who should be dead. He walks and talks like you or me, except he doesn't remember anything."

"Hmm. This sounds like a conversation we shouldn't be having in the middle of a reception," Aragon said.

"Here? Everyone is busy finding out who knows what, and who is allied to whom. I don't think anyone has time to spare for a doctor and an alchemist. And even if they did, it's hardly secret business." Unlike the other worry at the back of her mind.

"There's a legend in the Far East," Aragon said. "Tales of rebirth and of a potion of forgetfulness that makes you oblivious to your past lives. You'd have to ask Philippe." His tone implied, quite clearly, that he didn't believe in any of it.

"I don't want to ask Philippe," Madeleine said. "I'm asking you."

"Then all I can tell you, as a doctor and a Fallen, is that it's impossible. This person—is he a mortal?"

"No. A Fallen."

Aragon sighed. "No one knows what happens when Fallen die. We're not exactly in the official texts. Humans get sorted out into Heaven or Hell. We probably do, too."

Or perhaps you're reborn, she thought, chilled. *Perhaps God doesn't want you back in the City, and can't bring Himself to send you to Hell. Perhaps you keep being incarnated, time and time again, until you get whatever you were supposed to get right.*

But if that was the case; if Fallen could indeed be reborn on Earth, then why Elphon? Why now?

PHILIPPE had not expected to enjoy the evening; and in this at least, he wasn't disappointed. Emmanuelle, with the help of what seemed like an army of valets, had fitted him into formal clothes: a stiff suit and equally stiff trousers, which had obviously belonged to someone shorter and with much larger shoulders. He was . . . exposed, and not only because his white socks were amply visible below the hem of trousers that were too short.

He was the only Viet in a sea of white faces: Emmanuelle herself seemed to have vanished, though of course she'd be doing Selene's bidding, flattering the various players among the Houses, smiling at who needed to be smiled at. It was something he'd done, once, in the Jade Emperor's Court; smiling at Immortals, gracefully mingling with the newly ascended. Now things were different, and he had no desire to make any kind of effort at indulging his captors.

He sidled toward the buffet, helping himself to a mouthful of bland food. He missed fish sauce more than he'd thought possible, but here in Paris only an ersatz version of it was available, at a price so expensive he couldn't afford it anyway. There would be a dinner later, in the ballroom, where Selene had had huge round tables taken out of storage; draped with embroidered cloth and adorned with the best silverware of the House. The seating plan was on a wooden board at the other end of the room: separate tables for the children of course; and then a careful selection of groups that would not give offense to anyone, while still allowing fruitful exchanges. Not that he was interested at the moment; he'd find out soon enough where he was placed, and probably wouldn't enjoy the dinner any more than he'd enjoyed the cocktail party.

"You look . . . lost," a familiar voice said in his ear.

Philippe looked up, to see Samariel.

He hadn't changed—he wore formal clothes in gray and silver with effortless elegance, and his face was creased in that wide, perpetual ironic smile. But, of course, Philippe wasn't supposed to have met him at all: he was meant to know him distantly perhaps, as one knew the heads of Houses, but that was all.

"I'm not used to this kind of event," he said.

"Indeed." Samariel inclined his head, gravely. "To be fair, most people here aren't. The last such conclave—"

"Was a disaster."

Samariel's lips tightened. "Rather, yes," he said. "You weren't there, I take it?"

"I was brought in . . . afterward," Philippe said. When the war had gone badly, when the Houses had needed all the bodies they could spare, and had bled their colonies dry to provide soldiers for the slaughter.

Parasites, all of them; smiling and bowing in their lace clothes from another age; subsisting on blood. For this, Hoang had died, and Ai Linh, and Phuong, and the rest of his unit. The lot of them could go burn in the Christian Hell.

Except, of course, that it wouldn't bring back the dead, or free him from this captivity.

"Count yourself fortunate, then," Samariel said. He laid a hand on Philippe's shoulder, casually sliding it down to his wrist; like the last time, his touch was as cool as frost, but there was warmth at its core, slowly rising, burning fire held in a fist of ice. "It's a shame, really. I was told the view from the Hôtel-Dieu was beautiful, but I was given a room in the Old Wing."

"The Hôtel-Dieu is a hospital," Philippe said, not sure where Samariel wanted to go.

"A ruin." Samariel's voice was grave, but he said nothing more.

At length, Philippe spoke up, voicing only what was expected of him. "So, where did they put you up?"

Samariel's smile was wide and sharp, like broken mirrors. "The North Wing. At the end of the corridor on the ground floor, the first one on your right when you enter from the street."

Philippe nodded. "Not such a great view. You should go out more: in Notre-Dame, or around the market plaza."

"Oh, indeed." Samariel's fingers rested, lightly, on Philippe's wrist, like the points of claws. "That's an idea. But at night, I think it best that I stay there, and enjoy what might happen in the House. Silverspires is . . . such an interesting place." He smiled again, and withdrew his hand; and wandered away as if nothing had happened. But he'd been clear; too clear, in fact—Philippe turned around, unsure if anyone was watching. There was only the usual crowd. A middle-aged woman—Lazarus's alchemist, Anna, if he recalled correctly—was talking earnestly to a tall, red-haired Fallen from House Harrier, but neither of them appeared to have paid attention to him.

Where was Isabelle—? No, he didn't need to worry about her: her presence was a white-hot brand at the back of his neck, the same link that had drawn her to him when he met Samariel for the first time; the awareness that they were bound together even more tightly than he was bound to the House. He found himself walking through the crowd, until he reached a corner of the room; where she stood talking to Claire, a frown on her face.

Unfair. She was no match for Claire.

Claire was dressed in a low-cut black dress with golden flecks and the outline of a deer: a revealing confection that was meant for a much younger woman, but trust Claire to carry it off. She positively glowed—with a bit of Fallen magic, quite probably, and also with a sharp happiness that made him wary. All the heads of Houses looked like tigers who'd just caught prey—which boded ill for Silverspires.

He shouldn't have cared; not about a House that kept him prisoner, a House that he'd agreed to betray. But if Silverspires fell it would be like House Draken all over again: running away in the darkness and clutching his wounds, hunting in the blackened streets of Paris for food and magic and knowing that the Houses held all of it. "Lady Claire," he said, bowing.

Claire smiled. "Why, Philippe. How . . . uncharacteristic of you to interfere in another House's affairs."

Still angry at him, then; but he wasn't surprised.

Isabelle relaxed a fraction when he appeared, although she threw him a sharp glance that told him she hadn't forgotten about her threat to inform Selene. The three days she'd given him had passed; he'd waited, fearfully, for Selene to turn up at the door of his room, but nothing had happened. Perhaps she already had told Selene; but if that had been the case, why was he still at liberty, and not imprisoned some-where under the House?

"I was asking Isabelle about happenings in Silverspires," Claire said.

Isabelle looked ill at ease—Philippe could guess the sort of sharp, pointed questions Claire would make, trying to see what Selene was thinking; where she could gain the advantage. And he wasn't sure how much Isabelle knew—how much Emmanuelle and the others had told her.

"I see," he said. "I didn't know it was such an interesting topic."

"Oh, Philippe. Everyone is talking about Silverspires tonight. And with good reason." Claire smiled, that self-deprecating expression that made her look like a harmless old lady. It didn't fool Philippe for one moment. "Wondering what Selene will have thought of to entertain us." Her gaze wandered through the room, encompassing the faded peonies on the wallpaper; the dull color of the mahogany tables. She didn't need to say what was on her mind.

"People died," Isabelle said sharply. "It's not entertainment."

Claire smiled. "Of course not. Death is a serious matter."

Philippe doubted that she meant it. "What do you want, Claire?"

Claire's gaze narrowed. "You've changed, Philippe. I never thought you'd be quite so . . . domesticated. What do you owe Silverspires?"

"A roof over his head. Protection," Isabelle said, in a low but firm voice.

"Gratitude?" Claire laughed. "That's for the young and the naive. You'll learn better in time, I expect."

Isabelle, pale and flustered, looked as though she was going to say something. *Don't,* Philippe thought. He sought her gaze; locked with it. *Go away,* he mouthed. At least he was used to fencing with Claire.

Thankfully, she took the hint. "I . . . have business elsewhere," she said, and retreated through the crowd—Philippe saw Emmanuelle swoop from the conversation she was in and steer her toward the buf-fet. Good.

Now it was just him and Claire, and Claire was smiling widely. "Your pet, Philippe? You didn't use to be . . . so altruistic."

She'd asked him to join the House, seeing him as an asset worth having; even without knowing about his powers, she had seen a sharp, keen mind and the skills that had enabled him to survive on the streets for months. Like Selene, she'd seen him as a puzzle to be cracked; and as with Selene, he had refused her. She had never forgiven him. "She's my friend," Philippe said.

"You didn't used to have friends, either. Or should I say you were very bad with other people's overtures?" Claire said. "So powerful, and yet so young and frightened. By the time she masters her own powers, they'll have diminished so much she won't be much use. Perhaps that's the world's way of making sure Fallen don't rule us all."

"You mean, more than they do now? What part of the city do they not run? Lazarus?" It was unwise to bait her, but he couldn't help it.

"Lazarus is their equal," Claire said. "If anyone is under siege—not, of course, that you'll care; you never have—it's you, Philippe."

He was going to say something—something smart, something biting—when he looked at her hands—wrinkled and pale, loaded with expensive rings—and the darkness rose within him—a flash of something that tightened in his flesh, until he was staring at Claire's hands again—some of the same rings, but clearly the hands of a younger woman. She was holding the mirror; the polished pool of obsidian they'd found under the throne, except that the paper around it was brand-new, the ink still glistening in the light of a lamp Philippe couldn't see. . . .

What?

Another memory—another vision of the past? Had Claire handled the mirror at some point? She was mortal—no more than sixty, seventy years old, and the hands he'd seen weren't those of a young woman.

"You've been here before," Philippe said, slowly, carefully—the vision with the mirror wavering, fading—replaced by something else, a haze that seemed to descend over the room, a thin layer where everything was pristine, everything cast in light . . .

With all his strength, he willed the vision to go away—he couldn't afford to let Claire see him distracted, to let her even guess at the enormity of what he was carrying with him.

"Of course I have been here before," Claire said. "Heads of Houses do visit other Houses." Her voice was low, condescending; but she held his gaze—wondering what was happening.

"The cathedral," Philippe whispered, trying to ignore the way the entire room seemed to shift.

All you hold dear will be shattered; all that you built will fall into dust; all that you gathered will be borne away by the storm. . . .

"What of it?" Claire shrugged. "It's a lovely place. Well, it used to be—like so many things, it's fallen into disarray since the war. Selene should clean her House."

"Of what?" Philippe asked.

Claire shook her head. "Of the rot at its heart."

"I don't know what you mean," he spat, but he did know. His gaze moved, to encompass the guests on the floor; the little knots of elegant conversation; the sea of colorful dresses and swallow-tailed coats; the expectant faces those of predators awaiting the right time to pounce, everyone gossiping and making careful approaches, trying to see who stood where.

In his vision, the peonies on the wall were a vivid pink, a color so pure it almost hurt the eyes; the smell wasn't that of humidity and mold, but the sharp one of new paint; and people in old-fashioned clothes mingled by a buffet much as this one—save that the room was brightly lit, and that he who cast such light was standing by the buffet, raising a jeweled glass to study the wine contained within, with the effortless grace and contained power that made him the center of attention. . . .

No, not now. Not. Now.

Philippe closed his eyes. When he opened them again the vision had receded, though a hint of Morningstar's presence still hung over the room—a reflected, shadowy glory that only drove home how shabby everything had become. Claire was right; they had diminished so much.

Good. They were his enemies, and he wouldn't allow himself to forget for even one moment.

Claire was gone, and he was alone in a slowly widening circle of people. Before anyone could engage him in more inane conversation, he moved toward the buffet, grabbing a cocktail piece at random: something with shrimp imported all the way from Brest or Guérande—the price of this alone would ruin Silverspires more surely than the rival Houses.

Philippe was about to head over to the seating plan when, out of the corner of his eye, he caught a glimpse of something creeping across one of the room's huge mirrors. When he turned, there was nothing. Puzzled, he took a few steps; and again something noiselessly slid past, this time in the facets of the empty crystal glasses. Nothing again when he turned; though this time, when he moved again, he was ready for it.

He didn't catch anything—just a glimpse out of the corner of his eye, of something flowing like darkest ink, something large and shadowy that spread wings as sharp as knives—and a sense of pressure against his throat, an irrational fear that clogged his chest with shards of ice. What—?

He'd seen this before—a shadow, passing across the sun; the impression of huge wings over the ruins of the Préfecture—a memory of Samariel lifting his head to stare at the sky, as though it contained more than gray overcast. . . .

That day, Oris had died.

Forcing himself to breathe, he moved across the room, bumping into people in his eagerness to keep an eye on mirrors and glass. Every time he moved, the darkness seemed to flow across the room, in empty wineglasses, in mirrors, in spectacles, in diamond pendants and polished silver fob watches; but it disappeared as soon as he tried to focus on it. It was real—rising, searching, sniffing the air like a blind, monstrous worm—something that made the room seem smaller, its air a miasma worse than the polluted clouds near the Seine; something looking for a way in. . . .

He came to with a start. He was staring at the seating plan, his hand frozen over Selene's name—she was at the largest table with the other heads of Houses, of course, but that wasn't what mattered. Cautiously, he craned his neck to the left and then to the right: nothing but the glitter of light on wineglasses. The darkness was gone, as if it had never been.

But it would be back.

NINE
A FALLEN'S LAST BREATH

LATER, after the formal dinner was over, they had coffee and biscuits; and then, in groups of twos and threes, everyone headed for bed. The conclave proper—the assembly between the various delegations, where everyone would scrutinize the inner workings of Silverspires—would not start until the following morning. This was merely its opening salvo; that tense moment before battle was joined, when everyone checked the bullets in their guns and the readiness of their spells, knowing they would see use before long. Philippe was not a dependent of the House, and not privy to whatever had brought them all here; but what he'd gleaned from conversations was that it was serious business, and that several dependents might be taken aside for questioning by the other Houses. He didn't envy them the company of a dozen overarrogant Fallen and magicians, all trying to ferret out the secrets of the House.

Philippe and Emmanuelle walked Isabelle back to her room—then Emmanuelle left, and Isabelle smiled. "You're not going to sneak away like a thief, are you?"

Philippe shook his head. He was tired, and the shadows slid across the back of his mind like woken snakes—demons take propriety and ritual, he couldn't decently refuse her.

He found himself cradling a cup of tea while Isabelle hunted for biscuits through the drawers of her huge desk. One would expect her room to be cold, devoid of ornaments; but in reality it was like Madeleine's laboratory: a mess of papers on every available surface, pictures at angles on the walls, covering one another in their eagerness to decorate the room—everything from pictures of Notre-Dame before the war, to a more modern print she must have got from Javier's photographic darkroom (which must have taken a fair amount of seduction, because supplies were rare and expensive, and Javier didn't give his photographs to just anyone).

"You didn't need to walk me back," Isabelle said.

Shadows. Darkness. Morningstar's burning gaze in the facets of crystal glasses. "I did."

"I'm not a child!"

But she was—and thank Heaven for that. She was everything the House couldn't corrupt, gangly and ill at ease, as impulsive and disorganized as Madeleine—perhaps not quite the same as she'd been when they first arrived there, but close enough that he could remember a time before Silverspires, before the imprisonment that chafed at him. Speaking of which . . . "It's been over three days, and you haven't spoken to Selene."

Her eyes were bright, feverish in her shadowed face. "I will. Believe me. When the conclave is over and she can listen to other things than the intrigues of Houses. What do you think you're doing?"

"I told you. Looking for a way out." Philippe shivered. It was going nowhere: their conversation the same as it had been before, in the library. "Can we leave it at that? You disapprove, and I don't. There is nothing to be gained here." He shivered. And, because he couldn't quite ignore his conscience, he added, "You should be careful. There are . . . things in the darkness here."

Things that wanted them dead, or maimed—opened up like Oris, a smear of bloodied entrails on the pavement of the cathedral. Something was going to happen. *Tonight.* Where did that utter certainty come from? The shadow within him, the one that had leaped from the mirror? Was he part of it, too?

No. He was still his own self. In spite of the visions, in spite of Morningstar's enticements—in spite of Selene's chains—he still knew what he needed to do, and he still knew enough to be scared of the shadows.

Isabelle shrugged. "There are always things. Old Houses cast shadows, that's all. You're worrying over nothing."

But he knew he wasn't. "Isabelle?"

"Yes?" She had risen—dismissing him and his worries, her cup forgotten on the table.

"Stay in your room tonight, please."

Her gaze hardened. "Because you're planning something you'd rather I didn't see, like your meeting with Samariel at the market?"

"No! I swear it, Isabelle. I don't mean you harm, or Silverspires. Not tonight."

"Not tonight. Well, that's something to live by, isn't it? What will you swear on? The City? You don't believe in it." Her voice was angry, sarcastic—with shades of the unthinking arrogance of House Fallen, of their unshakable belief in their own superiority.

The old oath was on his lips before he could stop himself, its music familiar, as comforting as a poem learned by rote. "I swear by the flesh of the father who sired me, by the blood of the mother who bore me. By the Immortals in the mountains, and Quan Am, who listens to our ten thousand cries for salvation. . . ."

Isabelle's face twisted, in what might have been a sneer, in what might have been a peal of laughter—his fists clenched then, ready to meet contempt with equal contempt. But then she grew grave again. "I was going to say that nobody talks like this, anymore, but . . . it means something to you, doesn't it? Or used to."

Her gaze rested on him; he met it, steadily, feeling himself grow light-headed—the world slowly heightened into swaths of yellow light, as if he'd been meditating again, on the knife's edge of hunger and thirst. "Back when I was mortal . . . it was an unbreakable oath."

"Back when you were mortal." Her voice was quiet. "Don't you ever miss it?"

So many of her questions were about what he'd had; what he missed—not, he knew, out of a desire to hurt him, but because she was afraid—deathly so—of losing what she did have. She sought . . . reassurance that she could survive beyond that loss.

"Do I miss mortality?" He'd never thought about it. It had been so long; centuries ago in another land. "Not so much, no. You forget, when you're Immortal. I remember my body getting old, my fear of death, but it's like they happened to someone else."

"So your kind are cruel, too."

"What do you mean?" He hadn't expected that remark, either.

"Your kind doesn't remember what it is, to be fragile and lost." Isabelle rose to fill her cup again; the harsh, earthy smell of tea filled the room, so unlike the delicate fragrance he remembered. "And neither do Fallen."

"Or House-bound," Philippe said, finally. "When you've never been hungry, or naked; or never had to run for your life, you think that warmth, and safety, and power, are due to you. That anyone who doesn't have them doesn't deserve them." That was how Houses ruled; the source of their ease, their arrogance. "It's different in Annam—the Court of the Jade Emperor doesn't mingle with mortals. They don't seek to rule over them." He knew what she would say: that it might well be true, but that they still thought themselves better than mortals; and he wasn't sure what he'd answer her.

But she didn't say anything. She drained her cup, and stared at it for a while. "I don't have a choice. As Madeleine said—it's either this, or be taken apart in the streets. Even my power won't protect me." There was a hunger in her eyes he found disquieting; a hint she would seize anything that would help her.

"It's not all about power," Philippe said.

Her gaze rested on him; dark and expressionless. "Isn't it?"

She couldn't know—she couldn't know what he'd promised Samariel, to break free of the House's hold on him; to be his own man again. She said she'd warn Selene, but she really had no idea what was going on. She couldn't—no matter how strong their shared link was within her.

"I need to go," he said, rising, gulping down the rest of his tea—the strong, bitter taste making his stomach heave as he all but ran away from her. "Stay in your room, please." And, when she didn't answer, "There is something in the House. I think it's what killed Oris. Please. I just want you to be safe. This is the truth. Make of it what you want."

In his room, he tried to read, but the words in his book kept blurring, frustratingly out of reach—becoming Isabelle's sharp gaze, the growing seriousness of her expression. *You mean it, don't you? Every word of it.*

Of course he'd meant it. And of course it changed nothing. She was free, and he wasn't. She was going to remain inside her room, sleeping the sleep of the innocent, and he . . .

He had an assignation—that might as well be an order—from Samariel.

He couldn't focus. He hadn't learned anything since his first interview with Samariel—drafted into moving tables, washing cloths, preparing dishes in the kitchens. All he knew was that one of Morningstar's apprentices had left a curse on the House; that he had somehow become part of it, carrying memories that might be crucial to understanding it. But that wasn't something he could tell Samariel; there was no hold over Silverspires, no way to understand what was going on, when and under what rules it would strike—if it would strike at all, since so far its only effect looked to be the taking over of his memory.

He ought to stay in: to follow his own advice to Isabelle, and his own growing sense that something was wrong. He had been right: it wasn't a night to be out. He should make his excuses to Samariel, and walk the safe path.

But he couldn't.

He got up and wrapped himself in one of the heavy woolen cloaks Emmanuelle had given him—not only because the House was freezing at night, but also because it might prevent someone from recognizing him.

At this hour, the corridors in his wing of the House were deserted; though, as he came nearer to the apartments for the other Houses, he heard muffled conversations behind closed doorways: this part of the House, at least, didn't sleep.

But, as he walked through the corridors, the shadow rose again—questing, sniffing the air for its prey. He quickened his pace, throwing glances left and right, hoping to catch it; but darkness slid across the walls, spreading wings; and the air became unbearably clammy and moist, tightening in his lungs until he could hardly breathe. He started running then; though of course there was no outpacing it.

MADELEINE couldn't sleep. She'd spent most of the reception behind one of the room's pillars, talking to Aragon and praying that Asmodeus would not turn his head her way; and had only blurred memories of the dinner. She'd seen him and Elphon from afar; had seen Elphon, sitting by his master's side, in the place of a favored bodyguard; had seen him laugh at some jest of Asmodeus's, as though nothing was wrong.

How could he?

It wasn't hard, to get down from her bedroom; not hard, to let her hands roam into the drawers she kept locked; not hard to inhale angel essence and feel its fire expand into the hollow of her belly.

She closed her eyes, and let the power wash over her: the tingling sensation in her fingers; the sharp taste on her tongue; the sensation that she could cast any spell, pay any price demanded by magic; that the world lay at her feet, hers for the taking.

Was this what it felt like, to be Fallen? To know that anything you did or said was saturated with that magic—magic that would kill a man, reduce him to the bloated husks she'd seen in Claire's morgue—the harbingers of her own fate, when her lungs finally gave out. Not that she cared. All that mattered was feeling safe, now, forever.

Safe. That was what Morningstar had said, when she first met him, bowing low to her, unfailingly courteous even though she was just a minor dependent of Hawthorn. *"I hope you enjoy what you see here."* And when she remained silent, too awestruck by his presence to speak, he'd smiled. "This is the first and greatest of Houses, Lady Madeleine. The safest place in Paris."

At the time, she'd thought it courtesy, nothing more; had doubted whether he would even remember her name. But, nevertheless, for some reason she couldn't quite place, the words had stuck with her; to be remembered when, shuddering, struggling to breathe through the pain of shattered ribs, she'd dragged herself out of Hawthorn, and into the deserted streets—toward Silverspires and the impossible hope of salvation. Wounded, bleeding, she had crawled rather than walked— every gesture sending a fresh wave of agony in her chest—and she had known, even then, that she wouldn't make it; even before the world began to waver and fold itself into darkness. She had known that death was the only possible end of the journey.

She'd heard the footsteps, then; slow and measured; had felt the presence that seemed to distort everything with its warmth; had felt him bend down, picking her up in his arms, and starting to walk. Then all was darkness, until she'd woken up in the Hôtel-Dieu with Aragon's face looming over her; and started the long, painful apprenticeship that saw her rise from mediocre kitchenhand to apprentice alchemist, and later mistress of the laboratory.

That night, that lambent, bloody night, was the last time anyone had seen Morningstar; and she herself the last person he had met. After he had left her on the hospital's doorstep, unseen, he had taken his sword and his wings, and walked out of the House he had founded; and never come back. He was dead; had to be, and Selene had to know more than she let on—why else would she rule Silverspires in her own name?

A knock at the door made her look up. Startled, she got up, feeling the pain of her old wounds.

"Madeleine, Madeleine!"

Isabelle was on the doorstep, staring at her with familiar fear in her eyes. "There's something out there, Madeleine. Something bad. And Philippe isn't in his room . . . I think—I think it's what killed Oris and the others."

Once, she'd have gone out with a lamp, speaking reassuring words until Isabelle went back to sleep. But now she knew the darkness had never really vanished, that, like a snake in high grasses, it bided its time until it struck. "Come in," she said, and closed and locked the door.

Madeleine cleared one of the chairs of the paraphernalia on it. "I wasn't expecting anyone tonight," she said.

Isabelle shook her head. "Doesn't matter." She looked at the door, and back at Madeleine. "Can't you feel it?"

"I can't," Madeleine started to say, and then the words were crushed out of her. There was something—a growing pressure, a growing shadow, something that wouldn't let itself be pinned down, that wouldn't even hold still—something winged and fanged and clawed, seeking to destroy them utterly, to rend the flesh from their bones, to suck their skins dry until nothing was left but scattered remnants of what they had once been—bloated corpses in some morgue with eyes like dead fish . . .

The door was locked. She knew the door was locked, but to even think about moving was an effort. *It won't find us. We're safe. Safe, safe, safe . . .*

"Madeleine—"

Isabelle's face was white with fear. She'd backed away from the door, holding the chair as a shield—but she was sinking down with every passing moment, curling into the fetal position against the wall. "Please, please don't come here," she whispered with the intensity of a prayer. "Please, please, please."

The laboratory had been lit by a single lamp. Now that lamp cast dancing shadows upon the walls; and those shadows lengthened, moment by moment—there was nothing Madeleine could see, nothing that would come into focus—nothing but that awful sense that they were being followed, dissected—that any moment now, something would leap at them from the shadows. The door was still locked, but the wood was bending, bulging inward. It was standing on the threshold.

Her ribs ached with the growing pressure. She was afraid to look down; if she did she might see blood on them again, might find herself crawling through the streets again.

"Madeleine . . ."

No. She wasn't that powerless any longer. Fumbling, cursing, she forced herself to move, one agonizing centimeter at a time—where had she put her most powerful artifacts? The second drawer of the secretary desk, the third?

The light of the lamp wavered. Out of the corner of her eye, Madeleine saw shadows flow across the dozens of small mirrors in the room—scattered pieces of the same reflection, something inhumanly huge, and it wasn't even in the room yet—this was just what came ahead of it. There was a noise, a hiss like a hundred snakes—it was snakebites that had killed Oris and the others.

Do not think. Do not fear. She couldn't afford to waste time. Neither door nor lock would hold it for long.

She opened the drawer by touch—the room had gone utterly dark—her fingers scrabbled for a hold on the objects within, trying to remember what it had felt like.

Once, Elphon had given her a locket filled with his breath; but she'd used the last of the magic a few months ago—not even for something worthy, simply to remind herself, one last time, of what his presence had been like. How she wished she had it now, so she wouldn't have to use something else.

Found it.

Isabelle's soft whimpers in the darkness; and the creak of wood as the door bent yet farther; and the hiss like a thousand snakes. They couldn't let it in: its touch would be death. The thought of Isabelle—pale and lifeless, taken apart for scraps of magic—rose in her throat like bile. No. She wouldn't let her new apprentice go the way of Oris.

Her hands closed on cold metal, which flared into warmth at her touch; and then there was another presence in the room, something vast and terrible and infinitely more powerful than anything the darkness could conjure. The heat on her skin was searing now, but she didn't care. She wove the strongest spell of banishing she could think of, and hurled it, half weeping, half screaming, at whatever was trying to come through the door.

The door collapsed into a thousand splinters. Madeleine ducked behind a chair, but nothing touched her. On the threshold was . . . nothing, just a sound she couldn't quite identify, growing farther and farther with every passing minute. Retreating.

Then there was silence, broken only by the sound of Isabelle's breath. "What"—she asked, struggling to speak—"what did you do?"

Madeleine withdrew her hand from the drawer. The container she'd used came with it, now no longer fused to her skin, though it had left a perfect, circular scar on her palm. She felt . . . light-headed, giddy—as if she could do anything, and yet all she wanted to do was to lie down and empty her guts on the floor. Isabelle had almost died. And she— she had almost succumbed again to that gut-wrenching, sickening fear of Elphon's last night, had almost lost herself. It wasn't death that she feared, but that touch, that reminder of what it had felt like, crawling with blood sticking to her skin, to her hair, hardening so it could never be washed away—that inescapable knowledge that Elphon was dead, that she would soon be caught and brought back to Hawthorn, to hear Asmodeus's mocking voice before she, too, died. . . .

No. The past was the past. She couldn't afford to live in it, anymore. Death and its sleep awaited: rest, at long last; and oblivion, free from the grasp of fear. She pulled herself up, shaking; forced herself to breathe until the room came back into sharp focus.

"I don't understand," Isabelle said.

In her hand was a sphere of gold, topped by a crown. "It was the last thing I had of him," Madeleine said. "The last thing anyone had of him, perhaps—I don't know who kept what in this House. But I had to—" She shook her head, dazed. "Morningstar. It was Morningstar's magic."

But now it was gone in a burst of power, all spent like the gift of

Elphon's breath; and how would they defend themselves, if the shadow came back?

She looked at the door, at the walls; heard and saw nothing but the usual sounds of Silverspires at night. It was gone, whatever it was. But it hadn't been a hallucination. And—

"You said it was what killed Oris."

"Philippe saw it, I think," Isabelle said. Her voice was still shaking.

Madeleine took in a deep, shaking breath; thinking of bodies shriveling and burning under the assault of magic; of Oris, crushed under the weight of gravity on the floor of Notre-Dame. "It's killed six people, whatever it is. Come on. We have to tell Selene."

PHILIPPE ran. It was undignified, and possibly useless, but he was past caring. Doors flashed by him, indistinguishable—at one point a door opened, and he almost toppled over someone in Harrier's uniform. "Sorry," he said, but didn't stop. There was a noise at his back, a hiss like ten thousand open gas taps; a shadow, slithering across flat surfaces whenever he turned his head, just enough to make a fist of ice tighten around his belly—except that the shadows were growing larger and larger, and the lights in the corridors ahead of him were dimming, throwing his own large, distorted shadow across the wall like that of some monster.

Shadows. A creature of wings and fangs and of darkness—he'd wondered, back then, what he had summoned when he touched the mirror; but he didn't need to wonder anymore. He *knew*.

As he ran, he tried to gather *khi* currents to him. But, without the calm of his trance, it was too hard to see the few threads that would be in the House; and all he could manage was a feeble ring of fire around his hand—which did nothing much to either reassure him or light his way.

He turned one last corner, and found himself in utter darkness. The hiss had gone away, and so had the shadows. So early, so easily? Slowly, carefully, he gathered more *khi* currents to him, widening the ring of fire in his hand until it lit the way ahead.

It was just a stretch of corridor, going to two rooms at the end: Asmodeus and Samariel, of course, the two lovers being accommodated close to each other. There was no noise coming from either bedroom. Philippe crept closer.

It was a bad idea. He should go back to his room, forget the whole incident; and come back later. This was . . . not a good time to be there. Not . . .

There was a sound, as he approached the end of the corridor: a slight hiss like an intake of breath, already slithering away. The shadows danced, around his ring of fire—out of the corner of his eye he caught a glimpse of something folding huge wings, and sinking back upon itself, but it might have been nothing more than illusion.

The door to Samariel's room opened easily, swinging with the tortured sound of ungreased hinges—surely it must have been heard all the way to Indochina. But no one moved, or spoke.

"Samariel?"

A slight sound, coming from the bed; a slithering of wet things from the wallpaper; a fist of shadows slowly closing around the lone light in the room. He took one step, then another and another, and approached the huge canopied bed in the center of the room.

The furniture was from another age: two bedside tables with thin, elegant curved legs, their drawer handles in the shape of butterflies; a mahogany commode with a marble top; a vase in that chinoiserie blue and white that looked even worse than the cut-rate porcelain the Chinese had foisted on the Annamite Imperial Court. His feet barely made any noise on the thick Persian rugs; and the *khi* currents in the room seemed to have shriveled and died around him, as if they'd been burned at the root.

His light, unsustained by any fire, shivered and died, leaving him in shadows. Another, stronger light took its place, the golden radiance of Morningstar's hair and skin.

No. Not now. With all his strength he willed the vision to pass—it did not, but neither did it fully materialize. Instead, Morningstar remained where he was, standing by the farthest column of the canopy. He had his sword in his hand, and watched Philippe with burning eyes.

"I warned you," he said, and his voice was like thunder, strong enough to make Philippe's knees buckle. "I told you to seize power, or be destroyed. Do you see now?"

Philippe made no answer. There was none he could give—nothing, to this ghost of the past, this bitter, angry memory of whoever had cast the curse on Silverspires. He simply moved closer.

Samariel lay in bed, splayed like a puppet with cut strings; his legs and arms at impossible angles, curved like the corpses of eels, as if all the bones had been sucked out of his limbs. The sound Philippe had heard was the wet struggle to breathe through crushed lungs. Nausea, sharp and bitter, rose in his throat; he held it at bay, kneeling by the stricken Fallen. "Samariel?"

The skin—all that was left whole—was covered in bite marks; as if a snake had struck him, repeatedly; the same marks, by all reports, that had been on Oris's corpse. The eyes—the eyes were still there, with that same, familiar, sarcastic intelligence. The mangled mouth opened, shaped around something—his name? "I'll get help—" he said, but Samariel shook his head.

"What do you want me to do?" he asked; but Samariel said nothing, merely stared at him with those bright eyes; and magic rose in the room, a burning heat that picked at the strands of the spell around him, snapping them like burned matchsticks.

"You can't—" he whispered. More and more strands were vanishing, though the strain of it should have been too much for a dying Fallen. "You can't—"

"Seize power," Morningstar whispered, his image wavering and bending as if in a great wind. "Seize power."

He didn't move as the magic wrapped itself around him, the spell unraveling moment after moment; staring into those bright, bright eyes and knowing exactly why Samariel was doing it. He had told him, all those days ago.

"I imagine it would be quite a setback for Selene to lose you. . . ."

Behind him, the door opened again; and closed, with hardly a sound. "What do you think you're doing here, boy?"

The face of Asmodeus, head of House Hawthorn, was twisted out of shape by grief and rage. *I can explain,* Philippe wanted to say. *Ask Samariel. I can—*

But Samariel would not speak, not anymore.

TEN
OLD FRIENDS

THE night had not ended well; and the morning had not started well, either. Selene sat in her office, staring at the papers strewn on them; at the memoirs of journeys in Indochina she'd been reading, back when her only worry had been how to best use Philippe for the good of the House—in hindsight, how much simpler those times had been, such easier moments compared to the tangle that awaited her now.

A tinkle of beads announced Emmanuelle's arrival from her private quarters. She was holding two coat hangers. One was a long black dress with straps; the other was a swallow-tailed suit with straight trousers. "Which one do you want?" she asked.

Outside the room—in the ballroom, where Father Javier was making them wait—stood the heads of every House, all with the same intent: to hear an explanation for the evening's events, and to see what concessions they could wring out of her for failing to protect her guests. Damn this stupidity of a conclave, for putting her in that impossible situation. "Did you hear anything from Aragon?"

Emmanuelle grimaced. "Samariel's alive, but just barely, Selene. Aragon said there was nothing much to be done. Just make him comfortable—"

No miracle, then, but then, why had she thought there would be one? God seldom visited those on Fallen; the thought was so old by now that there was little bitterness left in it. She hadn't prayed in years, not since she was Isabelle's age, in fact. "And Philippe?"

"Confined to his rooms," Emmanuelle said. "In any case, he can't leave Silverspires. But I highly doubt Philippe would kill Samariel. What possible motive could he have for that?"

Madeleine and Isabelle, now both back in their rooms, had both reported to Selene about seeing the shadows in the laboratory, identifying them beyond doubt as responsible for the killings; and Isabelle had been adamant the original warning had come from Philippe. But it meant nothing—a warning moments before Samariel was attacked was utterly ineffective, and Selene couldn't decide if that had been deliberate.

"I don't know," Selene said. "But he was with Oris, too. In any case, that's not what's most important now."

Two things mattered now, both for the protection of Silverspires. The first, to prevent whatever it was from killing again. She had people searching the House from top to bottom; and Madeleine and Isabelle gathering the strongest artifacts and breath-infused mirrors, distributing them among the dependents of the House—whatever it was that was roaming the corridors, it had killed six people and left another one at the doors of death. Javier was coordinating search parties, trying to see if its lair lay within the House. But all of this would be for nothing if she couldn't achieve the second thing—to placate the other heads of Houses before they took Silverspires apart as retribution for Samariel's wounding.

"The Houses?" Emmanuelle asked. She raised her coat hangers again. "Tell me how you want to dress."

Selene shook her head. "Not like this." Those were the clothes of the past, the formal evening wear of the days before the war. There was no need to recall any of that today. "Bring me the turquoise dress. And the rest of the ensemble."

After she was dressed, she looked at herself in the mirror: over the turquoise dress, she'd put on a long, embroidered silk tunic that closed at the neck with a single clasp. The tunic, made in Indochina and traded through Marseilles, was a vivid scarlet, embroidered with birds and plum flowers; and it came with a matching shawl of silk so fine it was almost transparent: like many things, a statement of wealth and power in a ruined world.

As if that would fool anyone but the weakest Houses. . . .

She let the shawl settle in the crooks of her arms, and peered critically at her reflection.

"You look dazzling," Emmanuelle said.

"Ha," Selene said. She didn't feel dazzling; she felt small and frightened. "It'll have to do."

Emmanuelle reached out, and put a kiss on Selene's lips. "You'll do fine. I'm sure you will."

She had to; there was no other choice. Squaring her shoulders, Selene went out of her office, to meet the heads of the other Houses.

THEY were all waiting for her in the ballroom, amid the cadavers of last night's excesses: the tables lying bare without their magnificent clothes, the empty bottles and the glimmer of shattered glass, the faint smell of food and perfume, their mingling turning vaguely sickening.

Guy of Harrier, portly and his brown hair slick, with red highlights; Andrea, his wife, her dark eyes shining in the paleness of her face. Claire of Lazarus, for once without the posse of children that accompanied her—no, that wasn't true; there was one with her, a little girl dressed in a formal suit, the vivid blue in sharp contrast to the darkness of her skin. Bernard of Stormgate. Sixtine of Minimes; and a sea of other minor Houses, yapping terriers she hardly paid attention to in normal times— save that even terriers could turn nasty, once they had smelled blood.

Asmodeus, though, wasn't there. Should she wait for him? He was no doubt at Samariel's bedside; praying, perhaps, though the idea of the head of Hawthorn praying for anything at all was ludicrous.

One of the faces staring at her—or perhaps all of them; it wasn't unheard of—was responsible for this. One of them, or several, was working to undermine the House, utterly destroy it. She'd find them; and make sure they couldn't harm Silverspires anymore.

They were getting restless, all of them; still politely waiting for whatever she had to say—again, amusing to see how courtesy still held sway, even in moments like those, when they hung poised, once again, on the edge of a feud that could lay waste to the city.

"You know why we're gathered here," she said. A dozen faces swung to look at her, silent, watching. "There has been . . . an incident." She raised a hand to forestall the inevitable outcry, and said, infusing her voice with the strongest spells of charm she could conjure, "Lord Samariel is at death's door. Something attacked him in his bedroom. We're not quite sure what yet, but rest assured that we're investigating. Silverspires will not tolerate this breach of the peace."

"Won't you?" The speaker was Claire, as impeccable as always. "There have been other deaths, and you haven't done anything. One might think you remarkably inefficient, or insufficiently motivated, or both."

Selene went for bluntness. "I don't take the deaths of dependents lightly, and you know it."

Claire did not bat an eyelid. "I'd hate to see what you do when you take things lightly, then."

"It's abundantly clear that you need our help," Guy of Harrier said. "With Silverspires' declining status—"

"We're not dead yet," Selene said, more sharply than she'd intended to.

Claire's thin, self-satisfied smile was more than she could bear. It was because of the three of them—Harrier, Hawthorn, and Lazarus—that she was here now; that she had to defend her House's failure to protect its guests, to justify why her wards and magical protections had failed to stop whatever roamed the House.

"The young man is involved, isn't he?" Sixtine of Minimes asked. "The Annamite, the one they found in Samariel's bedroom."

"Don't be ridiculous," Guy said. "He's human, nothing more. How could he do this?"

"He's human, yes," Claire said. "It just means he has no innate magic. With the proper artifacts, a bit of angel essence—"

This was too much for Selene. "You know we don't use angel essence in this House."

Claire's gaze was frank, untroubled. "Oh, don't you?"

She sounded as though she meant something specific, but Selene wasn't about to let Claire catch her off balance. "I have no interest in your games." They needed to find the means of murder. Shadows. A dearth of magic, or an excess of it, Madeleine had said; and Aragon had confirmed, once given access to the other bodies Claire had been keeping.

Not that it helped, of course. Neither Selene nor anyone in the House knew of any creature, weapon, or spell that killed that way. She had Emmanuelle digging into the archives; and of course Aragon was examining Samariel right now, trying to find something, anything that would get them out of this mess. Selene said, "If the question is whether a human could have done this—then the answer is yes. Everyone here—human, Fallen—is a suspect."

There was silence, in the wake of her words. Then, as what she had said sank in, a babble of protestations rising to a deafening pitch: "—surely you don't mean—" "—this is an outrage—" All things she had expected and counted on. She raised a hand and cast a spell of dampening: a cheap trick, but one that never failed to have its little effect. All sounds around her hand gradually sank to a murmur, in a spreading wave of silence.

"*You* came *here*," she said. "All of you. You forced your way in, claiming you would help us find our attacker, and then you have the audacity to complain when someone else dies. I know you. I know you all—Guy, Claire, Sixtine, Andre, Viollet." A further shocked hush. She had them now; she had to seize the moment, while they were still cowering in fear, and gazing suspiciously at their neighbors. If she could break their fragile alliances . . . "None of you is above killing to further your plans. None of you would weep if Silverspires paid reparation for your murders, and sank into obscurity."

Silence spread in the wake of her words. Then someone clapped: slowly, deliberately, the sounds echoing under the stuccoed ceiling of the ballroom, each one as sharp and as penetrating as a bell tolling for funerals.

"Such a pretty speech," Asmodeus said in a slurred voice. He detached himself from the pillar he had been leaning on; and came forward, toward Selene, blowing the acrid smell of orange blossom and bergamot gone sour into her face. She didn't flinch. One could not afford to, with Asmodeus.

Once, he'd moved like a sated cat; now his movements were still fluid, but quickened with a manic impatience. He had taken off his horn-rimmed glasses: he held them in one hand, toying with them absentmindedly, except that Asmodeus never did anything absentmindedly. The gaze he turned on Selene was still amused, but underneath it all she could guess at the controlled fury.

"You're drunk," she said, coldly. "Go back to where you came from."

"My lover's deathbed?" Asmodeus's smile was terrible to behold, sharp and fractured and incandescent. "Let us speak of Samariel, shall we? Humans expect to die in their beds; Fallen do not. Should not."

"You know I don't condone what was done to him," Selene said. "We are looking into it."

"You're investigating? There's no need for investigation. The culprit was found, surely."

"Philippe?" Selene forced herself to laugh. Emmanuelle had been right: in the end, she couldn't be sure what Philippe could and couldn't do; and among the strange magics he could call on, perhaps one of them had the power to end Fallen lives. "I'm not in the habit of condemning people on hearsay. Unlike you."

"We've gone past hearsay," Asmodeus said, gravely. He dwarfed her in size; and the power that ran through him limned him in gray light, almost drawing the outline of wings, reminding her of Morningstar at his angriest—when she hadn't been quick enough with his lessons, or when she had forgotten the wards that kept them all safe. But, compared to Morningstar, Asmodeus was pale and insignificant, a candle to the unclouded sun. She could handle him. "Discovering an attack is not the same as being the attacker. Even so, I've had him confined to his room."

"Like a disobedient child?" Asmodeus laughed. "Not enough."

Selene stood her ground. After all, she'd had plenty of practice. "Until I find otherwise, that is all I will do. Rest assured that if I find him guilty, nothing in this world will protect him from my vengeance." She said this with a lightness she didn't feel; after all, the young man had absorbed one of her strongest spells and emerged unscathed. She very much doubted he would come meekly or quietly.

"Not enough," Asmodeus said. "Not timely enough. I have taken my precautions already."

"Precautions?"

"You were always too squeamish, Selene. The House has far better holding facilities than rooms with guards. Confined to his room?" He snorted. "As if that would ever be enough."

"You—" Selene took in a deep breath, forced herself to speak quietly. "You've moved him to the holding cells." They hadn't been used in almost twenty-five years—even before Morningstar disappeared, he had been mellowing, and whatever he had been doing down there had ceased. Selene remembered, with icy clarity, going down there to clean them up; finding sharp instruments on which blood had dried like rust; and breathing in the stale odor of body fluids.

"As I said—" Asmodeus smiled. "Your master had many flaws, but he wasn't squeamish."

"Neither am I," Selene said.

"Then prove it to me."

"This isn't a contest," Selene said. But it was, and Asmodeus had won the first round: he had broken her authority in her own House. "And I should think you've done enough, haven't you? Or perhaps you want to hop over to Lazarus, too, and see if you can improve their wallpaper?"

Claire's head came up sharply, but she said nothing. Nevertheless, even drunk or on whatever drugs he was on, Asmodeus was smart enough to recognize he couldn't push things much further. "I'll leave you to it then," he said, bowing very low.

Yes, leave her to it. As if she had the faintest idea what to do next.

MADELEINE sat by Samariel's bedside. She wasn't sure why, in truth—she'd gone in to talk to Aragon, and the doctor had irascibly wandered off, looking for some instrument or another; and she'd been struck, all of a sudden, by how terribly alone Samariel must be. It was exceedingly foolish: he'd had no need of her while alive and would probably have mocked her at every opportunity, and he was Asmodeus's lover. By staying there she was making sure that, at some point or another, Asmodeus would wander back in and find her; and then she didn't know what would happen, when the knot of fear in her belly spread to all her limbs, and she stood in front of Elphon's murderer, of the Fallen who had turned Hawthorn into a bloodied ruin. The smart thing would have been to get up and slip away while Aragon was gone.

But she couldn't bring herself to do so. She sat in the chair she'd pulled up—the same chair she'd have used, in other times, to collect an entry toll—and watched the dying Fallen. It was unclear by what miracle he clung to life; the thing in the bed seemed hardly human-shaped anymore, the body slick and fluid in a way no body should be, with just the ghost of its old face staring up at her—with dark, bruised circles under his eyes and the bones of the face bulging from beneath the translucent skin.

Nurses and orderlies slipped in and out of the room, bringing clean sheets, taking soiled cloths and charts away—coming with syringes and injecting their contents into Samariel, though it made no difference to the husk on the bed.

Madeleine had a nascent headache, perhaps a side effect of having used Morningstar's orb. It hadn't been angel essence, but the sheer power that had coursed through her had been like nothing she'd felt before. In that moment, she'd been quite ready to believe Claire when she said all angel magic would kill magicians bit by bit; and now she had the magician's equivalent of a hangover, with her tongue stuck to her palate, and a set of drummers that had taken up residence in her brain on a more or less permanent basis. Perhaps she should ask Aragon for an aspirin, though she could imagine his face if she did so.

"Still here?" Aragon came back with a tray of scalpels, which he laid by the bed.

"Yes," Madeleine said. "I'm surprised they trust you with this, instead of Hawthorn's doctor."

"Oh, they've gone for Iaris. She should be here at any moment, but in the meantime . . ." Aragon shrugged. "I've done business with Hawthorn, too, and Asmodeus knows he can trust me." He ignored the slight revulsion that went through Madeleine. "All the Houses are the same, Madeleine. You should know that."

"I know," Madeleine lied.

Aragon didn't insist. "Mind you," he said, "I'm sure not much trust is required to leave him into my care. It's not like I can make him worse."

"Do you—" Madeleine looked away from the bed, and back to Aragon. "Do you know what did this?"

"You mean the description? I thought you'd seen it."

"Yes," Madeleine said. "Shadows that move, that feel like they're picking apart your thoughts. But that doesn't tell me . . ."

"What it is?" Aragon asked. "Or how it can kill that way?"

On the arms, which hung limp and deformed, were the same marks Aragon had pointed out on Oris, the same marks Madeleine had seen on the other corpses: the perfect circles with a single dot in the middle, a livid blue against the paleness of the skin.

"I think it's some kind of creature, a summoning or something."

"Summonings are impossible," Madeleine said. She thought of the shadows again, moving as though they were alive; of the hissing sound just on the cusp of hearing. "Aren't they?"

"Summonings have a mind of their own, and rules of their own, which often end badly for the summoner. But you're right, broadly speaking. There hasn't been a successful summoning in centuries. There are legends, of course—people who went digging into the past of the city—the Middle Ages, the Greeks and Romans, even the prehistory—who summoned up harpies and unicorns and saber-toothed tigers."

"And they're untrue?"

"I . . . don't think so," Aragon said. "But they're old. Even being generous with them, the most recent one would have been four hundred years ago, and the Fallen in question spent decades just preparing his ritual. We just don't have the power—or the level of obsession—for this anymore. They require energy beyond even what a Fallen might produce; even with artifacts, even with essence."

Madeleine tensed, but the words didn't appear to be directed at her.

Aragon went on. "It does sound like a summoning—or a trained beast. Maybe a construct, modified with magic. It's clear that it's not human. Not, mind you, that anything human was capable of leaving those marks."

A construct. That didn't sound like a cheerful notion, either. Again, there were tales: memories of Fallen who had survived the war and seen constructs in action. There was a reason why no one dared to use them anymore.

"He doesn't look the same as—" Madeleine swallowed. "He doesn't look the same as Oris."

"No," Aragon said. "Oris didn't look as though every bone in his body had shattered."

"You said—you said Fallen bones couldn't support the body."

"No," Aragon said. "They're thin and built for flight. Like a bird's. Hollow inside." He tapped the head of the bed, thoughtfully. "Oris died when magic was removed from him. I think Samariel's magic was removed for a much, much longer time."

Madeleine would have felt sick, once upon a time. "More slowly perhaps," she said. So he wouldn't die all at once, but would linger for a little while. Except that no one, of course, should be alive in that condition.

"I don't know what the shadows are," Aragon said. His hands

tightened around the bedstead. "I don't know, and this is . . . alarming." His face didn't move, but Madeleine could read the fear in the depths of his eyes; in the hands that remained stubbornly clinging to the metal frame of the bed.

Aragon had never been afraid of anything or anyone. "You're worried," she said, slowly, carefully. It was . . . even worse than Selene being worried. Aragon was always detached and clinical—impatient sometimes, but certainly never scared.

"Of course I am," Aragon said sharply. "There is something that's killing again and again in this House, with as much ease as a child snapping kindling sticks. I'd advise you to be worried, too." He closed his eyes for a moment and then said, with a visible effort, "Sorry. It's been a long night. You shouldn't listen to my ramblings."

But it hadn't been ramblings—simply the truth; the mask of propriety and impassibility lifted to show her what lay beneath. "I'm scared, too," Madeleine said. She'd seen it, felt it, and would give anything to never see or feel it again in her life.

"Don't be," Aragon said, but she couldn't believe him anymore.

Her gaze drifted to Samariel's face: the eyes were closed, but no one would have mistaken this for sleep. Likely he was too far gone to even hear them. Time to leave. "I'll be back," she said; and turned, and saw Elphon in the doorway.

Oh God, no.

The thundering of her heart must have been heard all the way into Heaven. Elphon, blissfully unaware of anything amiss, walked into the room and bowed to her. "We've met before, I think," he said gravely.

Madeleine kept her voice level, but it took all the self-control she could muster. "We have met." Not just once; every day of his life— they'd worked side by side in the gardens of Hawthorn, cut branches and tended flower beds together—how could he not remember?

"You're the alchemist." His gaze strayed to the bed; he sounded vaguely disapproving.

"Oh. No," Madeleine said, shaking her head. "Of course I'm not here for that. Whatever happens to him, he belongs to Hawthorn."

Elphon said nothing for a while. "I guess that's one way of putting it."

Aragon had disappeared—slipped out the door in Elphon's wake, no doubt. Madeleine suppressed a curse. She should make her excuses and leave, too; but curiosity got the better of her. "Are there—no people from before, in Hawthorn?"

"Before?"

Madeleine shook her head. "I'm a refugee. Surely Asmodeus has told you that? I was in Hawthorn. Under Uphir."

Elphon's face froze. "Were you?"

She nodded. "I left the night of the coup."

"Oh." She couldn't read Elphon's expression. "Well, I wasn't there, but to answer your question, there are people left from that time. Not many—I think not everyone swore fealty to Lord Asmodeus."

Of course they wouldn't, and of course he would ruthlessly remove them. Madeleine shook her head, trying to banish dark thoughts. Well, there was nothing for it. She might as well be honest. "You . . . look a lot like someone I used to know, once. Someone who died the night of the coup."

"All Fallen look alike." His face was haughty, distant.

"Yes, you've told me that before. But the thing is, he was called Elphon, too. And I knew him well, well enough not to mistake him for someone else. We . . . we worked together." It seemed like such an inadequate way to encompass all that Elphon had meant to her; the exhilarating nights racing each other to the roof of the House; the quiet lunches that they'd had, hiding behind fountains and trimmed hedges; the night they had snuck down to the Seine, and watched the black waves lapping on the shore, trying to imagine that there, too, amid the polluted waters, there was magic and wonder. And, remembering, she measured the gulf between this other life and the one she had now. The river was dark and dangerous, like everything else in Paris: waters that would eat at your flesh, waves that would reach out, grab you from the embankments, and drag you under the choppy surface to drown. There was a power in the Seine, yes; magic and awe—not innocent wonder, but something as dark and as gut-wrenchingly terrifying as the God who had destroyed

Sodom and Gomorrah—a faction as strong as any House, ruthlessly destroying anything that intruded on its boundaries. Not even the major Houses dared to tangle with it; and yet she and Elphon had sat on parapets, dangling their legs over the black waters, and thought only of fairy tales. . . .

Kids, that was what they had been. Innocent, careless, stupid kids. "It was in another lifetime."

Elphon's face was set. "I don't remember anything. Nevertheless, if what you say is true—"

"It is," Madeleine said. "Why would I lie to you?"

"Then I have no doubt Lord Asmodeus has his own reasons."

"Of course he has. He killed you!"

If she'd hoped to provoke some reaction, she was disappointed. Elphon merely shrugged. "As I said—Lord Asmodeus has his own reasons, and I have no doubt he would act in the best interest of the House. It's not my business to inquire."

In another lifetime, she thought, sadly. They had both changed, immeasurably; taking the bitter, salt-laden paths to this dying room, where they spoke to each other as strangers. "You're right," she said, finally. "Just as it's not my business to inquire. Good-bye, Elphon."

She left without looking at his face; afraid of what she would see, if she turned round.

ELEVEN
ANCIENT HATREDS

THE cells were damp, and cold—and the *khi* currents in them flowed lazily: layers and layers of metal and fire with the strength of primal screams. They seemed to be one of the few things in the House that had not decayed, and Philippe could understand why: because the memory of pain and rage and the dreams of revenge and death that had pooled between the stone walls were too strong, too vivid to leach away, even in the midst of Silverspires' atrophy.

It wasn't only the *khi* currents, though; there was something inside him, too; something dark and angry, raging at the prosperity of the House, at the worship of Morningstar. If he closed his eyes, he would feel it roiling within him like trapped crows—a storm of claws and sharp beaks, and darkness at its heart; a hint of the shadows that had killed Samariel.

He was linked to the curse, to the memories, and—whether because of the cells or because of the recent murder—it was rising, threatening to drown Philippe in visions of the past.

He needed to stay awake. He needed to—he needed to meditate, as he used to do in Annam, back when he'd ascended. But what he'd told Isabelle was true: it was so far away in the past it felt like something that belonged to someone else.

He leaned against the wall, the harshness of bare stone against his back; and tried to feel optimistic about the future. It didn't work. Asmodeus's face had been terrible to behold, and Philippe was pretty sure that even Samariel's recovery—an unlikely thing, the stuff of miracles and desperate wishes—would not assuage his anger. Asmodeus hadn't had him brought here for his own good.

Funny. He hadn't thought he'd be so worried to be free of Selene's oversight, but he would have chosen Selene over Asmodeus, any day.

Her spell was almost gone by now: the few threads tying him to Ile de la Cité were spun thin, like fragile silk. A simple tug would snap them. He had what he wanted, except that now it was useless. He lay against the wall, and considered his options. With *khi* currents this strong, he could weave magic, but there was no spell that would shatter the doors of the cells. Whoever had designed them had reinforced them with enough layers of magic to be impervious, and Asmodeus's guards had added a few spells of their own to make sure he didn't escape. He could call for help, but he had no doubt the outraged Father Javier had gone straight to Selene after Asmodeus's men had seized him from his bedchamber. That left . . .

If he focused a little—no need for much drawing of *khi* currents, or for anything save the lightest of breaths—he could feel Isabelle, somewhere above him; worried, fearful. But why draw her into this? She'd be no match for either Selene or Asmodeus. No, if there was anyone he wanted to call for, it would have been Aragon or possibly Emmanuelle, or even Selene, but that supposed he had a plan.

He had none.

The door opened. Philippe rose, flowing into a stance akin to a fighter's. He was not surprised to see Asmodeus walk in, followed by two beefy humans in the uniform of Hawthorn.

The last time he'd seen Samariel's lover, he had been wild, and disheveled, and with the fires of some western Hell burning in his eyes. Now he was cool, composed, the eyes behind the horn-rimmed glasses studying him dispassionately. But Philippe wasn't fooled. The fires were still there; merely hidden under a thin layer of courtesy, like the almonds at the core of dragées: bitterness under the thinnest coat of colored sugar.

Once, Philippe had been one of the Jade Emperor's emissaries, carrying edicts with his official seal to the mortal spheres; he had even gone deep into a dragon kingdom, carrying the execution order of its underwater king; staring past generals with crab pincers and soldiers with fish tails with no hint of fright. He remembered the Dragon King—in human shape, his yellow robes billowing in the waves of his anger; each shake of his antlered head making the palace of coral and jade shake; the pearl under the king's chin, growing darker and darker, the hint of an approaching storm. Through it all, Philippe hadn't moved, had simply repeated Heaven's will—the time and place of the king's death and the righteous mortal who had been appointed executioner—all of it with the cool arrogance of one under heavenly orders.

He held himself with that same stillness, that same arrogance now. "I was expecting you," he said.

"Were you?" Asmodeus smiled: a mouthful of white, sharp teeth in a pain-filled grin. "Then you'll have thought of what you were going to tell me."

"There is nothing to tell. Samariel was like that when I found him."

"Was he?" Asmodeus did not move. "And you have an explanation, no doubt, for why you were in his room at night." He raised a hand. "Don't tell me it was an assignation. I know full well what Samariel liked, and it's not you."

"I had business with Samariel. Private." At this stage, disclosing his agreement with Samariel would only hurt him: Asmodeus would certainly not extend the protection of Hawthorn to the man he'd found with his dying lover; and to have the whole matter become public would merely make Selene give up on him for good. He needed Selene; she was possibly the only one who had any hope of bringing Asmodeus under control.

"There is no privacy, not anymore."

"He wouldn't have wanted—"

Rage flared in Asmodeus's eyes, strong enough to make Philippe take a step back. "He lies boneless and dying. Don't presume to tell me what he would and would not have wanted. Not that it matters. The living have secrets. The dead can have none, not if they are to be avenged."

Philippe thought carefully. He didn't have much that could deter the Fallen's wrath, but he tried it all the same. "I don't want to impede your vengeance. Our business has no bearing on his murder. I'll swear it on the City."

Asmodeus smiled. "You have a quick tongue. Take care; it's easily removed. You're Annamite, and mortal. An oath on the City means nothing to you."

Means nothing? Isabelle had said the same thing—he felt the same words of the old oath rising through him, and pushed them down. There was no point: Asmodeus wouldn't know what he was talking about. "I abide by my word," Philippe said, drawing himself to his full height. It was all nonsense—here he was, vexed because some murderous bastard Fallen wouldn't trust his word? That was hardly the priority.

Asmodeus came closer. As he walked, something gathered behind him—shadows, Philippe thought at first, his heart in his throat, shadows like the ones in the ballroom—darkness pooling from the walls of the place, all the despair and pain gathering into the shadow of huge wings; until Asmodeus stood close enough to touch him, and, as with Morningstar, the weight of his presence was strong enough to make Philippe's knees tremble. "Yes," Asmodeus said. "Fear me. I walked this earth before you were born, boy, and I've seen enough things to turn your blood to ice. I've done many of them, too, and I won't hesitate before doing them to you. All of them, do you understand me?"

That—that wasn't what he feared, but he couldn't get the words past his frozen lips. Beyond Asmodeus, he could catch glimpses of movement; flashes of wings and fangs; of biting, rending sharpness; and his chest was so tight with the rising curse, his ribs were going to burst into splinters—

"Do you understand me?"

The eyes, behind their glasses, the mad, fiery gaze; the pressure of the curse against his mind . . . *I was born long before you,* Philippe thought, trembling. *When you were still rebelling in Heaven, I had a family—father, mother, wife, children. I . . . ascended. I became Immortal. You're nothing compared to me.*

He had to believe that; to hold on to that thought—and not to dwell on where he was, in a cell under the earth with close to no recourse—he found the *khi* elements leaping into his hands, eager to do battle, though to reveal himself, now, here, was a double-edged weapon—there were no shortages of Fallen here, more than enough raw power to utterly extinguish him. . . .

"Asmodeus!"

Selene stood in the doorway, her eyes burning. Threads of magic spun around her, drawn from the House itself, like a hive surrounded by a hundred swarms of bees. "Get out. Now."

"I was just getting started," Asmodeus said. He turned to face her; the overwhelming aura lessened; and then died altogether, as the shadows around Asmodeus departed. Philippe took in a deep, shaking breath—fresh air, though was it going to last?

Because, after all, the curse wasn't going to go away; not when it was so tightly tied to him.

"I know you weren't far in front of me," Selene said, grimly, to Asmodeus. "You left your goons at the door to stop me, and a further two in the corridor."

"Oh dear. I do so hope they're not harmed." Asmodeus made it sound like a threat.

Selene did not smile, or move from her place on the threshold. "They slowed me down a bit. As did the other heads of Houses, as you intended."

"Of course." Asmodeus left Philippe's side, and bowed to her, though there was no respect in the gesture.

"This is my House, Asmodeus," Selene said. "You may mock it; you may think we're degenerate and doomed to fail—"

"I didn't say that." Asmodeus's smile was ironic.

"No. You worked on it, very hard." Selene raised a hand; and Asmodeus flinched: a fraction of a movement only, but clear enough that Philippe could see it. "As I said, this is still my House, and I'm still head of House. Philippe is under my protection, and I won't give him up."

Philippe had never thought he'd be glad to be claimed by a House. "Then consider this." Asmodeus's smile was cold. "You're responsible for this. Even if you're not the one who ordered the killings, you've still failed to protect your guests."

"Guests? You knew what you were doing when you were coming here, Asmodeus. You wanted to invade us and humiliate us, by showing we were incapable of investigating our own troubles. You *knew* Silverspires was under attack, and you brought more people here! It's hardly my fault if you got burned."

"You—" Asmodeus's face twisted, and for a moment Philippe thought he was going to lunge at Selene. He controlled himself with a visible effort; his voice, when he spoke, was cold and contemptuous. "I will demand reparations, Selene."

"And you will have them."

"Will I?" Asmodeus pointed to Philippe, who still hadn't moved from his place by the wall.

Selene didn't move. "He had nothing to do with it." But her voice lacked the force of conviction, and Asmodeus must have felt that. Or perhaps he would have reacted the same way regardless of what Selene said.

"Possibly yes, possibly not. But you know how reparations work, Selene. Eye for eye. Blood for blood."

"You quote the Bible now?" Philippe asked. He couldn't help himself: he should have been more afraid, since it was his fate they were debating. But they were passing him around like some magical parcel—weighing and dissecting and selling him like coffee or rubber or anything else they owned.

Asmodeus did not even turn. "You will be silent." And then, to Selene: "You know what I want."

Selene nodded, but her gaze was wary. She didn't protest Philippe's innocence again. Her dress rippled in the wind from the corridor as she bent her head left and right. "Reparations usually involve the guilty party, Asmodeus."

Asmodeus smiled. "That would be you."

"You know what I mean."

"And so do you. Reparations are a gesture of goodwill, Selene. If you do not meet my demands—well, I and the other heads of Houses have to ask ourselves how sorry you are, exactly, about the attack on Samariel."

Selene's hands had clenched into fists, but she didn't move. "Fine," she said. "I'll think on it. In the meantime, you will leave me access to Philippe."

"Oh, I wouldn't dream of impeding you. As you say, it's still your House." He left, without turning back, but the irony of his words hung in the air long after he had gone.

"Sorry," Philippe said to Selene.

"Not as sorry as you'll be if Asmodeus gets his way," Selene snapped. She came into the room, bringing the smell of expensive perfume with her: patchouli and a hint of some other scent he couldn't identify, a breath from an entirely different world.

Philippe took a deep breath, and spoke, trying to put everything he had into a casual lie. "I had nothing to do with it, I swear."

Selene did not answer. She was watching him, scrutinizing him from all angles. On show again; a freak; a man for sale. "My spell is almost gone," she said sharply.

Philippe bit back a curse. Of course she'd know how her own work had fared. "And I'm still here."

"That's not the question." Selene watched him for a while; and then she sighed. "I can't read you, Philippe, or whatever your real name is."

Gone. Dead in the war, like so many things. "I tried to break the spell on my own," Philippe said. "But it didn't work."

"Of course it wouldn't," Selene said. She glanced at the door, where Asmodeus's two guards still waited. Of course she wouldn't admit that Philippe was more than he seemed, not in front of them.

"I think—" Philippe shook his head, and went for the lie nearest to the truth. "Something happened in Samariel's bedroom. Something that undid it, but I don't know what. It was like nothing I'd ever seen."

Selene's gaze rested on him; he couldn't read her expression, much as she couldn't read him. Then she started weaving magic, frowning—a cool cocoon that wrapped around them both, magnifying sounds until all he could hear was the sound of his own breath. "There. This should keep Asmodeus from listening in."

"You—"

Her face was hard; almost alien in its bleakness. "I saw you and Samariel together at the banquet. You will tell me everything that happened from that moment onward."

LATER, after she was gone, Philippe lay back against the wall, winded. He wasn't sure whether his highly censored version of what had happened had passed muster with her: the tale he'd woven, of Samariel's being intrigued by him, had been barely plausible. In her normal state she probably wouldn't have swallowed a word of it. But she was preoccupied, and so was he. The only thing she'd been interested in was the shadows; she'd made him describe them several times; and bit her lips thoughtfully, as if comparing them with something else. An eyewitness to Oris's death? He had obliged, because it seemed to be his only chance to get out of the cell.

He'd mentioned he suspected Claire; though he wouldn't very well explain the vision he'd had of her with the mirror without explaining what the mirror was—and of course he hadn't mentioned the curse or the memories: he wasn't crazy enough to admit to *that*.

Whatever Selene had said, he wasn't one of her dependents. She'd never give up one of Silverspires' men or Fallen, even to save the House; but he was the alien, the one who'd tasted Isabelle's blood; the convenient sacrifice that would buy her way out of the diplomatic tangle she was stuck in. He recognized the signs of it all too well. If push came to shove . . .

She hadn't renewed the spell, either. He'd thought it carelessness on her part, though she'd never been careless before. Perhaps she thought he wouldn't go far from where he was. Or perhaps she foresaw that she'd have to take him away from the grounds of Silverspires quite soon, and that it wasn't worth recasting the spell only to have to undo it again. He didn't want to dwell on that; so he snapped the last threads himself, reaching out to the fire and metal in the *khi* currents to form blades that would cut through anything. Now he could run, if there was an opening.

Not that he believed there would be one.

He must have slept, at some point; sliding noiselessly into dark, fearful dreams shot through with shadows sliding across mirrors.

When he woke up, woozy-headed, he saw Morningstar.

The Fallen was standing in the center of the room, which was no longer an empty cell: there was a table with . . . something strapped on it, something that moved and wheezed and moaned, something he couldn't afford to think of as human anymore. Morningstar's face was cold, emotionless, as he reached for a knife. He'd come for Philippe— but no, Morningstar wasn't looking in his direction. "Tell me again," Morningstar said to the table. "All of it."

Another vision from the past. Another memory. His head ached: he couldn't be sure if it was the dreams or the awful presence that filled the room. He'd thought Asmodeus was bad, but he'd forgotten how . . . overwhelming Morningstar was, how the mere sight of him hefting a blade could trigger a mixture of fear and awe—how he could hunger for the magic to turn his way, to acknowledge him in any way, even if it was simply to flay him alive—he would revel in the exquisite sensation of pain, in the surge of power that promised he could be anything, do anything. . . .

A noise at the door; and Asmodeus stood there, escorted by two guards in Silverspires' colors.

He was younger, his swallow-tailed coat hanging awkwardly on his frame; though his eyes were still as cold and hard as pebbles, polished to a sheen by the rush of living in the mortal world. "Lord Uphir is waiting for you upstairs, my lord."

Morningstar was bent over his work, and didn't answer at first. He nodded to something Philippe couldn't hear, and then looked up. "Apologies. Important House business. Asmodeus, is it?"

Asmodeus bowed. "Yes, my lord." There was something, some of the same underlying energy he had now, the same harsh, unyielding core that suggested he wasn't going to call anyone "my lord" for long.

"Give me a moment," Morningstar said. And, then, turning to where Philippe crouched—the magic turning, focusing on him with the intensity of a naked fire—he said, "Do you see?"

Philippe didn't answer, but Morningstar shook his head. "That Fallen on the table plotted to overthrow my rule. We can't have that here. You must understand. We're only strong when we're united. Any strife among us is an opening for our enemies. I don't like this"—a bare smile that seemed to illuminate the entire cell—"but it has to be done. Cancers must be excised from the flesh." And, reaching out, he bent over the table once again. "As promised," he said, and the blade flashed down, and there was an end to the piteous cries.

Morningstar dropped the knife on top of the table. He moved toward the door, flexing his back. The enormous serrated wings moved with him, catching the light; every part of him exuding a peculiar *sharpness*, like blades forged by a master. "Come," he said.

"My lord—" Asmodeus was still looking in Philippe's direction. "Lord Uphir—" He took in a deep breath. "He wants to see you alone."

"He's never objected to the presence of my students before." Morningstar turned back for a second, puzzled. Philippe braced himself against the pain that spiked through his eyeballs, even as he welcomed it. "Oh. Your lord is a fool, kinsman—do you know that? Mortals are more than the equal of Fallen."

Kinsman. It was a rather peculiar way to refer to another Fallen; as if they were all brothers under the skin—something not even humans had managed.

Asmodeus said nothing. Morningstar laughed; a sound so loud and primal it seemed to push back the walls. "I won't force you to utter a word against him, don't worry. Come," he said again, and walked through the door—and, in the darkness that followed him, shadows gathered and flowed like liquid ink, a tantalizing, heart-stopping glimpse of wings extending to blot out the light. . . .

The scene faded, leaving Philippe in the cell once more, breathing hard. The shadows were gone; and the world had gone dull without Morningstar's presence—everything was a touch darker, every sound oddly muted, every smell less sharp than it had been—as though he moved like a ghost through offerings not meant for him, tasting only the grit of the earth and the bitterness of ashes. He wanted—craved another vision, even though his head ached as though it would split in two. Another parcel of wisdom, of something, of anything that would make sense of what he was going through.

But he'd heard Morningstar, quite clearly.

Mortals.

A mortal's memories. But that was impossible. Leander had been Morningstar's last mortal student, and he was dead. Magic could prolong a life, he supposed; could heal some diseases, repair some muscles and strengthen some bones, but not to the centuries-long life span of a Fallen. Humans lived at most a hundred years, a hundred and ten? Nothing more than that.

But the memories were in the mirror; and the shadows were linked to them—he had seen them drawn to Samariel's bedroom, had seen Morningstar's ghost leaning against the bedpost, keeping watch over the body—the shadows were what the mirror had summoned. And the memories, quite unmistakably, belonged to one of Morningstar's mortal students.

The shadows were a mortal's revenge.

Who, and why? And how? The dead didn't cast spells. They didn't summon killing shadows, or seek revenge on those who had wronged them; or the world would be full of angry ghosts.

It was impossible. And yet . . .

And yet it changed nothing. It was tentative, useless knowledge—if he told Selene he had a connection to the shadows, she would toss him to Asmodeus without a second thought. He needed a person he could trust to investigate further, and there was a short supply of those at the moment. He was at the bottom of a cell, praying that Selene would find a use for him; a reason to protect him from Asmodeus—throwing in his lot with the House he'd so desperately tried to get away from.

He might have laughed, if the situation weren't so serious—if he hadn't remembered Asmodeus's pure, incandescent rage, the desire to hurt someone, anyone connected with Samariel's death.

Heaven help him—he was going to need the Jade Emperor's own luck to survive the coming hours.

TWELVE
Bargains Made in Anger

SELENE had cleared her desk. No more maps or papers to mar the smooth mahogany, or hide the gilded flowers of the border. Now one could clearly see the way they wrapped around the writing surface, the way they delicately followed the contours of the curved legs: the work of a master, lovingly kept and lovingly restored when necessary. It was a deliberate testament to Silverspires' wealth; the clean desk the reflection of an uncluttered mind, one that made its priority to investigate the attack on Samariel.

If nothing else—she doubted it was working as well as she would like it to—it drew the attention. She could see Claire's gaze focused on the desk, on Selene's hands; wondering what could be read from them.

Not much, not anymore.

"You know why I'm here," Claire said at last, crossing her arms over her chest. Her blue eyes were wide-open, ingenuous. Selene wasn't fooled.

Claire had come accompanied by two of the ubiquitous children, and a bodyguard she had named as "Eric," and treated with a suggestive familiarity. She wouldn't be the first or the last head of House to sleep with a bodyguard.

Selene was wondering when Claire would get on with things. She had other preoccupations, like the matter of the shadows that had attacked Samariel and killed Oris and now threatened every dependent of the House; and how best to handle Asmodeus and his uncontrollable grief. And, so far, all Claire had done was repeat Asmodeus's arguments—about reparations owed, and how Silverspires must be seen to care about Hawthorn's loss, all things Selene had listened to until she choked on them.

"Do go on," Selene said with a bright smile. "I'm listening."

"I'm not . . . unsympathetic, of course," Claire said, putting both hands on the table, their veined backs catching the light of the lone lamp in the room. "Lazarus has always been an ally of Silverspires."

No. Lazarus thrived on its unique position, which meant they couldn't afford for any House to reign supreme. They would ally with anyone, as long as they could continue to sow chaos. It was harmless, she supposed. Expected, at any rate; after all, Houses were not good in the Christian sense, or in any sense at all.

"I'm not averse to paying reparations," Selene said, calmly, smoothly. "However, all of this is going to be pointless if we don't find out who is behind this." It was one of them, no doubt. Who else could it be? No one but Houses had that kind of magic available; gang lords were weak and scattered, and too busy killing one another; lone, unaffiliated Fallen kept their heads down, and would bear no grudge to Samariel, or Oris.

Philippe had mentioned something about Claire—some incoherent story about her hands and the cathedral, which made little sense to Selene. But there was always a chance she'd catch Claire off balance. "Philippe seemed to think *you* weren't entirely blameless in the matter."

"Oh." Claire actually managed an utterly guileless look of surprise; quite a feat. "I don't see what makes him think that."

The fact that she couldn't have looked more innocent if she'd tried—and God knew Claire was no innocent. Selene bit down on the angry thought before it could escape her. She had no proof; and no idea of what, exactly, Claire had done—which made a conversation in that direction all but impossible. "You and Asmodeus and Guy are well informed," she said. "Too well informed." Not to mention that she and Asmodeus seemed to be taking their cues from each other, giving her suspiciously similar arguments.

"Why, Selene." Claire's smile was wide. "We care about the city. We wouldn't want to see it in disarray, with people dying right and left, and Houses left open to attack."

"And about Silverspires?"

"Silverspires is part of that fragile balance, isn't it?" Claire smiled, again. "Houses that die . . . leave a hole that is difficult to fill."

But that she and Asmodeus and Guy of Harrier would rush to fill. Selene shook her head. "I see."

"I was sure you would. We're also investigating, as you know." Selene knew, all too well—dependents tied up in pointless questioning, clustered for hours with Guy and Asmodeus and Claire and all the others, coming out shaken and unsure of whether the House could keep them safe anymore. For this alone, she'd have Claire's head, one day.

Claire was still speaking. "I wasn't suggesting you should stop your own investigation, or stop keeping us updated on its progress." She smiled, widely. "Which appears to be rather fragmentary at the moment, but then, I can appreciate the difficulty of keeping a House together in those trying circumstances."

Bitch. Selene kept her bright smile plastered on, refusing to acknowledge the gibe. "I see," she said, again. And, because it was late, because she was tired; and because Claire had always got on her nerves with her holier-than-thou facade: "You know Philippe."

Claire withdrew her hands from the desk, obviously taken aback. "Yes. I'm not sure what you're getting at."

"Do you truly think him capable of this?"

Instead of laughing, Claire shook her head. "All right. I'll give you this, Selene. Because it's you. No, I don't think Philippe is capable of this. He's angry at us, at all of us for what the Houses did—he thinks we're responsible for wrecking Paris and the world, though why he should care is beyond me—"

"Of course he cares," Selene said. "It's his home. He's been here so long he's no longer Annamite."

"So long?" Claire's bright eyes were on her. "He's what, twenty at most? Not that old for a mortal."

Damn. She had tipped her hand. Claire hadn't known who or what Philippe was; now she suspected something amiss. Well, not that it mattered. Words could hardly be taken back. "You know he's not guilty," she said, and wished she could believe that he'd had nothing to do with the attack on Samariel. His story of how he'd come to be in Samariel's bedroom barely held water, and it was such a convenient coincidence that her spell on him had all but shattered. She disliked coincidence; in her experience, there was no such thing when matters of magic were concerned. "Where would he have got hold of such powers?"

"I have no idea." Claire looked past her, at the curtains that marked the entrance to Selene's private quarters. Did she know or suspect Emmanuelle's presence behind them? It mattered little. Selene wasn't about to apologize for any of it.

"You're a bad liar," Selene said, dryly.

"All right," Claire said. "I know where we stand, Selene. Asmodeus has the other heads of Houses baying for blood. That blood could be yours, or it could be Philippe's. In the scheme of things, it's a small sacrifice to make."

Easy enough, when you weren't the one being sacrificed. On the other hand, Claire was right. Even if by some miracle she changed her mind and supported Silverspires—and why would she?—that still left the other heads of Houses. "Mmm," Selene said. "I'm not quite sure why you, of all people, indulge Asmodeus. Hawthorn is on the rise."

Claire shrugged. "You might say we have found . . . common interests. And Silverspires hasn't fallen so far, has it? You still have many things to call your own; and Asmodeus hates that. Though, to be fair, he would seek to destroy any House, if they did this to Samariel. It's no longer strategic; it's personal. And that's why he won't back down."

"But it's not personal for you," Selene said. She hesitated—she didn't care for Claire—but there was an opening, and she took it. "In the long run, is this the best thing for your House?"

"In the long run?" Claire smiled, and lifted her hands, so that Selene could see the wrinkled, dotted skin. "There's not much long run for me, Selene. We both know it. Magic doesn't work miracles, and no one lives forever."

Mortals, especially: they grew up in a blur of speed and bloomed like flowers, expending in a few meager years all the energy Fallen put into centuries. Selene had seen so many of them come and go, in the years she'd been with the House. An infusion of enough angel power could prolong life, but beyond a couple of centuries the human body seemed to decay on its own, as if hitting some limit that had been there all along. The work of God, perhaps: they were, after all, His subjects, and Selene was the last one who would deny His presence; or rather the hollow, dull pain of His continued absence. "You still ought to think of the future," Selene said. She looked at the children; at Eric the bodyguard, who stared stubbornly ahead and refused to meet her gaze. "Of what you will leave behind."

The future. The House she had been entrusted with—Morningstar would have wished to see it prosper, but the best she could hope for, in the current situation, was simply to survive. But of course she was the student, the apprentice; and never truly the master.

"Maybe so," Claire said. "Let me be blunt, then: what could you offer that would convince me to side with you?"

Magic, spells, angel toll; all these flashed through Selene's mind, and were swiftly discarded. Asmodeus could offer the same. If there had been any of Morningstar's magical objects left, she would have put them in the balance; but Morningstar had been stingy in sharing his power, and she had exhausted her meager source of artifacts.

"My goodwill," Selene said. "And certain . . . techniques that Morningstar passed on to me, which you will not find elsewhere."

Claire pursed her lips. "I'll think about it." She rose from her chair and bowed to Selene. "You'd do well to think on what I've said to you, too."

"Oh, I will," Selene said, not bothering to disguise the irony from her voice as Claire and her escort left the room.

Then there was blessed silence—no Father Javier introducing further heads of Houses in her office, no emergency that required her immediate presence—nothing except a faint tinkle of bells as Emmanuelle drew back the curtain and stepped into the room.

"I heard her," she said. She carried a tray with dinner for both of them: veal blanquette with rice, the carrots peeking through the milky-white sauce; and a simple dessert of oven-baked apples with cream.

Selene stifled a bitter laugh. "Did you turn chef of Silverspires when I wasn't looking?"

Emmanuelle didn't rise to the aggressiveness in her voice. "Laure brought it up herself, as a matter of fact—she's worried, though of course she won't breathe a word of it. You need to eat. You've been running yourself ragged. It's not because you're Fallen that you lack limits."

"I know where my limits are," Selene said. *I don't need a nursemaid,* she started to say, but then she saw the anxiety on Emmanuelle's face. "I'm fine, truly. Thank you for the meal. And sorry for being a horrid killjoy."

Emmanuelle shrugged. "It's a stressful time. Here." She grimaced. "We shouldn't be eating at your desk. It's hardly proper."

Selene sighed. Emmanuelle, like Aragon, was always concerned with appearances, propriety, and all the niceties Selene used as loose guidelines or as weapons. "Let's move to the dining room, then."

The "dining room" was a small corner of the bedroom with a round table, two chairs, and a tablecloth of white embroidered linen that Emmanuelle changed every other week. Today, the embroideries were birds with their young: colorful feathers against the pure white of the cloth. Selene sat down, and took an absentminded bite of her food.

"Do you think she'll accept your offer?" Emmanuelle asked.

Selene shook her head. "No. She won't. She's prevaricating, but in the end she'll see that it's not worth her while."

"All that you said about Hawthorn—"

"Is true," Selene said. "But they're not that powerful, not yet."

"I don't get the feeling we're particularly powerful, either," Emmanuelle said, dryly.

"We're still the biggest threat to Lazarus."

Or rather, they were, but not for much longer. Not after this.

"You're not considering—"

"I am," Selene said. The food tasted horrible, drained of all sharpness. Had Laure forgotten the salt, or was she too tired to properly taste it? "It would get Asmodeus off my back." It wouldn't solve the murders—at least she didn't think it would, didn't think Philippe was responsible for them; but everyone would pack up and leave, and she'd get some much-needed peace and a chance to protect her own people, without members of the delegations crawling in every corridor and every room.

"It's *wrong*," Emmanuelle said. "You know what Asmodeus is going to do to him."

"He's not one of my dependents." She'd seen something, in that cell; as Asmodeus turned toward her, framed by the magic he'd summoned; she'd have sworn she'd caught a glimpse of something else; of something dark and chillingly fluid—shadows like the ones Philippe and Madeleine had mentioned, or merely her own imagination overacting?

But, if Philippe wasn't the killer—and he couldn't be, because if he'd had that kind of power he'd already be free—then what were the shadows doing in his cell?

Emmanuelle said, "He's only here because you imprisoned him. Even if he were guilty—which he's not—it's a horrible way to die."

There were no good ways to die, though. Selene set her fork down, ignoring the look Emmanuelle shot her—no, she hadn't eaten enough; she would catch up later. "It would save us so much trouble, though, wouldn't it?" She didn't need to look up to see Emmanuelle's horrified gaze. But, as she said, she was considering it. Morningstar had, more than once, advised her to be more ruthless; and certainly he had always been ready to sacrifice whatever was necessary for the House. That had included his own dependents, sometimes.

But Selene wasn't like that, surely?

Still . . . still, if she gave Asmodeus what he wanted, the House wouldn't be the poorer for it. In fact, it might earn her Hawthorn's goodwill, at least for a few months, and that was something in short supply at the moment. And it would certainly placate the heads of the other Houses; effortlessly show her as a ruler not to be crossed—and not as one of Morningstar's youngest students, desperate to fill the gaping void her mentor had left in the heart of the House. And it wasn't as though Philippe was innocent; whatever he was hiding from her, it wasn't for the good of the House. He hated Silverspires as much as all the other Houses; more, perhaps, since she had imprisoned him. "He is resourceful," she said aloud. "He might even escape."

"You know he won't," Emmanuelle said. "And even if he did, be honest: it would change nothing. You would still have given him up. That's the guilt you would bear. It doesn't depend on how well he survives. It's all about what you did or didn't do."

What she did or didn't do. Yes, that was what it boiled down to, in the end. To her conscience; Fallen shouldn't have had one, especially heads of Houses, and yet . . .

"You're right," she said at last. "I can't." *Sheer foolishness,* Morningstar whispered in her mind. *How will you ever be a good leader for Silverspires, Selene?*

She didn't have an answer for him. She'd never had one. She'd loved and respected him, but had always known that, ultimately, he had been disappointed in her, just as he had been disappointed in all of his students: Hyacinth too unambitious, Seraphina too needy, Oris too fearful, Nightingale too careless, Leander too disobedient; and Selene, of course, too squeamish. If he'd lived longer, he would have turned from her, as he'd turned from each of his students. She didn't hate him for it: he'd been a force of nature, and every one of them had been bound to fall short; to shrivel next to his forceful presence—to crack like flawed porcelain in the oven.

"We have to find something to give Asmodeus," she said. "I can't leave this hanging—"

A knock on the door; Father Javier, bowing. "Excuse me," he said, but Aragon pushed him aside. "Selene," he said. "You have to come down now."

One look at his face was enough for Selene. "Samariel?"

"He's dead," Aragon said. "I need you down there with the corpse, to help with the last rites—"

"No, you don't," Selene said sharply; and got up, pushing back her chair. "Where is Asmodeus?"

"I left him with the body," Aragon said. He looked puzzled. "Left him time to . . . compose himself. I expect he'll be waiting for you. Why?"

Because he wouldn't stay with the body; not right now. He grieved, of course; but, with people like Asmodeus, anger and revenge always came first. "We need to get down to the cells. Now."

But when they got there, the door was open, faintly creaking on hinges that hadn't been oiled in decades; and the cell lay empty— Philippe vanished, without a trace of where he might have gone.

"Now what?" Emmanuelle said.

Selene took a deep breath. "We—" She breathed in again, trying to keep panic at bay. They could search the House, but it would take them hours if not days: too many places where one could hide, too many nooks and crannies she wasn't familiar with, and of course he wasn't one of her dependents, didn't have a tracker disk or anything she could use to find him . . . "I don't have a clue where he is." She breathed in the smell of mold and old terror from the cell's walls. "We need to find him, and fast."

THERE had been no warning. One moment Philippe was sitting in his cell; the next two of Asmodeus's thugs had come in, one of them reaching out for something he couldn't quite see—pain spiked through his eyelids, and he fell forward.

He woke up in a chair. Or rather, secured to a chair; and no matter how hard he pushed, the ropes wouldn't give way. There were other restraints, too, pressing down on him, not like Selene's intricate network tying him to the House, but a rough spider's web of large threads—not very elegant, but certainly effective in keeping him confined to the chair.

Alone. And with Selene nowhere that he could see or feel. This was not good. This . . .

"Glad to see you're awake," Asmodeus said. He was sitting in another chair: an armchair with faded red plush, and why did Philippe have the feeling he'd seen it before?

Then he felt the *khi* currents in the room, roiling, the dreadful presence pressing against his skin. *Oh no.* Morningstar's teaching rooms. "How do you know about this place?"

Something contracted around him, squeezing his hand until he thought his fingers would break—he bit his lip so as not to cry out.

Asmodeus's voice was cold. "I ask the questions here." His eyes were different somehow. It took Philippe a moment to see the redness around them; the mark of tears.

"He's dead, then. Samariel."

Again, the squeezing feeling—something popped in one of his fingers, sending a wave of pain up his arms. When he bit his lip again he tasted blood.

"You forget already. I ask the questions. And you will answer them. Tell me what you were doing with Samariel."

The *khi* currents. He needed to—somehow, if he could get hold of them, if he could . . . He said, "It doesn't matter. It was all a game for him—a power play in Silverspires—" Pain again, squeezing his entire body, and it was all he could do to breathe—bands of red-hot iron were slowly tightening around his chest.

He needed to—he needed to find the trance. He needed Selene, because she was the only one who would be able to help. But Selene wasn't there, and he wasn't part of the House—not truly, not one of her dependents and not tied to the magic of the House; there was no way he could reach her. . . .

Isabelle.

He forced himself to think through the pain. He was tied to Isabelle. Flesh and blood and bone, the sweet taste of power on his tongue—her blood, his guilt, a tie stronger than any wards Asmodeus might have devised. He needed . . .

Isabelle could find Selene.

"You think I cannot do worse?" Asmodeus asked. "Tell me what you were doing with Samariel. Tell me."

Bands of red-hot iron around his chest; the sickly sound of ribs cracking. He couldn't admit to being in league with Samariel, or Selene would cast him out.

Isabelle.

He felt her, somewhere infinitely far away; a faint presence, as if she was resting or sleeping; separated from him as though by a pane of glass. *Isabelle, please. Please, please, please.*

"Darkness," he whispered through the haze of pain. "There was darkness in the room, shadows that slid across the mirrors and the crystals. They killed him."

Asmodeus laughed—for a moment the pain lifted, and he saw the Fallen's eyes, as hard and as black as scarabs' wings. "Fairy tales. And lies. You haven't answered my question."

Because he couldn't. Because he couldn't afford to, not now that he had picked his side, or rather that his side had been picked for him. He took in a burning breath, and said, "I'm telling the truth. I had nothing to do with Samariel's death—"

"You will not speak his name! You will not sully it with your voice." The mask of sanity was cracking; that boundless energy, that madness, barely kept in check—

Then there was pain again. The world tasted like blood and salt, and he couldn't feel his hands anymore; each knuckle of each finger seemed to have burst.

He tried to close his eyes, to find again the serenity of immortals, but they were gummed with tears. He tried to call the *khi* currents to him, to talk to Isabelle, but nothing would leap into the broken mess of his hands—but there was only Asmodeus's overwhelming presence, the growing pressure on his mind, a raging fire battering at his defenses until he thought his brain was going to explode.

He needed . . . he needed . . .

He'd done this before. He needed to focus, to find the sound of a waterfall in a land that was so far away it might as well be dead; to feel the wet tang of the air in the mountains at dawn, when the whole world was spread beneath his feet, tinged with the pink of clouds in the light of the rising sun—to ignore the sucking of wet breath in his lungs, the waves of red-hot pain in his arms, the frantic beating of his heart. He needed to—Serenity always remained frustratingly out of reach. He couldn't think, couldn't focus on anything but the pain.

But there was something else—the familiarity of a vision, a memory—a pain in the back of his mind that wasn't his. There was the memory of knives against flesh; of straining against restraints that only burned deeper into his skin; the bleak, hopeless despair that knew only death would end the agony, that no one and nothing was coming to save him, because they had already given him up. . . .

Asmodeus's face swam out of the morass, his mouth open in a question that he couldn't hear. Every word slid like drops of water on polished glass: the pain in his body had abated, but the other one was still raging on, a whirling storm of suffering and anger and the desire for revenge on all that had harmed him. In a rare moment of lucidity—clinging, desperately, to thoughts that were his, he understood. This was the heart of the curse. This was the tight knot of pain and rage and disappointment, the *khi* current of wood and water he had followed to this room, the primal scream that fueled the darkness.

Betrayal.

This was not his; not his rage, not a betrayal of him, but something far, far older; the event that called for justice; for revenge. This—this was not his pain. This was not the present where he was being torn apart by Asmodeus, but the past; the memory of someone else's pain; of someone else's death—except that knowing it didn't help him, not one whit—the memories were too strong, an overwhelming maelstrom of power and rage that dragged him along until he could no longer tell what agony and rage belonged to him, and what didn't.

One must seize power, Morningstar whispered, sitting in the fractured image of a red plush armchair, the wings on his back glinting like blades in the instant before they cut into flesh. *One must be ruthless and utterly dedicated.* And, nodding gravely, he said, *I gave everything to this House, and I expect my students to do the same.*

That same horrible pressure against his brain, that same exquisite and painful sensation, the rush of knowing he did his master's will, that he would die for it—all that complex and conflicted love sharpened to pure hatred, as he hung suspended in the chains of another House, traded away to buy peace.

He—Morningstar had given everything to the House—everything—ruthlessly sacrificed his own student to a long, painful death, so the House would be safe. . . . He—

Revenge. Hatred. Betrayal. All there bubbling up from the past, overwhelming his mind—no wonder it was so strong; no wonder it still drove that curse like a sharpened, salted blade—that a master should betray his own pupil, his beloved child. . . .

You understand, Morningstar whispered, except it wasn't Morningstar; it was the black maw of some huge animal—the faint outline of leathery wings and claws, a shape that kept going in and out of existence—that slid across mirrors and crystal glasses, waiting until the time was right to strike. . . .

No, no, no.

THIRTEEN
A Thread of Wood,
a Thread of Water

ISABELLE was in Madeleine's laboratory, gluing a panel of glass to the inside of a mirror frame, her face furrowed in concentration. Earlier, she had looked preoccupied and uneasy, working the fingers of her good hand into the hollow of her crippled one, as she always did when worried—though she'd shaken her head when Madeleine had asked her what was wrong. Not trusting enough—Madeleine, remembering Oris, fought an urge to ask her again, but it was useless. She couldn't pry words out of Isabelle, not if the Fallen didn't want to talk.

Madeleine turned her attention back to the vials, where Selene had stored a few breaths: not much magic, but enough to get someone out of trouble, if need be. She would need to seal those carefully, stoppering them with primed wax so the breath didn't escape.

A sound brought her out of her reverie: a knock at the door. Madeleine opened it, to find Selene, Aragon, and Emmanuelle on her doorstep. *What—?*

Selene was as impassive as ever, cool and composed and revealing nothing of her thoughts. But Emmanuelle's face was ashen, her hands shaking.

"What is it?" Madeleine asked. Something grave, no doubt, to bring the three of them to her laboratory at this hour of the night. Thank God she hadn't taken angel essence; she wasn't sure she could disguise its effects from Selene's sharp gaze; though she felt the lack of it keenly, her mind shriveled and small in a moment when she could have used all of her wits.

Selene's gaze moved past her, to rest on Isabelle. "I thought I'd find you here," she said. "Your dedication is commendable."

Supercilious and entitled, as always. "We all do our duties," Madeleine said, dryly. Some of them better than others—it was a frightful thought, but what had Selene achieved, beyond opening them up to Hawthorn again—to reduce the safe House Morningstar had been so proud of to a tottering wreck? She quenched the thought before it could betray her, but the anger wouldn't leave her. "What do you want?"

Selene completely ignored her. "I need your help," she said to Isabelle.

Isabelle looked startled. "My help? But I don't—"

"Don't underestimate your powers, child." Selene crossed the room and gently removed the mirror from Isabelle's hands. "Listen to me, but don't ask questions. There isn't much time. Samariel is dead. Asmodeus has vanished, and so has Philippe. I need to find them, but it's a large House and we can't afford to search every room."

Isabelle, as Selene had asked, did not speak up. Her face drained of color, in what seemed an eternity to Madeleine; but when she spoke, Selene was still waiting. "What do you need?"

"Your help. You're still tied to Philippe, aren't you? There's a bond between the two of you, one I don't quite understand."

Isabelle flushed. "It doesn't quite work like that. I can't locate him, precisely. I just get images, and feelings, and only at certain times, when my mind isn't busy with other things. . . ."

"Please, child. There isn't much time."

Isabelle closed her eyes. When she opened them again, she seemed to have aged—her cheeks hollowed out, her hands shaking. "He's in pain," she said. "So much pain, dear God, how can he bear it all?"

Selene grimaced. "That's not very helpful," she said; but Madeleine, who was more observant, was there to catch Isabelle as she swayed and fell. Her body had gone rigid.

"His pain," Madeleine said through gritted teeth. "That's all she's getting from him." She didn't even bother to hide her contempt from Selene. Isabelle was convulsing in her arms—her body arching backward while her skin turned deathly pale, the weight of her almost catching Madeleine off balance.

"I know." Selene's voice was cool. How could she keep her head, in a situation like this? "But I need her. Asmodeus is an old hand, and he'll have obscured his location. I don't have the time or the resources to search every room in the House." She came to take Isabelle's hand, her dark brow furrowed in thought. "Isabelle, I need you to focus. I can help you, but only if you let me."

Magic blazed through her: a light from beneath the skin that cast every bone in sharp relief, a feeling of warmth drawn from the entire House, so strong it made Madeleine tremble. She ached for that power to go through her instead of Isabelle, to fill the emptiness within her, to wash away the rot in her lungs.

"Isabelle."

Isabelle's eyes opened. The brown iris had disappeared: they were white through and through, the color and harshness of seagulls' feathers; and shining with the same unearthly radiance as Selene. "Pain," she whispered, and said nothing else for a while. Her hands were clenched, her fingers held at an angle that seemed almost impossible—another trick of Fallen anatomy? Selene's grip on her remained tight.

Gradually, Isabelle's hands unclenched; and brown crept back into her eyes. She sucked in a deep breath, wincing. "It's an old room," she said. "With big armchairs and a low table, and that wallpaper with the little white flowers on beige."

Emmanuelle spoke up, her voice as dry and rasping as Madeleine on her worst days. "The East Wing. Behind the cathedral. Only place where we still have that old wallpaper."

"Only seventy or so rooms to search then," Selene said, dryly. "Can you remember nothing else?"

Isabelle shook her head. "I'm sorry. I wish I could help more." Her mouth opened, and closed, as if she'd just remembered something she wasn't supposed to say.

"What is it?" Selene asked.

"I'm not sure," Isabelle said. "But I think I smelled the river?"

"Ground floor." Emmanuelle's voice shook. She kept it steady only through a visible effort of will. "Is that good enough?"

Selene's face was grim. "It'll have to be. I'm gathering search parties." She looked at Isabelle; and at Madeleine, who was still hovering nearby. "That includes both of you."

Isabelle tugged at Madeleine's hand as they went out. She still looked awful, her eyes ringed with gray, her skin as pale as the corpses Madeleine had seen in the morgue; and her hands twitching in movements not entirely controlled. "You're still in contact with him," Madeleine said.

Isabelle grimaced. "It's like I said. He's always at the periphery of my thoughts, but now that I've focused on him, he's . . . hard to ignore. But he won't last long, Madeleine. Not under this kind of strain. No one can."

Madeleine could imagine, all too well, what kind of strain they were talking about—this was Asmodeus, after all, and he had learned from the best. Her own skin felt cold, but she kept her voice level as she answered Isabelle. "I'm sure we'll be in time," she said, and did not even flinch as she uttered the lie.

Mother of God, look over him, please. She didn't like Philippe much; but no one deserved to go through this, no matter what they might or might not have done.

THERE was . . . pain. There were fingers that would not flex; ribs that hurt every time he tried to suck in a burning breath, and a wet, gurgling sound that didn't augur well for the state of his lungs—pierced, maybe? What could Aragon put back together, given enough magic? Perhaps not even that—perhaps it was too late, just as it had been too late for the poor student Morningstar had betrayed and left to rot—

their agony running red-hot through them like molten lead—the battered legs, the dislocated shoulders, the myriad exquisite cuts as their jailers tried to make them admit to secrets their master had never given them—the babble that ran out of their mouth, mingled with blood and drool. A few lucid, cold thoughts here and there, though he wasn't sure if they belonged to him. Or to the sharp, implacable will that had waited decades for its revenge.

Given away. Bartered away to broker a fragile peace between the House of Silverspires and the House of Hawthorn—a peace that would not last anyway, for a few years later the Great War would come and destroy everything Morningstar had ever hoped for.

Good.

All you hold dear will be shattered; all that you built will fall into dust; all that you gathered will be borne away by the storm. . . .

The voice, running over and over in his mind; no longer a human voice, but something darker, rasping and coughing and breathing a smell of brine, as if the old stories of the Christian Hell were true . . .

A door slamming open, in a world far, far away. Emmanuelle's horrified expression, her eyes two pits of darkness in the muddy-milk paleness of her face. "Philippe—"

"Untie him. Now." Selene's voice, cold and cutting. "I won't ask twice."

She—she hadn't sold him to Asmodeus? She—he started to say he didn't understand, but his swollen tongue wouldn't obey him.

Asmodeus, rising, turning—the words all blurred together, too low to be made out; but Selene's reply was sharp and clear, like broken glass. "I think you've done enough, Asmodeus. Are you happy now? I should think this is proper compensation, insofar as you're concerned—and I would highly suggest you leave us alone now. You're this close to going too far."

And Asmodeus's face turning again—his eyes as hard as beetle's shell, but the corners of his mouth turned slightly upward, in horror, in disapproval; he wasn't sure.

He had to . . .

Needed to . . .

"Let him go," Isabelle said, and the sound of her voice—and the power blazing from her—was enough to drag him back to sanity for a moment. For a moment—a single, suspended heartbeat—he was himself again, in a body that kept twisting and twitching in pain—but then he was calling the *khi* currents from the roiling, writhing mass in the room—and fire leaped into his hands, circling his wrists—incinerating the rope and blasting through Asmodeus's weakening protections.

From his armchair, Morningstar smiled, and raised a crystal glass as a salute—a glass in which shadows slid and merged and waited for their opportunity to leap. . . .

He was up, and tottering across the room, leaning against the doorjamb before either Selene or any of the Fallen could touch him. "Philippe!" Emmanuelle said, but she'd never had the power to hold him. She must have reached out for him, because he felt her touch on his skin—something reared, deep within him—a head, darting forward, a bite, and Emmanuelle falling back with an incoherent scream.

No. No. But he couldn't hold on to anything. All his thoughts seemed to be as fractured as the glass in Morningstar's hands.

Fire in his hands, fire in his veins—the sound of his heart, madly beating against his broken ribs—the strength of water around him, drawn in a protective circle—and he ran on legs that should have been jelly, losing himself in the bowels of the House, letting Emmanuelle's and Selene's voices fade to wordless whispers. *Away.* He had to get away from this room; from Asmodeus, from Morningstar, from whoever was behind this—from the House that had given away its own students, that kept betraying its dependents, over and over again. . . .

Away.

MADELEINE, out of breath, with the beginning of a cough in her wasted lungs, cleared her corner of the corridor, and saw—

No.

No.

Asmodeus, in the middle of an old-fashioned drawing room, as elegant and dapper as always—his long-fingered gloves dark with the cloying smell of fresh blood. He held a handkerchief between the tip of his index and his thumb, carefully wiping his horn-rimmed glasses clear of any stain. The animal smell of blood, the sharp, sickening tang of it, rose so strong everything seemed to be coated with it, like an abattoir; or the kitchens, the night Elphon had died. . . .

Blood. Fear. *No. Don't be a fool.* It had nothing to do with her, or with Elphon. Nothing. She took a deep, shaking breath; forced herself to look at him. He was speaking, wearily, to Selene—giving the impression of an adult indulging a small child. "I have no idea where he went. I notice you didn't make much of an effort to follow him, either."

Selene didn't flinch. "He'll turn up." Beside her was Emmanuelle—the archivist's face pale—and Isabelle, who looked as though she'd descended all the way into Hell. "We have to find him," she said. "He's hurt."

Who—? Philippe. The blood—the blood was his, not hers, not Elphon's. . . .

Asmodeus raised an eyebrow, looked at Selene with an eloquent expression. "Do you always raise them this dumb?" he asked. "Such pure and magnificent innocence." He pinched the temples of his glasses between index and thumb, and put them back on his face. The handkerchief, stained with two bloody fingerprints in a corner, remained in his hands. "Trust me, child," he said to Isabelle. "If you don't grow up, others will make you grow up, and it will be a far less pleasant experience."

Heart beating madly, Madeleine turned to leave the room as quietly as she'd entered it; but Asmodeus's gaze turned in her direction. "Ah, Madeleine. Do come in."

Her voice seemed to have deserted her, and so had her will. She should bow and make her excuses, go back to the safety of her laboratory. Instead, she found herself moving farther into the room, as jerkily as a puppet on strings—coming to stand by Isabelle in a futile attempt to protect her, with the monster in the center of the room smiling widely all the while.

"You've got your audience," Selene said. "Are you satisfied?"

Asmodeus's eyes were hard. "Satisfied? No, if you must know. I would have liked to kill him myself."

Emmanuelle took in a deep, painful breath. "He wasn't—"

"You saw him." Asmodeus's voice was curt. "You saw what was around him. Will you look me in the eye and tell me that had nothing to do with Samariel? Such angry magic . . ."

Emmanuelle's face was pale. She lifted her hand: the flesh of the back was raised and red, formed around a perfect circle with a dot in the center. The mark of the corpses. The touch that killed in the time it took to draw breath, like the five informants in Lazarus, like Oris.

No. That wasn't possible. "You're still breathing," Madeleine said, and couldn't keep the accusation out of her voice. "How can you still—"

"Because she's a stubborn idiot and didn't go to the hospital wing when I asked her to," Selene said. "Emmanuelle—"

Emmanuelle didn't move. Couldn't move, Madeleine realized, chilled: too weak to do so. Her instincts kicked in; filling in the void in her mind. "Selene is right. You need to get to Aragon, now. Come on—" She moved to support the weight of the Fallen; and was only half surprised when Emmanuelle let her entire body go slack. She propped her up—she weighed almost nothing, compared to Isabelle— and started to walk toward the door.

"Let me help you," Isabelle said, and took Emmanuelle's other shoulder. Isabelle's eyes rolled upward for a fraction of a second, and the radiance from her skin intensified. "I've asked Aragon to meet us halfway."

Madeleine nodded. Good thinking—she should have had the idea herself, but her mind was frozen, all her thoughts hopelessly scattered in the presence of Asmodeus, running ragged on fears that he would find her, that he would make her pay for leaving Hawthorn, for betraying her loyalties to him. . . .

Behind them, Selene and Asmodeus were still facing each other. "I ask again," Selene said. "Are you satisfied?"

"In the name of the House, as reparation for Samariel's death?" Asmodeus's voice was sardonic, each word grating on Madeleine's exposed nerves like sandpaper. "It will have to do. I know the signs. He's gone away to bleed his last somewhere. There's only so much abuse mortal flesh can take, after all."

"And what if he's still alive?"

An amused snort. "Highly improbable. But, nevertheless, since you're smart enough to ask—yes. If he's found alive somehow, I'll have my revenge on him, but that will be outside House business. I'll consider—honor"—he rolled the word around on his tongue, as if it were an unsatisfying piece of meat—"satisfied, insofar as we're both concerned."

"That's good enough for me," Selene said. "Now tell the other Houses."

"Oh, I'll make sure I do."

How could she be so calm, so focused, with her lover all but ready to collapse, struck by whatever had already killed seven people? On her shoulder, Emmanuelle cracked a painful smile. "Mustn't worry her," she whispered. "She has a lot of things to do."

The first of which should have been worrying about you, Madeleine thought, but didn't say, as they went deeper into the maze of the East quarter, looking for a way into the hospital wing—leaving the two bickering Fallen behind her, talking about honor and the price of revenge on a House, and all the meaningless things they were all so obsessed about—what was the point, when the shadows were still around—when they could still kill as they had killed Oris?

LATER, much later—when the burst of magic was all but gone, the pain in his body a song that wouldn't fade away—Philippe crawled. He was almost out of the House by then—he needed to get away from it, from the shadows and the curse and everything that had broken him—on the bloodied floor of Notre-Dame, where Oris had died, his hands brushing the burned remnants of benches, feeling the harshness of carbonized wood against his bloodied skin. The stone under him was warm; the stars above cold and uncaring, as they had always been—where was the Herder, where was the Weaver, where was the River of Stars and all the figures he'd delighted in as a child?

He'd expected them to chase him; surely they'd guess where he would go? But there was nothing but the silence of the night; and the fumes rising from the banks of the Seine. The Seine. The bridge at the back of the church. No one in their right mind would go toward the river, or consider the low bridge safe. But he had no mind, not anymore.

He crawled farther, his mouth filling with the salty taste of blood—every inch a struggle against the encroaching darkness. He'd find his old gang again, beg forgiveness of Ninon, impress them all with his knowledge of the great Houses. . . .

He must have blacked out again, because when he woke up again, the stars had all but vanished, and the gray light before dawn suffused the church, striking the throne. He'd half expected the ghost of Morningstar to be sitting in it, but the stone seat was empty. However, something was . . .

He felt it again then—that thin thread of water he'd first touched here—and then later in Aragon's office—that same bubbling, simmering enthusiasm. Dragons. A dragon kingdom.

There were no dragon kingdoms, not here in Paris; not in the blackened waters of the Seine. That dark, angry power they had warned him about could not be the graceful, generous beings he remembered from Annam. But, nevertheless, he crawled, following the thread—soon, it would be dawn, and people would exit the House; soon, someone would see him and raise an alarm, though what could they do to him that hadn't been done before?

There had been a little verdant square, once, but the grass under him was scorched and dark; and the elegant stone wall that had adorned the bridge was torn, the carvings shimmering with the remnants of the spell that had destroyed them. Hauling himself to the opening, Philippe saw the waters of the Seine, glinting as black as coal under the gray skies. The waves glimmered with an oily, malodorous sheen. No dragon kingdoms there, of course not. What a fool he'd been.

When he looked away, there was a woman, sitting by the bridge. "I didn't see you. I'm sorry," he said, but the words couldn't get past the taste of blood in his mouth.

The woman smiled. She was dressed in a long court dress—not of France, but with the long billowing sleeves of the Indochinese court. Her face was whitened with ceruse, but patches of it had flaked off, revealing dull scales; and the pearl she wore under her chin was cracked, its iridescence the same sickening one as the reflections on the waters of the Seine. "It's quite all right, Pham Van Minh Khiet," she said— effortlessly putting all the inflections on his name. And before he could ask her how she spoke such good Viet, she swept him up in the embrace of her long wet robes and plunged with him, deep into the waters of the Seine.

FOURTEEN
SICKBEDS

AS Madeleine could have predicted, Aragon was not happy. "Did I miss a note about wounding season?" he asked, turning to look for his trays of instruments. "Still, at least you're conscious, which is a huge improvement on the previous patient."

He was making light of it, but he was obviously still worried—his eyes deeply shadowed, with the same hint of fear Madeleine had seen him show at Samariel's bedside. She had her artifacts, her mirrors, and her infused containers—enough protection, if she needed to—if she could convince herself that she was safe from whatever stalked the House.

"I'm fine," Emmanuelle said from the bed. She lay propped on a pillow; her skin the color of muddy milk, her wounded hand painful to see: the circle a little smudged, sitting smug in the center of a swell of red, raw skin.

"No, you're not," Aragon said. He slipped into a white gown, and went to a basin to wash his hands. "To start with, you're running a high fever, and only a fool would insist that injury is a harmless wound. What happened?"

"I wasn't there. But she tried to catch Philippe as he ran out of the door." Madeleine couldn't take her gaze away from Emmanuelle's hand; from the circle of raised, red skin that wouldn't go away—the mark that killed.

No.

"Philippe?" Aragon asked, from what felt like a world away.

"He touched me." Emmanuelle spoke up. "And it was . . . I'm not sure. It felt like his fingers burned—and it traveled upward. I can't feel my arm, not so well."

Madeleine fought panic.

"You didn't see any shadows?" Aragon asked, slowly, carefully. "Nothing beyond his touching you?"

Emmanuelle closed her eyes, and opened them again with a clear effort. "Maybe a glimpse? I'm sorry. I don't remember. It felt . . . as though there was more of him than there ought to be, if that makes sense? His hand was heavier than it should have been."

It made no sense to Madeleine.

"It doesn't matter," Aragon said, gently, pushing one pillow under her back. "We'll find out." And then, to Madeleine: "I don't understand why Philippe would do such a thing."

"Me, neither," Madeleine said. She wasn't altogether sure she had pieced everything together. Had it been Philippe since the beginning, truly? If he'd had a secret agenda against Silverspires, he'd hidden it well, under what seemed to be an entirely understandable grudge against the people who had yanked him from his home and enlisted him into a war that didn't matter a whit to him. But still—still, the evidence was inescapable. She looked at the wound on Emmanuelle's skin, the perfect circle with its bloody dot in the middle. "Is she going to recover?"

Aragon turned to her. His face was the mask she knew all too well, cool and professional, expressionless. But she could tell he was worried. "She will, if you let me do my job."

"It really does look like a snakebite," Isabelle said. "Can I do anything to help? I have magic—"

"That you won't use," Aragon said, curtly. "Healing spells cast on unknown magical wounds isn't an experiment I'm ready to run, not until we know more."

"Waiting until we know more could kill her," Madeleine pointed out.

"I'd rather appreciate if you didn't talk about me as if I were already gone," Emmanuelle said, but it was an absentminded comment. Her attention appeared focused on the wound in her hand; her brow furrowed, as if she were trying to remember something.

"It'll be fine," Madeleine said. "Really." But, like Aragon, she was worried. This was something that killed—violently, messily—something that took apart a Fallen's body, breaking down bones and organs. She wasn't sure how long contact would need to be, but even that short second between her and Philippe seemed to have had a huge effect.

She'd live. Of course she would. She was strong.

But no one had lived. No one had survived, so far—that was all the truth she had, all the comfort she could offer herself.

For as long as she could remember—since even before she came into the House—Emmanuelle had been there, a solid presence at the heart of Silverspires—like Madeleine, seldom speaking up, doing her job as best she could. To think of her gone; to even consider that tomorrow would be a day when she wouldn't be found in the stacks, gluing together old books and poring over faded images as if they were treasures . . .

Aragon put a syringe in Emmanuelle's arm. "A mild sedative," he said. "You need rest more than anything else."

"And you need to talk away from my hearing. Really, you could have gone in the other room," Emmanuelle said, grimacing. "I'm fine." She laid her head back against the pillow, staring at the moldings on the ceiling. "It'll pass in the night anyway. . . ." Abruptly, her gaze focused on Madeleine. "Madeleine. I've seen that wound pattern before." Her voice was low, urgent, but her eyes were already rolling up again.

"Where?" Madeleine asked, but Emmanuelle had sunk down into sleep; and only an indistinct word escaped her lips. Madeleine suppressed a curse.

"She'll wake up," Aragon said.

"Are you sure?"

"No, of course not. I can't be sure of many things. She's running a fever, which means she's fighting it."

"People have died of fevers, Aragon."

"Samariel didn't have a fever," Aragon said. "Oris didn't have time to have one. She's alive, and fighting. See it however you want. I'm choosing to be optimistic." His voice was weary. "We've had enough death here for several lifetimes."

No disagreeing with that.

"I expect Selene will be along later." Aragon put the syringe back on its tray, and sighed. "And I suggest you both get some sleep. You look like you got about as much as I did."

IN the end, as on so many nights, Madeleine couldn't sleep. She drifted back into the library, staring at the pile of books Emmanuelle had been working on; and, on impulse, took a pile of them with her. If she'd indeed seen that circle, perhaps it was recent. Perhaps it had been in something that Emmanuelle had been reading.

After some hesitation, she also dropped by her laboratory, and took with her one of her strongest remaining artifacts: a nail clipping from Selene set in an amber pendant, a warm, comforting weight in her hand, like a live coal on the coldest nights. Whatever had stalked the corridors during those fateful nights seemed to be gone—vanished with Philippe's departure—but she wasn't fooled. Something that strong wouldn't be so easily banished; and they still had no inkling of what it was, or what it wanted. Why target Samariel? Had it been smart enough to know what his death would cause, how it would weaken the House?

It wanted Silverspires' downfall; and perhaps that of other Houses, too. Perhaps, like Philippe, an end to the whole system—"feudal," Philippe had called it with a sneer, as if he came from a more enlightened place, and not a distant land locked in internecine fights between regions. The nerve of him—but he was gone now, dead; or if not dead, as good as dead. Asmodeus's fury wasn't to be ignored.

In Emmanuelle's room, everything was dark. The bed was heavily warded: Aragon's work, no doubt, though how effective would the wards be against something that could disrupt magic? Beyond the wards, Emmanuelle slept fitfully; the mark on her hand still raw and angry. No matter what Aragon said, she didn't look well—her cheeks were flushed, and Madeleine would find her skin red-hot if she reached out—though to do so would also trigger Aragon's wards, and wake him up from what little rest he was getting.

With a sigh, Madeleine settled in an armchair, and started to read the books.

It didn't make for much excitement. The first was a transcription of a Greek manuscript, painstakingly copied out. It was some kind of play about Orestes, though Madeleine didn't know the language and couldn't read more than a few words. She remembered Emmanuelle working on it in the archives; it had apparently contained one of the first references to the morning star, the most radiant of them all—to her, an intriguing addition to the history of the House's founder; to Madeleine, an obsession that made little sense.

The second book was an account of an obscure Merovingian procession back in the eighth century—pages and pages describing religious rituals, and the presence of noblemen and Fallen—even, it seemed, a captured manticore, such an unusual occurrence that the writer had devoted an entire chapter to its description, even though it hadn't lasted long past the execution of its summoner—Emmanuelle had probably been only interested in the brief mention of Morningstar and the House of Silverspires, but the detailed description of what everyone had been wearing and in what order people had been ranked made for rather dry reading.

Madeleine turned to the next book in the stack, which was printed by a small university, and looked to be a medicine doctoral thesis about the effects of some medicine on the Fallen body. Her heart sank. Surely

Emmanuelle wouldn't have read this cover to cover? But of course she had.

It was tiring work: poring through diagrams adorned with spidery handwriting, and through paragraph after paragraph of nearly incomprehensible jargon, struggling to make sense of the subject. There were sicknesses and symptoms, and the results of experiments, and everything merged and ran together in her mind, like ink on wet paper. . . .

She woke up with a start. There was someone else in the room—her hand, fumbling, found the amber pendant, released its power into her before she could think—and then, in the growing light of magic, she saw it was only Selene.

The ruler of Silverspires looked awful. There was no other word. She was disheveled, and there was something wrong with her clothes. It took Madeleine a moment to realize that the black jacket hung slightly askew, and the shirt was slightly creased: negligible, except that Selene would rather be dead than be seen with a less than perfect outfit.

Selene exhaled when she saw Madeleine. "Oh. It's you." She sounded disapproving.

Madeleine put the book she'd been reading back on the precarious pile at the bottom of her chair. "I thought I'd keep her company," she said, obscurely embarrassed, as if she'd been a child again, caught out when stealing jam from the communal kitchens. "In case—"

"In case it came back?" Selene shook her head. "It's gone."

"What do you mean?" Madeleine asked.

Selene massaged her forehead for a while. "I know the signs. It's not Philippe who is doing this. It's something . . . some power he's the catalyst for. He let something loose in Silverspires. Something . . . deadly, and it's still loose."

"I don't understand." Slowly, stupidly.

"It's gone. For the time being." Selene came in, and watched Emmanuelle for a while. Her face did not change expressions; but her body seemed to sag a fraction, as if something had given out within her. "She doesn't look good." She pulled a chair, and sat down, watching her lover with that same curiously impassive face.

"Where were you?"

Selene didn't look up. "Negotiating with the other Houses," she said. "Making sure they didn't blame Silverspires for this mess, and that it won't find us defenseless when it comes back."

"Comes back?" Madeleine asked slowly, stupidly; feeling as though she and Selene walked in entirely different worlds.

"You didn't think it'd stop now, did you? That's why I asked Asmodeus what he'd do, if it turned out Philippe was alive."

"I thought you wanted to question him yourself."

"Question him?" Selene's face still did not move, but her hands clenched. "I would like to, though Asmodeus will find him first. In the meantime, I do know that powers like that don't die fast, or easily. No, it will be back."

"But you don't know what it is," Madeleine said. She'd shared everything she had with Selene; and Selene still hadn't found anything. Emmanuelle had been looking; but . . . "You don't know what killed Oris or why."

"I know it's threatening the House. That's enough for me. Do I need detailed motivation? No. Detailed motivation for whoever summoned that power would be nice, but isn't necessary, either. The motivations are always the same, after all."

"One of the other Houses—"

"Oh, it's one of the other Houses," Selene said, sharply. "Who else in the city has that kind of power? I would guess it's Lazarus. But I've already done what I can with them. If they will not negotiate or align themselves with me"—her face was hard—"then there isn't much I can do, save prepare us for more attacks. I will not lose this House. You know that, don't you?"

"I know you won't lose the House," Madeleine said. "But we need more than that." The words were out of her mouth before she could think; the light in Selene's eyes shriveled and died.

"You don't trust me, do you?" Selene asked. Her tone was mild, almost curious; but her gaze had the edge of a blade—asking Madeleine whether she would dare voice her doubts and her fears, whether she would face Selene's anger.

Madeleine knew she couldn't. She was an alchemist; not a ruler, and certainly not even close to Selene in terms of power. She spread her hands in a gesture that was as unthreatening as she could make it. "It's not that. It's—" How could she make Selene understand? "Forget it. I meant nothing."

"You didn't," Selene said, but she didn't speak again. She watched Emmanuelle with the intensity of someone dying of thirst in a desert. Clearly not a moment Madeleine should intrude on; and so she went back to her books, straightening out the stack, and prepared to go back to her laboratory.

But, when she got up, the pile of books precariously balanced on her arms, Selene was up as well. Already?

"You're leaving?"

Selene shrugged. "I have something else I must do."

Something—what could be more important than Emmanuelle? "You should be with her," Madeleine said.

"You presume." Selene was looking through Madeleine again, as if she didn't really matter. "It was good of you to sit with her, but don't think this entitles you to familiarity."

What was it that they'd whispered, at the banquet she'd attended? Something about decline, and Silverspires being inescapably weak? It had been a terrible thing to say, but perhaps it was the truth; perhaps Selene's vacillating leadership wasn't what the House needed, after all.

"You're right," she said, bowing to Selene. "I apologize."

But doubt, like a serpent's fang, remained buried in her mind, and wouldn't be excised.

PHILIPPE'S dreams were dark, and confused. He lay in a covered bed, watching light filter, opalescent, through a ceiling that kept shifting—there was a face bending over him, almost human, except that it had green, scaled skin, and a thin mustache, and teeth that were too long and sharp—there was another light, sickly gray, and a voice saying words he couldn't quite focus on, but with a lilt that was familiar, that ached like a wound in his heart. . . .

Attendants moved soundlessly beyond the veils that hung over the bed: men with pincers instead of hands, with scales and fish tails, with hair the color and hardness of mother-of-pearl, everything billowing in currents he couldn't see.

I was there once, he thought, struggling to dredge thoughts through the morass of his brain. Swimming through pagodas of coral and algae, in gardens of basalt where volcanoes simmered, making the water warmer for just a moment; going over bridges with fish swimming under the rail, watching octopi nestle on gongs and drums, calling the faithful to worship . . .

He had been there once: a familiar memory, except that it wasn't quite what it should have been. He couldn't pinpoint why, but there was something—something he should have remembered.

As the fever sank down to a whisper, he saw more and more: the patches of dead scales on the skin of the attendants, that same oily sheen on the mother-of-pearl; the curious deadness in their eyes; the broken nubs of antlers at their temples.

Beyond the veils, the darkness waited. In every reflection on dull nacre, shadows lengthened, stretched, gathered themselves to leap, and he lay on the bed, too powerless to stop them—and every now and then Morningstar's dreadful presence would press against his brain until he thought his head would burst. He wouldn't actually see the Fallen, merely guess at the massive silhouette, sitting quietly just beyond the bed: watching, reproaching him for not using his powers, for being weak; for being all but dead, lost to the world.

One morning, or evening, he woke up, and his head was clear. He lay in bed, too spent to move; but alive, and not hovering on the cusp of Hell. His ribs had been bandaged, and smelled of camphor and mint; his hands likewise, and though flexing his fingers was mildly painful, it was nothing like the excruciating pain he'd once had.

"I thought we had lost you," a voice said. The curtains of the bed parted, and a woman bent over him.

She was the same one he had seen by the bridge: dressed in a five-panel tunic, the pearl under her chin shining faintly in the gloom. Deer antlers protruded from her temples, and scales mottled her skin, here and there—here and there flaking off, like dried skin.

Dragon.

"There are no dragon kingdoms in Paris," he said, slowly. "You don't . . . You don't need a dragon king to oversee the floods and the rains. You don't receive prayers and offerings from anyone. How can you possibly—? How can you possibly live?"

The woman smiled, revealing sharp teeth. "You're not the only one to have traveled far from the land of your birth," she said. She opened her hand, to reveal three sodden incense sticks: they smelled like the rot of the Seine, with a faint afterodor of burned incense. "And there are still those who offer prayers, to stay the wrath of the Seine. Hawthorn, for instance, is built on low ground, and they have cause to fear floods."

It was all too much to take in: that, and his near escape, and the visions he'd had. . . . He closed his eyes, willing himself to breathe slower. "What's your name?"

"Ngoc Bich," she said. Her voice effortlessly put the accents on words, giving meaning to things he hadn't heard in years.

"Jade," he breathed. "It's a pretty name."

Ngoc Bich made a face. "Father is very traditional," she said. "At least it wasn't 'Pearl' or 'Coral.'"

"You knew my name," he said. Not the one House Draken had given him on the conscription grounds; but the one he'd worn, all those years ago when he was a child, which still rang true even though he hadn't used it in decades. "My real name."

"Of course. Did you think you needed incense sticks to send prayers?"

"I didn't pray to you," Philippe said, obscurely embarrassed. In daylight the room was no longer diaphanous or mysterious; he could see the darker patches on the walls, the places where pollution had eaten away at the coral; and Ngoc Bich's face, painted over with ceruse, couldn't hide the places where her skin had entirely sloughed off, revealing the pristine ivory of her cheekbones. They were under the Seine; and like the Seine they were tarred with the pollution of the Great War, the cancer that had penetrated everything in the city.

Fallen again, corrupting everything they touched. He'd been part of that war, too—under orders, yes, but that didn't make him less guilty of what had happened. "I didn't know—" he said.

Ngoc Bich reached out, and closed his hand over the sodden incense sticks. Her smile was wide—like that of Asmodeus, that of a predator, but a very different one—someone who *knew*, without doubt, her place; and who was secure in her power, there at the center of everything. "When you crawl bleeding under the Heavens, all prayers are sincere."

She was . . . old, not ageless in the way of Fallen; but with the weariness of someone who had seen too much, endured too much. "Ngoc Bich—"

"I'm not the one you should worry about, Pham Van Minh Khiet. Think of yourself, first." She pulled the curtains back from the bed, and sat on it. "You can sit up."

Philippe tried. He could; but it was an effort, and it was so much more comfortable to sink back against his pillow, staring into Ngoc Bich's face.

"You should be mostly healed."

Her prevarication was all too clear. "Mostly?"

Ngoc Bich grimaced. "The wounds, yes. The rest of it . . . I'm not sure what you have in your heart."

He wasn't sure either. A curse, a vengeance; something too strong to be exorcised, even by the magic of a dragon princess, it seemed. A dead human's vengeance, slow and implacable and which would not be turned aside, since there was no reasoning with those that had gone on.

Then again, he was free of Silverspires now. He didn't have to care about any of this. It should have filled him with joy; but like Ngoc Bich he merely felt weary, burdened with something he couldn't name. He'd always known the Houses were corrupt, that they maintained their power on death and blood; but to casually betray their own . . . "I owe you a debt."

"As I said—" Ngoc Bich closed her hand around his again. "Don't think about it now. It's not as though there is much here, in the way of entertainment."

He was thinking about it, trying to remember old protocols, old rules. Dragon kings were old and wise, and lethal; and here he was in one of their courts, powerless and without even the clothes on his back. "I ought to pay my respects to your father."

"Of course." Ngoc Bich shrugged. "When you can walk. There's not much hurry."

"No." Fragments of half-remembered lore wormed their way through Philippe's brain, burning like molten metal. "This is his kingdom, and I'm here as a visitor." An ambassador from the world above, he supposed, save that he no longer had any status they would recognize. "I should come to him bearing gifts: tree wax and hollow green weed and sea-fish lime, and a hundred roasted swallows, all the precious things from the mortal world, laid at his feet with the jade and the pearls. . . ." Snake pearls and deer pearls, and all the rarities that would speak to animals; and those shining with the luminescence of the depths; and the one that, put in a rice jar, would fill it up again with the fresh crop of the latest harvest, smelling of water and jasmine and cut grass. . . .

There was something else, too—something he ought to have remembered, precautions to be taken before entering a dragon kingdom. He was sure there were cautionary tales, the kind he'd heard ten thousand times as a child—except that his mind seemed to be utterly empty—wiped out of everything.

"You need rest," Ngoc Bich said, gently; and drew a hand over his face; and darkness stole across him with the same gentleness as when it stole across the sky, and he sank back into confused dreams, struggling to name what he should have remembered.

MADELEINE was in her laboratory, cleaning out the artifacts drawer, when a knock at the door heralded the arrival of Laure, two kitchen girls, and Isabelle.

Laure must have seen her face. "Isabelle didn't feel like going alone through the corridors, and I have to say I can't blame her."

Madeleine opened her mouth to suggest that Laure had better things to do in the kitchens; and then closed it. Laure obviously knew. "While I'm at it," Laure said, putting a basket precariously balanced on one of the tables, "here's the sourdough bread." She smiled at Isabelle—like a stern mother. "Your dough is a mess, but it's getting better."

Isabelle made a face. "You said that the last time."

"That's because it takes time to get genuinely better," Laure said. "Now I'll be off. You two have things to discuss." The kitchen girls left with her, leaving Madeleine staring at Isabelle. From the covered basket wafted the tantalizing smell of warm, just-baked bread.

"Am I . . . Am I disturbing you?" Isabelle asked.

"No, hardly." Madeleine laid a small wooden box at the end of the line. There was a small fragment of skin trapped inside, its magic almost spent. "I thought I'd catalog everything. If there ever was a time when we needed magic . . ." The heat of the artifacts' magic played on her fingers, as if she stood close to a flame in the hearth. This was the bedrock of Silverspires: the power that made Asmodeus and Claire and Guy recognize Selene as their equal; the power that kept them all safe.

Except that it was all useless, wasn't it, if Selene couldn't keep things together?

"Emmanuelle is a bit better," Isabelle said. She wore men's clothing, an unusual occurrence for her: a tweed jacket and creased trousers, and a stiff white shirt that looked as though it'd come straight from the laundry. "Aragon said the worst of the infection appeared to be over, but he didn't sound very confident." She didn't sound very confident, either—she kept worrying at the gap between her fingers, quickly, nervously.

"He's a doctor. They seldom commit to anything." She wished she could believe her own lies: it would have been so much easier, so much neater. So much more reassuring, without Emmanuelle's life hanging in the balance, and everything that made Silverspires slowly unraveling like frayed clothes. Damn Asmodeus and his intrigues; and Philippe and his pointless grudges.

"I guess they do," Isabelle said.

Madeleine hesitated for a moment. "Does Emmanuelle remember—"

"What she said before she went under? I asked." Isabelle flushed. "She didn't, not exactly. She looked at her hand again, and said she'd have a look in the books she'd been cataloging recently."

"I had a look already," Madeleine said. "But I suppose she'd know best."

"She said she'd have them brought to her and try to work on them." Isabelle forced a wan smile. "Always working, isn't she?"

"She is."

Isabelle took a deep breath, and opened her hand. "I found this."

It was a flat, black thing—an obsidian mirror, the sort of old-fashioned artifact that had been dated even before the war. Madeleine took it, absentmindedly; and then almost dropped it. It was . . . malice, viciousness, hatred—whispers that she was worthless, that Silverspires was worthless, doomed to be carried away by the wind—black wings blotting out the sun, that same slimy feeling she'd got when the shadows filled the room . . . "What *is* this?"

Isabelle blushed. "It was under the throne. In the cathedral. There was a paper with it." She took a deep, trembling breath; held it for a suspended moment. "All that you hold dear will be shattered . . ."

Madeleine's fingers worked around the curve of the mirror—seeking the catch, the point of release. There was nothing; just that terrible sense of something watching her, darkly amused at her feeble attempts; that faint odor of hatred that seemed to lie like a mist over the smooth surface. "I can't open it," she said, finally. "It feels like an artifact, holding some kind of angel magic—breath, perhaps?" One she would have liked to hurl down the deepest ravine in some faraway country; and even then, she wouldn't have felt safe.

Isabelle picked it from Madeleine's hand with two fingers, and laid it back in a handkerchief—careful never to leave her skin in contact with it for too long. It was as bad for her as for Madeleine, then. "I thought you could . . . Never mind. It doesn't matter."

"It does matter," Madeleine said. "It's connected to the shadows, isn't it?"

"I don't know," Isabelle said. "You can't open it."

"I can't open it now. It's locked," Madeleine said. Not that she was keen on releasing whatever was inside it—whatever remnant of darkness still clung to its innards. . . . "It doesn't mean that, with a little work or a little research or both . . . Can you leave it to me?"

"Of course." Isabelle's face hardened again—as changing as the sky on a spring day, when clouds pushed by the wind could blot out the sun in a heartbeat. When she spoke again, her voice had a determined, harsh tone Madeleine had never heard from her before. "Madeleine?"

"Yes?"

"I think we should go and help Philippe."

It took a moment for all the words of that sentence to realign themselves in Madeleine's mind. "He's dead," she said. "They found the trail of blood leading into the Seine, and there's probably a corpse somewhere, playing with the fishes." If Selene was right, the thing he'd let loose was still in Silverspires; but it didn't mean that Philippe had survived—Asmodeus's attentions had been thorough, and unpleasant.

Isabelle shook her head. "There is—I don't really know how to explain it, but there is something in the Seine. *Somewhere.*" She played with her hands—the fingers of the good hand in the crippled one, worrying at the hole.

She was tied to Philippe; inextricably linked somehow, though in the days before the banquet their relationship had seemed more strained than before. She couldn't help defending him; to her, it would be as natural as breathing.

Whereas as far as Madeleine was concerned, Philippe could go hang. "Let me be clear. He wounded Emmanuelle. He was the catalyst for something that killed Samariel. Something that wrecked the House. And you somehow think it's a good idea to go find him wherever he's hiding?"

Isabelle flushed scarlet. "I don't know what happened. I think it's connected to him, but he's not controlling it. He's not doing any of it."

"That's great comfort, but no. If he's alive somehow—"

"He is. I know it. And he could help Emmanuelle."

Unlikely. He was the one who'd harmed her, after all.

"I wasn't doubting your ability to find him," Madeleine said. She sighed, and massaged her brow, feeling the beginnings of a headache. "Selene should be the one to find him, not us." Just look at them. One washed-out alchemist, and one young Fallen too naive to see the political implications of the fight she was dragged into. Hardly the elite group of magicians it would have taken to keep Philippe's magic at bay.

"Selene won't go," Isabelle said.

"You asked?"

"I had to," Isabelle said. She bit her lip. "But she said no. She has too much to do; and she hates Philippe."

"With reason," Madeleine said. She didn't much care for Philippe, either; even before the conclave, he had been surly and uncivil.

Isabelle bit her lip. "He—he promised to look after me. He wouldn't attack me."

"He cut off two of your fingers. That's hardly—"

"That's the past," Isabelle said, more forcefully than Madeleine had expected. "Before he came to the House. And he's . . . not himself now."

"Which doesn't excuse what he has done. If he has done it," Madeleine said, grudgingly. She was willing to grant that all of it was a bit much for a young man; even if said young man was older than he appeared. Whoever had killed Samariel had known the effect it would have, and that spoke of familiarity with the city and its fragile equilibrium of warring Houses; something Philippe had been demonstrably uninterested in. "But I still don't understand why you want to go running after him. You're not—"

"In love with him?" Isabelle smiled. "I saw the thought cross your mind. Of course not, Madeleine. I know what I am."

"Fallen doesn't mean emotionless."

"Oh, no. I mean that he's still in love with his country above all else, and I—I'm still trying to figure out how things work."

"That would certainly give you a head start on how things work," Madeleine said, suppressing a smile; and raised a hand to forestall Isabelle's objections. "But never mind. If it's not that, then . . ."

"We're friends," Isabelle said. "He made a promise to look out for me, and I can't do any less."

"It does you credit," Madeleine said, slowly. "But—" *But what you want is insane,* she wanted to say. To go wherever she thought Philippe was, to confront what had killed Samariel and Oris and countless others . . .

"Don't you want to understand what's going on?" Isabelle asked.

No. She had no desire to; but then she thought of Oris, lying cold and naked on the slab as she took him apart—the only thing she knew how to do anymore. "I want justice," she said. "But I'm not sure how this would help me."

"Because it's not over," Isabelle said, at last. "It never was. Look at Selene. She's known, all along. She watches the darkness, knowing that it will return."

"It?"

"Whatever killed Samariel. Whatever killed Oris. It's not Philippe," she said, again, her voice low, urgent. "You know it's not, Madeleine. Behaving as though it's him—that's just refusing to acknowledge the truth. And *that* will kill you. That will kill all of us."

"I—" Madeleine took a deep, shaking breath. She could go on as she had always gone; keep her head down and inhale angel essence until all grief, all memories had been dulled to nothingness, wasting Morningstar's gift of life as she had wasted everything else. Or, before it was too late, she could do one last, small thing for Oris's memory.

"Let's go," she said. "Quickly, before I change my mind."

FIFTEEN
GHOSTS FROM TIMES LONG GONE

SELENE buried herself in work. It was the only way she'd found to forget Emmanuelle's pallor, or the deep, dark circles in her face; the shadow creeping across her eyes, making her seem gaunter and gaunter with every passing day. Aragon made optimistic noises, tried one treatment after another; but nothing seemed to take hold.

It reminded her of that other time; of those dark, desperate hours when Emmanuelle's addiction to angel essence had gone beyond control—when she lay wasting away on a hospital bed, and Selene prayed to a God she no longer trusted for any kind of cure. Months and months of battling against the drug; until at last Emmanuelle rose, her skin paper-thin, her smile brittle and forced; and they had slowly started picking up the threads of their old life; slowly accepted that, sometimes, for incomprehensible reasons, God did grant miracles. Emmanuelle would have called it an answer to prayers; Selene . . . she wasn't so sure. But she no longer made gibes at Emmanuelle for going to Mass, for who knew what kind of powers it was wiser not to antagonize?

She could have used Emmanuelle's faith, now; or a miracle. But her prayers were distant and insincere, born out of fear and self-interest; even if she hadn't been Fallen, God would have no time for them.

If Selene had still had artifacts infused with Morningstar's magic—or even angel essence—she would have used them then, in a heartbeat. But there was nothing of the kind; the last remnants of his magic had been used long ago, to shore up the House in its hour of need. Now it was just her; and Asmodeus was right: she was faltering.

Sometimes, she hated Morningstar; hated him for picking up his things and vanishing without a word of explanation, without even an apology. But then she remembered that he'd never explained or apologized for anything; and that—always—he'd radiated such warmth and magnetism one couldn't help loving him. Moth to a flame, Emmanuelle had said, with a fraction of bitterness; because Morningstar had never liked her. He chose the ambitious, the desperate, the *hungry*. Emmanuelle, perfectly content with her life among the books, fit none of those criteria. Selene, on the other hand . . .

She'd been young, and among the least of the hierarchy in Silverspires: practicing magic at night in her bedroom, making rumpled sheets smooth themselves out, flowers bloom on dry wood, rain splatter on her bedside table. It must have been those small magics that had caught Morningstar's eye, or perhaps his weariness with his previous apprentice, Leander—she was never sure. But she remembered the moment when he'd turned to her; when she'd walked into the cathedral and found him waiting for her in the light of the rose window. "Selene, is it?" he'd asked, and she'd only nodded, too awed to dredge up words. "Come."

She missed that now; that glow that would fill her whenever she mastered a complex spell, and looked up to see him smile; the light limning his fair hair and the curve of his wings, and remembering, in this moment, how favored she was.

You should be here, she thought, closing a file and putting it with the others. *Helping us hunt down whatever caused this.* She had Javier and the others patrolling, making sure that nothing stalked the corridors anymore, and all the children in the school slept with Choérine, who was a bit old but still more than capable of drawing protective wards. But it wasn't the same. It would never be.

You should be here.

Reparations had been offered; Houses had been appeased—it should have been a slow, intricate dance of negotiations and apportioning blame, but it had been surprisingly easy. In the wake of Samariel's death, the Houses quietly forgot why they were here in the first place—they might not quite believe Selene's assurances that the murderer had been dealt with, but it was not their immediate problem, and to remain in Silverspires would have been too costly and dangerous.

The delegations were leaving; the tense atmosphere gradually dying down. Guy and Andrea had left first, with their usual haughtiness; then Sixtine and Bernard, then the rest of the minor Houses. To all of them, she'd made the same reassurances—that Silverspires had settled compensation with Hawthorn, that the person responsible had been dealt with adequately—that they weren't all dancing on the edge of a worse conflict than the Great War. She'd smiled and prevaricated and lied until her face ached.

Which only left two Houses.

They came into her office together: a surprise, but not an altogether unexpected one. "Asmodeus," she said. "Claire."

Asmodeus wore mourning clothes: a black shirt under his jacket, a severely cut set of trousers, on which the simple white tie seemed almost obscenely out of place.

Claire had dressed as deceptively simply as usual: a gray suit with a knee-length skirt and an elegant coat with a fur trim on the collar. Her usual entourage of children had remained at the door; Selene was impressed she hadn't even had to ask. On the other hand . . .

On the other hand, there was Asmodeus.

His face was quiet, expressionless; his hands gloved. It was hard to imagine him angry, or covered in blood; but it was a mistake his former enemies had made. "You'll be leaving, I imagine," Selene said.

"Of course." Claire nodded. She readjusted her own gloves: a borderline disrespectful gesture, as if she were already out of the House. "I have things to do, Selene."

So did Selene, but she wasn't churlish enough to point this out. "I see. I won't hold you, then."

Claire's smile was bright, innocent. "Of course you won't."

Asmodeus was staring at her—grave, serious, with none of the usual sarcasm. "I ask your leave to remain."

What—? He couldn't—Selene bit her lip before that thought could escape her. "I must ask why," she said, keeping her voice as cold as she could manage. She'd hoped to be rid of them all; to have mastery of her House once more, to scour it to make sure the creatures were gone—to spend time by Emmanuelle's side without worrying about who might come in and how they might judge her.

Asmodeus looked up, with a fraction of his old sarcasm in his eyes. "Why, Selene. One would think you weren't pleased to see me."

"You know what I think," Selene said.

"I do know what you think. It doesn't matter much," Asmodeus said. "I have a body to prepare for burial, and a vigil to conclude."

"I thought—" Selene swallowed, unsure what to say. "You'll want to do this at Hawthorn, surely."

Asmodeus shrugged. "Some things will be done at Hawthorn; what we can do. But he died here, Selene. If there are ghosts to exorcise, they will be here."

Unbidden, a flash of shadows in her memory—of darkness sliding across the faded wallpaper and the polished parquet floors, like what she had seen around Philippe. Selene gritted her teeth. She knew the shadows hadn't left; she didn't need the distraction.

She looked at Asmodeus: impassive, elegant in his mourning clothes; though there was a slight tremor in his hands, a slight reddening of his eyes beyond the horn-rimmed glasses. Grief? He'd hardly cried when Samariel died, unless the . . . madness he'd inflicted on Philippe was his way of weeping. One could never be too sure, with Asmodeus.

But whatever he wanted to remain here for, it could hardly be sentimentality; not something he'd ever been known for. Though . . . though he and Samariel had been together for as long as Selene could remember—long, long before Asmodeus became head of Hawthorn. One was, perhaps, allowed a little sentimental lapse; but no, that was exactly why Asmodeus had risen so far; because people wanted to believe he had feelings, that he could be swayed by tender emotions.

It didn't matter, either way. She couldn't say no, not to a request framed this way, and he'd known it all along. "By all means," she said, not bothering to force sincerity in her voice. "Remain a few days more, if you think it'll help you find peace."

Claire smiled. "So glad to see everything is settled." She pulled on her gloves, again. "I thought for a moment it would be war."

Thought, but hadn't been worried by. "Don't be a fool," Selene said. "Who wants to go to war?"

"You're the fool." Asmodeus shrugged. "Who wouldn't want to? We all cherish the illusion we'd easily defeat all the other Houses. That was the reason we got into the last mess."

"But you know," Selene said softly, feeling the fist of ice tighten around her heart, "you know that war would simply devastate us further?"

"Yes," Asmodeus said. "For the right gain, though—"

For standing in a field of ruins, crowing victory? Selene bit down on the angry answer before it could escape her lips. There was no point. They didn't see things her way. They never would. "I'll see you on the parvis, then," she said to Claire. "For the formal leave-taking."

"By all means," Claire said. She smiled again: that soft, vaguely pleasant smile that sent waves of dread down Selene's throat. "I was hoping Madeleine would be there, too."

"I think you've seen enough of Madeleine," Selene said, sharply. "I warned her against you."

"Ah." Claire paused, halfway to the door. "But who warned her against herself?"

"I don't follow your meaning." It was a mistake, exactly what Claire had expected, but Selene couldn't help herself. She was acutely aware, as she stepped closer to Claire, of Asmodeus, who hadn't yet moved from his chair and was staring at the desk with an odd, predatory intensity. This alliance between them was . . . unsettling.

"Oh, Selene. I did warn you, didn't I? About cleaning your House. But no, you have to take in the strays and the defectors—"

So *that* was what it was all about. She could feel Asmodeus tense beside her. She'd always assumed Madeleine was beneath his notice: a mortal with little magic, and no great position in Hawthorn, and God knew he'd had so many people die in the bloody night he'd taken Hawthorn. But perhaps he still considered her his property; and still demanded from her the same loyalty he demanded of all his dependents.

"You can talk, Claire," Selene said, pointing to the pack of children waiting outside, frozen in uncanny intentness, even as they played among themselves. "I thought Lazarus prided itself on its . . . inclusiveness."

"Of course." Claire's smile was the toothy one of a tiger. "We'll take in the poor and desperate, but we'll make sure they clean up first."

They could go on like this for hours, but Selene had no patience for prevarication anymore. "The hour grows late. Say what you want to say, Claire, instead of talking in riddles. Surely you've thought it over a thousand times already. What about Madeleine?"

"Ah, Madeleine. A sweet, sweet child, the apple of your eye—"

Hardly. Selene snorted, and crossed her arms over her chest, waiting for the sting.

"I warned you," Claire said. "Do you know where she is now, Selene? She's inhaling her life away in some corner of Silverspires, like some junkie on the streets."

Inhaling. Selene said nothing, but she felt as though she'd been doused with a cold shower.

"Don't tell me you haven't noticed," Claire said. "Her lungs are wasted, and she's never had much magical talent. How much easier to steal it away—"

"You will stop," Selene said, slowly, coldly. "This . . . allegation has no truth." But she'd heard Madeleine cough; had seen the circles under her eyes become larger; had felt the power that filled her alchemist from time to time, far larger and fiercer than any magical talent Madeleine might have shown. For a mortal and an alchemist, she was shockingly undertalented. Selene had assumed sickness; there were more than enough of these going around.

"No?" Claire said. "My mistake, then. I'll leave you to your House and the handling of your dependents."

Madeleine. Angel essence. That . . . was not possible. She would have known. She should have known, if she'd been paying attention.

Someone came to stand by her side; with a shock, she realized Asmodeus had left his chair. "You'd do well to leave this alone," he said to Claire.

"Why, Asmodeus." Claire's voice was coquettish. "One would almost think you cared for her."

Asmodeus did not answer; but did not budge, either. There was something in his eyes: anger, fear? How could he possibly care about Madeleine?

By the looks of it, Claire couldn't work it out, either. "As you wish," she said. "I've said all I had to. Good-bye, Selene. I'll see you on the parvis."

After she'd gone, Asmodeus bowed to Selene, with the same old, usual irony. "And I shall see you later."

"Asmodeus," Selene said, when he started to move. He didn't bother to turn around. "She's right. You don't care."

A silence. Then, in a voice as cold as the chimes of winter: "Don't presume to tell me about what and whom I should and shouldn't care."

And, with that, he was gone.

For what felt like an eternity, Selene stood there, trying to make sense of what he had said; knowing she was wasting her time, that he wouldn't explain anything to anyone, least of all her. And now he was in her House looking for God knew what.

Great.

A knock on the door announced the arrival of Father Javier and Aragon, both in a mess and with the pale look of the sleepless. "Any news?" Selene asked.

Aragon shook his head. Father Javier said, "We've turned the House upside down. I think it's gone—"

No. She didn't have the strong link to the House Morningstar had had, another item on the long list of why she wasn't and would never be Morningstar—but she was still linked to it, had still had toll taken from her and bound to the substance of the House. If she called the magic of the House to herself; if she held it, like a trembling breath, she could still feel the darkness that had slain Samariel; could taste it like bile and blood on her tongue. "It's here," she said. It hadn't gone with Philippe, though there was but little doubt Philippe had been its catalyst. But he'd released something; something large and angry and deadly; and she had no idea where it could be hiding in the vast spaces and corridors of those disused buildings.

"I'll need you to prepare," she said to Father Javier. "And tell Choérine to do the same with her students."

Javier had gone pale; though with his dark, Mediterranean countenance, it was merely a slight change of skin hues. "I have a few spells," he said, "but you know the position of the Church—"

Selene smiled, bitterly. "I have faith. But faith isn't always enough. And, to Aragon, "I'm sorry."

Aragon shook his head. "I'm the one who should apologize. But it would be good if—"

"I know," Selene said. Asmodeus be damned, she needed to see Emmanuelle; even if she was afraid of what she'd look like, of the new hollows the sickness would have carved into her cheekbones. "I'll be by later."

Aragon nodded, and withdrew. After a while, Javier did the same. He was too well-bred to say what he thought, but he wanted to protest. She could feel the mood of the House; knew what they all felt but wouldn't say. They needed strong leadership, and they didn't feel Selene was providing it, not anymore. It had been easy to head the House in the years of its power—or in as much of its power they could salvage, after the war and Morningstar's departure—but now that the storm had come . . .

Well, she was all they had, and short of a miracle that Selene didn't believe in, they'd have to weather this together.

Selene shook herself, and went to see Madeleine.

She shouldn't have had to. There were far better uses of her time, and myriad things that needed to be done. But she was rattled, and the laboratory wasn't far, and she was sure that just a few words would be enough to dispel Claire's suggestions. All she was trying to do was set them at each other's throats; to weaken Silverspires from within after failing to undermine it from without.

The laboratory was deserted: no sign of Madeleine, or Isabelle, though the latter's red cloak lay on one of the large armchairs. An assortment of magical artifacts lay on the table, all of them shimmering with the potency of stored magic. There was a sheet with Madeleine's painstaking, precise handwriting, making a note that some of the ones at the end would need to be emptied and renewed soon. Good. In times like this, it was better to know what they had; though they should think about storing more magic. She herself had been remiss on that, lately, with the various emergencies. . . .

They couldn't have been gone long, or planned to be gone for very long, given the state of disarray; though, to be fair, Madeleine's laboratory was *always* in a state of disarray.

There was nothing in the laboratory to vindicate Claire's suspicions. At least, nothing visible. Selene took a deep breath—what was she doing, giving in to suspicions?—and gathered to herself the magic of the House. For a moment, she hung in a timeless space; feeling the connections between the House and its dependents, the ghosts of the dead and the roiling, anguished magic spread throughout Paris; tasting blood on her tongue, and the darkness around them, barely held at bay by Morningstar's wards.

There was . . . something in the laboratory, or rather the remnants of something. Selene spoke the words of a spell of retrieval, and let the magic guide her to a drawer in the secretary. When she opened it, it was empty, but a slight shimmering indicated a ward. She punched through it and the ward disintegrated, but the drawer was still empty.

Selene let go of the magic. Suspicions, nothing more; Claire playing them all for fools. She shouldn't have entered her game; whatever secrets Madeleine was keeping, they were none of her business. God knew everyone from Javier to Aragon to her was keeping secrets—she might not be taking in all the strays, as Claire had accused her of, but many people in Silverspires had come here because it was a refuge—and one could seek refuge from many things, not all of which could be freely admitted.

She was about to leave the room when something caught her attention: something that jangled in the subtle tracery of magic, a feeling like something scraping her skin raw. She followed it to a smaller cabinet, which she opened. There was nothing there, either, in any of the compartments; but when she put her hand in one of them, she felt the scalding heat. Something powerful had been kept there: a pendant, judging by the empty jewelry box still bearing its imprint.

"Show me," she whispered, and put her hand in the box. When she withdrew it, there were minute traces, like dust. Without the magic, she wouldn't have seen them, but with it, they burned like raging fire. An intimately, obscenely familiar touch: a power that required its users to take always more, always more often—to find more bones, more Fallen corpses to strip—a power that fueled its existence on the death of her kind, an abomination that shouldn't have been allowed to exist.

Angel essence.

Claire had been right, then, damn her.

Selene reached into the cabinet, and incinerated the jewelry box and every trace of essence it had contained: an empty, grandiloquent gesture, but it made her feel better.

Angel essence. How could Madeleine be so stupid? It was forbidden in Silverspires, because all it did was beget more deaths, more junkies clamoring for a fix; all that for a power they were too drugged to properly master. Morningstar had despised it, and she was no different. She would not have it in her House. Not now, not ever.

MADELEINE stood on the bridge, staring down into the waters of the Seine—fighting her instinct to take a few steps backward, to be safe from whatever might come up from the river. "Here?" she asked. Below her, black waves were lapping at the embankment. The stone was stained dark, with the oily residue of the water still clinging to the mortar; and the water itself was foaming, far more than it should have been—much as if you'd poured soap into a bath, though she very much doubted it was similarly innocuous. She wouldn't have leaped into that water, even if you'd paid her. "That's really not attractive—"

"I think it's here." Isabelle bit her lip. "That's where he is, but they have to grant us entry."

"You're not making sense," Madeleine said. She carried her bag close to her, the weight of the artifacts a reassurance that she could handle whatever they happened to find. Isabelle hadn't been forthcoming with any information; or rather, the little she'd given Madeleine had added up to no coherent picture. She should have been scared, if she'd had any sense; but the memory of Asmodeus's fingers, still stained with blood—of being unerringly picked out from where she stood, as if he'd had eyes on the back of his head—left her no room to fear anything else.

The river. Everyone in their right mind avoided the Seine; and here they were, headed straight into its heart—to the frothing insanity it had become, corrupted by the remnants of spells and magical weapons. "Isabelle?"

Isabelle said nothing for a while. Her eyes were closed, and the low-key radiance that emanated from her body intensified—until everything around her, from the stunted trees to the broken benches, seemed slightly grayer, slightly less colorful. The light spread, slowly, softly, engulfing the embankment, the patches of dirty, foamy white on the river; the overcast sky above. Everything seemed limned in that curious illumination, everything somehow diminished, bereft of something vital.

"Speak to me," Isabelle said, and her voice rang like a bell tolling for the dead.

There were stairs, leading down the embankment onto a small stone dock, where boats would sometimes moor. But, on the last step of the flight of stairs, a shadow caught the light: a hint of something that wasn't quite there. "Speak to me," Isabelle said.

The shadow solidified, became the outline of an Annamite pavilion: the elegant curve of the roof, the sharp, brittle brightness of lacquer, the flowing lines of calligraphy on the wooden pillars.

Impossible. This was Paris, not the colonies. There could be nothing like this here. . . . But Philippe had come to the city, and perhaps other things had. Madeleine found, by touch more than by sight, the pendant around her neck, filled with angel essence, let the warmth of its power wash over her until nothing of fear remained. Oris. She was doing this for Oris, and for Emmanuelle; and so that the Silverspires she knew could continue to exist.

Isabelle opened her eyes. They were white, filled with the same light that flowed out of her. "Come, Madeleine."

The air changed as they descended the stairs. It was still clogged with the acrid smell of magic, burning the lungs, but it acquired a peculiar tang, something salty and electric that Madeleine could not place, until she remembered standing by a well in a disused garden, breathing in the smell of rain after the storm. It wove in and out of her lungs, until she felt almost—not healed; nothing could do that, but healthier, the damages of the drug covered by a thin coating of seawater and algae. Nothing should have been able to do that. And she could feel something else, something weaving in and out of her mind, fingers like the teeth of a comb, raking thoughts out of her almost as soon as they surfaced—she fought it, but it was a constant effort to keep everything in place without that alien tampering.

What *was* this place?

"It's a dragon kingdom," Isabelle said, as if she read her thoughts.

"Dragons don't exist." The insignia of House Draken had been a rearing dragon, but it was a mythical animal, nothing more. Summoning creatures was impossible.

"Maybe not. Maybe." Isabelle had that peculiar smile again, half-amused, half-bewildered, as if she knew something but couldn't remember how she'd come by that knowledge.

At the bottom of the steps, the pavilion had taken on body and heft: no longer a silhouette, it towered over them, its colors vivid in the gray light—red and gold and the deep brown of mahogany. Closer, though, it didn't quite look as impressive: patches of mold and gray foam had eaten away at the paint; the lacquer, cracked and damaged, had flaked away; and the pillars smelled of rot and damp. So even that dragon kingdom, whatever it was, hadn't been spared by the war. It made Madeleine perversely glad, that nothing had been spared; and yet . . .

And yet, what would it have been like, at the height of its glory? As blinding as Silverspires, a refuge for Philippe's kind in the city: bright and welcoming and so terribly unsettling, with that odd tang in the air, that nameless feeling sinking its claws into her, digging into her brain like a worm; making her feel healed, making her feel whole.

Serenity, she thought, and the word was like ice in her mind. She couldn't afford that, couldn't let go of fear. It was what kept her alive, for what little time she had left. It was what kept her away from Asmodeus.

"It's old," Isabelle said, pausing, for a moment, with awe in her voice, before turning and walking straight on, between the two pillars. As soon as she'd set foot under the temple, her image wavered; became fainter, billowing like a water reflection in a windy day; disappeared altogether from view.

Madeleine looked up. The steps of the embankment, too, had vanished, and she stood within a circle of perfect silence; breathing in, breathing out, a salty taste like tears on her tongue.

Well, there was nothing for it. She reached for the pendant around her neck, opened it; and in a single, practiced gesture, inhaled the angel essence from it.

Fire, in her belly—light, radiating from her outstretched hands—she could do anything, challenge anyone, defend anyone and anything. Slowly, carefully, she rode the crest of the wave, soothing the magic within her until it lay quiescent, ready to be called on at a moment's notice.

Then, without looking back, she stepped under the pavilion, and followed Isabelle into the dragon kingdom of the Seine.

SHE'D expected many things, but not a palace—a fragile assembly of courtyards and pavilions of nacre and jade, with marble steps and red-lacquered pillars—all spread below the hill on which she stood. Everything shimmered and danced; and the people moving in the various courtyards all but disappeared from sight as the waters around her shifted.

She could breathe, but that somehow didn't surprise her; or at least wasn't any more surprising than anything in the previous hour. As she walked, she felt again the place getting at her—soothing fright and surprise out of her, trying to make her feel at ease. No. She couldn't.

Had to fight it, had to remain on her guard—

A flight of stairs cut into the hill led downward. They crunched underfoot, and she realized as she descended that she walked on thousands of fish scales—dark and dull, with none of the iridescence they should have had. Below her stretched a vast plain: a palace in the foreground, in the midst of a city arranged on a grid pattern, with narrow houses crammed together, and small silhouettes carrying water pails, fruit, and wooden boxes.

Everything was . . . charged, saturated with that curious energy of the embankment steps: something that wasn't magic, that had no business healing or reviving, but that still soothed her hollowed lungs; that still sought to dig its way into her thoughts. The place set her on edge; or rather, it should have, but again there was that relaxing, soothing atmosphere about it that kept damping down her fear.

At the bottom of the steps, Isabelle was arguing with two guards. As Madeleine walked closer, it became clearer neither of them was human. They had the same dull and dead fish scales on their cheeks, and thin, curved mustaches like catfish, though they shared Philippe's dark complexion. Their eyes, as they turned to take her in, were like nothing she'd seen: pearly white, gleaming in all colors like bubbles of soap.

"And who is this?" the taller of the guards asked. Madeleine had expected him to speak Annamite; but he spoke French, without a trace of an accent. That odd magic that wasn't magic again, translating for her benefit? Or, like Philippe, enough years spent in France or in its colonies to speak fluently?

"She's with me," Isabelle said. "Now will you listen to me?"

The guard said nothing. He was watching her, holding a spear with a curved blade at the top—afraid, Madeleine thought. Afraid of what she could do, in this kingdom that was no longer young, or powerful, or undamaged.

"We don't have a policy of welcoming strangers," the guard said.

"I found the door," Isabelle said.

"A party trick," the second guard said, frowning. "Do you have the gifts?"

"What gifts? I already told you—"

"Fallen magic isn't welcome here," the taller guard said. He hefted his spear; his grip on it was white. "Play your power games above the surface, but don't bring them here. There has been enough destruction, my lady."

"I told you," Isabelle said, "I'm just here to find a friend, and then I'll leave."

"Your friend enjoys the hospitality of the king." The guard smiled at that, a not entirely pleasant expression, as if he'd remembered a joke at their expense.

"So he is here," Madeleine said, aloud.

"Of course," the guard said. "It's hardly a secret."

Isabelle was obviously getting nowhere; not that Madeleine was more gifted in diplomatic matters, but by comparison . . . "Who rules here? The king?"

The two guards looked at each other, and then back at her. The pearls under their chins pulsed, faintly, to the rhythm of Isabelle's light. "The king is . . . indisposed."

"Then his son," Madeleine said. "Or his daughter." She tried to remember the little she knew about Annamite society, but her thoughts slid away from her. Damn this place—she could barely focus here. "A prince? A princess? Take us to them." She bent toward the guard, letting the magic trapped within her roil to the surface. "Or do you want us to bring the devastation of the surface world your way?" It was a lie, of course; judging by the rank darkness of the waters, and the unhealthy look of the guards, the surface had already intruded. The pollution of the Seine had spread to the underwater kingdom.

The guards looked at each other again, and then back at Isabelle—who waited with arms crossed on her chest, the water around her getting warmer with every passing moment. The taller one swallowed, a sound that rang like a gunshot underwater; resonating for far longer than it would have on land. "We'll take you to Princess Ngoc Bich."

The palace turned out to be a maze of courtyards with small buildings. Everything was open and airy, the roofs resting on lacquered pillars, and the gardens filled with water lily pools, and a distant music like drums or gongs, moving to the same slow, stately rhythms as the touch on Madeleine's thoughts. At last, they reached a squatter, larger building; its windows slit faience, drawing elegant characters in a long-forgotten script. They entered it, and found themselves in darkness. Gradually, as they walked forward, Madeleine's eyes became used to the dim light, and she was able to make out the room.

It was huge and cavernous; in a palace made of coral and mother-of-pearl, something that seemed to hearken to a more primitive time, its walls carved of black rock, its floor skittering sand instead of square tiles.

At the center of the room was a throne, raised on steps covered with ceramic tiles: a riot of blue and yellow and other vivid colors, painted in exquisite, alien detail, under a delicate canopy of glass, though there, too, rot clung to the tiles, and unhealthy-looking algae had crept over the painted characters and landscapes. On the throne, a golden statue of a man, seated, dressed in ample robes and looking straight at them. Like the guards, he had a pearl at his throat, and a thin mustache, and a scattering of scales on his cheeks.

"The Dragon King," Isabelle whispered.

There was another, similar dais a bit farther down; still being erected, with workmen carrying in tiles and wooden planks. An artisan was working on a matching throne, carefully laying gilt over the intricate wooden carving. He was doing so under the gaze of a woman, who turned as they came in. "What do we have here?" she asked. She smiled, but it was a thin, joyless thing: a veneer of courtly politeness that ill masked her annoyance.

"They said they wanted to see you, Your Majesty," the taller guard said.

The woman—Ngoc Bich—looked at them, carefully, like a hound or a wolf, wondering how much of a threat they were. "Visitors. It's not often that we have them." She wore white makeup, which didn't cover the places where her skin had flaked off; the bones poking through her flesh were an obscene, polished ivory on a background of vivid red. "Fallen. And"—her gaze rested longer on Madeleine, and she smiled again—"not Fallen, but partaking of their magic. You shouldn't, you know. It's a cancer."

Madeleine certainly wasn't about to be lectured by anyone, least of all a dragon princess from some nebulous, unspecified realm that kept grating on her nerves—never mind that they'd stepped into that realm and were at her mercy. "I'm quite all right, thank you."

"We're not." Ngoc Bich's hand trailed, encompassed the entirety of the place; the pervasive rot, the workers with their mottled skin; the golden man on his golden throne. "You'd do well to remember it was angel magic that did this."

"Precisely." Isabelle's smile had the sharpness of a knife. "We'll be on our way when we have what we want."

"Don't tell me," Ngoc Bich said. "If you came here following your head of House, you'll be sadly disappointed. He left some time ago."

"We're not here—" Isabelle started, but Madeleine cut her off.

"What do you mean?" They'd only had two heads of House, and only one Fallen who had manifested as a man. "Morningstar came here? When?"

"Some years ago," Ngoc Bich said. "It's hard to keep track—time wanders and meanders here, away from the mortal world." She paused, made a show of remembering—clearly she had no need to do so, even to Madeleine's untrained eyes. "Twenty years ago."

Just before he had vanished for good. "I don't understand," Madeleine said. "Why was he here?"

Ngoc Bich smiled, showing the fangs of a predator. "Because like speaks to like. Power to power. He wanted power like a dying man wants life."

"Your power," Isabelle said, flatly.

"Anything that would have helped him," Ngoc Bich said. "There was a ritual he wanted to attempt; something he needed my help for. He wanted to keep his House safe, you see." She smiled, again—a wholly unpleasant expression.

"From what?"

"A threat."

The shadows. The ones Philippe had brought into the House. "Shadows? The shadows that kill. What are they?"

"I don't know." Ngoc Bich shrugged. "He left when I couldn't give him what he wanted. He was going to attempt his spell without my help. I presume it worked—you're still here. The House is still here."

Still here—such a casual assessment, failing to encompass Morningstar's disappearance; the gentle decline of Silverspires; and the quicker, bloodier deaths of the previous days. "What spell?" Madeleine asked.

"A beseeching." Ngoc Bich's voice was emotionless. "An offering of himself as a burned sacrifice, to safeguard his House and forever be delivered from darkness."

None of it made any sense to Madeleine. She was going to ask more, but Isabelle finally lost patience.

"The past is all well and good, but it doesn't concern us," she said to Ngoc Bich. "You know that's not why we're here, or what we want."

"Which is—?"

"Philippe. And you know exactly who I mean. Don't lie."

"I have no idea what you mean." Ngoc Bich turned toward one of the workers, who was dragging a wooden statue of some god with a halberd. "I gave you enough, I feel. Now if you'll excuse me—"

"I won't."

Madeleine drifted away from the conversation. There was something about the first dais that attracted her gaze, and she wasn't quite sure what;

but the angel magic sang in her veins and in her bones, drawing her irremediably to the golden throne and the figure seated on it.

It was a good likeness—idealized in the way all statues were; but staring at the broad, open face creased in its enigmatic smile, she could almost get a sense of who he was—no-nonsense, disinclined to be patient or diplomatic, with the sharpness of a razor. So why the dais, and why the statue? She knew little of Annamite customs, but this looked like a throne room; except were throne rooms meant to be this subdued, this somber? Something was . . . not quite right.

At the back, behind the dais, was what looked like a secretary of wood inlaid with gold tracings, adorned with two large porcelain vases, and a large three-tiered bronze container with elaborate handles, and a crouching lion at the top of its dome, and two incense sticks in a hollow halfway up the structure. Two bowls held bananas and mangoes, and a candle burned on the right side. An altar, though she didn't know to what god: there was a red sign with characters over it, but of course Madeleine couldn't read it.

Madeleine found herself reaching for the fruit, stopped herself just in time. Instead, she nudged her stolen angel magic to life, willing it to pick up what scraps of meaning it could from the table and from the emotions that had to be roiling in the room.

There was . . . hope, and love, and awe—and a sense of loss, of grief so powerful it overwhelmed everything else. The red sign over the table—no, not a table; an ancestral altar—the red sign said THE KING OF DRAGONS, THE EMPEROR OF GREAT VIRTUE, ADMIRABLY FILIAL, LONG-LIVED AND PROSPEROUS, ADMIRER OF THE ARTS, DESTINED TO UNIFY THE WARRING PEOPLE, and the fruit and the candles were offerings, so that the soul of the dead might look kindly upon their descendants. She had a vision, for a split moment, of a younger Ngoc Bich bowing before the altar, lighting a stick of incense; saw the tears streaming down her face. Which meant—

Which meant this wasn't a throne room.

It was a mausoleum.

Which meant—

Her heart in her throat, Madeleine looked at the second dais; and found, among the artisans, one working on a second red sign, carefully filling in the outline of characters with golden paint. THE PRINCE OF DRAGONS, PHAM VAN MINH KHIET PHILIPPE, ADMIRABLY FILIAL, BLESSED WITH HEALTH AND CONTENTMENT, WHO WAS BORN IN THOI BIEN IN TIMES LONG GONE BY, AND CAME TO US FROM SILVERSPIRES.

Philippe.

There was no time. Isabelle was still embroiled in her bitter argument with Ngoc Bich, futilely trying to get her to admit where Philippe was.

Whereas Madeleine *knew*.

She drew her power to her like a mantle, and ran toward the dais.

SIXTEEN
THE DRAGON KING

PHILIPPE woke up in darkness, and remembered the stories about dragon kingdoms.

There was always a princess in those stories, and an absent king; and a fisherman who found, by mistake, entry into the dominions of dragons; who rescued the princess in her shape as a human or a fish, who performed a service for a beloved general, who threw back a bauble that turned out to be invaluable treasure. The stories were all the same, and they all ended the same way: the fisherman met the princess and was smitten by her unearthly beauty; and married her, ruling by her side as a human consort. In some stories, they came back to land and founded a human dynasty.

This was not one of those stories.

He was lying on something dark, and damp—the smell of rot was more pervasive here, wherever they had brought him; and there was another smell, a sharp, unpleasant one that brought tears to his eyes.

Cave. It smelled like a cave; like the temples of the Five Elements Mountains in Annam, the smell of incense drifting over that of dampness. He tried to rise, but an unbearable pain flared in his wrists and ankles, pulling him back to his bed. It wasn't rope they had bound him with—spikes, nails?

He tried to see the *khi* currents in the room: water, of course, and a hint of wood, but all of it was claimed for. He tried to call some of them to him; to soothe his wounds, to pull the spikes from his limbs; but the currents remained where they were, obstinately pointing leftward, where Ngoc Bich or the dragons were, no doubt. He needed to—he tried to sit up again, but the pain was too much; he didn't have the guts to pull the things from him, not in his weakened state.

Within him, the darkness rose. Philippe could guess at the shape of Morningstar, crouched against one of the far walls, ready to impart his fake wisdom, his platitudes about power and its uses—it struck Philippe, suddenly, that his human self might well be older than Morningstar, that all the Fallen's so-called wisdom might well be nothing more than the fraud of a youngster—a darkly amusing thought, save that it was all so terribly tempting to prolong the vision for a little longer, to feel Morningstar's terrible, seductive presence, that hunger of a moth for a flame, that easy magic that would reduce his bonds to dust, if only he reached for it. . . .

He needed to . . . Ancestors, he wasn't that much of a fool—not a Fallen or one of the magicians, giving in to weaknesses like this—he'd risen to Heaven on abstinence and strength of will, and he could do it again. Just find the place, the perfect place within him where everything was quiet and still; with the pull of water, the memories of blue-misted mountains, the soft rocking of a boat in a river . . .

"It's stronger than you," a voice said, next to him.

What? Philippe almost backed away; and stopped himself in time, remembering what would happen to his body if he did.

There was a man, standing by him—no, not a man, a dragon, with green skin and antlers at his temple, and a beard that fell in braids around the pearl under his chin. He looked for all the world like the images of Khong Tu in the temples, though he wore, not court clothes or scholar's robes, but ceremonial armor. He was, quite unmistakably, dead, with the particular translucency of ghosts.

Philippe had had enough of ghosts, vengeful or not. "Look," he said. "Wherever you came from—"

"I didn't come from anywhere. I was always here. Or nearly always," the man said. He reached out, and touched Philippe's wrists—Philippe couldn't shift himself out of the way in time. A cold, oppressive feeling stretched from the dragon's fingers, until the pain had been numbed away. "You'll forgive me. I'm not what I once was."

"You're—" Philippe looked again at the pearl, at the strength of its radiance; at the headdress with its nine five-clawed dragons. "Why couldn't I see you before?"

The man smiled. "Being there doesn't mean being obvious. There's . . . value in remaining hidden."

"You're the Dragon King."

"The Emperor of Great Virtue," the king said, forlornly. "There's an awfully long posthumous name, but I'll spare you that. Why don't you use Rong Nghiem Chung Thuy?"

No. One did not name the dead; especially not dead emperors. "Chung Thoai," Philippe said, adroitly replacing syllables—it had been such a long time since he had to do this, his brain felt full of cotton. "If you wish."

The king smiled. "Chung Thoai, then. And you're Minh Khiet?"

"Does everyone here know my name?" Philippe asked, of no one in particular, and the king didn't answer. There was no need to. "How about what I'm doing here? I'm not—" He stopped then, looking into the darkness. "I'm not dead yet, am I?" The boundaries between life and death were fluid, but surely he'd have known. Surely there would have been servants of the King of Hell coming with a mandate, to take his soul away?

Chung Thoai shook his head. "No, but you're close. It's as I said: it's stronger than you. Whatever it is you have within you."

A dead student's revenge. A ghost's last, angry thoughts; the ones that never dissipated. "I don't want it, or need it," Philippe said, acutely aware of how childish he sounded. But after all he'd been through, maintaining decorum wasn't a priority.

"I know," Chung Thoai said. "That's why you're here. Because my daughter thought I could . . . exorcise it."

In all the tales, the Dragon King laid hands on the sick, on the deformed; brought them back to health, cleansed of the injuries evil spirits had caused. "And—?" Philippe asked.

The king's gaze was grave. "As I said—it is stronger than you. Stronger than even I, I fear."

UNDER the dais. That was where she needed to go—Madeleine resisted the temptation to send everything flying, since there would surely be awkward explanations to give afterward. She held at bay, effortlessly, the guards who tried to stop her, though the angel essence within her was faltering, unused to such demands. Her body would pay for it later, but she was used to it; inured almost.

Show me.

There was a passage, under the steps—hidden under three of the colorful tiles. She opened it with a gesture, and ran down—another set of steps, going downward into another vast cave, plunged in darkness.

At first, she thought the man lying on the stone slab was Philippe; but he was older, and too desiccated to be anything but ancient. She hadn't thought she could be creeped out by a corpse, whether Fallen or human; but this body wasn't either. A tightened, pinched face that was almost featureless; a skin of a green like algae; and curved, sharp claws reminiscent of a bird of prey—this was the fluid alienness of Ngoc Bich laid bare; every unfamiliarity heightened until it seemed she was staring at the withered corpse of a monster.

The Dragon King, the Emperor of Great Virtue . . .

God, how she hated this place.

"Madeleine?"

There was a second slab, behind the first: judging by its location, it was under the second dais. Philippe lay on it; or rather, was nailed to it with spikes of coral. His face was ashen, and the shadows around him stretched farther than they should have. Madeleine approached warily, remembering the mark on Emmanuelle's hand. "Give me one good reason why I should free you."

"I'm not sure you should," Philippe said. He said something else, in a language she didn't recognize—Annamite?—it was clearly not addressed to her. She realized he was completely unaware of her presence.

The angel magic died abruptly, leaving her weak and shaking, desperately trying to remain standing. Behind her, running steps: the guards, no doubt, coming to drag her away.

"Wait."

Ngoc Bich walked into her field of vision, followed by Isabelle, who looked ashen, too. "Is this how you treat your guests?" she asked.

Ngoc Bich ignored her, and turned to Philippe. "My apologies," she said. "I thought you needed better healing."

"With the dead?" Philippe's smile was terrible to behold.

"With my father," Ngoc Bich said. Her voice was softer, almost pleading. "You have to see the . . . curse within you is not going away; not without help."

"Oh, I know, believe me. A peach-wood sword, a drum, and a gong for a proper exorcism . . . You don't have any of this, do you?" He smiled again. "It didn't work."

"I saw," Ngoc Bich said, sharply. She reached out, and touched the spikes in his wrists and in his ankles—they crumbled into thin dust, carried away by currents Madeleine couldn't see. "I do what I can with the little I have. Like everything here, we've been much diminished."

"Indeed. I wasn't aware dragon kings could die."

Ngoc Bich's face, for a moment, became contorted with hatred. "He was the Seine," she said, finally. "You know how it goes. The waters filled with oil, with chemicals; with spells and artifacts cast into them like so much chaff."

Philippe pulled himself up with a grimace of pain. "I'm sorry. I . . . spoke without thinking. What . . ." He paused then. "What do you want with me?"

"What we always want, in the stories." Ngoc Bich's voice was sad.

"A husband on the throne; a fair and powerful queen with a wise and enlightened king by her side . . ."

Philippe's laughter was bitter. "Me, a wise king? You have the wrong person. You could have asked. You could have explained."

"That your salvation lay with a ghost, and that the kingdom lay in disarray, with no king and no power? Would you have said yes? Would you have trusted me?" Ngoc Bich held his gaze, until he looked away.

Isabelle found Madeleine, steadied her. "How did you find this place? I could feel the power flowing through you—what did you do?"

"What you brought me along for, no?" Madeleine said, more sharply than she intended.

Isabelle's gaze rested on her—how much could she see, or guess at? "I can see that," she said. "We need to talk."

"There is nothing to say."

"Philippe tried that one," Isabelle said, with a mirthless smile. "It didn't work very well."

What—what was her game? What did she want out of life? Madeleine made an effort to stand up straighter, and gave up as a bout of coughing racked her entire body. Everything spun and shone, slightly, with that yellow tinge that came before faints. Should have brought sugar; though sugar wasn't going to patch up the Gruyère holes in her body. "Just stop asking questions. Please. I know you need to understand everything—"

Isabelle shook her head. "You misunderstand me. I'm not interested in knowledge. I merely need . . . leverage." Again, that soft, sly smile that was too old to belong to someone like her. "If you find the right place, you can move the world."

"And what would you do with the world?"

"Defend myself against it." Isabelle's voice was low, intense. "I lost two fingers. I will not lose anything else, not if I can help it. And you—you need to think on what you're doing."

"I am doing nothing but what is expected of me."

"Were you?" Isabelle raised an eyebrow. "What was in that locket?"

A power you will never wield. "The most powerful thing in my laboratory. You said you wanted my help. Are you going to deny that it was useful?"

Isabelle grimaced. "It was, but—"

Madeleine made her voice as firm as she could. Selene would have seen through it in a heartbeat, but Isabelle wasn't Selene. "We have more than enough worries without our being at each other's throat."

"Mmm," Isabelle said. "A truce, then, for a while. It makes sense." But she didn't sound wholly convinced. It wasn't the end of it, not by far; but Madeleine was too weary to do more.

PHILIPPE could see Chung Thoai: the Dragon King was standing beside his body, looking faintly apologetic. "You can't see him, can you?" he said.

Ngoc Bich stared at the darkness by his side, in the opposite direction to Chung Thoai. "No." Her eyes shone with tears. "I don't speak to ghosts. The only thing I have is the *khi* currents. I don't think he intended me to rule."

"I did," Chung Thoai said, but she couldn't hear him.

"I'm sorry," Philippe said, again; rubbing at his wrists, at the marks of the coral spikes. "But I would have appreciated a warning, all the same." It wasn't every day one found oneself nailed to a stone slab in a tomb, after all: some of his compatriots would have thought it bad luck, but he'd long since left all such considerations behind him.

Ngoc Bich shrugged. "We did what was necessary. What will you do now, Philippe Minh Khiet?"

"I don't know," he said.

"They have come to take you home," Ngoc Bich said. "The Fallen in particular was most insistent."

"I'm not surprised," Philippe said, wryly. Isabelle looked to be haranguing Madeleine, though he wasn't clear why—knowing her, he suspected the whole trip was her idea. Madeleine was too . . . staid for such a thing.

"What will you do?" Ngoc Bich asked again, and he had no answer. Whenever he thought of Silverspires, he thought of the darkness, of vengeful eyes behind horn-rimmed glasses, of bright and cruel and knowing smiles; of a pain that seemed to spread through his entire being, laying him flat on the ground and holding him there, as surely as coral spikes.

He swung himself away from the slab, and found Isabelle. Her gaze met his without flinching.

"I can't come back," he said.

Isabelle shook her head. "You must. You owe Silverspires."

"For a cage?" Philippe said. He raised his hands—almost shocked to find that they worked, that his once broken fingers flexed, that his shattered bones held everything together; and, in answer, Isabelle raised hers, showing him the gap where two of her fingers were missing—and nausea rose in his throat, sharp and biting.

Some things, after all, could never be healed. "No," he said. "This isn't that debt."

Isabelle's smile was bright, terrible; the same as Morningstar's, in the visions. She had known, or suspected. She had seen Samariel; had warned Philippe—though presumably she hadn't had time to see Selene, or it would have been quite a different story. "You wounded Emmanuelle," she said.

"I—what?" He vaguely remembered running out of the room, shoving the archivist out of his way; losing himself in the darkness, crawling his way through a haze of pain. "You're lying."

"She's not," Madeleine said. The light of the tomb played on her face: she looked terrible, gaunt and drained of all vitality, ten or twenty years older than the woman he remembered. "You left a mark on her. A circle with a dot in the center."

"I don't see what you're talking about."

"The dead," Madeleine said. "The other ones. They all had the same mark." She looked at him, angrily; and he still had no idea what she meant.

He shook his head. "Madeleine—"

"Never mind," Isabelle said. "Will you come back to Silverspires, please? For Emmanuelle's sake."

"By now they've all left," Madeleine said. "The other Houses. Selene was seeing them all off. Asmodeus won't be there anymore."

"I— Look, even if I wanted to, I can't do anything for Emmanuelle. I can't—" He didn't understand what he had in him; or if he was really the only carrier. There was something else loose in Silverspires, something that went beyond his visions and memories.

"He shouldn't go," Ngoc Bich said, gravely. Behind her, the ghost of her father had spread his hands, mouthing again what he'd said to Philippe, that it was stronger than him.

Philippe bristled. "So the alternative is? Staying here?"

Ngoc Bich didn't blink. "I had hoped you would," she said. There were no tears in her eyes; she held herself with the pride of a queen. "But if you don't want to—then I would leave, if I were you. Go home, or elsewhere; but don't take what you have back into Silverspires. You might live, then."

"Should I take it back to Annam, then?" Philippe said. He'd dreamed, once, of returning home—the dream Isabelle had instilled back into him—but, alone with Chung Thoai under the mausoleum, he had tasted the darkness at the heart of the curse; and had seen that it would not go away. "Is that your idea, Ngoc Bich?" To think of Morningstar striding across the land of his birth, of his casual arrogance while watching the women bowed under shoulder yokes, the peasants in their rice paddies, the colorless imitations of Chinese porcelain sold to the ruined imperial court . . . "No. It's not a possibility."

Ngoc Bich shrugged. "As you wish. But you have been warned, Philippe Minh Khiet. The thing within you—it will be satisfied with nothing less than blood, the blood of Silverspires."

"I don't care about Silverspires," he said, and both Isabelle and Madeleine winced. "It's not my home. It's a place where I was imprisoned and tortured and betrayed and left for dead. Tell me, where in there do you see a cause for gratitude?" It could go hang, for all he cared; could burn itself to ashes, or go to war with other Houses and be destroyed, like Draken. He owed it nothing.

Ngoc Bich's eyes were unreadable; the shade of mother-of-pearl, illuminated only by the lanterns on either side of the door to the tomb. "Then don't go back to Silverspires. As I said, that would be wise. The thing within you wants blood. It might take yours."

"You're just going to let Emmanuelle die." Madeleine's voice was low, angry; for a moment, as she moved toward him, something shifted, and she was larger than life, lit by a radiance that burned everything it touched. "She's in a hospital bed, burning up. Like Samariel."

"Look, I said it already. Even if I saw her, I'm not sure what I could do! I didn't do—"

"You know something," Madeleine said. "Don't try to shift the blame. You know some, or all, of what's going on, don't you?" It was like watching a kitten grow fangs and muscles and venom; becoming the tiger that could eat you, if it so chose. It was frightening, and shocking.

"If he goes back," Ngoc Bich said to Isabelle—who hadn't said a further word, but simply stood, biting her lip as if trying to come to a decision—"if he goes back, he will bring it back into the House."

"It's already inside the House," Isabelle said, softly. "It leaped from the mirror into the cathedral, and from the cathedral into everywhere, didn't it?" She reached inside her jacket and held out something to Ngoc Bich. "You're wise and old, aren't you? Tell me what this is. Tell me how to unlock its secrets."

Ngoc Bich shrugged, and took it—as Philippe had suspected, it was the mirror they'd found in Notre-Dame, its malice undiminished by the atmosphere of the dragon kingdom. She turned it over, slowly, her gaze fixed on Isabelle; as if she wasn't quite sure what to make of her. Philippe wasn't sure, either. Her face had that terrible, ageless smile that seemed to be the province of Fallen. She scared him, even more than Madeleine did.

At length Ngoc Bich smiled. "A sealed artifact," she said. "I could show you how to open it"—her hands danced, for a bare moment, on its rim, in the beginning of a pattern that seemed to have Isabelle hypnotized—"but it would avail you nothing. This was the source of your curse, but as you say, it has moved elsewhere. It is now within the

House, and its darkness is in its corridors, climbing up toward the light. Opening this won't gain you anything, except perhaps the release of the last few scraps of darkness contained within."

"You're lying," Isabelle said.

Ngoc Bich held out the mirror to her. "Why should I lie? The problems of the surface aren't mine." A quick showing of teeth, pointed and sharp like those of crocodiles. "I defend my territory, but I have no interest in what Houses do, above. No one can touch the river. You know that."

"I don't." Isabelle's face was pale, resolute; as if she were really ready to take on the entire dragon kingdom by herself. Philippe found he was holding his breath, waiting for an explosion that never came. Instead, she merely took the mirror back, wrapped it in its grubby white cloth. "But I believe you."

"How good of you." Ngoc Bich turned back to Philippe. Behind her, Chung Thoai watched him, his hollow gaze sorrowful—but of course the dead couldn't weep. "You heard my words. You know I'm right, Philippe Minh Khiet."

Isabelle's attention had turned back to him; her smile was wide, mocking, like the goad of a cattle driver. "Do you want to run away, Philippe?"

He ought to—he really did. He wasn't one of them, to think that some quaint version of honor demanded he face the enemy. He'd always been sane about this: if outnumbered and outgunned, one should run to ground, not rely on versions of honor thought of by knights in dust-covered books.

Emmanuelle—Emmanuelle had been kind to him, in a House where not everyone was kind, or gentle—but, in the end, she still belonged to the House, to Morningstar. He'd be quite happy for the vengeful ghost to have its way, for the House to split open like a bloated corpse.

Except . . . except the darkness was within him, too, as Chung Thoai had said; the link to the curse and the ghost he couldn't run or hide from, that he would always carry within him. He would, in the end, have to face it; or be entirely consumed by it, ground down into dust until no trace or memory of him remained within the city.

And there was Isabelle. Who stood, watching him; he could feel her through the link, her worry, her anger; her anxiety about the House, about him. He owed her—for finding him when he was being tortured, for coming all the way into the dragon kingdom, determined to bodily drag him back—and all he had given her so far was pain; and trouble—and two missing fingers.

Blasted conscience. It never worked the way it was supposed to.

"All right," Philippe said. "I'll come back with you. But only for a short time, mind you."

If he said it firmly enough, he might even believe in it himself—though Chung Thoai's ghost, looking wistfully at him and making a gesture of blessing reserved for those in dire predicaments, would have reminded him of how insane it all was, to plan to go back to Silverspires.

IN the end, as she had known, Selene found herself drawn back to the infirmary; just as she had been drawn to it, years ago, when Emmanuelle was fighting her addiction to essence.

It was a foolish idea, with Asmodeus poking and prodding, looking for God knew what in the House—a weakness, per the terms of his agreement with Claire? It didn't take that much intelligence to guess what Selene's weakness would be.

A nurse—Bellay, the slender Fallen with the intricate tattoos—showed her into the room—which was awash with a surprising number of flowers.

To her surprise, Emmanuelle was up, reading a book; with deep, bruised circles under her eyes, and lips the pallor of watered-down paint. She didn't look as though she'd slept at all; though Selene knew from Aragon that all she did was sleep, except for rare waking moments. On Emmanuelle's hand, the circle was still there: fainter now, ringed with other faint circles. Aragon had frowned when he saw this, had reluctantly admitted it might be a good sign; that Emmanuelle's sleep was that of recovery, not the first step on the long drawn-out road to death.

A good sign.

Selene didn't have Emmanuelle's faith, and hadn't prayed for many, many years; but if she'd thought it could help Emmanuelle, she would have abased herself in Father Javier's chapel, or in the privacy of her room. Except, of course, that Fallen had never been the favored of God, would never be.

Javier would berate her if she confessed to this; though she suspected he'd lost his own faith long ago. Most of them had; or, like Madeleine, had lost the conviction that God was loving and kind. Only Oris and Emmanuelle still prayed with anything like conviction. Surely God would save the worthy, those who kept the faith when all around them faltered and fell by the wayside?

And then she remembered—like a shard of ice driven deep into her heart—that Oris was dead.

"Oh. Selene," Emmanuelle said. She took one last look at her reading and closed the book. She was good; the tremor in her fingers was almost invisible. "How are you?"

Selene breathed in through the vise on her lungs. "I should be asking you that. Bellay said you didn't lack for visitors."

"If visitors' good wishes could heal, I'd already be up and about," Emmanuelle said, with a tight smile. She pointed to a series of smudged drawings by the side of the bed. "But it was good to see the children— even though Caroline is still as impertinent as ever." She chuckled. "One day, the little scamp is going to give me lessons on how to run my own library. I'll look forward to it."

Selene knew deflection when she heard it. "Emmanuelle—"

Emmanuelle shrugged. "Don't worry about me. Aragon is hopeful. How is the House?"

Selene couldn't help it. "Aragon hopeful? Now, that would be quite a sight. Was he smiling?"

Emmanuelle's lips quirked up. "He might have been. You're right, it's quite a sight. I should have made sure I had proof."

"Think of it for next time." Selene took Emmanuelle's hand, ignoring the trembling heat of fever that seemed to spread to her own hand. "The House is fine. Don't concern yourself with that."

"Liar." Emmanuelle's voice was light, as if they were merely having a conversation over tea and biscuits. "Terrible one, too. Tell me what's happening out there."

Selene spread her hands. Where to start? "They've gone. All of them, except Asmodeus. He made a pretty show of grieving, but I think we both know that's not why he's staying here."

"It's a pretty good reason," Emmanuelle said. "And the . . . shadows?" Her voice caught a bit on those words. Selene shivered, remembering darkness, spreading behind them like pools of ink, the hint of claws and fangs; the overwhelming, reflexive fear that men must have felt, seeing eyes shining like beacons beyond their primitive campfires.

"We've searched the House." Selene felt weary; out of control, for the first time in decades. Where was Morningstar when you needed him? "I haven't found anything." Or felt anything. "But they're still here."

Emmanuelle nodded. "They don't die so easily." She closed the book she'd been holding, carefully, as if it might break; though she was the one who looked as though she might break, if so much as breathed upon. She said, finally, "I've been thinking. About Philippe."

"You—" Selene started to say Emmanuelle should rest, and then stopped.

"I can still think," Emmanuelle said, with an amused smile. "I felt . . . hatred, when he touched me. A scream like primal pain. The shadows hate the House."

"You felt his hatred," Selene said. "He has no love for us."

"No. Philippe hated Houses, but as part of a system. And Silverspires a little more, because we imprisoned him." Emmanuelle's voice was clinical, detached. "I don't think it's a House doing this, Selene. Or if it is, it's someone with a grudge against us. A personal one."

"That doesn't really narrow the field, does it?" Selene asked. "We have many enemies." The House did what it had to do, and not always compassionately, or fairly. "I'm sure Claire and Asmodeus are part of it. They're too well informed."

"But they don't hate Silverspires."

She was right: they only saw the House as an obstacle to be removed; heedless of the chaos that would happen in Paris's fragile magical balance, if Silverspires should fall. "They could be in league with the summoner."

"I think they are," Emmanuelle said. "I—" She thought for a while. "Philippe came to me, back when he was still new to the House. He wanted to know about the history of the House. I think he was looking for something."

"A weakness," Selene said. She didn't blame him. No, that wasn't quite true. She understood him, because in his position she'd have done the same; but he was the reason they were in this mess, and if he hadn't been dead she might well have strangled him herself.

"I—I'm not sure," Emmanuelle said. "He sounded worried."

"Do you remember what you gave him?"

"Yes, of course. I can look at the books, but it won't tell me what drew his attention. He knew some of what was going on."

"And he's no longer in a position to tell us." *Good riddance.*

"He was the catalyst," Emmanuelle said, at last. "But no longer. The game has changed, Selene. We must find out who really is behind that spell." She lay back against her pillows, breathing heavily.

"You'll exhaust yourself. Get back to sleep; and you can ask Aragon for those books tomorrow, if you want."

"Don't baby me, Selene. You've got much better things to do."

Entirely too many, Selene thought, but didn't say it: there was no point in worrying Emmanuelle. She'd save all the worries for herself, and chew on them until she choked.

SEVENTEEN
GRAVE MATTERS

THEY came up in the mortal world near the Pont de l'Archevêché, where Philippe had first seen Ngoc Bich. It was night again, with the low, diffuse glow of pollution over the city, the glistening of oil on the waves that lapped at their feet.

"We weren't gone that long," Madeleine said, shocked.

Isabelle's voice was distant. "Time passes differently there."

It wasn't only time. Philippe could feel the tug of the House again now, could feel the roiling anger within him. Morningstar stood on top of the flight of stairs, limned in his terrible light—hefting, in one hand, the large sword that he always carried. Was he defending the House against them? Of course not, he was simply a vision, a memory.

He hadn't told Madeleine or Isabelle about the vision he'd had while Asmodeus had tortured him; not because it seemed like a fancy of his sick mind, but because he had no intention of helping Silverspires beyond healing Emmanuelle and ridding himself of the curse.

"We'll go around the cathedral," Madeleine said, biting her lips. "There's a maze of disused corridors there."

A maze where he'd lost himself; where he'd found himself. The world seemed raw to his senses, the light too harsh, the sounds jangling in his ears; even the touch of Isabelle's hand on his shoulder scraped like a blade across his flesh. He longed for the dark and quiet of the dragon kingdom already, even knowing that it was but a mirage.

You could have stayed, Ngoc Bich's voice whispered in his ear, and he didn't know what answer to give her.

They crossed the small garden behind Notre-Dame: corrugated benches, skeletal trees in the midst of scorched earth; and walked toward one of the side doors of the House, a postern that gave access to the East Wing.

You could have stayed. Would it have been so bad, to be her consort? She was smart and fierce and beautiful, and doing honor to her devastated kingdom; but then again, what wasn't devastated, in this day, in this place? He would have ruled with her, renewed and rejuvenated daily by the *khi* currents. He would have found a manner of peace; and, with Annam unattainable, it was probably the closest thing to coming home.

He didn't deserve it. He was nothing but a disgraced Immortal, his offense so old and so papered over, it barely stung.

The Court of the Jade Emperor was beyond him; and, as Ngoc Bich had known, there would be no return to Annam; not even if the way magically opened, not with this curse within him. Aragon was right, he ought to make a home here in Paris, in this city of murderers who sucked the resources of Annam like so much lifeblood. He ought to . . .

And then the shadows shifted across the burned-out trunks of the trees, like blacker dapples on birches—vanishing every time he focused on them, but quite unmistakably flowing toward them.

SELENE felt it long before she saw it, of course. The shadows had been one thing—scurrying at the back of her mind, a blot on the power of the House that slowly sank to an annoying whisper. This . . . this was something else: a feeling that something was not quite right, that something was gnawing away at the foundations of the House's power.

Javier had come back with one of the search parties: they all clustered in her office, looking glum—but at least they were alive and un-harmed. One of the previous parties hadn't been so lucky: their brush with the shadows had sent a man to the hospital with a flesh wound eerily similar to Emmanuelle's. Aragon didn't expect him to survive the night. One more confirmation, then, that Philippe had been the cata-lyst; but that the shadows had a life beyond him and were, in fact, spreading faster now that he was dead, as if he had been the only thing holding them in check—his mortality the only curb to their frenzy.

She'd have been in a better position to appreciate the irony if her House hadn't been coming apart around her.

"Tell me again," she said to Javier, fighting back the urge to snap at him.

"It's not what you think," Javier said.

"I have a very good imagination." The House, its power and repu-tation diminished after the Samariel "incident," could hardly afford another emergency. And she—she needed to be the rock they all stood on, not a Fallen shattered by the sickness of her lover. It would be fine, if she focused; if she forgot the awful pallor of Emmanuelle's face, the dark circles under her eyes like bruises, everything Aragon wasn't saying in his silences. *We're all mortal,* Morningstar would have said, and he would have smiled. Secretly, he wouldn't have believed anything like this would ever apply to his Fallen. What a fool he had been, some-times. "Now tell me again why I can't go to Asmodeus's rooms and ask him what is going on?"

Javier's face was pale. "Because you need to see this first."

Selene dismissed the rest of the search party with her apologies—and summoned two of her bodyguards, Solenne and Mythris; as well as the butler, Astyanax. Then she followed Javier.

It had once been a bedroom on the first floor of the East Wing. Now its floor was shot through with . . . "Plants?" Selene asked. What-ever she'd expected, it wasn't that.

They were slender green shoots with long, elegant leaves: she could imagine using one of them as a boutonnière, its vibrant green in stark contrast to the dark gray of the suit, a welcome note of freshness. They didn't sound harmful, exactly, but they were *plants*. Growing on dusty parquet floors.

"That's . . . not natural," she said.

"No. They're only in this room, though," Javier said.

So far. "I assume you've tried pulling them out."

Javier gestured toward the nearest shoot, which grew inches from the curved legs of a low marble table. "Be my guest."

Selene reached out, felt the tingle of magic on her hands. Apart from that, it looked like a usual plant; though not something that would ever be found in French gardens. It was a jungle thing, blown in from Guyane or Indochina or Dahomey; longing for warm, humid weather in which to grow. That it could take root here, under the perpetual pall of pollution from the war . . .

She tried to pull it out; and her fingers slid through it, as though it hadn't been there. And yet . . . and yet she could feel the silky touch of its leaves on her hands; could feel the sap pulsing through the stem, the slow ponderous heartbeat of the plant . . . She reached again, this time drawing to her the power of the House, whispering the words of a spell to start a fire. Again, her hand did not connect with the plant; and the fire died without fuel to consume. It was . . . it was as though the thing didn't exist; or more accurately, wasn't properly part of the House.

But it was part of the darkness. It was what she had sensed, lurking around the wards; circling, like vultures waiting for a dying man to breathe his last—for any weakness in the structure of the House.

And now it was in—taking root in the structure of the House itself.

That was more frightening than anything else. The wards, laid by Morningstar when he'd founded the House, should have held. It was the wards, in fact, that made the House; their slow, painstaking accretion transforming unremarkable buildings into a shelter and a source of magic, a fortress that protected them all against attacks. Morningstar's absence would not have changed anything—they would have been flimsy things indeed, if they could not survive their creator's leave-taking. Morningstar was no fool: he had known that most Houses survived far longer than their founders.

But if the wards were still there, what, then, was this?

She had no idea what was going on, but she didn't like any of it. "Fine," she said to Javier. "You're right. We're not going to Asmodeus's room."

Javier nodded. "The foundations," he said.

There was no locus of the House, no single point of vulnerability an attacker could have used to disable the wards. Other Houses were rumored to have one: House Draken had, if the testimony of survivors could be believed; House Hawthorn, though Madeleine had been tight-lipped about it. Selene wasn't sure if it was ignorance, or a reluctance to sell a past she would not talk about.

Madeleine. She remembered angel essence on her fingers; Emmanuelle's pale, skeletal face; then, as now, the nights sitting by her bedside, praying that she would recover, that the preternatural thinness wouldn't turn out to be the beginning of a long, slow slide toward death. . . .

No. That was a weakness she couldn't afford. She needed to be as tough and as uncaring as Morningstar, focused only on the good of the House.

Morningstar had been old, and clever: the wards he had made could not be easily dispelled—Selene would not even have known where to start, if it had been her stated mission. The wards were carved into the foundations; baked in the bricks of its chimneys; ground to dust, and made into the mortar of the walls. There were places, though, where the fabric that hid them was thin and translucent; where, stretching out a hand, one could almost feel the energy surging under one's fingers.

Selene headed for one of these: a patch of wall at the back of one of the wine cellars. She grabbed another three guards on her way with a wave of her fingers; just to make sure there was an escort in case something turned sour.

The cellar was at the end of a long corridor, beyond more disused rooms: all empty, the dust blown under their feet as they walked, with that sense of entering the mausoleum of a king. Empty and dead; lost since the heady days of the House's glory, though . . .

Something was off. Something . . . not as it should have been, a feeling she couldn't quite name. Slowly, carefully, she moved to one of the doors in the long corridor—it was ajar, and she only had to push to open it.

"Selene?"

Nothing but a reception room: an upholstered sofa, its flower motif tarnished by layers of dust, a handful of elegant chairs with curved legs, a Persian carpet stretching away toward a grand piano.

"Selene?"

"It's nothing." She looked again at the room, trying to see what had bothered her. Just dust, and the smell of beeswax; and a faint, familiar smell of flowers.

Flowers. Bergamot. "Asmodeus was here."

Javier said nothing, though his face made it all too clear he thought she was imagining things.

He didn't know Asmodeus. "You do have people keeping an eye on him, don't you?"

Javier looked affronted. "I do," he said. "He hasn't left his room."

Or had already left it; and returned, with no one the wiser.

Selene suppressed a sigh. One thing at a time. She had to worry about Asmodeus; she couldn't afford not to; but, first, she had to know what was going on. "Let's go."

The butler, Astyanax, opened the door of the cellar for her, the creak of the key in the lock resonating like the groan of tortured souls. "Here you go, my lady."

The cellar was bone-dry, and relatively clean—the wine for the conclave's banquet had come from here, after all—but still, it exuded the same pall of neglect as the rest of the House. Why was she so sensitive to it, all of a sudden? It wasn't as though anything had changed; but, perhaps the setback they had suffered had finally exposed the truth—as if, with Silverspires' reputation in shambles, she had suddenly discovered that she couldn't lie to herself anymore: the House *was* in decline, and it would never, ever claw its way back to its former glory; not even if Morningstar himself were to come back from whatever obscurity he had vanished into.

If he wasn't already dead, or worse, imprisoned somewhere. But no, if he had been imprisoned somewhere, whoever had him would have used it against the House by now. No, it was either dead or gone to some other project of his own. She'd have liked to think he wasn't capable of such casual betrayals, but she knew him all too well.

"There."

Between two of the wine bottle racks, there was a slightly clearer patch of wall: a place where the plaster had peeled off, revealing the stone of the cellar walls; nothing much, either at first or second sight, or even with magic to boost one's darkness-encrusted eyes.

Selene reached out, drawing for a suspended moment the scraps of magic the House could spare, from Madeleine's deserted laboratory to the wards of the school; from the hospital wing where Emmanuelle fitfully slept, to the ruins of the cathedral and the shattered throne; from the dusty corridors and disused ballrooms to this place, here, now, where she and Javier and her escort stood, breathless and skeptical and praying that it would work, that it would still work. . . .

The chipped stone of the wall gradually went blank, as if a hand had reached out, melted it to liquid, and smoothed out every single imperfection from it. Light spread from its center, slowly, gradually: a soft, sloshing radiance like that of a newborn Fallen, until every wine bottle seemed to hold captured starlight; and a slow, comforting heartbeat traveled up Selene's hands; the reassurance she'd craved for, with no hint of faltering or of weaknesses.

The wards still held, then. The House still held.

Javier must have seen her face. "Selene—"

"It's going to be fine," she said, slowly exhaling. She withdrew her hands from the wall; but the light and the heartbeat persisted for a while yet, balm to her soul. She might have failed everything else, but not that. Never that. They still stood strong. "The wards are intact."

"Thank God," Javier said. Such fervor in his voice; had he found his faith again, then? "We're still safe."

Selene thought of the sour smell of bergamot in a disused room, and of the ghost plants that she couldn't touch, or tear out. "Yes," she said, "we're still safe."

And tried to ignore the small, fearful voice in her mind: the one that knew all about lies, and the things they denied until it was too late, and all the masks and the faces beneath them had crumbled into dust.

NO one spoke as they walked back to the House. Madeleine kept an eye out for anyone; though Asmodeus would have left with everyone by then, surely? She hoped so; because if he found them, he would take his revenge; and it was quite unlikely he'd bother with minimizing loss of life, especially since it looked as though they were all in it with Philippe.

Which they might well be. She wasn't sure if she believed him; if he was merely, as he said, a victim of something he'd accidentally released into the House; or if it was part of a longer game he was playing with all of them. But if he could help Emmanuelle; if he could shed some light on what was happening . . .

"You heard what Ngoc Bich said," she said to Isabelle, as they walked toward the postern. "Morningstar wanted a powerful spell to protect the House against something."

"It was twenty years ago. I can't imagine—"

"It was a threat large enough that Morningstar had to look for help," Madeleine said. "It could be unrelated to the shadows, but it would be one hell of a coincidence."

And he'd disappeared shortly after coming back from the dragon kingdom. So either he was imprisoned somewhere; or he was dead—and, either way, it had to be linked to the spell. If they could find him—if they could get his help . . .

What was it Ngoc Bich had said? A beseeching. An offering of himself as a burned sacrifice . . .

A cold wind rose across the ruined gardens, bringing with it a sharp, familiar tang. It took Madeleine an agonizingly long moment to realize it was the animal smell of fresh blood. The clouds over them had darkened, as if a storm were coming; the sun still shone, but its light was weak and sickly: that of a winter's day, with no power to warm or comfort.

"Madeleine." Philippe's voice was low, urgent.

"I can see."

"No, you can't. They're here." The fear in his voice was bad; what could he be scared of, when he'd seemed to shrug off whatever Asmodeus had done to him?

"We have to find shelter."

"There's no shelter that will hold against them," Philippe said.

They came out of the ground; great splashes of shadow that seemed to move just below the charred earth—circling them, like wolves—large shapes flowing across the walls of the cathedral, extending huge leathery wings.

Was this what Oris had seen, before he died?

A burned sacrifice. Forever delivered from darkness.

Burned offerings.

A prayer.

He was offering a prayer to God—and where else would you pray to God, but in a church?

"The cathedral," Madeleine said.

Morningstar wasn't in the cathedral—not in the razed church that had been searched, again and again and with growing despair, in the past twenty years. But . . .

"The cathedral didn't help Oris." Philippe's voice was bleak.

"No, that's where they came from." Isabelle rolled up the sleeves of her shirt, staring speculatively at the faint light emanating from her hands.

If they could find Morningstar, or the refuge he'd hoped for, or the spell he'd cast—something, anything . . .

There was a sound around them, like a hiss of snakes. Madeleine kept a wary eye on the ground, where the shadows were flowing like ink stains; curling and curving in a slow dance, forming circles with a dot in the center like the one in Emmanuelle's palm. It was . . . almost beautiful, if one didn't remember Oris; didn't remember Samariel; didn't remember the five corpses in the morgue. Had it hurt, when magic overflowed every cell of a mortal's body? Or was it like angel essence, a slow, heady feeling of rising power, until all life had burned away?

"We have to get to the cathedral," Madeleine said. "Morningstar . . ." She couldn't voice the thought. He'd been gone for twenty years; what made her think she could find him, when the entire House had failed?

"Morningstar is gone. He won't help you," Philippe said, softly.

Isabelle looked at Madeleine for a while; then she shook her head. "No, but it's no worse shelter than elsewhere," she said. She was running already, moving toward the ruined arches of Notre-Dame.

Madeleine barely heard them. There was something . . . hypnotic about the circles, some half-remembered thing, perhaps an image she'd seen in Emmanuelle's library? She watched them coalesce and vanish, watched the single dot like a thousand unblinking eyes. . . .

"Madeleine!" Philippe's hands grasped her shoulders, and shook her. "Come on!"

They ran. After just two steps, Madeleine's breath seared her lungs, and the desire to stop, to bend over, to cough out phlegm, was an almost unbearable, agonizing weight.

There was a hiss, like a knot of a thousand snakes; shapes that she couldn't quite make out, at the edge of her field of vision; vague images of fangs, of huge wings like a drake's, slowly beating like a dying heart; if she could only turn her head, she would see them clearly; would be able to name what was after them . . . No. She didn't look back, or aside. She dared not. Like angel essence, this was a power that subsisted on the forbidden.

Had . . . to . . . run. Had to take in a searing breath, and another one—to put one foot before the other, time and time again. The courtyard wasn't very large, but it felt as though it contained the entire city now—the postern never growing any nearer.

"This way," Isabelle said, somewhere from the left. "Not the postern!"

Madeleine turned, almost blind. She could feel Philippe, dropping behind to check on her. "I'll—be—fine," she breathed through lungs that seemed to have collapsed; but he didn't hear her. "A few more meters," he said, softly. "Come on, Madeleine."

"Come on, come on, come on." It was a prayer now, each word stabbing the fabric of Heaven. A shadow loomed over them, solid and reassuring this time, the bulk of the ruined cathedral. There had been a side door, somewhere. . . .

No time for that. Isabelle had plunged into the ruins; they followed, weaving their way between two walls supporting the shards of stained-glass windows.

They stood, panting, just under the dais with the throne, the ruined altar only a hand span away. How much protection was it, really? Did God still look at unrepentant Fallen, at desecrated places? Except, of course, that the place had never been deconsecrated; it had simply fallen into ruin with the rest of the House. . . .

The shadows circled, under the benches, deeper pools of darkness; reaching out tendrils to touch the charred wood, spreading wings on the arches. The hiss was stronger; and behind it she could almost hear—words, a litany like an obscene chanted prayer.

Philippe had closed his eyes; his face had gone pale and slack, as if he were asleep; but in his outstretched hand a green light was growing stronger and stronger: faint traceries, like lines of power, came and went through the skin of his palm.

Madeleine took a deep, trembling breath, staring at their surroundings. The glass windows were dark and dull, their colors and brilliance drained away; the remnants of the ribbed vault weighed down on them, like the fingers of a giant hand pressing them down into dust. She forced herself to look away, opening the pendant at her throat. There was nothing in it but scraps of essence; a bare hint of a power that had once been strong. Like the cathedral, she thought, fighting the urge to retch.

If only they knew where Morningstar was—if only they could call on him—

But that was impossible. Why had she even suggested they go there? *Give it up, Madeleine—no time for fancies or flights of the imagination.* When this was done—if they survived, she'd have time to go back into the dragon kingdom—no matter how uncomfortable it was—she'd have time to ask Ngoc Bich what she knew. . . .

The shadows appeared reluctant to reach the dais. They circled it warily, tentatively sending tendrils to touch the steps; withdrawing as if burned. Perhaps they'd be safe.

And perhaps she was the messiah come again.

"They're waiting," Philippe said. He hadn't opened his eyes. The light had now spread to both his hands; he held it against himself, cradling it like a child.

"For what?" Madeleine said; and wasn't so sure she wanted to know. "What are you doing?"

Philippe's face was pale. "Keeping them at bay. Can't . . . do much. The power . . . is weak here."

Isabelle was kneeling, inscribing a ward across the dais, a blinding radiance streaming from her skin; rushing through the now translucent stone, illuminating every crack and every blackened spot from within. "They're shadows," she said. "Every shadow is cast by something."

She'd been right. She didn't want to know; or to inquire how either of them knew. The noise was stronger now; there *were* words, if she paid attention; whispered curses, vicious hatred . . .

"All you hold dear will be shattered; all that you built will fall into dust; all that you gathered will be borne away by the storm. . . ."

"You said he was here," Isabelle said. "Where?"

"I don't know!" Madeleine said. He'd gone there, yes, twenty years ago; but the church was a ruin now, with barely any shelter she could see. "I didn't say I had the answers!"

Philippe was standing, pale, disheveled, before the throne, watching the shadows pool together in the aisle between the ruined benches—a rising smell like rotten fruit, a cold, biting wind that seemed to flay them to the bone. . . . "It's Morningstar's dead apprentice—I don't know who they were, but they died betrayed, and now they're taking their revenge."

"I don't understand," Madeleine said. She breathed in the last scrap of essence; tried to believe in the comforting warmth that spread through her belly and lungs.

"Morningstar betrayed one of his students," Philippe said. "He loved and cherished them, and then gave them away to buy peace with Hawthorn, left them to rot in the cellars of the House. They died . . . angry." He shivered.

No. Morningstar wasn't like that. He wouldn't . . . She thought of the leisurely footsteps, the warmth of hands lifting her; the slow, sure sound of his breath. He'd rescued her when he didn't have to, had welcomed her to the safety of the House. "He wouldn't . . . ," she started, and then stopped. It was pointless. He might well have liked her, might well have shown favor to her—on a whim, a moment's thought on his way to nowhere—but she'd heard enough during her time in Silverspires to know he'd been Fallen through and through.

Isabelle's eyes were jewel-hard. "He did it for the House." On the floor beyond the dais, the shape was becoming clearer and clearer: wings, an elongated face, hands that curled like claws . . . She *knew*, instinctively, that they didn't want to be there when it finally became defined. But still . . .

Still, there was something about that shape; about the leathery wings, the hiss of snakes, the perfect circle . . .

"Of course. Isn't that always the excuse? 'For the House.'" Philippe's voice was biting. He leaned against the throne, cradling his light between his hands. "Anyway, that's what they want. The destruction of Silverspires, the deaths of all of us if they can manage it. The unquiet dead." He laughed, bitterly.

The death of Silverspires. Violence begets violence, death begets death: a perfect circle around that single point, that unthinkable break in the skin of the world, pressed tight until blood welled up, dark and red and still quivering with the memory of a heartbeat . . . And Madeleine knew where she had seen the circle, after all; not in the medicine thesis, but in the Greek play Emmanuelle had been so painstakingly restoring. Orestes. Clytemnestra. Kin betraying, murdering kin. And what was a House, after all, but an overlarge family? "Not revenge. Justice."

"That's not different," Isabelle said, forcefully, but Philippe stilled her with a gesture of his hands.

"What do you mean?"

"Erinyes," she whispered. Justice for the murdered, the betrayed, the silenced; the unquiet dead, hungering from beyond the grave. "The Furies. That's what they summoned."

"And that helps? How do you stop them?"

"I don't know!" Madeleine said. "It's not even supposed to be possible!" Sentences from Emmanuelle's books swam in her head, a jumble of information she could hardly keep a leash on. She knew about the Furies; every child in every House learned about them; but as a remnant of the past, of the things that were gone and could no longer be summoned.

How did you stop the Furies?

Spilling blood; granting them revenge . . . all things that seemed beyond them now.

But . . .

Morningstar had come there once, to stop them. To cast a spell, Ngoc Bich had said. A ritual of power, to safeguard the House.

There was nothing here—just broken stained-glass windows, the burned remnants of pews, cracked stone, and cracked columns—nothing that could serve as a shelter or as the basis for a spell.

Nothing *aboveground*.

The Furies were the past; the buried creatures from the history of Paris, so deep they were beyond the reach of Fallen and humans alike—and where else would you defend against them but underground—near the foundations of the House you'd sworn to protect?

Within the earth. Underground.

All churches had crypts, and how come she'd never heard of one in Notre-Dame?

Madeleine closed her eyes, and called up power; scrounged every scrap of it from the rawness of her lungs, from the fragility of her bones—it coalesced within her, drop after drop, her limbs growing cold and heavy with its withdrawal.

The shadow was peeling itself free of the stone floor; unfurling wings large enough to darken the sun.

It was now, or never.

"Morningstar. Show me," she whispered; and cast everything she had—not at the Fury, but at the throne on its dais—thinking of the darkness under the earth, the musty smell of the grave—willing the cathedral to give up its secrets. . . .

A thin line of light snaked from where she stood, zigzagging across the stone like a flame dancing on the edge of a paper. It passed from her outstretched hands into the throne; and then expanded outward, blossoming into a huge incandescent flower. There was a blinding light; an explosion that sent her, retching, toward the floor—as the sound of tumbling stones filled her ears.

"Madeleine?" Isabelle pulled her up—there were other hands, Philippe's, propping her up. "We have to move."

"The . . . Fury . . ." Every word seemed to leave a trail of blood in her mouth.

"Stunned, but not for long," Isabelle said. "We have to go."

Where? She tried to ask; but then there was no need.

Behind the dais—where there had once been graven tombstones covered in rubble, with faded litanies beseeching God to have mercy on sinners—there was now a huge, open space gaping like the maw of a monster; and within that darkness, the glimmer of steps, leading down into the bowels of the House.

IT was damp, and quiet; too quiet, like the day, ages ago, when he had crawled into the ancestral chapel and had stood before the altar, feeling the weight of the dead, of his death, like a yoke on his shoulders. There was little light, but the *khi* current of wood he had called up was enough to walk without stumbling. It wasn't the darkness of the flowing shadows, though; but rather what was left when the sun turned its face away from the world, with not a hint of fangs or claws or snakes, and only a peaceful, almost contemplative silence.

Madeleine was a sagging weight between Philippe and Isabelle, her breath going fainter and fainter as time passed; her weight a hindrance. He feared they'd both let go, and she'd tumble down the stairs to Heaven knew where.

"They haven't followed us," Isabelle said, beside him.

Philippe shook his head. He'd half expected to see ghosts again, but even Morningstar wasn't there. It was eerily unexpected. The *khi* currents there weren't faded as they were in the rest of the House; they gently lapped at one another in a never-ending circle; and there was a vague sense of magic, nothing major. Just . . . silence. Waiting, though he couldn't have told what for. "They won't come. Not here."

Isabelle took in a sharp breath, but did not ask him how he knew. "But they'll be waiting outside, won't they?"

"Of course."

"Why are they trying to kill us?"

"I don't know," Philippe said. He pushed his shoulder upward, to readjust Madeleine's weight. "I'm just the vessel, and probably even less than that."

"But you knew what it was."

"No, Madeleine did."

There was silence, at those words. "Yes. She did."

A further silence. He needed to speak up: it was now or never. "Thank you," he said.

Isabelle turned, surprised. "Why?"

"For coming for me."

"You mistake me." Isabelle's voice was cold, but her hands shook. "I came because Emmanuelle needed you. Because it was the only way."

"You're not a good liar," Philippe said, before he could stop himself. There was no answer from her; not the explosion he had half dreaded. "You could have come on different terms. Selene gave me up, didn't she? She thought I was dead. She thought I was guilty."

"I don't care about what Selene thinks." Isabelle's voice was low and fierce. "I know you wouldn't—"

Wouldn't he? He wasn't sure. If it was the way forward; if it could open the way to Annam . . . He was honest enough to know he would do whatever was necessary. "I don't have your scruples," he said, though he wasn't sure if she still had any.

"No." Isabelle laughed, shortly and without joy. "You don't. You're fortunate."

She was Fallen, and she would pull away from him eventually; she would take her cues from Selene and the House. And yet . . .

She had come back for him. Had argued with Madeleine for him; had casually swept aside all of Selene's suspicions and doubts as if they meant nothing; and had stood for him over standing for the needs of the House. That counted for something, surely? Surely she wouldn't turn into another Morningstar or Asmodeus. . . .

They reached the bottom of the stairs, hearing their steps echo in a space that was far vaster than the little they could see. Philippe tried to call more wood to him, but there was nothing there; just that breathless, expectant pause after someone had spoken; an answer, waiting to be uttered.

"There is something," Isabelle said. She shifted so abruptly that Philippe almost didn't react in time, and Madeleine slid down halfway to the ground. He caught her, the muscles in his arms burning.

"I can't see—" And then he didn't need to strain, because the soft radiance from her skin increased a thousandfold; not slowly like the rising of the sun, but with the speed of a shutter removed from a lamp; from darkness to light in heartbeats. He closed his eyes; it was almost too much.

When he opened them again, he was alone with Madeleine; Isabelle was a few paces ahead, moving toward the center of the room.

Like the church above, it was a room of pillars and arches; smaller and more intimate, the arches pressing down on the ground with the weight of the earth, the smell of damp and rot almost overbearing. It was not large, and most of it was filled with graves: the stones of the floor were meticulously laid out, each with a name and a prayer, and letters whose gold had flaked away with time.

In the center . . .

In the center was a stone bed, not unlike the one he'd been pinned to in the dragon kingdom—except that this one was occupied already, by an ivory skeleton lying in the darkness with its arms crossed over its chest, one hand over the other, as if protecting its rib cage from depredations.

"Isabelle?"

She didn't turn. "Can't you feel it?" she asked.

It trembled in the air: a touch of heat, a butterfly's wings of fire, caressing his cheeks; an irresistible attraction to the locus of power in the center of the room. Bones. Angel bones.

He was halfway to the stone bier before he realized he'd left Madeleine. He turned back. She was lying in shadow, on the folded edge of his cloak—at least he'd remembered to wrap her in something, to keep away the damp—and then it had hold of him again, was reining him in like an unruly horse, pulling him to the center of the room.

Power. Magic, all that he had ever wanted, with the prickly incandescence of a thornbush. It would hurt if he grasped it, but once he did so the world would be at his feet; he would dispel the pall over his heart with a wave of his fingers, would go back to Indochina in less than the time it took to draw breath; would make Asmodeus scream and writhe as he had done with a mere look. . . .

Chung Thoai's sad, regal face swam out of the morass of his thoughts. *It's stronger than you,* he said, shaking his head, his chipped antlers shining in the darkness.

The Dragon King hadn't referred to the bones, of course; but still . . . Still, a part of him stood, trembling; remembered what it had felt like to be hungry and not eat, to be thirsty and not drink; to feel power in every bone and sinew, and not use a drop of it.

This.

This was *weaker* than him.

When he opened his eyes, he stood mere inches from the stone bier, watching the bones. They looked old, though that hardly meant anything: slight and fluted, with the reinforced rib cage clearly visible; fused in odd places, a skeleton that was almost, but not quite, human, with the ridges, tapering off, that had once marked the beginnings of wings. A Fallen; but then, there had never been any doubt of that. There was no visible wound, no indication of how their owner had met his end. Merely magic, burning raw and naked, a fire he dared not touch.

"Isabelle—"

He couldn't see her face, but he could feel her: engrossed, as he was, in the power that emanated from the bones, reaching out to touch them. "Isabelle," he said. "Wait—"

Her hand had already connected. Fire leaped from the bones into her; so that, for a moment, she stood with vast wings billowing behind her, wreathed in smoke that shouldn't have been.

A noise, like a soft patter of rain: the bones were crumbling one after another, falling onto the stone table: mere dust, not angel essence, just the remnants of something that had died long ago.

"Isabelle."

Slowly, she turned, her lips stretching in a familiar, arrogant smile; and in that moment, looking at the power that streamed from her like water, he knew exactly who the bones had belonged to.

Morningstar.

EIGHTEEN
THE SALTY TASTE OF TEARS

FOR a moment Philippe stood frozen, looking at Isabelle. The light was already trembling, on the cusp of extinguishing itself, its persistent whispers fading into silence, its secret traceries absorbed into her skin. He tried to whisper her name, but the light held him fast—the light, and the ageless reflection in her eyes, the same storm of power he'd always seen in Morningstar's gaze, a conflagration that promised him anything he'd ever wanted.

There was something behind her, a shadow that was growing, even as the light sank down and died, even as the dust on the stone bed scattered under the breath of a wind that came from nowhere: something that wasn't wings, or light. Something . . .

And then the light was entirely gone, and there was only Isabelle, bewildered and lost, staring at him as though he could make sense of it all; and behind her, a translucent figure, like a ghost: Morningstar, arms outstretched as though to embrace her, a mocking smile on his face.

A cry echoed under the arched ceiling; mingled anger and triumph, even as the shadows deepened around them.

At last! the voice screamed. He had never heard it, but the burden of its presence was one he'd lived with for days; and he knew exactly who it belonged to: the ghost who harried them from beyond its restless grave. Nameless, featureless, weightless—too many things he had no hold on—as Chung Thoai had said, how could he hope to fight it? Why had he come back here? It was futile.

Darkness pooled on the scored floor: the shadows, as thick as ink or tar; raising tendrils like the heads of ten thousand snakes, hissing and snapping at the air. But they never reached Isabelle: they met a circle on the floor—runes that Philippe hadn't seen in his rush to get to the bones, finely graven into the stone—a protection that seemed to be an impregnable barrier to the shadows. The tendrils thickened and merged, until they became three human-shaped shadows—except that each wore a crown of snakes. Their hiss deepened, became a voice that made the earth tremble.

Kinslayer.

Behind Isabelle, Morningstar stretched and smiled, his serrated wings catching the light. He bowed, an old-fashioned gentleman showing his respect to ladies of good family. *Erinyes.*

The floor was pulling apart: cracks appeared on the stone pavement, outlining the circle's boundary, as if burning-hot fingers were pressing down all around the circumference.

Did you think you could escape? the Furies asked.

Philippe's chest—it, too, felt as though it was going to pull apart, as if the storm of crows roiling within was going to break free in a welter of beaks and blood-soaked claws—but Morningstar merely smiled. *On the contrary, I knew I couldn't. There is always a price to be paid, isn't there? In blood or lives or both . . .*

The circle was bending inward—the shadows at the feet of the Furies pressing it out of shape—the cracks getting wider and wider—until, with an earsplitting sound that sent Philippe stumbling to the floor, the protections broke.

The Furies surged forward; and Morningstar, detaching himself from Isabelle, walked to meet them. He was still smiling—and the smile didn't waver as the snakes wrapped around him; and their voices grew into a scream of mingled rage and satisfaction—and the light in the crypt grew so bright that Philippe had to cover his eyes.

When he opened them again, everything was silent; and Isabelle stood, watching him, by the side of the empty stone bed. She looked unharmed. "Isabelle!"

"I'm fine."

The air had changed: no longer pregnant or oppressive, that sense of breathless waiting gone. "He's gone," Philippe said, aloud.

And so, it seemed, were the Furies.

Isabelle shook her head, dislodging a few strands of errant hair from the tight mass wound at her nape. "What was that?" she asked; but he saw in her eyes that she knew. "He was dead," she said, slowly.

"Not yet. But now, yes." Dead and gone on, to wherever the Fallen went, the last trace of him removed from this Earth.

"And the . . . Furies?"

"I don't know," Philippe said. He couldn't hear anything from the cathedral anymore; even the faint pressure at the back of his mind was gone. "They got what they wanted, I think." Kinslayer. The Fallen who had sent his student to slaughter. Blood or life or both . . .

And now the House, once protected by Morningstar's bones, lay vulnerable.

"He died for the House," Isabelle said.

"Do you—" He shook his head. "Do you have his memories?"

"No. Just images. Glimpses." She smiled wryly. "It's just as well, isn't it? I get the feeling that the full version would burn my eyes clean out of their sockets."

Philippe forced a smile. Ngoc Bich had warned him about coming back to the House—but she had been wrong. He drew a deep, trembling breath—no, too much to expect. The curse was still there. The shadows—the Furies—had only been part of it. There was . . . something else to it, something bigger and larger that still sought the destruction of the House—the anger and rage and betrayal of Morningstar's student.

And still linked to him, obviously.

"But you have it. Morningstar's magic." The link they shared had faded, become fainter and fainter with time; and his plunge into the death shadows of the dragon kingdom had all but killed it. But he could still feel it; the distant heat of molten metal, a sense that it would all become unbearable if he were to come closer.

Isabelle took a deep, trembling breath. "Yes. If I don't hold it in—like a wild horse, like a breath—then I don't know what will happen."

She'd destroy the crypt, and the cathedral, and perhaps a good part of the House around them, but he didn't tell her that. Either she'd worked it out for herself and there was no point; or she hadn't, and he didn't need to add that kind of pressure to the balancing act in her mind.

Philippe walked back to Madeleine, to check on her. Her breath came in slow and deep; her eyes were closed, bruises in the oval of her face. She was shaking. No, it wasn't her; it was the ground under them. Something was moving, deep within the earth: not a quake, something far slower, far more persistent, like some kind of burrowing worm. . . . Morningstar had kept it at bay, whatever it was.

"How is she?"

"She'll live." Philippe grimaced. "Though she'll probably spend some time in the infirmary with Emmanuelle."

Isabelle grinned. "Aragon will be furious."

Philippe couldn't help the smile that came to his lips as he imagined the uptight doctor's face. "Oh yes." He rose, drawing the cloak back over Madeleine. "We should go . . . Wait."

He walked to the circle he'd seen earlier. Now it stood like a crack in pristine porcelain, surrounded by broken pieces of the floor. It had been large, wide enough to encompass the bed; and the letters themselves hadn't been disturbed by the Furies' attack. He walked toward it; looked at the letters—a crabbed, prickly handwriting, though the writer had clearly been in supreme control: not a letter was smudged or out of place, and they all had the same expansive curves. He'd never seen Morningstar's handwriting, but he imagined it would look something like this. A scuffed noise behind him: Isabelle was kneeling on the floor, running her hands on the letters, her eyes shining with a reflection of the light that had engulfed her earlier on. "He carved them," she said, the wonder in her voice that of a child—it had used to make him smile, but now he felt vaguely queasy—was it Morningstar that she was awed by, or was it the lure of power that, in the end, drew all Fallen?

"I know. Can you read them?"

It was an incongruous sight: crouching in a crypt and betting that his senses were right, that the Furies were gone: there were so many smarter things he could have done, starting with running away, far from Silverspires and its ghosts. . . .

Isabelle frowned. "No," she said at last, sounding surprised. "But it's a spell. A very powerful one."

As if anything handled by Morningstar would be pale and faint, running like old dyes. Philippe closed his eyes. There hadn't been any mark on the body; though it was hard to remember anything more but the blinding radiance that had surrounded it. *You,* he thought to the ghost of Morningstar, hovering in the room. *You never make things easy, do you?*

There was no answer, but then, he had never expected one. He bent forward, letting his hands rest on the carvings, the coolness of the stone on his fingers; and the slow thrum coming from below the House, the worm that was gnawing at its insides. Something growing, ever patient, ever persistent: step after step after step, until it was all done, the House swept from the memory of men. . . .

Let it be, he thought, savagely. *It doesn't deserve to be remembered.*

He could feel Morningstar's disapproval, but with Ngoc Bich's healing it was faint, barely perceivable; not the storm that would have caused him to bend the knee in abject submission.

There were *khi* currents, clinging to the inside of the circle: wood, for spring; fire, bright, ever-expanding. Protection, warding; and the desperate love one feels for the doomed; the feeling that would seize a man on seeing a beautiful flower, a perfect sunrise, a piece of sculpted ice, knowing it was all destined to wither and fade.

He died for the House, Isabelle had said. Had sat there, painstakingly carving all those letters by hand: there were no marks, no scuff traces, nothing to indicate that he'd done anything but sit down, and written the words of a perfect circle into the stone. A spell; a powerful one, controlled only by the ruthless force of his will; something that had kept the House safe through the long years after the war.

But even safety, it seemed, came to an end.

He rose, brushing the dust of Morningstar's bones from his trousers. "Come," he said to Isabelle. "There is nothing left here."

They were halfway to the stairs, carrying Madeleine between them, when he heard the footsteps—he didn't turn aside, or move; what would have been the point, in a confined space with no other exit?—and they'd almost got to the exit when the first head came into view—Father Javier, his face carefully blank as he descended, and behind him . . .

Selene.

The Lady of Silverspires wore incongruous clothes, an orderly's white overcoat tossed over embroidered silk pajamas. She must have come straight from the hospital, with no time to put on anything more appropriate. It would have been a comical sight, if not for the pressure of the magic swirling around her, gathered from every room, every corridor, every ruin of the House. She was followed by three guards, one of whom held a light.

"You—" Selene took a deep breath; her gaze pausing, for the briefest of moments, on Madeleine, though she didn't appear to be entirely happy to see her. "You will explain. Now."

Philippe would have spread his hands, in a gesture of peace; but he would have had to let go of Madeleine. "I came back," he said. "To see if I could—"

"Finish what you'd started?" Selene remained where she was. The light from above pooled around her head, like a memory of what she must have looked like in the Heavens; in another lifetime, centuries ago.

"You—" Philippe took a deep breath. "You bound me. You treated me like a curiosity to be dissected and discarded. Do you really think you have any kind of authority over me?"

"The authority of power." Selene's voice was mild, but the pressure in the room had intensified; a wrong word, a wrong gesture, and it would push outward, shattering the pillars and stone bed, burying the crypt out of sight. "I thought you'd be able to recognize that, if nothing else."

Philippe pulled fire from the ground, let it dance on the tip of his nose.

Selene's face didn't move. "Party tricks," she said.

Party tricks that had absorbed her magic, once. *Let her try . . .*

Javier's voice floated back to him, out of the darkness. "This place is old. I had no idea—"

"Javier. This isn't the moment."

"Oh." There was silence for a while; the sound of feet scraping on stone. Then Javier said, "I think you should come and see, all the same. You two can kill each other afterward."

Selene raised an eyebrow. Philippe didn't, but he was as surprised as she. In all the time he'd been in Silverspires, he had never once heard Javier defy her. "What is here?" she asked; it wasn't clear if the question was to Javier or to him.

"A circle," Philippe said, cautiously. "A grave."

Her face was tight, her lips pinched to a sliver of gray. "Whose?"

"Morningstar's," Isabelle said, before Philippe could stop her.

Selene didn't move. Her face didn't, either. It seemed to have frozen, in the exact same configuration as a moment before: the eyes unblinking, staring rigidly at the darkness, the mouth set in its thin line against the pallor of her skin. "Morningstar," she said. Her voice conveyed some emotion, but Philippe couldn't name it.

"His bones were on the stone bed," Philippe said. "They're dust now. The magic is gone."

She should have asked where; if she'd been in anything like her normal state, she would have. But she still stared ahead of her with that same eerie stillness to her face, her lips the only part of her that still seemed to have life. "He's dead," she said.

"He died for the House. He inscribed a circle. . . ." Isabelle's voice was low and fierce.

Selene raised a hand, and a wave of silence spread through the room: magic unfurling, pushing the words back into their throats with a taste like bile. "I don't want to know," she said. "Javier?"

"Yes, my lady?"

"Bring them to the ballroom," she said. "And get Choérine or Gauthier and a few guards to watch over them." Her eyes drifted to Madeleine, who still lay limp between Philippe and Isabelle. "Belay that. Get them to the hospital wing. And make sure Asmodeus doesn't find out about them. Not yet." She didn't have to work very hard to make it sound like a threat; and Philippe didn't have to work much, either, to find the fingers of his hands clenched, and to feel a convulsive shiver take hold of his entire body—remembering Asmodeus's face, twisted with hatred; the methodical snapping of his fingers one by one—the nightmare memories of dying that had seized him, that had sent him crawling and weeping into the night. . . .

Asmodeus? *No. No.* "You told me he was gone," Philippe said. "You said—"

Isabelle started to say something, but Selene cut her off.

"I don't know what your game is," she said. "Right now, I don't want to know. We'll talk more *after* I'm done here."

There were too many people, and they could no doubt summon more. Better to obey.

For now, at any rate.

AFTER they were gone, Selene walked to the center of the room. She stared, for a while, at the stone bed, on which the wind lifted the remnants of dust; at the circle inscribed on the ground, with a handwriting she would have known anywhere, inscribed boldly and without apology. There were cracks all around it—on the outside, as if something had smashed itself, time and time again, trying to get beyond it.

A grave, Philippe had said.

And, from Isabelle: Morningstar's.

It couldn't be: Morningstar was as long-lived as the planet that had given him his name; a rock she could cling to even in his absence. He would not die so softly, so easily; would not have been lying under the House for those twenty years, silent and unmourned.

She picked up the dust in her hand, let it flow between her fingers. It was utterly inert, the ashes of a spent fire: nothing that was or had been magical, though from Philippe's confused explanations she gathered it had once been the body of a Fallen.

You can't be dead, she thought, slowly, fiercely. It was, had been, someone else they'd seen, some other corpse on that stone bed, a sacrifice for the spell inscribed in the circle.

And yet . . . yet, in twenty years, he had never come back. Had never sent word, or given a sign of life.

She walked to the edge of the circle and knelt, tracing the letters with her hands. They needed him in Silverspires, so badly it was like a fist clenched around her heart; a hollow in her chest only his presence would fill. *She* needed him; the force of his presence; his sardonic amusement at her efforts; his grudging praise when she did do something right; his effortless strength, keeping them all safe. But there was nothing; her fingers, brushing against the tip of the stone, felt only the coldness of the carved letters. She traced them, one by one: not the language all Fallen learned to read, but an older, colder alphabet that she had seen so many times in her brief apprenticeship: the language of Morningstar's desires.

Through those words I shed aside all desires but one. . . .

Through those words I send my prayers to the City, for the good of the House and the good name of Silverspires. . . .

Let me be the one shattered, let me be the one that falls into dust, let me be borne away by the storm. . . .

Through those words I shed aside all desires but one. . . .

And on and on, around the entire surface of the circle, an intricate network of sentences crossing one another, words that mingled with one another until the spell became a litany—a secret tracery of patterns that spoke to Selene, reminding her of long afternoons practicing the gestures and words that would unlock the magic within her. *"Power,"* Morningstar had said, smiling—sitting in the red armchair of the room where he taught, that room now soiled by the memory of what Asmodeus had done in it. *The world shapes itself around power, and this is its language.*

She remembered kneeling, tracing letters similar to the ones on the ground in her own blood; the air trembling with the force of the power she was calling; a perfect moment when everything seemed to be frozen, waiting for the gust of wind that would sweep everything away. . . .

Yes, this was Morningstar's work, no doubt about it. A spell of . . . self-sacrifice—the thought made her sick to her stomach, because it meant that Philippe was right, that Isabelle was right; that he was gone beyond retrieval, beyond the reach of any magic or miracles. Gone. Dead; perhaps back to that City they all dimly remembered, though she found it hard to believe forgiveness would be so easy to earn.

They needed him so badly, and he wouldn't be here. Wouldn't ever be coming back.

Gone. Dead. Forever.

Selene knelt in the dust, one hand on the circle Morningstar had so painstakingly traced; and felt the cool, salty taste of the first tears on her cheeks.

WHEN Philippe and Isabelle entered her hospital room, Emmanuelle was waiting for them. She was sitting in a battered old chair, her hand lying on one of the armrests, so that the mark on it was clearly visible. It pulsed in Philippe's vision; but only mildly, like a dying heartbeat. "It's almost gone," he said, before he could stop himself.

Emmanuelle smiled at him: her face pinched on itself, around the hollows of cheekbones, as if, lifting a shroud, he had seen the face of death staring back at him. "Philippe. I wasn't expecting—"

Philippe felt himself grow red. They'd pushed him to see Emmanuelle, as if it would make any kind of difference; as if he could do anything for her. "I'm sorry," he said. "I shouldn't have come here."

Isabelle was watching the guards lay Madeleine down on another bed; though she would be listening, he was sure.

"Why?" Emmanuelle asked. She did not move from the chair. He suspected she could not; that it was the only thing keeping her upright at the moment.

"They told me—" He took a deep, deep breath, cursing Silverspires and its ancient, irrelevant intrigues, struggled for words that should have come easily to him. "They told me you were dying. I—I thought I could help. Seeing that I was the one responsible for it."

"But you're not, are you." It wasn't a question; and her gaze had the sharpness of broken glass.

Not a question he was ready to answer; and he couldn't quite stop glancing at the door, worried Asmodeus would walk in, with that easy, dangerous smile. . . .

His hands had tightened into fists again; again he was surprised that they didn't hurt. "Let me have a look at it," he said. "And then we can talk. Please?"

Emmanuelle shrugged. "If you want."

He knelt before her, touched her skin. The raised area was surrounded by a circle of dried skin like lizard scales. There was a little magic under his fingers; a little of the same sense of oppressiveness he remembered from the shadows' presence—it leaped when he touched it, reawakening the same feeling within his chest—for a moment shadows wavered and danced on the edge of his field of vision; for a moment he waited with his heart in his throat, but there was nothing more; it was all fading fast. . . .

They were gone. The Furies were gone.

He moved to the secondary rings; they were all but reabsorbed back into the skin. "You're healing." He could be done with this; find the source of the darkness and—then what? Face it as he'd faced Morningstar's bones?

He had no idea what to do.

"So Aragon says. I could do with less fatigue," Emmanuelle said. She smiled, tightly. "Now you should leave the House."

"Ha."

"Selene has expressed interest in our staying," Isabelle said, behind him.

"Madeleine?" Philippe asked.

"They've sent for Aragon, but at this hour he's not in the House anymore," Isabelle said. "They'll see if Gerard or Eric . . ."

Emmanuelle was not to be deterred from the earlier thread of conversation. "So you're a 'guest' of the House once more."

Never. "Not if I can help it," Philippe said, more sharply than he had intended.

"You're not bound." Emmanuelle shrugged. "I would advise you to slip out the door—I'm sure you can," she said, to the too-quick denial she must have seen on his face.

Philippe had not moved; was still kneeling, holding her hand. It would mean leaving with the darkness still inside him; it would mean leaving Isabelle—but he couldn't hope to remain here, not with Selene aware of his presence. He needed . . . he needed to be free. "At least let me have not come for nothing."

She raised an eyebrow. "What—"

He called fire then, and wood, and gently entwined them on her skin. They were weak and faded, nothing like the *khi* currents he'd played with in Annam, but still, there was a memory of the strength of the House. Still, it was enough.

On Emmanuelle's hand, the rings faded away one by one; last to go was the central one, its blackened outline shifting to dark red, and then to inflamed brown; and then gracefully merging with Emmanuelle's dark skin.

She was looking at him, mouth slightly open. "No Fallen magic—"

No Fallen magic could heal that fast, that easily; or not without costs. But his magic was different—just as Ngoc Bich's magic was different, and thank Heaven for that, or he'd still have been a broken body in a bed, awaiting the death that would extinguish his pain. "Party tricks," Philippe said, gently; rising, and releasing her hand to fall, limp, at her side. The color was back in her cheeks; her breath came in fast bursts, as if she were bracing herself for flight; and she could have fled, too; with that infusion of strength she could easily have risen from her chair and walked without shaking.

But she didn't. Instead, she watched him, warily. At length, she spoke in the silence of the room. "What threatens the House?" She didn't ask what he was, or what he could do; merely took it all on faith. He wasn't quite sure how to feel about that. He was sorry he had wounded her, accidental as it was. She was House, true; but she was graceful about it; generous to a fault, even to those who weren't dependents.

See, there were positive sides to a House.

But of course there were. Of course there would be good people like her, like Laure—within Silverspires, within Hawthorn—even within House Draken, where Theophraste the tailor had been kind, and sorry to see the Annamite troops drafted in the war, and made his best effort to cut them uniforms with flowing patterns like those on Annamite silk, and handed them scraps of cloth they could use as blankets against the killing cold. It hadn't changed a thing. Such people's lives were richer, easier because of the House system. And in turn, the House system existed only because such kind, gentle people kept pledging themselves to it and strengthening it from within. They were all complicit, without exception.

And so was Isabelle.

"What threatens the House?" Emmanuelle asked again.

Philippe shrugged. "A ghost," he said, feeling the memory of darkness within his chest. "Anger. Revenge."

Not revenge, Madeleine had said. Justice. But was there such a difference to be found in Paris, anymore? The Houses were their own enclosed systems, making their own laws; and bowing only to he who had the greater power.

Morningstar was hovering on the edge of his field of vision, smiling that terrible seductive smile, his wings gilded with the last of the dying light. *My world,* he whispered. *From beginning to end. Will you not play by the game's rules?*

Never.

Then the game will crush you, and grind your bones into dust.

But Philippe wasn't the one whose bones were dust; wasn't the one whose dreams had come to an end in the crypt beneath the altar. He was alive.

Emmanuelle was still watching him. "A ghost. One of the dead. Someone we wronged." She didn't sound surprised, or shocked. Of course. She was still part of the House. She still knew about what it did, for its supposed own good.

"One of your precious Morningstar's students." He hurled it at her like an insult; weary of it all; of Morningstar and his senseless plots, of Selene and her damnable pride, of Asmodeus and his casual cruelties. "You betrayed them. Sold them like a pound of flesh."

To buy peace.

As if that had ever been a reason for anything.

Emmanuelle said nothing for a while. Her eyes were closed; her face pale. When she spoke again, her voice was level. "Sold to Hawthorn, wasn't she? In reparation for two murders that Lord Uphir threatened to turn into a bloodbath."

"Who? How did you know this?"

"I can read." Emmanuelle's voice was mild. "And you asked for books when you came into the library, some time ago. History books. I had . . . a refresher course on who might have cause to hate the House."

"What was her name?" Philippe asked.

"Nightingale," Emmanuelle said. "It was a long time ago, Philippe. Before the war."

"And you—" She didn't seem to see anything wrong with it, with what Morningstar had done.

Isabelle said, "I remember her. She was quick to smile; quick to anger; like a beloved child."

"How—how do you know that?" Emmanuelle asked.

"I don't know." Isabelle looked bewildered for a while. "I had this image—and then nothing else." An image from Morningstar, Nightingale through his eyes.

Philippe took a deep, trembling breath; forced himself to think.

He couldn't afford to jump at fancies; because the darkness was with him, and it was real, and deadly.

"I need to know," he said, pulling a chair; and felt as though he had set a foot on loose rock; and stood, perilously balanced, in the instant before everything came tumbling down. "Who is Nightingale?"

"You must understand that I don't remember her," Emmanuelle said. "Her name was Hélène, I think, before Morningstar chose her. She was mortal. She studied with him for a couple of years. He'd have grown bored with her, in time; dissatisfied, as with any of his other students. But something happened first."

"The betrayal."

"There were two murders," Emmanuelle said. "It was . . . messy, I remember. Two dependents of Hawthorn, in broad daylight, as they came out from Notre-Dame." She frowned. "Uphir thought it was our fault. That, even if we weren't behind it, we should have protected them better."

"And were you? Behind them?"

"How should I know?" Emmanuelle said. "Morningstar never admitted to anything. But yes, it might well have been him. Who else would have had the gall to commit murder on the steps of his own House?"

"Go on," Philippe said. He felt the darkness, rising within him; the room, growing fainter and fainter; the memory of pain; of anger; of disappointment. He wanted to ask how they could do this; how they could sell their own; but he knew the answer she was going to give him.

"There's not much else," Emmanuelle said. "That I know of. Morningstar went to negotiate with Uphir. He might have accused Nightingale, because she was convenient. Expendable. I assume . . ." She paused; Philippe only saw her through a haze of rage like a living fire. "He must have left tracks. Traces of his own magic that Uphir saw. And he pinned it on Nightingale—"

"Because she was his student and had learned his magic." Isabelle's voice was sharper than usual.

Memories. Visions. Philippe closed his eyes—the room was receding, and he could feel only Nightingale's thoughts, drowning his.

They'd come for her one day in the courtyard; Morningstar smiling like a sated cat; telling her she needed to go to Hawthorn, to sort out something for him; a minor detail in an agreement with Uphir. And she had gone, trusting him; until the gates of Hawthorn closed on her, and she saw Uphir's cold, angry smile . . .

"They thought she was responsible for it. In Hawthorn."

"Yes," Emmanuelle said. She exhaled loudly. "I can understand why she'd be angry. But she's dead, isn't she?"

She'd hung in chains for days and days on end, endured pain without surcease—blades that opened her flesh, burns, spells that turned her innards to jelly, all of that to make her admit to something she hadn't done—and she could scream and accuse her master, but in the end, it hadn't made any difference, had it? Because Uphir hadn't cared, so long as the price was met. "She died in Hawthorn."

Isabelle said, "The dead don't walk the earth, Philippe. They don't leave mirrors with curses, or trace summoning circles on the floor."

"They speak to the living, though," Emmanuelle said, slowly, carefully. "To magicians foolish enough to summon them, if it comes to that. Death is not necessarily an obstacle. There are precedents . . ." Her arms gripped the side of the chair, so strongly her skin went pale.

"A ghost, then. With human agents."

"Yes. Claire. Perhaps Asmodeus. And others, quite probably. You would not lack for people with a grudge against the House," Emmanuelle said. "But I doubt she has need of them any longer."

Claire—his vision of her hands; the mirror—she'd probably left it in the cathedral, years and years ago: it would be just like her, to try to give Silverspires a nudge in the right direction, to patiently wait for the curse to take hold. Asmodeus was . . . more direct. "I don't make a habit of studying ghosts," Philippe said, a tad stiffly. Ghosts were bad luck. Their walking the earth was against the natural order of things, and he certainly had no intention of being in the same place as one, if he could avoid it. The ghosts of dragon kings were one thing; those of indentured mortals, House dependents at that, quite another. "I—" He spread his hands, unsure. "I can't give you much more. Madeleine knew what they were—the figures in the crypt."

"Erinyes," Isabelle said, in the rising silence.

"Furies?" Emmanuelle looked at her hand; and then at the pile of books on the chair next to her. "Of course. The circle that crushes the original offense. The bites of snakes. But no one has summoned the Furies in—"

"You forget," Philippe said. "Morningstar taught her."

"How did she die?" Isabelle asked. She was standing by one of the bay windows, staring at the courtyard outside; at the daylight, slowly eclipsed by the coming of the night.

"Not well," Philippe said. He could breathe—he could keep her at bay; keep her memories out of himself. He had to. Because, as he spoke, it was within him again—the darkness, rising within him; the growing rage, mingled with the memory of the awe Morningstar had generated as effortlessly as he breathed—with a burning sense of shame that she was revolting against her master, betraying his trust— such a terrible thing, that even hanging in her chains in the depths of Hawthorn, she'd been capable of such devotion. "They broke her piece by piece in the name of their justice, but it wasn't them she died thinking of."

"Thinking of?" Isabelle asked. "Hating?"

"Hate and love and all those things intermingled," Philippe said. It was hard to focus, remembering that rage; remembering that sick feeling within him, that desperate desire to please, even after what Morningstar had done . . .

Emmanuelle's face was pale; drained of all blood. "I didn't know," she said. "None of us did."

"I know you didn't," Philippe said. "But it doesn't change anything."

"Morningstar is dead," Isabelle said, softly. "Does that not—"

"The Furies are gone," Philippe said. He felt, again, the tightness in his chest; the sense that he was larger, stretched thinner than he ought to have been—the darkness below him, burrowing toward the foundations of the House. "But Nightingale hasn't disappeared. Her revenge is still happening. It will destroy you, in the end." It would destroy him, too—he'd been a fool; he wasn't strong enough to resist her—he was being torn apart, piece by piece, bones cracking in the furnace of her anger, his brain spiked through with the strength of her implacable resolve. . . .

He . . . he needed to get out of here. Now.

Emmanuelle shook her head. "There's nothing we can do to atone for this. Nothing that will . . ." She took in a deep, shaking breath. "I didn't know," she said, again, as if she still couldn't quite imagine it. Morningstar had taught them well; hammered loyalty into them until they could barely see themselves anymore. "Philippe, you have to—"

"I'm not the one you should convince."

"No," Isabelle said. "But ghosts aren't convinced anymore, are they? They're exorcised."

"Isabelle!" Emmanuelle said, sharply. "You can't—"

Philippe stifled a bitter laugh—and he wasn't sure whether it came from him or Nightingale. "See what you have?" he said. "See what Morningstar shaped; what all Fallen are, in the end? Perhaps your House doesn't deserve to survive. Perhaps none of them do." He rose, brushing his hands against the cloth of his trousers, as if he could remove the dust he'd breathed in the chapel. "I'm sorry, Emmanuelle. I don't have more than this."

He left, without looking back.

ISABELLE caught up with Philippe in the corridor. "You can't leave."

Philippe turned, stared at her. There was no illumination in the corridor, but, every two or three breaths, Isabelle's skin would gradually brighten: a slow, lazy radiance that would throw underwater reflections on the flower wallpaper. It was . . . eerie, not least because she had never done that, not even at the height of her powers; back in that single, bloody night in the Grands Magasins where his life had changed.

"I can if I want to," he said. And he had to. Before Selene found him and imprisoned him, once again. Before this House—and the rage Nightingale felt when he stood within its walls—was his undoing.

"You—" Isabelle shook her head. "You made a promise, remember?"

He had, but it had been to a different person. And perhaps he shouldn't have made it at all. He owed nothing; not to her, not to this House. "I promised to help you. To keep you company, until you could work things out." Philippe shook his head. "You're all grown up now, Isabelle."

"Why? Because of what happened in the crypt? Because I touched a body? Is that what worries you?"

No, not that—it was her entire behavior: the light, streaming out of her, the ageless glint in her eyes, the way she held herself. What she had said, to Emmanuelle and Madeleine; the casual way she spoke of exorcising a ghost that bothered her, not understanding any of Nightingale's suffering, or the magnitude of Morningstar's betrayal. Nightingale had been *wronged*, and all she could ask herself—instead of questioning the House and its ways, or the acts of Selene's master—was how to remove this inconvenient obstacle from her path.

Like them. She had become just like them.

No. She had always been like them, and he had been too blind to see it.

"I'm still the same," Isabelle said. "I—" She raised her hand, the one with the fingers missing; worried at the gap with her other hand, as she always did under stress. "Why can't you see it?"

Because she was changing, and she scared him stiff. Because he couldn't be quite sure when it had happened—when, in the seemingly endless night that had sharpened his entire being to a thin pretense of what he once had been—she had become a Fallen in her own right, like Selene, like Oris.

Like Asmodeus.

Was it when she'd touched Morningstar's bones? A simple answer, that—that power was its own corruption, but of course there were no simple answers. "You've changed," he said, simply. There was nothing else he could say that she would understand.

"I haven't." Isabelle's voice was grim. "I warned you once before: this is my House, Philippe, and the only place where I feel safe. I will defend it."

"You weren't this"—he struggled for words—"categorical before. You didn't go to see Selene back then, did you?"

She held his gaze, unflinchingly. "Perhaps I should have."

He sighed. "It hasn't got much to do with you in any case, Isabelle. I'm just—" Tired. Tired of it all, of their stupid power plays and reputation games; tired of wondering where he fit into all this and never finding an answer. "I can't go on like this."

And of course, it wasn't true. Because it wasn't just weariness, but also her. What she had become; the power she effortlessly wielded—and the effortless cruelty that surfaced, like a scorpion sting, in the moments he least expected it.

He couldn't face that, not anymore.

Isabelle's face was a mask, all emotions smoothed out of it. "You—you could offer Selene your help. I'm sure she would pardon you, take you into the House—"

"I don't want to be in a House!" He hadn't meant to shout it, but the words slipped out, as treacherous as a wet knife blade. "A House took me, once. Tore me from my home and marched me all the way here, to fight in a stupid, senseless war; and left me with nothing, not even a mouthful of food or a scrap of cloth to call my own."

Isabelle's voice was quiet. "A House took you. It wasn't this House, Philippe."

As if it made any difference—how could she not see it? How could she—? "No," Philippe said. "It wasn't. But, deep down, they're all the same. Can't you see? Morningstar betrayed Nightingale for what? Two deaths? An advantage with Hawthorn that didn't last the winter? Houses all think lives are cheap." Pointless. It was all so pointless, their little games like children's fights in school, with no more rhyme or reason than their meaningless professions of charity and care for the weak.

They didn't deserve anything—except to crumble and fall.

"We don't," Isabelle said. "I—I—"

"You don't, or you don't think you do." He sighed. She looked bewildered once more, her preternatural maturity gone. She'd always been like that, hadn't she, a child who had seen too much to remain one? But children were cruel, too; casually tearing the wings from flies, mocking and hurting one another and never knowing when to stop. What would she do, with Morningstar's powers, and some of his memories? What would she think of? He didn't want to find out. Better leave now, with some of his illusions intact.

"I'm sorry. I can't help you. How do you appease a ghost, if they're right? I can't believe the House is worth saving."

"I have to believe." Isabelle drew herself up, gathering light around her like a mantle; appearing, for a bare moment only, as she must have when in the City, her black hair ringed with radiance, and with the shadow of huge, feathered wings at her back. Like the wings of Asmodeus in his prison cell, he thought, hands shaking. Even if everything else had been different, he couldn't live with that. "Don't you see, Philippe? I have nowhere else to go."

"I know." They wouldn't budge, either of them. It was futile. "Let's agree to disagree, shall we?"

Isabelle said nothing. He could have done something then; could have found words to comfort her, could have laid a hand on her shoulder and told her that it was all going to be all right. He didn't, because he couldn't lie to her anymore. Because there was still darkness in his heart; and underneath the House, the soft, crushing sound of that huge thing hungering to reduce the foundations to dust. Because the sound of the wind through the corridors was no longer a lament, but that of an oncoming storm.

She'd be strong enough to weather it—she had Morningstar's magic; and the protection of the other Fallen in the House. He didn't need to worry; or to listen to the treacherous voice in his heart that reproached him for leaving her. "Be well, will you? I—I would hate for you to come to harm."

Isabelle shrugged. "It happens," she said. "To Fallen."

"To mortals. You're not anything special."

Her smile was bitter, wounding. "Hunted for magic in our bones, in our breath? We didn't *ask* to be made special, Philippe. But we have to live with it, all the same."

While he—he had asked to become an Immortal, of course; had starved himself until he was whiplash-thin, meditated until all the mountains blurred and ran into one another like watercolors under rain. He couldn't blame an accident of birth; he had made a deliberate choice.

But then, so had she, one she couldn't remember—the one that had driven her from Heaven. "I guess this is good-bye, then. Fare you well, Isabelle."

"And you." Her gaze was clear, distant; the radiance of the wall soft, like water, like tears. "Fare you well, Pham Van Minh Khiet. I hope we meet again."

They both knew they wouldn't; or that, if they did, it would be under very different terms.

SELENE might have wished to keep her grief private, but news of Morningstar's death filtered through the House, leaving dependents in a state of stunned shock. No one had believed Morningstar could die, just as the sea or the wind couldn't die—and, if he could die, was the House truly as invulnerable as Selene assured them?

The news filtered elsewhere, too—and in another part of the House, a dusty, disregarded cellar that hadn't been opened in twenty years, other people set to work.

Asmodeus knelt in the center of a circle much like the one that had been traced in the crypt; with the same kind of flowing tracery that had adorned its edges, the same alphabet that was the language of power. He had removed his usual, elegant finery; the letters flowed across his broad torso, like writhing snakes outlined in the light of another world—slowly descending along his arms toward his hands, and from there into the floor, linking the two halves of the circle together.

At one point, halfway through the work, he raised his head, sniffing the air like a hound scenting blood; and bent back with a white-toothed smile, intent on his spell. He whispered words, as the letters filled the empty space on the floor: a litany that seemed to be at once a mourning chant and a prayer.

When he was done, he lifted his hands. For a moment, there was nothing: silence, filling the room as the last echo of his words faded into nothingness, and every letter going dark. Then a pure, single note rang, like a plucked harp string. Asmodeus smiled, and got up.

His attendant, Elphon, was waiting for him at the entrance to the room. He handed Asmodeus his shirt and jacket, which Asmodeus slipped into effortlessly. As he buttoned up his shirt, Elphon spoke up. "My lord, if I may?"

Asmodeus didn't say anything. Elphon went on. "This is a circle of rebirth, isn't it? I'm not sure I understand why—"

Asmodeus smiled, white and sharp, like a tiger prowling the woods. "You mean, because Silverspires is my enemy?"

Elphon blushed, obviously bracing himself for further rebuke. "Yes."

"You think this is going to benefit them? Oh, Elphon," Asmodeus said, shaking his head. "I had a bargain with someone else for . . . a ritual. For a weakness in Silverspires' wards, at a key point in time—which required us to be here, in the House, in order to undermine it from within. This isn't a gift I'm making them. Quite the contrary. This, my friend, is their downfall."

And with that, he turned away, leaving that single note behind him. Unlike the words, it didn't fade away into silence, but gradually was joined by others, until a faint but clear chorus of voices echoed under the vault.

In the room, in the center of the circle, light danced on motes of dust; and then the light died down, and the dust settled, slowly accreting itself into the shadowy shape of a human being.

And something else, too: on the edges of Asmodeus's circle, tendrils of leaves and wood started to grow—plunging so deep into the floor that the stone itself began to crack.

NINETEEN
The Oncoming Storm

MADELEINE woke up, and wished she hadn't.

She was lying in an infirmary bed. She would have known that peeled, faded painted ceiling and its flower-shaped moldings anywhere. When she tried to move, every joint in her body seemed to protest at the same time, with a particular mention to a crick in her neck that seemed to have become permanently stuck. What— There had been the strangeness of the dragon kingdom—the flight to the cathedral—

"Oh, you're awake. Good." Emmanuelle's face hovered into view. She looked better, but distinctly worried.

"What did I miss?" Madeleine said, or tried to. Her tongue was as unresponsive as a lump of wood—her mouth felt full of grit and ashes, and her words came out garbled. She tried again, felt something shift and tear. "What—?"

"Aragon said you needed to rest," Emmanuelle said.

"You're—you're fine," Madeleine said. "You're healed."

Emmanuelle nodded.

"I'm glad," Madeleine breathed. At least they had succeeded in that. At least . . . "Philippe—"

"He left. Isabelle went after him," Emmanuelle said. "She has some foolish notion that she can change his mind." Her eyes—her eyes had changed somehow. They were . . . older, as if something had made her age in the space of a few hours. What had happened? Had Philippe healed her? She was standing, and didn't seem to be in any pain other than extreme weariness. Surely that meant they had succeeded; but then, why did she seem so distant? Something . . .

The House, she realized, and felt as though something was squeezing her heart. Something was wrong with the House. She could feel it, even through the tenuous link she had with it.

The House's magic was coming apart.

A commotion: Aragon's raised voice, and then steps, getting closer to her. "I know she's awake," Selene said. "You should have notified me before."

If Emmanuelle looked ill at ease, Selene looked unchanged. She was dressed in her usual men's swallowtail and trousers, regal, apparently unaffected by whatever seemed to have oppressed the atmosphere. "Madeleine." Her voice was cold, cutting. "Will you leave us?" she asked Emmanuelle.

Emmanuelle winced. She cast a hesitant glance at Madeleine, but withdrew; her mouth shaped around words she never did get to pronounce. An apology? But what for?

"You're going to chastise me for lacking to do my duty," Madeleine said. "We were trying to help Emmanuelle."

Selene said nothing.

"Isabelle thought that, if we could find Philippe, we could convince him to help—" It sounded small and pitiful, when she said it; with none of the hard-edged certainty she'd felt when she went with Isabelle; as if whatever magic had flowed out of her had utterly, finally gone, leaving only the taste of ashes in her mouth.

Selene's face had not moved. She let Madeleine's awkward, spluttering speech fade into silence. Only then did she speak, and her voice was entirely emotionless. "I would reproach you for that in ordinary circumstances, yes. I expect the alchemist of House Silverspires to be available when I have need; and not gone into God knows what senseless adventure with her apprentice, whom you're supposed to keep an eye on, not indulge, may I remind you?"

"In ordinary circumstances." Madeleine struggled to think through the layers of cotton wool that seemed to fill her mind. "I don't—"

Selene raised a hand, and power crackled in the room like the prelude to a thunderstorm. "You will remain silent. How could you be such a fool, Madeleine?"

"I don't understand—"

"Don't insult my intelligence. You knew. You knew the rules, and you flaunted them. How long has it been going on?"

"I—" She knew. The only thing that came to Madeleine's befuddled mind was the truth. "Five years. Nights are hard, when you remember the past. It's—" She took in a deep, burning breath. "The dead and the dying and the bloodbath at Hawthorn—"

"Be silent. I don't want your excuses, Madeleine."

"Then what do you want?" She knew, even before the words were out of her mouth, that they were a mistake; knew it when Selene's face hardened like cooling glass, impossibly brittle and smooth at the same time.

"You know exactly what I want. I'm not throwing you out of the House in your current state, which Aragon tells me is probably so poor because of your use of angel essence. But I want you gone, Madeleine."

Gone. Cast out from Silverspires; stripped out of her refuge, her last rampart against Asmodeus and the nightmares of the night Uphir had been deposed. Her worst nightmare coming to meet her, and she couldn't even seem to muster any energy for fear; for anything but the sick feeling in her belly. "But—I have nowhere else to go."

"You should have thought of that before you got addicted to essence," Selene said. She snapped her fingers, almost absentmindedly; and something was gone from Madeleine's mind, a noise she hadn't been aware of, but whose lack was overwhelming, a glimpse into the abyss. "I withdraw from you the protection of the House. Go your own way." And with that, she turned and left—that . . . that bitch. Emmanuelle had been an essence addict, once; and she'd been allowed to clean up her act, to go on as if nothing were wrong; but Emmanuelle was Selene's lover, and of course she'd be favored over everyone else. Of course.

She couldn't seem to think straight—as in the dragon kingdom, except that it wasn't serenity that plagued her this time. Her thoughts kept running around in circles, around the gaping wound left by the loss of the House; couldn't seem to coalesce into anything useful. But still . . .

Still, she was damned if she'd let Selene have her way. "Selene?" She forced the words through a mouth that felt plugged with cotton.

Selene didn't turn, but she did pause for a moment.

"You're not Morningstar," Madeleine said. "You're not even a fraction of what he was."

"Perhaps not," Selene said. "But I am the head of this House, Madeleine. And nothing will change that."

PHILIPPE came out of the House under the same gray, overcast skies of Paris. He barely could remember a time when they hadn't been thus, when he had come in from Marseilles under a sun reminiscent of the shores of Indochina, a long time ago, in another lifetime.

He carried a basket of figs, dry-cured sausage, and bread that had been forced upon him by Laure when he went to the kitchens to say good-bye—Laure hadn't said anything or accused him of anything, merely shaken her head sadly, like a mother whose chicks had had to flee the nest far too early. He'd tried, then; to warn her; to tell her she should leave the House before it collapsed around her, and realized that she'd lived for so long in it that nothing existed outside its boundaries. It had been . . . sobering—and made him think, again, of Isabelle and what she had become.

He stood, for a while, on the boundary between the House and the city, by the raised parapet of Pont d'Arcole, watching the oily waves of the Seine. He had feared the river once, like everyone in Paris; but now his eyes were opened to its true nature, and there was nothing to fear. Dragons ran sleek and superb beneath the water, elegant shapes racing one another; if he frowned hard enough, he could forget the broken-off antlers, the patches of dry scales on their bodies, the dark film that made their eyes seem dull, like gutted fish at a monger's stall. For a moment; an impossible, suspended moment, he was back on the banks of the Perfumed River; with the smell of jasmine rice and crushed garlic, and the sweet one of banana flowers, all the things he should have set aside when ascending.

Past, all of this, gone by. There was no point in grieving for faded things.

Aragon had said he should forget it all; that the way to Annam was closed forever; that he should accept that his new home was in Paris, and act accordingly. But Aragon, who liked to call himself independent and unbound by loyalty to any House, still lived through his services to them; still drew a salary from Silverspires, and the lesser Houses he helped. Aragon could no more envision a world without Houses than he could stop breathing.

And Isabelle . . .

No, he couldn't think of Isabelle now; or of what she might have meant to him. He couldn't afford to.

What he was sure of was this: he would rather die, or forsake any hope of ascending ever again, than be forced into service once more.

Isabelle might have given in, but he wouldn't. He threw a piece of broken stone into the river, and watched the ripples of its passage until they faded away. Then he shook himself, and went to look for the nearest omnibus stop.

MADELEINE tried not to brood, but it was all but impossible. Her mind was an empty place; a yawning abyss opening onto the night of the coup; and now she had neither angel essence nor the House's protection to dull the knife's edge of memory. In her dreams she smelled blood, the thick, sluggish, sickening odor of a slaughterhouse; and remembered Morningstar's measured steps: the fear, shooting through her, that he would pass her by, that he would leave her to die in the darkness. In her dreams she never made it to Silverspires; or she stood on the Pont-au-Change and watched the ruins of the House, with the acrid smell of magic in her nostrils. In her dreams Asmodeus laughed, and whispered that he had won.

She lay alone in her room. She supposed Selene had given orders that no one could visit her; it would be just like her, drive home the sheer soul-destroying misery of her situation. Or perhaps no one wanted to see the pariah; to think on how their own existence within the House depended on its master's whims.

Aragon, when he did come, was brusque. She gathered she wasn't the only one he needed to take care of, or perhaps it was the atmosphere of the House, finally getting through to him even though he wasn't bonded to it.

"I can't do anything for you," he said. His lips were two thin lines in the severity of his face. "Your lungs are all but gone."

Madeleine suppressed a bitter smile. "How long do I have?"

"You know as well as I do. A few years maybe? Unless we're talking some kind of miracle."

"Miracles never happen here," Madeleine said, with terrible bleakness. "Not in this city, not in this House." She had felt it; the change to the fabric of Silverspires; the worm, gnawing away at the layers of protections Morningstar had painstakingly laid out during the founding of the House. Perhaps it was better if she left; soon there wouldn't be any refuge here anyway. But where else would she go? There was nowhere, nothing; and the thought of taking Claire's charity in Lazarus was a draft too bitter to be swallowed.

"You should have told me," Aragon said, finally, as he was about to leave: the professional reserve peeled away, to reveal—what? Anger? Hurt? She couldn't read him, never had been able to. "You didn't have to—"

Madeleine thought of Elphon; of blood, warm and sticky on her hands; and the ghost of pain in her hip, the acrid memory of fear as she crawled out of Hawthorn. "There are some things I can't live with, Aragon."

"There are some things that will kill you, and you should have known that." Aragon stared at her for a while. "See me before you leave. I can give you a few addresses and names. You don't have to head into the unknown."

"Thank you," Madeleine said, but she was too drained, too hollow to care. Silverspires had been her life, her refuge; and now, soon—all too soon—it would be gone, leaving only a bitter memory in her thoughts. She needed . . . a plan, something she could cling to; but nothing seemed to penetrate the gloom around her.

THE omnibus was crowded, but the crowd lessened as they drew away from the major attractions. They passed the empty space where Les Halles had once been, the charred trees on rue de Rivoli, under the watchful gaze of the dome at La Samaritaine: the shop, like Les Grands Magasins, had been nuked in the war, and an upstart House whose name Philippe couldn't remember had settled in the wreckage, making grand claims of restoring the art deco building to its former glory. Like most grandiloquent claims, this one had never materialized.

Then, in the distance, the dome of Galeries Lafayette, and the roofs of House Lazarus and its counterpart, Gare Saint-Lazare—where trains had once departed for Normandy, but which hid nothing more than beggars and essence junkies. The crowd was no longer House dependents, or middle-class shopkeepers, surviving as they could; but younger, more haunted faces: children with nimble hands doubling as pickpockets, mothers carrying their entire belongings on their backs; old women smoking pipes, tobacco the only luxury they had left.

Philippe left his ornate cloak and Laure's basket of food to one such woman, bowing very low to her; and ignoring the puzzled, suspicious glance she threw him. Suspicious or not, she would sell the cloak: he hoped for a good price, though it was all out of his hands. Then, at the next station, he got down.

La Goutte d'Or had been a workers' neighborhood before the war, the hands and arms toiling away in factories, making the luxuries the Houses gorged themselves on. Now the factories functioned at part capacity only, and the workers sat on the pavement, drinking absinthe when they could afford it, or other alcohols that were much less kind on the eyesight when they could not. They watched Philippe, warily; not because he was Annamite—there were plenty of Annamites there, the descendants of those sucked in by the maw of war—but because, with his quiet, confident walk and his clean cotton clothes, he stuck out like a sore thumb.

Philippe ignored them, except to answer when a mocking voice would greet him. He was unfailingly polite and courteous; but, nevertheless, he called fire from the wasteland around him, and held the *khi* element in his clenched fist, ready to finish an argument with more than good manners.

The building hadn't changed. It was still where he remembered it: at one of the edges of a triangle-shaped square, its limestone walls overgrown with ivy, its wooden shutters discolored and cracked. The bottom floor had once been a vendor of sewing materials, but had since long fallen into disrepair; the little drawers with cloth samples and ribbons now held pilfered artifacts and containers, anything that could be sold for a price.

It hadn't changed. But then, why had he expected it to?

He waited outside until the usual crowd had all but gone, as the evening deepened around him, and the wind picked up. Then, shrugging his scarf around his neck, he walked into the shop.

And stopped, for it was Ninon behind the counter—who watched him, openmouthed. "Hello," he said, into the growing silence. "I've come back."

SELENE had hoped it would get better, but it didn't. Asmodeus was shut in his rooms, claiming to be grieving and refusing all her polite requests for a meeting. Emmanuelle was back with her, but given to odd bouts of melancholy; back to her old self, before she'd completely given up essence, grieving for something neither she nor Selene could name. Despite their intense searches, Philippe could not be found anywhere, though there had been the occasional glimpse of him on the margins of the House, like a ghost she could not exorcise.

And Selene knew the name of her enemy now, though it did not help her.

Nightingale.

She had been young then, in the days of Nightingale's apprenticeship; young and naive and self-centered, paying little attention to the things that didn't concern her. Nightingale had given way to Oris, and Selene had barely noticed; nor had anyone within the House ever talked about the transition.

Given away, Emmanuelle had said. Betrayed.

How could he—? He was cold, and cruel, and ruthless, but she'd always thought he would do right by his students; that he discarded them for weaknesses, but not that he would turn them out of the House; bargain them away on shadowy things, use them as pawns in his war of influence.

Not her. He never would have. He didn't love her, or even feel more for her than the casual affection of a man for his pet, but he . . . He never would have—

But, if she closed her eyes, she would see, again and again, that amused glint in his gaze, would feel again that terrible sense of oppression; that primal fear that tightened all her leg muscles at the same time, primed for fighting or fleeing—fleeing, for what else could she have done, she who had never even been close to equaling him?

He never would have—

And her mind paused then, hanging over the precipice, because she knew, deep down, that he was perfectly capable of it. That he had always been.

"You can't appease a ghost," Emmanuelle had said, with a tired sigh. *"She's dead, Selene, and she's been working on her revenge for decades. The dead don't easily change their minds."*

She knew, but still she had to try.

While Emmanuelle was sleeping, she stole away, wrapped only in a thin cotton shawl, the cold wind on her skin like the beginning of a penance. She had put two guards outside Emmanuelle's room, but though she wouldn't be such a fool as to requisition them, neither would she be fool enough to go off on her own. She dropped by the mess hall, and asked which bodyguards were available. Two of the idle ones—Imadan and Luc—leaped up at the chance to follow her, abandoning a spirited discussion on the proper way to sketch the human body.

The crypt where Morningstar had lain was all but deserted. The stone bed was still empty in its circle of power—*do not think of the bed now, not of the grave or whom it belonged to*—but the place had changed. Along every column holding up the ceiling, something crept downward: great buttresses like snakes, moving so fast she'd have sworn she could see them shifting; encircling the pillars so hard and tight that the stone had cracked. Selene walked closer, touched them. They were as hard as rock, but the material wasn't rock. It was wood.

She thought of the plants in the East Wing; of the leaves she couldn't touch or pull out. Green things. And, like all green things, they had roots; roots which were now choking the foundation of Silverspires. If it couldn't be stopped . . .

Of course it could. It was silly to think that any ghost could affect the oldest and most powerful of Houses . . . But this ghost had summoned the Furies—killed Oris and Samariel and others; used Philippe as a catalyst to enter the House; and perhaps Asmodeus and Claire to wreak its havoc. This ghost had led Morningstar to sacrifice himself in order to exorcise her; in vain, for he had only kept the danger at bay, not eradicated it.

A worthy student, Morningstar would have said; except that, of course, it was his House being torn apart, and he who had been killed.

Selene knelt in the circle, touched her fingertips to it: nothing but cold, inert stone. Dead, all dead, and yet . . .

She brushed her fingers against the stone bed, and, calling to her the magic of the House, pulling in every strand like a weaver at her loom, spoke the slow, measured litany of a spell.

Something stirred, in the dark; large and unfathomable and not feeling human anymore. "I would speak with you," she said, slowly.

Darkness; and the wind, howling between the pillars with their weight of tree roots. "I know Morningstar harmed you, but he is gone. I—I am mistress of his House, and would offer amends in his name."

Amends, the darkness whispered to her, in her own voice. A cold, unpleasant feeling, slithering across her hands. *Amends. There are none.*

"Whatever you desire—"

All that you built—destroyed. All that you hold dear vanished. All that you long for—borne away by the storm.

"What storm?"

It is coming. Can you not hear it?

Selene could hear nothing *but* it; the sound of the wind racing between pillars; the distant noise of branches bending against its onslaught; the tightness in the air, a cloth stretched taut, almost to snapping point. "Your storm?"

There was no answer from the darkness. "What do you want, damn it!"

She had already had her answer; had already seen what was happening. Not a House, but something else; the foundations of a new building, a new garden, its roots in the wreckage of Silverspires.

Never.

It wasn't Morningstar's voice in her mind, but it could have been: it was that same cold, dry feeling of steel against the nape of a neck, that same feeling of unbreakable promises. The House was hers, now that Morningstar was dead; wholly hers, with none of the whispers that Asmodeus and Claire had started, none of the doubts about her ability to rule. It was hers; and, because no one else could protect it, that duty fell to her.

"I will crush you," she said to the darkness, her voice taking on the singsong of chants and litanies, and powerful spells. "Hack off your roots and suck the sap from your leaves, and burn your seeds before they can ever land." The air was taut again, as if listening to her promise; but what could it know of fear? It wasn't even human, not anymore.

"Selene?" It was Javier, pale and untidy. His creased face had the same expression as when he had waved Asmodeus into her office.

Her heart sank. "What's happened?"

"Asmodeus is leaving," Javier said. By now, she knew, all too well, his expressions and what they meant; and could read what he didn't say in the tightness of his clenched hands, in the thinness of his stretched lips.

"Asmodeus. That's not what I ought to be worried about, is it?"

Javier winced. "You—you have to come and see. There really is no good way to explain it."

MADELEINE wrapped her things carefully; not that there were many of them, of course. Isabelle watched her in silence, leaning against the doorjamb of the laboratory: she'd come in the middle of Madeleine's packing, and had settled in her current position without a word. At last she said, "You don't have to—"

Madeleine winced. She'd scoured her drawers before Isabelle had arrived, and had found only one small locket with a little angel essence; nothing like what she'd have needed to take. A vague edge of hunger seemed to overlay everything she did. It wasn't a craving, not something irresistible that would have left her in tears; merely a faint sense of discomfort that seemed to be slowly increasing. She refused to think about what it would mean for her, out there. "Selene gives me no choice."

Isabelle's hands clenched. "Selene can't drive everyone away."

"Philippe, you mean?" Madeleine asked. She'd never liked him, so she couldn't say she was sorry for him. But anything that would rile up Selene had her approval at the moment. How dare she—how–

Her throat was closing up. She took a last look at her laboratory: at the old, battered chair she'd sat in during her wild nightmare nights; the secretary desk, with the first drawer that always jammed—if she closed her eyes, she could still see Oris, sitting at the table with a frown on his face, trying to understand what she wanted from him.

Oh, Oris.

She blinked back tears. She'd never been one for sentimentality: she and Selene had that in common, at least; and she wasn't about to collapse in tears in the middle of her laboratory.

"Madeleine?"

"I'll be fine," she said. She had her bag. All the containers within belonged to the House, but she didn't think Selene would begrudge her a battered leather bag, so old it could have seen the days of Morningstar. "You should—" She closed her eyes. She couldn't feel the House; couldn't even reassure herself that she would be safe. And she'd had so little time to know Isabelle; but she and Emmanuelle were the one shining spot left in the desolation. "Take care of yourself, will you?"

Isabelle smiled sadly. "That's what Philippe said. Do you all think me such a child?"

"No," Madeleine said. She laid one of Isabelle's containers on the now-empty table. "But you'll be House alchemist. That's a big responsibility, trust me." One that she'd never been quite up to, she suspected; but she'd done better than her predecessor, at the least. And she'd trained a successor, in all too short a time. If only she could have stayed longer . . .

"I know." Isabelle shook her head. "I didn't . . . There was no time, Madeleine."

"It doesn't matter." Madeleine sought words; never something she'd been good at. "You'll do fine. Believe me."

Isabelle laughed bitterly. "Perhaps. You will write, won't you? Send news—"

Madeleine shook her head, unsure of what to say. Tears blinked at the corners of her eyes; she didn't move. No sentimentality. "Of course." It was a lie; why bother Isabelle with the remnants of a sad, washed-out alchemist, a teacher who couldn't even provide enough knowledge? "Of course I'll write. If it makes you happy."

Isabelle's smile seemed to illuminate the entire laboratory; no, it wasn't merely an illusion; it was a radiance from her skin, so strong it cast dancing shadows upon the walls. "Not as well as your staying, but I'll take it," she said.

Madeleine's heart clenched in her chest. She couldn't do anything more for Isabelle; couldn't protect her, or even give her more than a modicum of the knowledge she'd gained. It would have to do; because

Selene had left her no choice; but oh, how it hurt, as if she were betraying Oris all over again.

She hadn't had much, and hadn't hoped to bequeath much; save for the hope her apprentices would do better than her.

She left Isabelle in the laboratory, moodily staring at the container, and took the shortest way out, toward the ruined cathedral and its parvis.

There was something—something in the corridors that wasn't quite usual. On her way, she bypassed the school. She could hear Choérine's voice, explaining the finer points of Latin, and the giggles of some of the girls, but the noise was overlaid by something else, some other sound she couldn't quite identify. A breath, a tune she couldn't quite catch; voices whispering words on the cusp of hearing—but, no, it wasn't voices. It was . . . a sound that was the creak of a mast on the sea, a rustle like cloth; a breath like the wind in outstretched sails.

None of her business, not anymore.

People stood on the parvis. At first, Madeleine thought only to push past them on her way to the Petit-Pont; but then she saw the uniforms of silver and gray, and the sickeningly familiar insignia, the crown encircling the hawthorn tree. No. Not them, not now. She would have turned in blind panic, to find her way back into the House; but there was no safety there, not anymore, only the cool welcome they would reserve for strangers.

Breathe. Breathe. Do not think about blood, or the hollow pain of ill-healed ribs, the old wounds that never stopped twinging. She was going to walk past them, cross the river, get on board the omnibus that stopped before the Saint-Michel Fountain; and at last be rid of Hawthorn's ghosts in her life.

Her breath seemed to come out in short, noisy gasps as she crossed, on the other side of the vast plaza where the market was held, now all but deserted, with only a few House dependents hurrying about their tasks, their gazes studiously avoiding her. Halfway through, she threw a glance at them: so far away, they seemed like dolls, their faces all blurring into one another. They were talking animatedly, paying no attention to their surroundings. A leave-taking, that was what it had to be—she remembered something about the Hawthorn delegation staying on—a funeral, had it been? Or something close to it.

Ahead, the bridge beckoned, and the omnibus was waiting at the stop, its horses pawing at the ground, fresh and nervous, at the beginning of their hour-long run through Paris. She was going to make it—she was—

"Ah, Madeleine."

She never even heard him. One moment there was nothing; the next he stood between her and the bridge—with Elphon and another Fallen one step behind him. His glasses glinted in the sunlight; the expression in his eyes light, mocking. "Leaving so soon?"

The wind blew the smell of bergamot and orange blossom into her face, so strong that her entire stomach heaved in protest. "Asmodeus." She got the word out; barely. "It's none of your business."

His smile was bright and dazzling. "Oh, but it is. When a House rids itself of a most talented alchemist, I cannot help being interested."

There was no one else; or rather, everyone was giving them a wide berth, heedless of Madeleine's feeble attempts to signal for help. She was on her own, and she had never felt so alone. "Go away."

"I think not. I have a vested interest in you, after all."

Because she had once belonged to Hawthorn, because the House never let go of what it had once possessed, because she'd woken up at night, shaking and fearing that they would come to take her back, and now it was happening, and she was powerless to stop it. "Please—" she whispered, and Asmodeus smiled even more brightly.

"My lord." It was Elphon; for a wild, impossible moment Madeleine thought he had remembered, that he was going to speak up in her favor. He would— "We need to return to the parvis."

Asmodeus did not turn around. "For the formal leave-taking? Selene is half an hour late, and I see no sign of her coming."

The world had shrunk to Asmodeus's face; to his eyes behind their panes of glass, sparkling as if they shared some secret joke. She couldn't—she had to . . .

Her bag. The box with the remnants of angel essence. If she could find it. Slowly, carefully, she moved her hand, creeping toward the pocket where she had put it.

Asmodeus was talking to Elphon, and his full attention wasn't on her yet. "I expect the House to be . . . somewhat in disarray right now. I'll send someone with our excuses, to apologize for the impoliteness of leaving without the formal ceremony."

Madeleine's hand closed around the box; undid the clasp, plunged into the essence—warmth on her fingers, a promise of power. If she could raise her hand, and swallow it. If she—

"I'm sure Selene won't begrudge us our departure," Asmodeus was saying. He reached out, almost absentmindedly, and caught Madeleine's hand in a vise. His index finger pressed down, unerringly, on one of her nerves, and her fingers opened in a shock, sending the box clattering to the pavement; and the essence wafting onto the breeze, the wind picking at her palm and fingers with the greed of a hungry child.

Asmodeus's hand went upward, toward her shoulder; and effortlessly slid down the strap, divesting Madeleine of her black leather bag. "I think not. Where you're going, you'll have no need of this."

HE sat on a bed in Selene's room—Javier had spluttered and hemmed on the way, saying something about privacy and the need to keep this a secret, but Selene had been barely listening.

Javier closed the door behind her as she entered, leaving them in relative privacy. Emmanuelle was there, too, her eyes two pools of bottomless dark in the oval of her face. "He was wandering the corridors," she said, slowly, softly; as though everything might break, if she spoke too loud. "Stark naked." There was not an ounce of humor in the way she spoke: in spite of the incongruity, the hour was not one for laughter or light-spirited comments.

For a good, long while, Selene did nothing but stare.

He had the radiance of newborn Fallen: a light so strong it was almost blinding, so oppressive she fought a desire to sink to her knees; and the eyes he trained on her were guileless, holding nothing but the blue of clear skies. "Selene?" he asked, quietly. "I was told you were Head of the House now."

Selene swallowed, trying to dispel the knot in her throat—she wasn't sure if it was relief, or anger, or grief, or a bittersweet mixture of all three. "Glad to see you, Morningstar."

TWENTY
LIKE SEEDS, SCATTERED BY THE WINDS

EMMANUELLE came in with Javier: the priest looked much older, much more brittle than Selene remembered. "We found the place," Emmanuelle said. She looked grim; her sleeves slashed in multiple places. "A cellar with a circle—like the one under the cathedral."

A circle of power, like the one he had originally traced. Had he always intended to come back, then? Had he . . . engineered his own death and resurrection? "I see," Selene said. She didn't look at the curtain that separated her living quarters from her office; afraid that she'd see Morningstar in repose once more, with that serene, otherworldly expression: innocence personified, jarring from someone who had never been innocent, or even young.

"No, you don't." Emmanuelle's face was hard. "It was full of roots, Selene. I think . . . I think the circle was a crack between life and death; and a crack in the wards, too—an opening big enough for the curse to exploit. The roots must have descended from the first floor and gone into the foundations through the circle."

"Morningstar would never do that," Selene said, startled.

"No," Emmanuelle said. "If I understand correctly, he was dead at that point." She bit her lip. "He had a plan, I'm sure, Selene. I just don't think it played out as he wished it."

No; or he would be back as he had been. But the dead didn't trace circles, or cast spells. Someone else had done this for him.

Asmodeus. Her hands clenched, in spite of herself. "Has Hawthorn left?"

"They're gone," Javier said. "With apologies for taking their leave so . . . abruptly."

And no wonder, if what she suspected was true. Except, of course, that she had no way to prove it—and what would she do, even if it were proved? Accuse Asmodeus—who would no doubt laugh at her, and tell her that spells of resurrection were a fantasy? In any case—she had bigger problems on her hands.

"Did you—" Choérine swallowed. "Did you learn any more?"

Selene shook her head. "He says he doesn't remember anything. As if he were a newborn Fallen." And she was inclined to believe him. If it was an act, some game put on for their benefit, it was an impossibly good one.

Choérine shook her head, once, twice; her dark eyes burning against the porcelain-white tones of her skin. "What's going to happen, Selene?"

I don't know, she wanted to say; she wanted to surrender to the pressure, to bow down and admit that she wasn't worthy of this mantle, that she never had been. But she stopped herself, with an effort of will. Ignorance or indecisiveness was not what Choérine needed to hear. "We will talk," she said. "See where the future of the House lies. It's a good thing he's back; we could badly use his insights."

"Yes, of course." Choérine smiled, some of the fatigue lifting from her eyes. "I'll go see to the children."

After she was gone, Emmanuelle pulled away from the wall she'd been leaning on, and came to rest her head against Selene's shoulder. "A good lie," she said.

Selene breathed in Emmanuelle's perfume: musk and amber, heady and strong, a reminder of more careless days. If she closed her eyes, could she believe they would go to bed now; would kiss and make love with the fury and passion of the desperate?

But, of course, there had never been any careless days. There was war, and internecine fights; Emmanuelle's addiction, and Selene's hours of crippling self-doubt. "What else could I have told her?" Selene asked.

Emmanuelle didn't move. "It wasn't a reproach. But if you think you can fool me . . ."

"I would never dare." Selene gently disengaged herself from her lover's embrace, leaving only one hand trailing in Emmanuelle's hair, running braids between her fingers like pearl necklaces. "But you can't fool me, either. What didn't you tell me?"

Emmanuelle grimaced. "I underplayed it, Selene. It wasn't easy to search the cellars. Everything was . . . covered in roots. And they weren't exactly friendly."

"What do you mean?"

"Try fighting your way through a thornbush. One that hits back. And it's big now. Entire corridors are starting to look like the underside of a particularly nasty kind of tree, yes." Emmanuelle picked at her torn sleeves, her face grim and distant. "At this rhythm—"

"I know," Selene said. "The entire wing will become unusable." She didn't need Emmanuelle to tell her that: the magic of the House was flickering, being squeezed and choked into nothingness in so many places. In too many places.

All that you hold dear—vanished.

"That's assuming it stops at the wing," Emmanuelle said.

Which was, on the face of it, rather unlikely. "It said, in the crypt, that it would destroy us all." Selene stared at her hands. What could she do? She should wake Morningstar, ask him what they should do. Surely, even amnesiac, he would know. . . .

Pathetic. He had said it himself. She was head of the House now, and it was her responsibility. "Get me Isabelle," she said to Emmanu-elle. "We need to destroy this before it destroys us."

LATER, much later—or perhaps it wasn't, but time seemed to have blurred between a series of unbearably sharp tableaux, like teeth, biting over and over into her flesh—walking over the Pont Saint-Michel, watching the omnibus she'd hoped to catch move away from her, the sound of the hooves like thunder in her ears—a brief conversation be-fore a line of black cars, Asmodeus gesturing to her, Elphon prodding and pushing her into the same one as his master—the car pulling away, and the spire of the ruined cathedral dwindling farther and farther away in the distance.

"You're much better off with us," Asmodeus said. He was polishing his glasses with a yellow cloth; his eyes on the window, on the House that was his rival and enemy. "See? Over Notre-Dame?"

There were . . . clouds, but clouds didn't gather so dense and dark, didn't form that almost perfect circle that ringed the two ruined towers like a crown. And clouds didn't reach down: those were extending ten-drils, wrapping themselves around the ruined stone, until the entire cathedral seemed tethered to the Heavens.

"It's survived such a long time, hasn't it? Fire and floods and war. But this, I think, will finally break it." He sounded thoughtful, not gloating or satisfied, as she would have imagined. His eyes rested on her; in earnest for once, with none of the mockery she was used to. "So silent? Have you nothing to say?"

Madeleine, too weary for words, rested her head against the pol-ished, darkened glass of the car window, and watched her safe haven of the past twenty years vanish into the distance, leaving her alone with the master of Hawthorn.

ISABELLE, when she came, didn't seem entirely happy, or entirely at ease with her new charge as alchemist. "Madeleine knew better than I," she said.

Selene shook her head. The last thing she needed was people questioning her decisions. "Madeleine is no longer with us. There are only a few laws in Silverspires; and she broke one."

"So you don't forgive," Isabelle said, slowly. She was more sharply defined, somehow, the light from her body radiating more strongly than it should have. Was she on essence, too? But there were no signs of any external sources: merely Isabelle as she'd always been, impossibly young and impossibly old at the same time. "That's good to know."

"Do you have objections?" Selene said. She hesitated, for a fraction of a second only, and decided to make this her show of strength. "You can leave if you disagree. I'm sure there are other Houses that are far less vigilant about enforcing their laws."

Isabelle looked thoughtful. For a moment Selene thought she'd misjudged, that Isabelle would indeed leave, seek out Hawthorn or Lazarus—but then she nodded. "Your House, your law. I don't approve, but it's only fair."

Something in her tone was sharper than it should have been—as if, for a brief moment, she'd seriously considered challenging Selene for the leadership of the House. "Tell me what you know."

"I don't," Isabelle said, serenely. "Madeleine knew they were the Furies. Philippe and Emmanuelle figured out it was Nightingale. I—" She shrugged. "I don't know much, other than that Morningstar died." The light around her flickered, throwing distorted shadows on the walls.

"About that—" Emmanuelle said, but she didn't have time to finish, because, in that moment, Morningstar pulled away the curtain that separated Selene's living quarters from her office. "I heard something about my death?"

Isabelle stared. So did Morningstar. Black gaze met blue; and remained stuck there, as if they recognized something in each other, a connection that went beyond anything Selene would have expected.

What—how could they even know each other? Morningstar had been dead for *years* before Isabelle was born. There was no way they could recognize each other, no way that Morningstar should be paying attention to a minor Fallen of the House.

Emmanuelle laid a hand on Selene's shoulder, squeezed gently. "Do you know each other?" she asked.

Morningstar tore himself from his contemplation of Isabelle. "I don't remember," he said, thoughtfully. "Perhaps I did."

Isabelle didn't speak. At length, she shook her head. "I don't think so. But all the same . . ." She was silent, for a while. "I saw your corpse."

"Possibly." Morningstar shook his head. "I don't remember, you see."

But he'd remembered Selene. He'd lost everything else; most of the memories that would have made him more than this blank slate; but he had still recognized her.

"That's all very nice," Selene said, "but it doesn't help us."

"I'm not sure what we need help against," Isabelle said. "A ghost?"

"Ghosts can be exorcised." Morningstar lay back against one of the walls, his gaze blank, making merely a timid suggestion, so far from the maelstrom of power she had once known. He hadn't always been that way—back in a time when things had been simpler, easier, when the House had been prosperous; and when solutions had not required so much agonizing over what they could and couldn't do. There was a vise in Selene's chest, squeezing her heart to bloody shreds.

"Not so easily," Emmanuelle said. "And neither will what she summoned vanish."

"The Furies?" Isabelle asked.

"No, the Furies are dead," Emmanuelle said. "I was speaking of the tree choking the magic of the House."

"How do you stop a tree? Or a ghost?"

"You don't," Selene said. "Morningstar—"

"Yes?"

"You really don't remember, do you? What you did to Nightingale?"

Only polite interest from him, a raised eyebrow. Perhaps it did mean nothing to him, after all. Or perhaps it did, and there was so little emotion attached to it that he could so easily lie.

"It was done," Isabelle said. "Are we going to stand here debating the morality of it? At the time, you judged it right for the good of the House."

Another raised eyebrow. "No doubt."

The image of Asmodeus rose like a specter in Selene's mind, his eyes and the horn rim of his glasses sparkling in some unseen light. *Your master had many flaws, but he wasn't squeamish.*

I am not.

Then prove it to me.

They could stand all night discussing this, with no more progress— none of them, save perhaps Isabelle, would take the authority to make decisions. And it was the decision that mattered, not its rightness.

Selene took in a deep breath. "Emmanuelle, can you research exorcism? All the others, we're going into the East Wing, to see if we can stop the roots. I don't know what Nightingale's game is, but I won't let her swallow the House."

MADELEINE had expected to be shut into one of the cells: they'd existed back in Uphir's day; and she had no doubt Asmodeus would have kept them all. But Elphon merely showed her into a room on the first floor—one with a little private staircase leading into the depths of the House's huge garden. "Someone will be by later. I wouldn't try anything funny if I were you," he said. "Lord Asmodeus isn't known for his patience."

"Wait," Madeleine said.

Elphon turned, halfway to the door, politely waiting for her to speak. His face was blank, and there was no hint of recognition in his gaze. He didn't remember her. He would never remember her.

"Nothing," Madeleine said, slowly, carefully. "It's nothing." She'd have wept; but there were no more tears to be wrung out of her. Miracles didn't happen, did they?

"As you wish," Elphon said, bowing to her. "I'll leave you to speak to Lord Asmodeus."

And he was gone, leaving her alone in the room.

The House hadn't changed; or perhaps she didn't remember it well enough: it had been twenty years, after all, and she was no Fallen. The brain decayed; memories became as blurred as scenes seen through rain. The green wallpaper with its impressions of flowers was the same; the elegant Louis XV chairs were the same she'd once had in her rooms; and the covered bed with its elaborate curtains was, if not familiar, entirely in keeping with the rest of the room.

She was back.

There was no escaping that fact; or the memory of that car ride with Asmodeus, so close the stink of his perfume still clung to her clothes. Back, and powerless; and entirely at his mercy, a fact that no doubt amused him. Probably the only reason she was still alive.

A fit of coughing bent her double, left her gasping for breath; her lungs wrung out, emptied of everything except bitterness. She needed essence, needed its familiar warmth to keep away the memories, to smooth over the bare, inescapable fact that she was back in the last place in Paris she wanted to be; to keep her from imagining her future, which would be short and nasty and brutal.

Does it really matter? Your future was always short. You've always known that.

But there was the long, slow slide into an oblivion fueled by drugs—and—this. One of her choosing, the other one emphatically not.

Selene, no doubt, would have lectured her about the need to be strong, to keep her head. Madeleine wasn't Selene, and saw little point in any of this. This was Asmodeus's House; and there wasn't a corner of it he didn't master. He had hundreds of dependents, a hundred rooms like this one; and a vast reservoir of artifacts from his predecessors in addition to his own power.

She lay on the bed, and tried to sleep, to banish the smell of orange blossom and bergamot from her clothes; although she already knew both attempts were doomed to fail.

MAGIC didn't harm the roots. Fire did, but they immediately grew again, more numerous, as if they'd cut off the hydra's head. Emmanuelle suggested axes infused with angel breath: that worked better than fire, but with the same drawbacks.

And the tree fought back. Roots uncurled, far faster than anything vegetal had a right to—and strangled the unwary, or knocked them against the wall so hard their bones broke.

Selene lost two bodyguards, Solenne and Imadan; and Isabelle, reckless and heedless of the danger she put herself in, almost got herself killed.

In the end, nothing really seemed to make a dent in the inexorable engulfment of the House.

Selene stood in what had once been the entrance to the East Wing: the corridor was now a dense mass of roots and branches—not exactly inaccessible, but certainly not a part of the House anyone would run through.

She kept a wary eye on the labyrinth of roots blocking the corridor; but the tree appeared to be quiescent for once. Emmanuelle had theorized that it was most active at transition times: at twilight, or at dawn, or when the moon moved away from a quadrant of the sky into another. Which, as insights went, wasn't very helpful.

"Please tell me you've found something useful," she said to Emmanuelle, who only grimaced.

Morningstar hovered by—hesitant, ill at ease—even more useless than Isabelle, who didn't master her powers but didn't hesitate to use them. It broke her heart: he looked like him, and sometimes the odd mannerism would surface, but there was nothing left, not one useful memory, not one bit of deeper comprehension of magic, or of the predicament they found themselves in. "I can't exorcise her," Emmanuelle said. "I would need access to her grave for that."

Said grave was either in Hawthorn—where the chances of Asmodeus giving them access were so slim they might as well not exist—or in an unknown place in the city, wherever Hawthorn dumped its bodies—again, Asmodeus might know; and again, he would not tell them a thing.

"Morningstar?" She hoped—she prayed against all evidence—that there would be a miracle, that he would recall something of use. But there was nothing.

"I don't—"

"It's fine," Selene lied, swallowing the words like so many shards of glass. "We'll find another way."

"There is another way," Isabelle said, detaching herself from one of the walls. Disheveled and wild, she looked for a moment like one of the feral women from legend; and the radiance she cast flickered fast and out of control, from soft to almost blinding.

"I'm not sure I see one," Selene said. Something had changed in Isabelle; something that made her ill at ease, though she couldn't have told what.

Isabelle looked at Morningstar, who gazed steadily back at her. "You don't remember anything."

"No," Morningstar said, his voice holding nothing but mild, polite interest.

"I could fix that."

"You could—that's not possible!" Selene said. Spells that tinkered with the mind weren't *impossible*, per se. They were just very complex, and had a higher chance of frying a brain than actually working.

Isabelle smiled, as slow and as enigmatic as an Asian idol. "Why not?"

"Because—because it won't work," Selene said. "Because you'll damage his mind—" She stopped, before she could say "even further than it already is," but the words hung in the air, regardless.

Morningstar was looking curiously at Isabelle. "What makes you believe you can do that?"

Isabelle came closer to him; and bent, briefly, to whisper something in his ear. Morningstar didn't move; his face remained emotionless; but his hands clenched. "I see," he said.

Selene didn't. And didn't like it much, either. "Do tell."

Isabelle shrugged. "I learned a few things, that's all."

From Philippe and his mysterious magic, which made no sense to

Emmanuelle? Or from whatever had happened when she and Madeleine left the House, whatever conflagration had left Madeleine on a sickbed, Philippe missing, and Isabelle secretive and withdrawn?

"I don't think you should—" Selene said, but Isabelle had already put both hands on Morningstar's temples. "No!"

Neither her cry nor Emmanuelle's came soon enough. Light blazed, a radiance like the heart of the sun, so strong she had to close her eyes. When she opened them again, Isabelle stood in a circle of charred parquet; and Morningstar was stock-still, his face the color of bleached paper, his blue eyes as vacant as those of a corpse. Selene's arm completed the movement it had started, and pried Isabelle's hands from Morningstar: they were warm, quivering as if with fever. "Morningstar? Morningstar?"

His eyes swung to look at her, but life didn't come back into them. What had Isabelle done? How could she, heedless of everything, go blazing in, eager to number him once more among the dead? "If you have harmed him . . . ," Selene said to Isabelle, who only shook her head.

At length, Morningstar drew a deep, shuddering breath. Selene could almost hear his chest inflating, could almost trace every ounce of color coming back to his skin, every smidgeon of red flushing his cheeks. "Selene," he said. His eyes had unclouded; but they were still clear, guileless.

"Do you—" She forced herself to breathe through the obstruction in her throat. "Do you remember anything?"

"Images," Morningstar said, after a pause. "Memories, things that make no sense." He closed his eyes, opened them again—there was something in his face that hadn't been there before, a slightly harsher set to the boyish features. "No," he said. "I don't remember much that would be of use. Sorry."

Selene shook her head. "Forget it." She'd hoped, against all hope . . . But no, miracles didn't come to Fallen, not so easily. "We'll need to take another look at our options." She'd sent messengers to Minimes, one of her traditional allies; though she doubted anyone would come. Draken, Hell's Toll, Aiguillon—when these had fallen during the war, not a single House would have lifted a finger to help them. In the world of Houses, being vulnerable was merely a reason for people to abandon you, like rats fleeing a sinking ship—no, she had to be fair there. Had Minimes fallen so low, she would have looked the other way. Allies didn't mean friends. "And the tree?"

Emmanuelle's voice was grim. "I have no idea about the tree. Selene?"

"Yes?" Selene asked. "You're going to make a suggestion I won't like."

"You know me too well," Emmanuelle said.

"Of course."

Emmanuelle took a deep breath. "You should ask Philippe."

No. "Philippe is the one who got us here. Did you forget that?"

"No," Emmanuelle said, but she had forgotten. She'd forgotten those agonizing hours when she lay with labored breathing—when Selene wasn't sure if she'd lose her or the House first, when she'd only had Aragon's reports to track the progress of the infection. She'd forgotten, and forgiven. Emmanuelle had always been too nice.

And Selene wasn't. "He brought the Furies here, Emmanuelle. And he was the one who disturbed the crypt, which got this—this mess started." She wanted to say something other than "mess," some stronger word that would encompass the fear that gnawed at her entrails like a carrion eater, that would take her, unaware, in a moment when she'd felt herself safe, when she'd forgotten, for a bare minute, that the House was collapsing around them.

"Be fair. Asmodeus and Claire are equally responsible for this mess. And he was also the one who helped us figure out the identity of Nightingale. He has a connection to her—he could find her grave, if moved to it. Or give us another way to go around her."

Selene looked at the mass of roots that blocked the corridor—that spread through open doors, tearing holes through furniture, lifting wallpaper like snakes—was something moving, in the darkness? Branches and roots; and something deeper and darker, crouching behind it all like a spider in the center of a web? "We should head back to my office," she said. "But you know I can't countenance this."

Morningstar had moved; was leaning against one of the walls—he reached out, absentmindedly, as a root attempted to wrap itself around his wrist—and snapped it cleanly in two. The neighboring roots shuddered as if stung, and fell still; almost as though they'd decided he wasn't worth the trouble.

Something had changed. He was . . . stronger than he had been. But still not strong enough.

"I don't see how the situation can be made worse," Emmanuelle said.

Selene sighed. "That's because you lack imagination." They still stood. It was small and insignificant—and likely would become false within a week or so—but she clung to this like a lifeline. As long as they stood, there was hope.

IN the end, two guards came for her and took her through corridors, down a vast staircase that led back into the hall; and into the gardens.

In an era of charred trees and blackened skies, the gardens at Hawthorn were the pride of the House. The grass was emerald green; the trees in flower, with the sheen of rain-watered plants; and there were even birds gracefully alighting on the lakes and ponds—one could almost forget their torn feathers and dull eyes, and see a fraction of what Paris had been, before the war. Statues of pristine alabaster stood around the corners of impeccably trimmed hedges; and the gravel crunching under Madeleine's feet was the soft color of sand, with not a speck of ash or of magical residue to pollute it.

That hadn't changed, either. If not for the two thugs at her side, she could believe herself back in happier days; could remember Elphon catching water from one of the ponds deeper into the gardens. . . .

No. She would not go there.

At the bottom of a knoll was a circle of gravel, and at the center of the circle, a fountain depicting Poseidon's chariot emerging from the sea: the four horses surrounded by sprays, and the water glistening on the eyes of the statue, an unmistakable statement that the House of Hawthorn could afford to waste such a huge amount of clean drinking water to keep the gardens running.

Asmodeus was sitting on the rim of the basin. He was wearing a modern two-piece suit in the colors of Hawthorn: gray with silver stripes, and the tie a single splash of color at his throat, the vivid red of apples; a city man through and through, looking almost incongruous against the pastoral background of the gardens. Except, of course, that he still exuded the lazy grace of predators in the instant before they sprang.

"Ah, Madeleine." He gestured to the two guards. "Leave us, will you?"

On the rim of the fountain beside him was a spread-out cloth, a picnic blanket with a selection of things that wouldn't have looked out of place in the cells, knives and hooks and serrated blades, still encrusted with blood, and it didn't take much imagination to know what they would be used for—Madeleine just had to close her eyes. . . .

"Sit down, Madeleine."

Madeleine's hands were clenched, though she didn't remember how they got there; didn't even remember sitting, yet there she was on cold, harsh stone, her clothes soaked with frigid water like the touch of a drowned man.

"You've been uncharacteristically silent since your return," Asmodeus said.

Madeleine stared, obstinately, at the grass at her feet; but she could still feel his presence; could still smell the orange blossom and bergamot carried by the wind; could feel magic in the air between them; though he had no need of a spell to hold her, trembling and motionless, on the rim of the fountain.

He was silent, mercifully so—except that she could hear the sound of a blade, negligently scraping on stone—scratch, scratch, scratch, a sound that seemed to grow until it was her entire universe—each movement peeling her as raw as if it had been her skin under the knife, her muscles and veins laid bare to the water's biting kiss.

The last thing she wanted was to speak up, but he wouldn't be satisfied until she did. "What—what do you want?"

"Why, what has always been mine to take. Did you not know that?"

The knife was still moving; the stone still scraped raw. Madeleine tried to calm the trembling of her hands, and failed.

"No," she said. And, because she had nothing else to lose: "You have Elphon." She didn't need to look up to imagine his smile, lighting up his face like a boy's.

"You've noticed, haven't you? As loyal to me as if nothing had ever happened."

"Something happened." Madeleine laid her hands in her lap, tried not to think of the twinge of pain in her unhealed leg. "You killed him."

"I prefer to think of it as the result of an unfortunate picking of sides," Asmodeus said. "One cannot rise to the top of a House without bloodshed."

"You didn't have to rise to the top of the House!"

Silence; and a cold touch against her hand; and the smell of orange blossom, sickeningly close. Raising her gaze, she found him holding the knife against the back of her hand, driven down until he'd broken the skin. "You forget yourself," Asmodeus said. His hand, wrapped around the knife's blade, was utterly still; but why would he have trembled? "But never mind. It's not Elphon I am concerned about."

"Me?" Madeleine watched the blood—a vivid red, like Asmodeus's tie—smear itself against the paleness of her skin. She ought to have cared. She ought to have felt pain, but she was just so tired. "What could you possibly want with me, Asmodeus?"

"A washed-out alchemist addicted to angel essence?" He smiled at her shock. "Do credit me with a reasonable information network, Madeleine. You belong here. It's high time you came back to us."

As what, a corpse in a coffin? As a blank-minded, obedient fool like Elphon? But she'd known all along—Hawthorn, and Asmodeus, never let go of what was theirs—and what were twenty years to a Fallen, after all? "You might save yourself the trouble," she said. "Kill me and resurrect me, like Elphon."

"I would, if it worked on mortals." He smiled, again. "Which leaves me with . . . more prosaic tools." The knife tensed against her hand, but did not draw further blood.

"You ought to know that won't work," Madeleine said. She wished she had the confidence to believe that; and he knew it.

"You'd be surprised what does work. In the depths of pain and darkness, what kind of spars people can seize and never let go of . . ." Another sharp-toothed smile; and then, to her surprise, the knife withdrew. "But I have other means."

Magic? Could he use a spell to render her docile? Not impossible, after all; there were precedents. . . .

But he cast no spells. He didn't move. She felt the air between them fill up with magic, with radiance and warmth like a summer storm; a feeling she remembered from her meeting with Morningstar; that sense of vast insignificance and terrible satisfaction at the same time, that transcending joy that someone like him should have noticed someone like her . . .

No.

"A truth like a salted knife's blade . . . Tell me, Madeleine, does your calf still pain you?"

Madeleine's hand moved toward her leg; stopped.

Asmodeus bent forward, the warmth becoming so strong it was almost unbearable. "I know every wound you bear from that night, Madeleine—the knuckle-dusters that shattered your ribs, here and here and here . . ." His hand lingered, quite softly, on her three broken ribs, the ones that hadn't quite healed, that would never heal. ". . . the knife that slipped into your calf, here and here"—a touch on the scars of her calves, heedless to the trembling in her entire body—to have that obscene parody of love, of friendship that wouldn't stop—to *know* he wouldn't stop, even and especially if she said anything, the effort of holding herself silent and still through her rising nausea—"and the other cuts, the ones on your arms and chest, the ones that healed"—a touch here, a touch here and there; his hand, with fingernails as sharp as a blade, resting on her chest, just above the heart. "You haven't asked me how I know."

She spoke, dragging her voice from the faraway past. "Why would I?"

"Oh, Madeleine." Asmodeus shook his head. He didn't withdraw, or make any effort to move his hand. "It was a dark, lonely night, and the citizens of Paris were keeping their heads down, as they always do when it's obviously House business."

"Someone was there," Madeleine said. If she moved, if she pulled away from him, would he drive that knife into her chest? And would it matter quite so much? Perhaps that was the cleaner ending, after all, the death she'd craved for all of twenty years. "What does it matter, Asmodeus?" She didn't say she had no more patience or fortitude for his games, but if she had broadcast the thought, it would have been a scream.

"Because *I* was there," Asmodeus said.

"I don't understand."

"You heard me quite correctly. I was there. I carried you, all the way into Silverspires."

"That was—that's a lie," she said, more sharply than she'd meant to. "Morningstar—"

Asmodeus's laughter was darkly amused. "Morningstar was away. Do you really think he came halfway across the city to find you dying on the cobblestones? Why? Because he smiled to you once, gave you the charm treatment? He was like that with everyone. He wouldn't have known you two seconds after his back was turned."

He had been kind to her; had offered her the asylum of the House—no, no, that wasn't it—memory, merciless, conjured the scene again; Morningstar's distant, distracted courtesy.

"This is the first and greatest of Houses, Lady Madeleine. The safest place in Paris."

A boast, nothing more: as Asmodeus had said, a grandiloquent statement of pride in himself, in his House.

No. No. That couldn't be.

She'd heard—footsteps—she'd felt—the warmth of magic—hands, taking her, the grunt as her body shifted and he bore her full weight— and the world spinning and fading into darkness. "No," she said. "No." *That's a lie,* she wanted to say, but what reason would he have for lying?

"You were in Hawthorn," she said.

Asmodeus still hadn't moved. His eyes behind the horn-rimmed glasses were unreadable. "You remember nothing, do you? It was almost dawn when I found you, Madeleine. It was over by then, in Hawthorn; had been, for a long time. I was head of the House." He said it quietly, calmly, with no inflection to his voice; not even pride.

"Why would you—"

"I had business. In Silverspires. Did you never wonder why you had lost the link to Hawthorn?"

"I—" Madeleine took in a deep, trembling breath. "Uphir died—"

"Oh, Madeleine. Do you think it's that easy to break a link to a House? I broke it—before I dropped you off."

"I don't understand," Madeleine said again. Stupidly, like a lost child. "Why would you—" *Why would you carry me to Silverspires? Why would you let me live?*

His smile was wide, dazzling. "Call it . . . a whim. Or a loan, for safekeeping, while I purged the House of all remnants of Uphir's days. But all loans are called, in time. All whims run their course."

He withdrew, but the feel of his hand on her chest remained, sharp and wounding and *God, oh God* . . .

She was going to be sick, this time: the cough was welling up in her lungs; and she was on her knees in the damp grass, not sure if she was vomiting or coughing—breathing hard when she was done, nauseated and drained and utterly unable to move. "Ah yes. The little matter of the angel essence. We'll have to do something about that. Can't have you addicted this badly."

"Why—" Madeleine whispered. He shouldn't have heard her, but of course he did. Of course he always did.

"To remind you," Asmodeus said. "That you owe nothing to Silverspires, or to Morningstar. Your place is here, Madeleine. It's high time you accepted it."

TWENTY-ONE
For the Good of the House

SELENE sat in her office, staring at the wall. In her mind, low-key yet inescapable, the melody of the House's destruction played itself through, from its insignificant beginnings to where they stood now, beleaguered and besieged.

They had lost the East Wing, and the North Wing; and in the Hôtel-Dieu Aragon's office was a mass of impassable roots. On the upper floors, branches and leaves were sprouting, a verdant mass that wouldn't have looked out of place in a tropical country. In the buildings that remained, people were jammed together, three or more to rooms that hadn't seen use in decades or centuries: the children sleeping on unrolled mats on the floors of sitting rooms, the corridors a mass of refugees, the ballrooms hastily rearranged to accommodate makeshift tents.

Aragon had muttered something about working conditions, and had left. He might be back; or he might not: after all, he wasn't a dependent of the House, merely doing them a favor in the name of some long-forgotten debt to Morningstar.

Emmanuelle came in; and Isabelle, and Javier: all of them looking as though they had not managed a night's sleep. They probably hadn't.

"Morningstar?" she asked.

Javier shrugged. "He said he had something to do, and that he would come by later."

Selene nodded. She wasn't sure she could look Morningstar in the eye these days—because she'd lost him, because she was losing his House; because, if she'd had any thoughts to spare, she would have wept, for how far he had diminished from the Fallen she had known.

There were whispers, of what Morningstar's return meant; but no time to prevent their spreading, or to coach people into an acceptance not tinged with fear. She would have to see to it later, if there was a later. If there was a House by then.

How could this have happened? Weeks before, they'd been a proud House: teetering, like all other Houses, on the edge of an abyss opened by the war, but it was nothing that should have worried them. And yet. And yet . . .

"Tell me," she said to Emmanuelle.

Emmanuelle shook her head. "I don't have much else to report. You know about the North Wing."

"All too well," Selene said, wryly. "And the Hôtel-Dieu. And the parvis?"

"That's still free of roots," Javier said, pale and with the taut features of the sleepless. "They just might not like sunlight."

They might as well have had faith and believed that God and His angels would swoop down and save them. Selene bit her lips to prevent the words from escaping them. They did not need, or deserve, her sarcasm.

"I don't have any artifacts left," Isabelle said, in the silence.

"I'll have every Fallen drop by the laboratory, later."

Isabelle nodded, but she didn't look happy. Probably worried raw, like all of them: she was the closest thing to an alchemist the House had, and woefully untrained, with one dead predecessor and one banished one.

"You're doing great work," Selene said, and it wasn't a lie. Isabelle was reckless, and ill inclined to take advice, but she seemed to have come into her powers at last—they wouldn't have made it this far without her.

A knock at the door heralded the arrival of Morningstar: he came holding a wrapped package that was twice as large as him, and half as tall again. "What is that?" Selene asked, and then Morningstar let fall the cloth that served as a wrapper, and she forgot she had ever asked.

Once, the head of House Silverspires had had wings, and a sword. Both had been lost when he vanished—gone with him, Selene had assumed—what would have been the point of looking for them, when only he had known how to wield them?

Beside her, Emmanuelle drew a sharp, wounding breath. "I didn't think—" she said, softly, slowly.

The wings were huge, and unadorned: they were not a toy or an accessory, but the rawest embodiment of a weapon; their serrated edges catching the light like the blades of scimitars: it was all too easy to imagine the wearer lunging, shoulder extended forward; and the sound of flesh tearing in the wake of a wing's passage.

Morningstar laid them on the floor, gently, keeping only the matching bladed gauntlets in his hands. They looked like the spines of a fish, except that was a faintly ridiculous comparison, and there was nothing faint or ridiculous about those, either. Everything about them seemed to hunger for blood. "I remembered," he said. "I hid them once. . . ." He frowned; and for a bare moment he looked like his old self again, tall and fair and terrible to behold; and so achingly familiar Selene's world blurred around her. "Buried them in the earth for safekeeping, so that no one would lay claim to what was mine." And then the moment was gone, and he was just a newly born Fallen, bewildered and lost—and Selene blinked back her tears. It was a hard thing, to stand by the side of the dead.

"And the sword?" Emmanuelle asked, slowly, softly.

"The sword wasn't there," Morningstar said. He frowned, again. "It doesn't matter."

It did matter, because they would need to find it eventually, to know if it was merely Morningstar not remembering what he'd done with it, or someone else moving it; but right now, they didn't have the time. . . .

"These will cut through anything, if properly used," Morningstar said.

Properly used. With muscles that only a Fallen could have: muscles, unused in years or decades or centuries, that still remembered what it meant to fly. "You remember?" Selene asked, not daring to hope.

"Some," Morningstar said, curtly. Beside him, Isabelle was watching the wings, fascinated; reaching out to touch them, and withdrawing as if their mere sharpness had drawn blood. "I'm not sure it will be enough."

"It won't be," Emmanuelle said, gently. She pushed aside a mahogany chair to kneel by the wings; like Isabelle before her, she ran a finger on the serrated edges, heedless of the risk—Selene fought the urge to snatch her away, before she cut herself too deeply for mending. "Don't you remember, Selene? They were infused with magic, once."

Oh yes. Like Morningstar, they had radiated the terrible warmth of raw power: what else could they have done, bathed day after day in his presence?

"It's all gone," Emmanuelle said.

"Then we'll give breath, and whatever else is needed," Selene said. "Isabelle—"

"I can't!" Isabelle's eyes were wide; her words halfway between a protest and a disappointed cry. "I'm no alchemist."

God, the last thing they needed was her falling to pieces. Selene said, gently, "You were my choice, and the House's choice. You have the skills."

"I don't. We all know I don't. It was meant to be Oris, except that he died, and that left only me. There was no time, Selene." It wasn't despair, after all; merely a bald statement of fact. "Madeleine could—"

"Madeleine is no longer part of this House," Selene said, more sharply than she'd intended to. She had no desire to be reminded of her failure—she probably wouldn't have been able to stop Madeleine's addiction, but she could have found out earlier. She could have avoided Claire using it against her, at a time when the House was already in disarray. Her fault. "She's probably part of Hawthorn again, by now, if Choérine is right." Certainly she had left at the same time as the Hawthorn delegation, and in the company of Asmodeus and his henchmen.

"I doubt by choice," Emmanuelle said dryly.

Selene didn't say anything. Whether it was by choice or not, there was nothing she could do for Madeleine. The House was certainly not in a position to go making demands of anyone. And she had abdicated responsibility for Madeleine. She had to remember that. If she did not stand by her decisions, who would? "Whatever the case," she said. "We can discuss this when we survive. *If* we survive. Isabelle, I'm sorry. I know you deserved more time. I know you didn't have it, but right now you're my only choice, and our only hope."

Isabelle said nothing. She nodded at last, but didn't sound remotely happy. "I'll try," she said. "Will that do?"

As long as she didn't do anything rash. Selene made a mental note to ask Emmanuelle or Javier to keep an eye on her. "As to the rest—" She took a deep, deep breath, not looking at Morningstar. One had to recognize when one was beaten, and plan accordingly. "I'm sorry it has come to this, but we will have to evacuate the North Wing as well, and regroup around here."

Here. Her office. Her living quarters. The center of the House; and, it seemed, the place where they would make their last-ditch attempt to defeat Nightingale's curse.

PHILIPPE'S return to the gang had been anticlimactic. Bloody Jeanne had smiled, and hugged him; though perfunctorily, with an expression that suggested she would stick him in the ribs if it served her purposes. Baptiste and Alex had been more circumspect, but everyone had seemed almost happy to have him back. It ought to have touched him; or to make him feel wary, or something—anything, but it didn't.

He sat down in the little courtyard at the back of the shop, watching the flowers on the arbor, as if, with enough attention, he still had time enough to watch them grow: he had done this once, in another lifetime, in another land; but this felt so far behind him it might as well be dead.

Aragon had been right: for him, there would be no return to Annam. That dream was gone, nipped in the bud before it could ever blossom; crushed in the egg before it could stretch legs or wings.

"You look thoughtful," Ninon said. She slid down, easily, by his side, all loose limbs and easy smiles. "You've hardly said a word since you came back."

"Yeah, I know," Philippe said.

"Is it because of what happened in the Grands Magasins?" She bit her lips. "I shouldn't have left you behind—but I thought you were dead. I—"

"It doesn't matter," Philippe said. He was thinking of Silverspires; of Isabelle, restless and angry, somewhere at the back of his mind. Why could he not be done with her; with the continual, distant awareness of where she was, of the power running red-hot through her—through her bones and her lungs and every sinew of her body? He could feel her; could almost taste her worry about the House, about Selene— about Madeleine. There was something about Madeleine; a glimpse of a fear he couldn't quite focus on.

He . . . he had left her behind; had left the House and its buried darkness behind—and yet, he kept thinking about her—kept expecting her to walk up to him, to reminisce about Annam with him—to argue with him about what he needed, about what he ought to do in that infuriatingly direct way of hers. He . . .

It was none of his business. The House was none of his business. They would fail, and fall, because ghosts like Nightingale couldn't be stopped; because what fueled her was nothing human or Fallen, just the relentless anger and love she'd felt when she died. For this, there was no exorcism; merely prayers to guide her to rebirth, and a better life—and those would have required a monk, or a priest; and he was neither. He owed them nothing, save his stiffened hand, save the memory of a night when he had been taken apart piece by piece—the same thing that had happened to Nightingale in Hawthorn.

Most of all, he owed Isabelle nothing. She had chosen, too; chosen the House and its darkness; the House and the secrets that would choke it—Morningstar's grisly and unjustifiable legacy. They were worlds apart now; in fact, they had always been. He'd been a fool to hope otherwise.

He . . . It had all made sense, back at the House, back within its oppressive boundaries, when all he could think of was how fast to leave it; but now he sat outside, under overcast skies—breathing in the smell of flowers, with Ninon worriedly looking at him, trying to apologize for leaving him behind—when he was the one who had left Isabelle behind. . . .

"Philippe? Philippe!"

But he didn't need to close his eyes to guess at the silhouette of Morningstar, sitting beneath the arbor; didn't need to meditate to feel the darkness trapped within his chest, the remnants of the curse even Chung Thoai hadn't been able to banish.

"If you go back, you will die."

He had gone back, and got out, and he was still alive.

He ought to stay out; to rebuild whatever life he could out of the shattered remnants of his time in Silverspires; to learn as much as he could from this experience, to make of himself a living blade that nothing and no one could harm. He should forget Isabelle, forget her betrayed look as he left her, her presence at the back of his mind like a wound that wouldn't close. . . .

Someone was shaking him; Ninon, he realized with a start. "You haven't spoken for an hour," she said. "Just staring off at the sky. . . ." She shook her head. "What did they *do* to you in that House, Philippe?"

"You wouldn't understand."

That clearly stung. "Try me."

He opened his mouth, saw only Morningstar's bottomless eyes— felt a twinge of pain in the hand that Asmodeus had disjointed; and remembered the slimy feel of shadows sliding across bare walls, across the facets of crystal glasses—and, on his skin, Samariel's heavy breath, whispering the spell that had set him free. No words came out. "I need to go for a walk. Sorry."

"Philippe!"

Outside, it was no better. The pall of pollution seemed to hang heavier on La Goutte d'Or, or perhaps it was just him, feeling sweat run down his body in rivulets. Perhaps he was the only one with that hardening mixture of panic and resolution within him; who couldn't tell, anymore, if it belonged to Isabelle or to him.

Stay out of this. It was a House struggle, like House Draken, and he'd lost enough to Draken and Draken's fall; it was a ghost more powerful than him, a House that he had no cause to love. *Keep your head down.* Rebuild, always with the darkness at his back, haunting him as surely as it haunted House Silverspires. Always, with the memory of Isabelle—of stepping away from her, and leaving her to fend for herself—to die—in the storm that was engulfing Silverspires.

He couldn't do it. He couldn't be free of her. He—

He had to go back.

MADELEINE sat in the gardens, watching water pool on the rim of the fountain. If she closed her eyes, she would see Asmodeus again; feel the heat of his radiance on her hands, hear his voice again, level and emotionless, calmly stating the obvious.

A truth like a salted knife's blade . . .

Do you really think he came halfway across the city to find you dying on the cobblestones?

She had believed; or had wanted to believe, so much; that she had been chosen by Morningstar himself, that her presence in Silverspires had meaning. That there was safety there, yes—that it was the oldest House—but that he had known. That he had extended his hand as his last act in this world.

And it was a lie. It wasn't kindness that had saved her, but merely a whim. Worse than that; a whim of the Fallen who had killed Uphir, who had killed Elphon—who had destroyed her world—and who had decided, because it cost him nothing, that he could spare her life.

It would cost her nothing to deny him his victory.

A knife's blade, or a noose, or a pool of water: so many ways she could leave. He might stop her once, or twice, but he couldn't keep her forever. In the end, she would win.

No one would miss her. Selene would be glad to be rid of her, and the House at Silverspires had already forgotten her. In a way, the sentence had already been passed, long ago, her twenty years nothing more than suspended time, a miracle that had had no right to exist. No one would—Isabelle would weep. But no, Isabelle was young, and naive—give her a few centuries, and she'd be as hard as Selene.

She stared at the water, knowing she didn't have the courage for any of this. If it had been essence, perhaps she'd have gone on, slowly killing herself. But every other solution required fortitude she didn't have.

In this, as well, she was a failure.

SELENE was staring at the wings, wrapped in a corner of her office where Isabelle had left them. She'd looked distinctly unhappy, muttering something about shoddy work; and had left abruptly. Even for her, that had been beyond politeness. Whatever the case, it was done. The wings were now infused with magic; with the combined breaths of every Fallen in the House from Choérine to Alcestis to Morningstar—God grant that it would be enough, though she knew all too well the futility of prayers for such as she. Now all that remained was . . .

Her thoughts, as usual, drew back from the abyss: she knew what had to be done, the only thing that they could do, but . . .

"Selene?"

"Come in," she said.

It was Emmanuelle, dressed in a simple white cotton tunic that set off the darkness of her skin. "There's a sprig of green just around the corridor."

"I know." And, more softly: "I will give the order to evacuate this wing. And I will go with them."

"The parvis?" Emmanuelle asked.

"Yes." There was no choice. Because a House was not merely a fortress of spells and wards, but a collection of dependents, and she couldn't wait for them to be picked off one by one. The parvis remained clear of roots; and yet still within the protection of the wards: that was where she would tell them to assemble, Javier and Choérine and Gauthier and Geneviève and all the others, from the youngest children to the eldest mortals, grown old in the service of the House. And she would go with them; because it was more important that someone defend them than a last-ditch, desperate attempt to stop a ghost who had almost already won.

She had thought herself unworthy as the head of the House; she hadn't expected to be the one who saw its demise. Unless . . . Unless.

Morningstar was behind Emmanuelle, watching the office with bright, curious eyes. Selene looked away, unable to meet his gaze. "It doesn't matter, Selene," Emmanuelle said. She reached out, but Selene evaded her grasp.

"You didn't come here for that, did you?"

"Oh no," Emmanuelle said. "I came to tell you I'd found something."

"Nightingale's grave?"

Emmanuelle grimaced. She pulled one of the chairs to her: one of the old Louis XV ones, with a pattern of embroidered flowers on red suede. "Forget the exorcism," she said. "A ghost like this, with this kind of power, enough to summon the Furies in the hour of her death . . . you can't exorcise, not that simply. But you can destroy her curse."

"How?"

Emmanuelle bit her lip. "I know what kind of tree this is, Selene. It's a banyan."

"And—?" The name meant nothing to Selene.

"It's a tree from the tropics. He was, after all, the catalyst for the spell—it quite probably drew from his memories."

Selene scowled, but forced herself to listen. Emmanuelle regularly forgot how much the subject of Philippe was a sore point.

"The point is, it's a strangler tree. Starts as a seed borne by the wind into a tree's branches, and then extends roots until the tree it encases shrivels and dies."

Just like Silverspires. Selene shivered. "I don't want to think on that." She shook her head. That was childish, and beneath her. "How do you destroy a banyan, then?"

"Destroy its roots," Emmanuelle said. "But most of all—because this is no ordinary banyan, Selene—there is a place that's of particular significance."

"Which one?"

"The hollow," Emmanuelle said. "The place left by the encased tree when it dies. You could say that's the banyan's secret. In the Far East, they say that's where the spirits of the tree reside."

In the Far East . . . Perhaps they should have found Philippe in the end; but no, she didn't want to think on Philippe. It was only because of him that they were here.

Because of him, and Morningstar, a treacherous voice whispered in her mind. *If he had not betrayed Nightingale . . .*

But no, she couldn't think that: because, without Morningstar, there would be no Silverspires, no refuge in Notre-Dame. He had done what was necessary to maintain the House, and so would she, if it came to that. Because it was her duty as head of the House. Because the Fallen now staring at her, puzzled and without any comprehension, was nothing like the distant, radiant head of the House; the powerful magic wielder who had taught her, who had worn wings as a reminder that he was the only Fallen who had dared to wear what they had been stripped of; who had dared to use it as a weapon.

"The hollow," she said. "What about it?"

Emmanuelle handed her something, which she almost dropped, because the malevolence contained within was almost palpable. But she wasn't about to be defeated by a mere artifact. "A mirror," she said, aloud. Made of obsidian and not glass, an odd affectation that placed it somewhere two centuries ago, perhaps? When anything from the New World had still been new and fascinating.

"Isabelle gave me this," Emmanuelle said. "She says she and Philippe found it, and that it's what started it all."

Selene closed her eyes. "The source of the curse?" She didn't ask whether Isabelle could be trusted; how the loyalties she still very obviously held both for Philippe and for Madeleine impacted on this. She *had* to trust Isabelle, because she had no other choice. "You mean to destroy it?"

"Symbolically," Emmanuelle said. Her face was set. "In a place of power, in the hollow of the banyan. If that doesn't work—"

If that didn't work, then they'd all be out of a House, but it was all they already faced. "Even if you could get there—" Selene's lips moved, silently, as she contemplated the consequences. "She will be there, won't she? You said it was the place of the spirits." Of ghosts; and of the restless, unavenged dead. "Waiting." And Selene doubted it would be easy to defeat her. The Furies might be gone, but Nightingale would have other tricks up her sleeves.

"Nightingale?" Emmanuelle nodded. "That's almost certain. I haven't found a solution to distract her."

Selene turned her gaze to Emmanuelle, resolutely; refusing to stare at Morningstar or at the wings that so fascinated him. "I have," she said, slowly, carefully.

They were his weapon, and he had retained the mastery of it. What they cut would not regrow—she knew it in her heart of hearts. And, more important, he was the only one who could provide what they so desperately needed.

A distraction.

"Morningstar?"

"Yes?" Faint bewilderment, nothing more, in the voice. Isabelle might have unlocked some memories, but he didn't know; he couldn't know what it had been like, when he was head of the House.

She thought of Asmodeus, telling her she was too squeamish to be head of the House; and of the enormity of what she was about to do.

They barely had had time to get used to his presence again, and here she was: a jumped-up apprentice who had become head of the House only because everyone else had died or disappeared, and she would dare . . .

She had to. It was the only choice. "You have to go," she said to Morningstar. "It's what you started. It's you who should fix it."

Beside her, Emmanuelle took a deep, shocked breath; held it. "You know—" she started, and Selene squeezed her shoulder so hard that Emmanuelle gasped. *Not now,* she mouthed.

Morningstar's face was puzzled. "Go where?"

"Inside," Selene said. She looked up at last. There was only guileless innocence in his blue eyes, and she tried to swallow past the salty taste in her mouth. "I need you to open the way to the banyan's heart. They're your wings. You're the one who should wield them."

Morningstar looked puzzled—for a moment she thought he would see it; that he would comprehend the magnitude of what she had just done, but he simply nodded. "I see. Is there no one else?"

"You're the most powerful Fallen we have," Selene said, simply; the lie tasting like ashes on her tongue. He *was* the most powerful, but also the most naive, the one who couldn't master his own powers. He was the one they could spare. "We need you."

Surely he wouldn't believe that—who did? Surely . . .

But he merely nodded; and she knew, then, that her old master was dead and buried; that she had already grieved for him in the crypt beneath the chapel; and that there would be no return. "I'm honored by your trust."

Emmanuelle spoke up, at last, her voice as dry as dust. "Selene— you'll still need someone—"

"I know," Selene said.

"You can't go," Emmanuelle said. "I'll do it."

Selene shook her head. "I'll find Isabelle. Or someone else." Someone powerful, someone else they could spare—as if there was such a thing. "I'll send them right after you," she said to Morningstar.

It was enough. It would be enough. Nightingale thought Morningstar was dead; taken away by the Furies. She would be surprised; and they would have a chance.

A small, insignificant chance they'd need to grasp in the moment it was offered; but it would be more than anything they'd had so far.

Morningstar shrugged. "Don't wait too long."

"I know," Selene said.

Emmanuelle closed her eyes. "Isabelle isn't on the grounds right now."

"What—?" God, not another loose cannon somewhere. She was tired of dealing with those. "Does no one in this House know how to obey orders?"

"It's a House, not an army," Emmanuelle said. But then her face grew more serious. "I could go."

"That's out of the question."

"I can do my duty to the House, just as you do."

No. She had lost the House, or almost as good as; she wasn't going to lose Emmanuelle as well. It was selfish and ill-placed, and she was aware that she would have sent Emmanuelle if there had been no one else, but in this case . . . "Locate Isabelle, wherever she went; tell her she is to come to Silverspires, immediately."

"I will. But if she doesn't come back in time . . ."

"Let's not talk about it," Selene said.

"As you wish," Emmanuelle said, but she sounded dubious. And disappointed. Selene knew the feeling: powerlessness, slowly watching the House being choked to death. For once, they could do something— even if it was such a stab in the dark, even if it was just a likelihood of success rather than a certainty. . . .

She watched Morningstar heft the wings; and slowly and awkwardly adjust them onto his back; watched him assay a few thrusts here and there: they were astonishingly graceful, proving that the body, if not the mind, remembered something of what it had been before. She could have looked away, but she didn't.

After all, she'd just sacrificed him, as callously as he'd once sacrificed Nightingale.

You'd be happy, she whispered to the memory of Asmodeus. *I have taken the decisions that needed to be taken, for the safeguarding of the House.*

And, in her mind, Asmodeus merely smiled, showing his pointed white teeth; and said nothing.

TWENTY-TWO
MORNINGSTAR'S HEIR

MADELEINE didn't know what she'd expected when Asmodeus summoned her again, but she certainly hadn't bargained for Isabelle.

They were in a room of the House that she couldn't place, a sitting room with a harp and pale green conversation seats. It certainly wasn't part of Asmodeus's quarters, merely a place he had chosen to talk to his current guest; by the looks of it, trying to make it as uncomfortable as possible for her, giving her a metal chair with a high back, set in the middle of unadorned parquet floor. He lounged, as satisfied as ever, in a much more comfortable chair, his hands gracefully resting on the teak desk in front of him.

Something was wrong with him, though: it took Madeleine a moment to realize that the unreadable expression on his face was as close as he would ever come to showing shock.

Isabelle, by contrast, looked utterly out of place; and yet not—radiating a magic that had passed beyond Asmodeus's reach long, long ago. Something had changed; or perhaps it was something that had always been there: a harshness to the planes of her face, coalescing into sharp focus through the last few days. "You have some nerve," Asmodeus said, softly, "walking in here and asking me this."

Isabelle smiled; a sharp, wounding expression that Madeleine had never seen on her. "What bothers you so? It's business between Houses."

At length, he raised his eyes to Madeleine; pinned her where she stood, fighting the urge to turn away, the rising nausea in her throat. "You are aware," he said, slowly, softly, "that to bargain from a position of weakness is demonstrably inefficient."

"Weakness?"

"Your House collapses, even as we speak." Asmodeus did not even smile. "Morningstar's little schemes have finally borne fruit; and behold, it's as rotten as the heart of Silverspires."

"Do you truly think there is a House whose heart is not rotten?" Isabelle didn't look at Madeleine. She sounded—old, weary, cynical; Madeleine ached to wrap her into her arms, to tell her everything was going to be all right. But of course it was too late; had been too late for a long while.

Asmodeus laughed. "Of course not. We are all equal, are we not? One day, the many schemes of Hawthorn might bear the same kind of fruit as Silverspires'. But I would be a fool to intervene while a rival is removed."

"Only if you're sure that's how things will work out." Isabelle smoothed her silk skirt, with that same smile that was like a knife twist in Madeleine's heart. "If we should survive, in any fashion—" She let the words hang in the air for a bare moment. "—then we would remember those who helped us in our hour of need."

"Your survival is unlikely," Asmodeus said, dryly.

"But then again, I'm not asking you for much, am I?"

Asmodeus's eyes had not moved; they were still on Madeleine, with a peculiar expression she could not name. "I went to some trouble to recover her," he said, still not talking to her. "It wasn't to let her go at the slightest threat."

"Do you fear she'd never return?"

Her. They were talking about her. Madeleine turned her eyes from Asmodeus's horn-rimmed gaze, and took a deep breath, trying to steady herself. Isabelle had come back for her. She had—"I know she wouldn't," Asmodeus said. "Would you, Madeleine?"

She didn't know what was expected of her; what would help, what would hinder Isabelle. Negotiations had never been her strong suit, and she struggled to understand most of the undercurrents in the scene before her. Asmodeus's fingers drummed, lightly, on the surface of the desk.

"Answer me." The voice was light; the threat unmistakable.

She ought to have lied; but she couldn't. Nothing but the truth would come, springing from some deep place, as uncontrollable as the first flow of a spring. "I'm not your toy. I'm not your whim or your project. You spared my life; that doesn't mean you own it." She was angry, and frightened; and she wasn't even sure if she ought to return to Silverspires; to a House that wasn't hers, that might well be fading away—once her perfect refuge, her dying place, her quiet and undisturbed grave.

There was silence, in the wake of her words. She turned her head, slightly: Asmodeus was watching her with the same faint, amused smile on his face. Isabelle might surprise him; but it seemed Madeleine didn't—couldn't. *You don't own me,* she repeated to herself, and wasn't sure how much of that could be true.

"Commendable," Asmodeus said, "but I own the keys to your jail. And did you truly think that Selene didn't own you? We're all, in the end, the toys of someone else."

"And whose toy are you?" The words were out of her mouth before she could stop them.

Asmodeus raised an eyebrow, but didn't flinch. "Samariel's, once. Hawthorn's, once and now and always." His voice was toneless; Samariel's name barely inflected. Had he taken another lover? It didn't sound as though he had. Perhaps in his own, twisted way, he had genuinely cared for the other Fallen; enough to still grieve. But she couldn't afford to think of him that way.

"And the city's?" Isabelle asked, softly. "Do you even know why Silverspires is falling?"

"I suspect," he said. "But it is of no matter."

"Of no matter." Madeleine laughed, bitterly. "Morningstar's little schemes, as you call them, involved Hawthorn. She died in Hawthorn, didn't she? Morningstar's betrayed apprentice, to pay the price of a treaty. Whose hand struck the blow?"

Asmodeus raised an eyebrow. "Before my time, I'm afraid. Uphir's, perhaps. But I would not have shied from it. I told Selene as much already: House business is not for the squeamish. If you have no heart for it, then do not rise so high."

How could he—how could he sit there and say this to her face, knowing what he had done? "That's not my point," Madeleine said softly. "You should ask yourself what will happen should Silverspires fall. Do you think vengeance will stop at our doors?"

"No longer your doors. You keep forgetting you're no longer part of Silverspires," Asmodeus said; but it was reflex. At length, he took his glasses, and carefully wiped them clean. "I should think we are adequately protected; and while the points you make are valid, I don't find them quite compelling enough, I'm afraid." He turned again toward Isabelle; smiled: a thin line that had nothing of amusement in it. "I would suggest you leave, and return to your House, while there is still a House to save."

Isabelle bit her lip. "I see," she said. She rose, making her way toward the door—Madeleine's heart sinking with every step she took, watching the only miracle that would have freed her from Hawthorn leaving. At the door, Isabelle turned, slowly, and stared at Madeleine. There was a light in her eyes: something ancient and fey, and wholly unlike the Fallen Madeleine remembered. "Asmodeus?"

Asmodeus looked up, mildly curious; but then something hardened in his face, and he stared at her; the light from her body glinted on the rim and arms of his glasses. "Yes?"

"Uphir was a fool, and so are you. You remember a day long gone by, don't you?"

"Do tell," Asmodeus said, softly; but he no longer looked flippant or sardonic. What had been so frightening about Isabelle's words?

"Do you truly wish to antagonize me, kinsman?"

Madeleine had never heard anyone call Asmodeus "kinsman," especially not with that derisive familiarity. For a moment she thought Asmodeus was going to strike Isabelle down where she stood, that he'd find a knife or some magic and drive it all the way into her heart; but that didn't happen. He sat stock-still, staring at Isabelle. At length, he said, "So you set yourself up as his heir, do you? That's a dangerous position to occupy."

Isabelle stood, framed in the doorway, limned in an old, terrible light that haloed her dark hair, and drew the shadows of great wings over her shoulders—surely . . . Surely that was impossible. "I don't set myself up as anything, save that which I already am. But you would do well to remember that I have survived this far."

"Indeed." There was cutting irony in Asmodeus's voice. "Very little of it being my doing, I should say." He looked at Madeleine again. "I won't release her, and you know it as well as I do. It's high time Hawthorn got back what is due to it. But let's talk."

"There is no talk." Isabelle's face was serene, otherworldly so. They were going to fight. Here, now, in this room, in the heart of Asmodeus's and Hawthorn's power.

Madeleine, struggling for breath, found only a memory of what Asmodeus had said, tumbling over and over in the emptiness of her mind like a dust ball adrift in a storm. "Call it a loan," she whispered.

"Of twenty more years? I think not."

"A day. A week. What would satisfy you, Asmodeus? I will return. As you pointed out—I have no House of my own anymore."

A silence; and his presence at her elbow, strong and nauseating, the smell of orange blossom and bergamot as overwhelming as always. "You're wrong." Arms, encircling her but not touching her; his fingers on her hand, over the scab from his earlier knife stroke—warm, suffocating skin; she would have pulled away, but he held her, effortlessly—a touch of warmth, and suddenly she was part of Hawthorn again, the House's magic a muted rhythm in her mind; the presence of Asmodeus like the points of a thorn tree—both in her mind and against her body. She pulled away, spluttering—retching, still feeling his touch on her skin like a pollution. "Who gave you the right—"

He smiled; a knife's width between two bloodred lips. "I take it. Have you understood nothing about me yet, Madeleine? You were the one who promised me a return. I'm merely giving you now what you would have had then."

Hawthorn was fast and impatient, nothing like the steady, reassuring presence of Silverspires, the background to her life for the past twenty years. Had it always been like that? She didn't even remember losing her link to Hawthorn—she remembered kneeling in front of Selene, being welcomed into Silverspires; but with the gloss of things long past, almost as if it had happened to someone else.

Asmodeus smiled. "A week. Run along, Madeleine. I'll know where you are."

But he always had known, hadn't he?

"Here." He threw her something. She caught it by sheer reflex: a familiar warmth spread to her fingers. It was a small ebony box, inlaid with mother-of-pearl, and she knew what it contained.

"Why?" she asked.

"I would hate it if you got yourself killed," Asmodeus said. His face was unreadable. "But don't think this is a license to continue this foolish addiction. Merely . . . a convenience, until you come back."

Until she came back. If she ever did. But she'd survive; she'd proved she didn't have the recklessness or bravery needed to endanger her life.

She walked out behind Isabelle, with the shadow of Hawthorn at her back and the House's presence in her mind, knowing that she would never again be rid of it.

SOMETIME later—much, much later, when the sun had started to alter its course downward and the light darkened to late afternoon— Philippe must have reached the Seine, crossing the ruins of the Halles, each pavilion clearly delineated in its rectangle of charred ground. He stood, breathing hard, before the Pont-Neuf, in the shadow of the Samaritaine, hearing distant noises of laughter and feasting from the House that occupied its grounds.

Ahead, in the dim light, was House Silverspires. It looked different somehow, less threatening; he wasn't sure how; but then . . . Over the ruined towers of Notre-Dame, burned until only the charred shell remained, something else had spread. In the darkness, it was hard to be sure, but . . .

No, his vision hadn't betrayed him. It was the crown of a huge banyan tree: the towers and the buildings were its buttresses, and its aerial roots seemed to dig deep into the House itself. A banyan. For botanists, a strangler tree; for Buddhists, the symbol of the Buddha's preaching. His people had a different legend about the banyan, though; about Cuoi, the boy who had once seen a tiger mother lay her dead cub in the hollow of the tree, and feed him the banyan's leaves until he had sprung back to life.

A banyan meant rebirth; meant the dead walking the earth once again. Meant that ghosts, perhaps, could be brought back into this world, given enough power; and how much power would there be, in the death of an entire House?

Selene had no means to know this. But did he truly want to warn Selene? Did he truly want to save Silverspires?

No. He didn't. But . . . Isabelle wouldn't leave the House; and neither would the curse—and if saving the House was the price of helping her, then he would pay it.

In the river, dragons flowed like the wakes of boats, sleek and elegant and deadly, and so removed from anything in the world of mortals. One of them looked up at him with intense eyes, the color of dull nacre; he thought he recognized Ngoc Bich, with her broken antlers, but he couldn't be sure. *Come with us, Philippe. Do you truly think you belong here? In any House, in any gang?*

Come with us.

Their song was close to one he'd heard once; to the music that had always played in the background of the Jade Emperor's Court: he could almost imagine himself bowing to a courtly lady, acknowledging an official's respects, back in a world where he knew exactly his place, and how to behave according to it. He only had to find the staircase again; to sink below the waves of the Seine and be lost forever to the mortal world—and it wouldn't be home again; it wouldn't even be the status of Immortal he'd once craved, but it might be something close enough, even with ruin encroaching upon the kingdom. He'd be her consort, and was that such a bad thing?

Come with us.

But on the stairs leading down to the river, the translucent shape of Morningstar stood guard, his wings sharply delineated against the night sky, his large sword held upward without apparent effort. And he could push past the Fallen—he was a ghost—no, worse than a ghost, a memory of a ghost that could no more stop him than a breath upon the wind—but, even in the depths of the dragon kingdom, Silverspires and its curse would still have him in an unbreakable hold. And, even as consort, even as Immortal, he would still remember Isabelle; and how he had failed her.

Come with us.

"Not yet," he whispered to the encroaching night; and turned away from the stairs, to cross the bridge toward House Silverspires.

OUTSIDE, in the gray light of late afternoon, Madeleine turned to Isabelle. "Thank you," she said.

Isabelle shook her head, pulling her toward a black car. "Don't thank me. I need you, Madeleine—I gave Selene something, but it's not what she needs—you have to come—"

"You make no sense," Madeleine said, but she let Isabelle pull her toward the car, where Javier waited, a frown on his face. "Good to see you again," he said. "Let's go."

She asked for explanations in the car; but Javier was distant, and Isabelle uncommunicative.

As they approached Silverspires, she held her breath. The cloud over it had now extended tendrils all the way into the cathedral; and there was something around the ruined towers, a canopy of . . . leaves?

"You have to explain," she said, playing with the box of essence.

"I don't have all the explanations," Isabelle said. "But the House is dying."

Dying? She'd left it in bad shape, granted, and Asmodeus had seemed so sure it was about to fall, but . . .

"Trust me," Isabelle said, and half dragged her, half pushed her into corridors overrun by huge roots and branches. There was an open door; and before she could realize it was Selene's office, now invaded beyond recognition, Isabelle had pushed her in.

It was empty; or almost so: Emmanuelle turned as they entered, surprised. "Madeleine? I thought—"

Madeleine felt the presence of Hawthorn in her mind, a weight dragging her down. "Emmanuelle? Where is Selene?"

"Overseeing the evacuation," Emmanuelle said; and in the face of Madeleine's blank stare: "You came in through the North Wing? If you'd gone to the other side, you would have seen everyone else. Everyone still alive, that is."

"I—" Madeleine took a deep breath, struggling to balance her sense of panic. "I thought—"

"This is a dying House," Emmanuelle said. Her smile was bitter. "But she hasn't won yet, not if I can help it. Selene's first duty is to her dependents, but I—I have no such compunction."

Isabelle was looking left and right, frantically. "Where are they?"

"The wings?" Emmanuelle took a deep, slow breath; let it out again. "Morningstar took them and went inside, to open the way. You just missed him."

Morningstar? But Morningstar was dead. Surely . . .

"Then I'm too late." Isabelle slumped. "It can't have worked, the power I infused them with. I brought Madeleine because she'd know how to do it properly. Emmanuelle—" She almost looked as though she was pleading, but without the tone that Madeleine would have associated with that. She looked and spoke as though she was head of the House.

Asmodeus had asked, *"So you set yourself up as his heir, do you?"*

The heir of Morningstar; but there was only one heir, and she was head of the House.

"That's a dangerous position to occupy."

Selene would be livid. Then again, Selene had no part in what they were now doing.

Emmanuelle said, "You got my message?"

"You know messages aren't that clear," Isabelle said. "Merely an intimation to come back, and that there was something here for me."

"Yes," Emmanuelle said. "Selene had a mission for you."

Madeleine merely stood, and listened; everything sliding past her. The box Asmodeus had given her was warm in her hands. "It can't be this easy—"

"Of course not. Morningstar . . . should provide you with time."

"With a distraction, you mean," Isabelle said. "Did Selene expect him to survive?"

Emmanuelle's voice was low, bitter. "She did what had to be done."

Isabelle said nothing for a while. At last, she said, and her voice was cold, and wholly unlike what Madeleine remembered, "Blood and revenge and death. She is truly head of the House."

"Of course." Emmanuelle sounded exhausted. She opened her hand: in it was a small, blackened thing. "You didn't ask what Selene wanted of you. You will take this to the heart of the tree, and kill the curse. If it can still be done."

Isabelle looked at it, intently. "Why are we not going through the parvis? That would be simpler, wouldn't it?"

"Because the door of the cathedral is where we're evacuating," Emmanuelle said, "and we'd rather not have a fight conducted among our refugees."

"I see." Isabelle bit her lips. "It might work."

"It might not," Emmanuelle said.

"Of course it will. I will come back," Isabelle said, carelessly. "But I have accounts to settle, first."

With a ghost. With someone she had never known, except that this same someone had doomed Philippe; and turned the House she had always thought of as a refuge into—this.

Emmanuelle held Isabelle's gaze for a while; at length, she nodded. "For the good of the House," she said. She reached out into one of the drawers, and picked up a small knife. "Here. You'll need this as well." And as she handed the knife and the mirror to Isabelle, she added, "You've changed."

"I've had to," Isabelle said. She bit her lip. "Like wildfire—if I let go for even a moment . . . ," she whispered; and for a moment she sounded bewildered and lost, once more the Fallen Madeleine had taken under her wing. "I'm sorry, Madeleine. But you should go."

Emmanuelle was already halfway to the door. "Madeleine?"

Madeleine remained standing where she was. She couldn't have told what moved her now: the melody of Hawthorn within her mind, the memories of Isabelle; the pain in her hip and in her ribs that would never truly go away? *"Try not to get yourself killed,"* Asmodeus had said, knowing that she would be safe. She was not one for rash decisions. She—"I'll go with you," she said.

Isabelle smiled. "Are you sure?"

Madeleine shook her head. "No. But it's as good as anything. But I wasn't sure about the dragon kingdom, either, was I?"

Isabelle forced a smile. Charge in, and then see later. As if that had worked out well: the root of all their problems, Selene would have said, her voice acid.

But Selene wasn't there, anymore; forced out of her own House and her own office by the magic of revenge. "Let's go," she said; and walked out of the room, refusing to look back.

TWENTY-THREE
THE PLACE OF REBIRTH

THE corridors were empty, overrun by the huge, fibrous roots Madeleine had already seen—though in places, huge chunks of them had been removed, leaving easy passage.

"Morningstar," Isabelle said, curtly.

"You're going to have to explain this."

Isabelle shook her head. "I can't really explain. He was dead, and then he was not."

Like Elphon, Madeleine thought; and shied away from the implications. Asmodeus could resurrect his own Fallen from within Hawthorn, but surely he couldn't . . .

She touched one of the cut places; sap dribbled down, wet and sticky: it pulsed with a slow heartbeat, like some huge being; and the warmth of her hand was magic. The magic of the tree; or that of the House? Behind the roots, she could see cracks in the wallpaper; no, cracks in the wall itself. "It's choking the House," she said.

"I know." Isabelle's face crumpled, became harsher, as if she were thinking of something unpleasant. "Destroying everything that is Silverspires. I—I will not stand for that. Come, Madeleine."

They ran, in the flickering light provided by Isabelle's skin; though, as they went deeper and deeper into the House, the light grew and grew, until it seemed to Madeleine they were moving within Heaven itself—until, between the roots, she caught glimpses of graceful tiered arches; of the golden glimmer of icons on painted domes; and the hint of music, harp and violin and voices that squeezed her heart into bloody tatters.

The City.

Bright and terrible, and wholly out of this world; the warmth around her reminding her of Asmodeus's touch on her skin, as his passionless voice explained why he had saved her life; why he had not cared, and would never care.

Bright and terrible; like Isabelle, like Morningstar. Were all Fallen like this, with the harshness of their Fall at the core of their being? No wonder they were merciless, and cruel, if that was all they saw and remembered. . . .

Isabelle had stopped in the middle of an intersection of corridors. The light around her was tinged with the green of the East Wing. Morningstar, or whoever he really was, was taller than her, and the humanoid-shaped hole he had left on his swath of destruction to the heart of the cathedral surrounded her like the sarcophagus of a mummy—slightly larger than her, perfectly shaped—even taking into account the shadows of wings at her back.

Morningstar's heir.

Madeleine was already running out of breath; not that she'd had much to start with. They hadn't seen anything so far; merely the silence of the grave; and even the tree itself seemed to have been shocked into stillness. Whatever Morningstar had done . . .

Selene had sent him ahead as a distraction. There was no other interpretation possible—she had known, sending him, that there was only one possible outcome to his charging in alone—even with all the magic the House could spare at his back.

"Are you all right?" Isabelle asked.

"I don't know," Madeleine said. She leaned on one of the descending roots to catch her breath, felt the warmth leeched from the House; and withdrew her hand.

She was Hawthorn's now. It was no longer her business.

There was a sound around them; a huge tightening of something, so hard that the walls audibly cracked. "What was that?" Madeleine asked.

"Something that has no right to happen," Isabelle said coldly. "Come on, it's this way."

The cathedral had changed. Instead of pillars, a host of fluted trunks; and an impassable canopy of branches and leaves masking the view of the Heavens. Here there were few or no cuts from Morningstar's wings; but also enough space for them to wend their way through the maze of roots and trunks and green leaves. The smell of a tropical jungle became overpowering: loamy earth and the peculiar sharpness that comes after the rain. Madeleine's hands tightened around the box; should she inhale its contents? No, she wasn't going to give Asmodeus that satisfaction.

Over the altar was the largest trunk of them all, covering seemingly everything from the throne to the entrance to the crypt. But Madeleine had no time to take it in, because the trunk was halfway open; and someone stood there, bending over a body.

The body was Morningstar's. Even though she hadn't seen him since he came back to life, there was no mistaking the fair hair, or the serrated wings that the other person was busy removing from him.

In front of her, Isabelle's light grew harsh. "Stop!"

The other rose, taking the wings with her; dropped them, as if they were fundamentally distasteful. "You fool," she whispered, and her voice carried under the vault. "Did you really think they would serve you, in the end?"

Then she turned, and looked at Isabelle.

She was small, and thin; her hair a dull, mousy brown; her eyes wide in the delicate oval of her face, with the same familiar harshness to her features that Madeleine had seen in Isabelle and Selene. She wore a simple white shift, reminiscent of the robe of altar boys; leaves were still caught around the collar, and scattered twigs clung to the hem above her bare feet.

"That is unexpected," she said. She walked downstairs, leaving Morningstar behind her. Her gaze raked Isabelle and her from top to bottom, leaving Madeleine with the distinct impression they'd been found wanting. "Is this what the House sends to defend itself? You're too late."

"Nightingale," Madeleine whispered, and the woman smiled.

"I'd thought it would be someone I would remember."

I don't, Madeleine thought. *I wasn't even there when you died. I—damn it, can't the dead remain where they are, safely away from us?*

"You have no right." Isabelle walked toward her; stopped, in a perfect triangle with her, Morningstar's body and Nightingale.

Nightingale's gaze swung toward her. "Right? You do know what he did, don't you? I would hate to think his House produced someone so naive."

Isabelle drew herself to her full height. "It's not his House any longer."

"It's Selene's." Nightingale's gaze moved, rested on Madeleine. "Don't look so surprised. I don't come into this world like a blameless fool. I'm no Fallen."

No, that she patently was not. How much did she know? Was it through the Furies, through Philippe, or something else entirely? She had been born of the House's magic: their own sword, turned against them; Morningstar's own sins, brought back full circle; and she would not be stopped.

Except . . . Behind her, to the right, lay the discarded wings; and Isabelle had claimed her right to inherit Morningstar's mantle. If anyone could stop her . . .

Madeleine took a step forward, her heart hammering against her chest. Before she could think on what she was doing, she raised the box to her face; and, opening it in one swift movement, inhaled its entire contents.

It was like inhaling liquid fire: an irrepressible feeling of suffocation that rose in her, sending her to her knees, struggling to breathe—even as warmth exploded in her chest, spread to her arms and legs—and climbed upward, a stab like a spike driven into her brain, whiting out her vision for a bare moment.

When she opened her eyes again, Nightingale had moved; was standing almost over her. Madeleine pushed herself upward, stood. Nightingale watched her, unmoving. "So you set yourself to fight me, then?"

No, no, no. She wasn't that much of a fool. Isabelle had to understand, had to get the message. "Someone has to stand against you. I wish it wasn't me, but there is no one else." Each word she spoke hurt, lodged against her tongue and palate like serrated blades, like flame butterflies. If she moved too fast, or spoke too soon, she was going to burst; so much power within her, so much raw potential. Once, she would have felt safe, away from Asmodeus, but now she had Hawthorn at the back of her thoughts; and she stood in the destroyed heart of Silverspires, facing a dead woman come back to life. There was no safety left to her.

There had been no safety for such, such a long time.

"I see," Nightingale said, and reached out, power blossoming within her. Madeleine stepped aside, instinctively raising wards that the power tore to shreds. She wasn't made for this: she wasn't Isabelle; she wasn't Selene or any other Fallen. She was an *alchemist*, not a fighter!

She tried to see Isabelle, but Nightingale blocked her field of vision, smiling. "You're not much of a challenge."

She had to—Madeleine reached within her, felt something shift; and magic flowed through the floor, raising little bumps like a hundred fingertips poking through the stones. Nightingale stepped aside, but not in time: she stumbled, mouthing a curse, and leaves scattered from her shift.

Her response was a cold wind, flowing through the trees. Madeleine dived behind one of the fluted trunks, but the wind tore through it: her fingers were locked into place, and everything was frozen within her.

Where was Isabelle—she couldn't keep this up for long; she'd never been trained . . .

Nothing. Silence.

She bent around the trunk; and saw, like a response to her prayers, that Nightingale's attention had shifted to Isabelle; who was straightening from her crouch, with Morningstar's wings spreading wide behind her.

She was bright, and terrible: light streaming from her skin, her presence so palpable, so vivid, a pressure in the air that made Madeleine want to prostrate herself; for what else could she do, before Morningstar's heir? Behind her, the wings fanned out, as sharp as sword blades, and she had picked up a knife from the wreckage: Morningstar's knife, or perhaps the one Emmanuelle had given her in Selene's office?

Nightingale was watching her, a mocking smile on her face. "Commendable," she said. "But not, I think, enough, in the end."

She flung her arms outward; Isabelle moved faster than Madeleine had thought possible and was almost upon her, the wings scraping against the trunks, leaving deep gouges as they did so. Nightingale dodged, and sent a trail of fire streaking through the air, which Isabelle caught in her hands and flung away. . . .

Madeleine, watching them, was reminded of nothing quite so much as dancers, moving with inhuman fluidity, as if to a rhythm only they could hear, some slow and ponderous music played on a now defunct organ.

She crawled, instead, to Morningstar; fearing, with each jolt, that the magic within her would tear her apart. It would fade, eventually, the sense of coiled fire within her sinking down to dull embers; leaving her once more craving its touch, once more staring at the aimlessness of her life. It would go away. All she had to do was wait.

Neither Isabelle nor Nightingale paid her any attention, too engrossed in their fight. Nightingale's fingers were moving fast, as if playing on piano keys, and Isabelle was leaning on a tree trunk, breathing hard, eyes closed, while frost coalesced around her fingers. . . .

Madeleine had seen Morningstar in life, a long time ago. In death he looked almost ordinary, his hair the color of freshly cut corn, his hands long-fingered, with nails that curved almost like claws; his skin with a faint glow, not like Oris, whose corpse had lost its luster . . .

No. Wait. Fumbling, Madeleine looked for the heartbeat in the wrist and in the chest—then gave up and called on the magic within her. It rose, wringing her lungs out like a cast-off floor cloth: a jolt that traveled from her heart to her fingers; and, as she touched Morningstar's wrist, she felt the magic earth itself; felt the slow, regular heartbeat under her fingers. Alive, then. Barely so, if it took magic to hear it.

There were healing spells; and ways to keep him farther away from death's door. She knew none of them; only Aragon's gloomy warnings that one did not meddle with human or Fallen biology. Anything she did risked making matters worse. But—she raised her eyes. Nightingale and Isabelle were fighting a little farther away from her, throwing magic at each other with abandon. Isabelle's face was flecked with sweat; Nightingale's hadn't changed as she flung trails of fire at Isabelle.

Isabelle, obviously weary of the spells exchanged, lunged at Nightingale: once, twice, the wings following her every movement. Nightingale dodged two moves that should have slashed her from shoulder to hip, smiling. "Is this all you have?" she asked.

"You have no idea." Isabelle shook her head. "This is my House. The place that took me in, that gave me space to grow and learn and be safe. I—will—not—lose—it." Her knife sliced; Nightingale leaped away again, and the knife scraped against the edge of a ward she'd put up. She was smiling, not even out of breath.

"You forget. It was my House, too." She extended both hands; looked at Isabelle, her gaze intent, her eyes two huge black holes in the oval of her face. "Just as it was yours." Her hands shot forward; the air seemed to crumple in front of her; and she drove them, effortlessly, into Isabelle's chest.

Isabelle froze. She stared at Nightingale, her eyes widening, slowly glazing over. Her mouth opened, but no sound came out.

No, no, no.

Slowly, gracefully, Isabelle fell back; and a spray of blood fell forward, onto the stones of the cathedral.

No.

Madeleine rose, and ran, screaming, the magic streaming out of her, uncontrollable—fully expecting to have to fight Nightingale, too; and to fail as Isabelle had failed, to fall as Isabelle had fallen. . . .

But when she reached the body, Nightingale was already gone, walking away without a backward glance toward the entrance of the cathedral; the roots opening in front of her in an obscene parody of the sea parting before Moses's staff. Madeleine knelt, shaking, pouring all the magic she had left into Isabelle's body, trying to find a way, any way, to heal her.

Nothing happened. A glance should have told her—as she looked up, weak, trembling—that it was useless, that no one recovered from two bloody holes of that size in the chest. Isabelle's eyes were wide-open, vitreous; her breath inaudible; her skin already losing its luster, becoming gray and fragile and mortal.

No, no, no.

Fallen outlived mortals. Apprentices outlived teachers, not the other way around; and Madeleine had lost so much already, so many people in her care. She . . . It wasn't fair.

The last of the magic left her; now it was just her and her meager skills, trying to shake some life into a corpse. Trying to make Isabelle move, to make her say something, anything. *Please, please, please, let there be a miracle.*

Useless, all of it. As it had always been.

Madeleine knelt on the cold, hard floor between the fluted trunks, and wept.

PHILIPPE was halfway across Ile de la Cité when he felt it. He was crossing a deserted avenue, heading in the vague direction of the Hôtel-Dieu or the parvis—hard to tell, at night—when Isabelle's presence in his mind flickered and weakened, and went out like a snuffed candle.

He stopped, then. The bond between them was strong, sealed in Fallen blood, and nothing should have been able to remove it.

Nothing, save one.

No. That wasn't possible. He took in a slow, trembling breath; and heard only silence in his mind. Gone. She was gone; back to the City she'd had so few memories of, or to whichever destination awaited Fallen, after their time on Earth was done. He hoped she got the answers she'd craved for in life; or the rest that had been denied to her.

He—he needed to keep moving, to find Emmanuelle or Selene or someone who would have some idea of what was going on; to warn them about Nightingale. He needed to— But for the longest time, he simply stood rooted to the spot, watching the darkened skies above him blur; like rain running down a glass pane until the entire world seemed to have vanished into a maw of grief.

SELENE sat in the center of the market's square, listening to Javier report on the evacuation of the House. Everyone appeared to have made it out, which was a relief.

"So he went in."

Emmanuelle grimaced. "Yes. That worked, it seems."

"Yes." They both knew what that meant; and she had no regrets. "And the rest—"

"I don't know."

The House's magic was flickering and weak in Selene's mind. Earlier, she had heard the cracks as the roots tightened around the walls, and felt the magic slowly squeezing out. Like a pressed lime: it would have been an incongruous comparison, if only it hadn't been her walls; if she hadn't seen, in her mind's eye, the familiar corridors bend out of shape, the furniture in her office crack into a thousand pieces, the beds in the hospital heaving and shattering . . .

Aragon would have been angry; but then, Aragon, not bound to the House, had left them. She couldn't blame him; though part of her wished he had stayed. She certainly could have used his help.

Even if it did work—even if they could banish the curse—the House would still be as it was: all but destroyed, its magic gone, channeled into the roots of that huge tree, into all the damage the curse had wrought.

Some leader she was.

"You look gloomy," Emmanuelle said.

Selene forced a smile. "Of course not," she said, because Javier was listening. "Come on, let's go and see everyone."

People had settled where they could on the market square. Some bright enterprising soul, probably Ilhame, had rigged up a huge tent from metal poles and a few sheets. Selene spoke with those she saw, dispensing reassurance where she could, forcing a smile she didn't feel, mouthing platitudes about the future of the House. She reassured them that the protections still stood; barely, but they were still within the wards, and the House was, if not a building, still a shield that kept them safe from the others.

Not that anyone, save scavengers, would be interested in Silverspires now.

She found Choérine minding the children, who were possibly the only ones finding the evacuation fun: half of them were playing tag in the shadow of the East Wing, and the other half, toddlers still, chasing a ball. She forced a smile when Selene arrived. "It's been a trying time. I have half the parents out of their minds with worry, and the children feel it. It's difficult to distract them."

"I know," Selene said. "Believe me, I know."

She kept a wary eye on Emmanuelle, who had found Caroline and a group of other children—the little girl had pelted straight for her, dragging Emmanuelle back to the circle where she and her friends had piled a dozen books—all they must have been able to grab in the evacuation, and even then it must have been a heavy load—God only knew how Caroline had managed to talk them into them. Caroline was proudly waving a book at Emmanuelle, and saying it would be all right, that they had managed to save some of the books and the library would be fine. Selene looked away then, not willing to see Emmanuelle's face.

"At least we're all alive," Choérine said. She didn't sound happy about it, or cheerful.

"We'll rebuild," Selene said; and paused then, seeing the crowd part ahead for something she couldn't quite see: not what she had expected, because whatever it was came from the side of the island opposite the cathedral. "Excuse me a moment, will you?"

As it turned out, she didn't have to wait for long, because he was making straight for her.

"Well," she said, staring at Philippe.

He looked as though he'd been through Hell and back, his clothes black with soot and torn in places, his eyes ringed with deep, dark circles; but he still stood in front of her with the bearing of a king, utterly unapologetic—he had destroyed them, and he didn't care; he had never cared. "You dare come back here."

Philippe shook his head. "That's not important. Listen, Selene—"

"Not important?" Her hand moved, encompassed the wreck around her. "*This* is what we are now, what we are reduced to. All your fault."

His gaze was steady. "I meant no harm."

"You did it regardless."

"Oh, for Heaven's sake," Philippe said. "We can argue about responsibility later, Selene. Listen." His words came fast now, one after another with hardly a breath, his voice expressionless. "Isabelle is dead. The banyan is a tree of rebirth—it took the magic of the House and used it—"

"Isabelle?" Selene asked, her heart sinking, just as Emmanuelle asked, "Rebirth?"

"Yes. You have to—"

But in that moment, the cathedral exploded.

A huge noise deafened Selene; she dived, reflexively, even as bits and pieces of the tree were sent into the air. She barely had time to see Emmanuelle put up wards around herself; she reached out, raised her own in a wider circle, hoping there wouldn't be too many people in their path; and then the world was a welter of dust and flying things, and she couldn't see anything, anymore.

She rose, slowly; reached for the mirror at her belt, inhaling the stored breath until magic coursed through her veins again. Then she turned toward the cathedral.

Notre-Dame's doors were gaping holes, surrounded by dying roots. And in their center . . .

Selene recognized her immediately, though it had been many decades. She had barely changed, in the sense that her physical features were the same: that same harsh cast to her face, those same huge, driven eyes that gave the impression of seeing straight into your soul. But other things had changed: her skin now held trapped light, as though she were a Fallen; and she moved with fluid, inhuman grace as she walked to the edge of the parvis, surveying the devastation she had wrought.

Her gaze met Selene's, and she smiled. "Hello, Selene."

Selene walked, slowly, toward her, the world reduced to nothing but the hammering of her heart, like a hummingbird's wings straining against a cage of ribs. "Hello, Nightingale."

TWENTY-FOUR
HEAD OF THE HOUSE

THE huge explosion had deafened Madeleine, but it had turned out to be nothing more than the doors blasting open. Dust had risen thick around her, a cloud that racked her lungs. Now it was subsiding, leaving her barely enough light to guess at the shape of Isabelle's corpse.

Isabelle.

She had gotten Madeleine out of Hawthorn; even if it was only for a moment, even if it was only a loan. She had known about the angel essence; about the addiction; and had still come back. Had still believed in Madeleine's skills as an alchemist; in her as a teacher and as a mentor, and as a friend.

And in return, what had Madeleine done for her?

Nothing.

If only she'd had more time . . .

But it was a lie. One made do with the time one had; and this—from the beginnings in Hôtel-Dieu to this unbearably warm jungle—was all they had been given.

She had failed Oris. She had failed Isabelle. And—she had failed Silverspires, too, in the end; had given the House nothing but her slow dying.

Morningstar might not have saved her, but Silverspires had been her refuge and her sickbed for all of twenty years.

Light streamed from the hole Nightingale had opened in the tree's roots, too bright for her to guess at more than silhouettes. Light, like the bright and terrible and unforgiving light from the City—she knew what it was now, what Fallen carried in their hearts, the unbearable knowledge that there was no absolution that would wash away the taint of what they had done; nothing that would reopen the pathways to Heaven and let them immerse themselves in the glory of God.

She closed Isabelle's eyes, mouthing a prayer that the Fallen would find her way home, and rose. Her eyes were dry; her lungs and whole being wrung out, as if she had run for an entire night. She might as well return to Hawthorn: there was nothing left for her here, nothing in the whole world that held meaning for her.

No. That wasn't quite true.

She reached out, and found, by touch more than by eye, the mirror that Emmanuelle had handed to Isabelle. It burned her hand as she touched it, the trapped malice within it almost palpable. If that was only a fraction of what Philippe had unleashed . . .

"Destroy it," Emmanuelle had said, *"in the hollow of the tree."*

She didn't know if it would make a difference, but she had to try.

ON the steps of the cathedral, Selene faced Nightingale. "It's been a long time," Nightingale said, with a wide, insincere smile.

"Indeed." Selene kept her voice low. "And what will you do now, Nightingale?"

"Do?" Nightingale raised an eyebrow. "I have nothing left to do, have I? I've won. Your House lies in tatters."

"No, not quite," Selene said.

Nightingale's gaze raked the market square; the mass of people that looked like a refugee camp. "You're right," she said. "But it won't matter, will it? You'll be easy pickings, Selene. I could destroy you all; but it will be more satisfying to see others do it for me. Then everything Morningstar fought for will be gone."

"Did you hate him so much?" Selene asked; and Nightingale's face darkened.

"You're not the one he betrayed," she said.

"I know." Selene thought of Morningstar; now lying dead and cold somewhere in the bowels of Silverspires. "But he did it for the good of the House."

"And that excuses anything?" Nightingale turned. Light streamed out of her, making her a living beacon against the churning of the darkened skies. "Shall I tell you what they did to me in Hawthorn, Selene? Every cut of the knife, every broken bone, every wound that wouldn't close . . ."

"No more than what Morningstar did," Selene said. The cells had gone dusty in her time; because she wasn't Morningstar. Because she wasn't hard enough, and look where it had got them. "I grieve for what happened to you, Nightingale, but it doesn't give you the right to destroy us."

"Of course it does. The House is based on lies, Selene, on selling its own dependents to further its own interests. Do you truly believe you deserve to survive?"

Justice. Blood. Revenge. Had she been so naive, once? "All the Houses are the same."

"Then perhaps no House deserves to survive." It was Philippe's argument; and Philippe's face, closed and arrogant; and the same desire she'd felt then, to smash his high-mindedness into wounding shards.

"And that would be your mission?"

Nightingale's face was serene. "Who knows? I don't owe you anything, Selene. Least of all accounts."

"No," Selene said. "But I owe you something, Nightingale. Excuses."

"You made them. I have accepted them, but they change nothing. You're not Morningstar; of course you're not. No one can be, Selene. No one can loom as large as he did; no one can hold an entire room to attention by merely stepping into it." Her face was soft then; some of the intensity smoothed away, as if she recalled happier times—as if they had ever existed. Morningstar hadn't been a kind master. "And you certainly couldn't hold the House he built together."

Selene bristled. "I am head of the House." Within her, almost nothing; the magic sunken down into cold ashes, the protections almost stripped away. The House was dead, or dying; and she had presided over its demise; had failed to see the danger until it was too late.

"Oh, don't blame yourself." Nightingale shrugged. "He took us all, didn't he? Saw something in us and tried to remake us into more than we were. Some of us broke; and all of us failed. All disappointments."

She was his heir. The head of the House. But of course she had always known that it was solely because there was no one else; because he was gone and she was the latest apprentice. There had been no designation, no transfer of power; merely everyone looking to her as the nearest thing they still had to a leader.

And what a leader she'd been: truly unworthy of anything he had left her, a child playing with adult tools and burning herself.

"Of course it wasn't you. It was him and his standards no one could live up to. He was firstborn, Selene; the oldest among you, the first Fallen. What made you think you were worthy to even follow in his footsteps? I forged my own path; so should you."

"A path of revenge and madness," Selene said. "Look where it got you."

"Indeed. Look where it got me." Nightingale turned, slowly, taking in the ruined cathedral drowned in a mass of tangled roots and branches; scattering leaves from her white shift over the cracked stone of the parvis; ending her rotation so that she was once more facing the scattered remnants of the House in the square. Selene could see figures moving, picking themselves up from the devastation: Emmanuelle helping a limping Philippe, Javier rallying the guards—but they would be too late. It was here; it was now; just her and Nightingale, the last two surviving students of Morningstar facing each other.

And of course Nightingale was right. Of course she was a failure; of course her fears had always been right. She was a small candle to Morningstar's bright star; a drop of water to the churning ocean; a fallen leaf to an oak tree—a pale reflection of the Fallen who had taught her, unable to even hold the House safe; to hold it together against all dangers; and, when the time came, finding her own ruthlessness too late, much too late.

Of course.

WITHIN the hollow of the tree, everything lay in shadow—none of the radiant light from outside, simply a strong smell of churned earth; and a heaviness in the air, as if before a storm. If Madeleine raised her eyes, she could see the stars through the top of the column: the trunk itself was merged roots with a thin coating of thinner bark between them, a wall peppered with holes where the bark hadn't quite closed.

Just enough light to go by.

Madeleine headed to the ruined throne, circling the gaping hole of the entrance to the crypt. Then she sat by the side of the throne, thoughtfully staring at the mirror.

Emmanuelle hadn't been very precise in her instructions, because she hadn't known how—because she'd guessed some things about the spell, but not enough to understand its true workings. But Madeleine remembered something else—the dance of Ngoc Bich's fingers on the rim, back in the dragon kingdom, a pattern that held the key to opening this.

A sealed artifact, Ngoc Bich had said. Madeleine ran her hands over the surface of the mirror. There was that familiar spike of malice, but also something else: a rising warmth, a feeling she knew all too well. The imprint of trapped Fallen breath. Whoever had helped Nightingale lay this in the cathedral had contributed to the spell that had cursed the House.

A sealed mirror—an artifact infused with Fallen breath and Fallen magic, the same as the ones Madeleine had handled for decades.

She didn't need to destroy it: merely to open it, and empty it of all its magic until it was once more inert and harmless, the curse defanged and spent into nothingness.

It was sealed, of course—Nightingale would not have made this so easy. Sealed and locked, and Madeleine hadn't been able to open it, back when Isabelle had handed it to her. Ngoc Bich had said they shouldn't try; that it would avail them nothing. But Madeleine was there, in the birthplace of the curse, in its only point of weakness. This might, of course, not work at all; but what choice did she have?

Madeleine's fingers moved on the rim in slow, half-remembered gestures—as Ngoc Bich's fingers had once done, the first steps in unlocking it—seeking the place that kept it all together.

"GIVE it up, Selene. No one will ever be Morningstar. You know it."

Yes, she did know it. No one would build the House from nothing; or the city, if legend had it right; no one would ever loom as large as he had done, before he died.

From where she was, Selene could see Emmanuelle, could guess at what she was thinking. *You're not giving up now, are you?*

Nightingale smiled. "See, Selene? I will leave you to your ruins. Unless you want to fight? Your dependent did, and it brought her nothing." She turned away, and started going down the stairs; planning, no doubt, to leave the island and strand them all in the middle of nowhere.

Isabelle. She knew more than Isabelle; but in the end, it would probably avail her nothing. Nightingale had the power of the entire House behind her now; the magic that had enabled her to defeat Isabelle and Morningstar. Because she had asked them to go; because she had known, all along, that this was where it ended.

She ought to have grieved; but there was no space in her heart anymore—nothing but a growing, roiling anger. *The storm is coming,* the Furies had whispered in the crypt.

Yes, it was.

A tree of rebirth, Philippe had said: gathering the magic of the House to allow Nightingale to walk once more upon the earth, the House's destruction the price of her resurrection. Selene could not hope to stand against such magic—except for one small thing.

No one could be Morningstar.

But she was head of Silverspires, and it mattered. Here, now, she was all they had; and that was all the worth she needed. She was their head because there was no one else, and that wasn't a badge of dishonor.

She did what she had to. Always.

And she knew exactly what needed to be done.

"Wait."

Nightingale turned, a half-mocking smile on her face; saw Selene standing, surrounded by magic. "Yes? You will fight? I expected better of you."

"No, not fight," Selene said. "You forget. I am head of House Silverspires."

THERE.

Madeleine's hands, twisting and turning, found a slight yield; pressed it.

The breath trapped in the mirror flowed straight into her—an unstoppable river—so much hatred and rage and malice and suffering—*no, no, no*—a raging whirlwind that invaded her mind and carried her along into deeper darkness, where it snuffed itself out—taking her mind with it.

NIGHTINGALE paused; raised her head toward the cathedral. "What is going—"

In that moment, Selene struck.

At Nightingale, but not where she expected it: not any spell, not anything that could have been dodged or parried, but a primal strike, one that stripped from her the link to the House, as Selene had once removed it from Madeleine. She was surprised at how easy it was: there was no resistance, because Nightingale had never thought that this could be done; that the magic she had stolen would be taken away from her.

"You—" Nightingale stood, watching her. The light was fleeing her, like clouds borne away by the wind, rushing across the surface of the sky.

"I am head of the House," Selene said, softly, almost gently. "This is my prerogative."

"I see." Nightingale raised a trembling hand as one wound, then another, appeared on her: great open gashes that bled only a fraction of what they should have; fingers crooked out of shape, broken ribs poking through her shift.

Shall I tell you what they did to me in Hawthorn, Selene? Every cut of the knife, every broken bone, every wound that wouldn't close . . .

Everything that had killed her, in the end. Selene watched, unmoving, as the wounds appeared one by one upon a body that had no right to exist. Nightingale didn't appear to feel them; or perhaps she had transcended them. Her eyes—her large, piercing eyes—rested on Selene all the while, bright and feverish and mocking.

You would style yourself Morningstar's heir, wouldn't you? Say that you defend everything that he stood for? In the end, I still win, Selene. In the end, your House still teeters on the brink of extinction. . . .

Even when she sank to her knees—even when she bowed her head—even after she had turned to dust, borne away by the wind—her eyes still remained in Selene's memory; and her challenge, too; a reminder that she was and had always been right.

PHILIPPE took the steps of the cathedral two by two; running through the ruined benches, the fluted tree trunks that were slowly losing their radiance, toward the altar and the throne. He almost stumbled on another body in his eagerness; stopped, then, staring at it.

There was no mistaking it, even lying in the debris with his eyes closed, and none of the towering presence that he remembered.

Morningstar. But Morningstar was dead. He had seen the corpse. . . .

Almost in spite of himself, his hands lifted Morningstar's limp arms, bared the black shirt to uncover the skin; and he laid a finger in the hollow of the wrist bone.

A slow and steady heartbeat like a secret music; and, when he bent over the Fallen, there was a slight intake of breath, and the ghost of an exhalation on his face. Alive, then, if barely so.

Unfair. The dead would not remain dead, and yet Isabelle was gone: her presence an emptiness in his mind like an open grave.

Unfair.

He left Morningstar without a backward glance, and went on, to find Isabelle.

Her eyes were closed; she lay on her side, with the bulky wings on her back resting on the ground, looking so much like an angel that he could have wept. He found, by touch, her left hand; and rested his fingers in the hollow where two of hers were missing.

Where to start—what to say? "I'm sorry" didn't cover anything; didn't even begin to hint at what they'd had and how it had ended. He still wasn't entirely sure what had drawn him back to the House, a mixture of self-pride and pigheadedness; and the desire to prove that he wasn't ruled by the curse that still lay within him; and a will, in the end, to help her. To turn back time, and not be the one who had failed her, time and time again, until she turned into the symbol of all that he despised.

"I wasn't fair to you," he said, at last, holding her hand tight in his; his eyes dry and fixed on her still, vacant features. "I should have—"

But he had come too late; and there was nothing he could have done. "I wasn't fair to you," he said, again. Wedging his hands under her, he rose, taking her full weight in his arms; and walked through toward the side door he remembered from his night of endless, bloodied crawling.

He didn't know where he was going; only that he couldn't leave her in the House, where she would be dissected for her magic, everything collected by the alchemist who would come after her: skin reduced to powder, hair cut and saved in jewelry cases, all inner organs weighed and cataloged, every scrap of magic put into service again.

She had done her duty to the House, to its bitter end; and he would give her the rest she deserved.

WITH Nightingale dead, the roots stopped growing and regrowing; and they at last managed to cut away some of them. The hollow trunk of the banyan, though, remained, completely wrapped around Notre-Dame, a grim reminder of what they had survived. Aragon returned, grumbling, as though nothing had ever happened; and took Madeleine and Morningstar, neither of whom had woken up, to the hospital wing.

They didn't find Isabelle's body, or Philippe. Selene gave some thought as to whether they should search further; but Isabelle had died for the House, and Selene didn't feel callous enough to hound her after death. Morningstar's wings were a loss, but one she could deal with.

Ironic, given that she had been callous enough to watch Nightingale die—and sent Morningstar to die—the fact that he had survived it didn't change anything.

Selene walked back into her office, which was a little worse for wear, with cracked walls and unusable furniture, though Javier found her a chair from the less damaged part of the House. She sat down before her broken desk, and stared at the wall for a moment.

Morningstar's heir. Heir to a rotten throne, a rotted House, while all around them vultures circled, eager for their pound of flesh.

Speaking of vultures . . .

A knock at the door heralded the coming of Emmanuelle; and behind her, Asmodeus.

He had dressed soberly for once, with a white shirt and minimal amounts of ruffle; and pressed, impeccable trousers that conveyed quite effectively the fact that Hawthorn had suffered no damage whatsoever in the affair. "Selene. What a pleasure."

"I'm sure," Selene said, sourly. "Do make yourself at ease. I'd offer you a chair, but I'm afraid we're a little short."

"On many things, I should think." Asmodeus smiled. "I won't bother you for long. I'm here to collect my dependent."

"Your dependent? Oh. Madeleine. Emmanuelle told me something of this." She wasn't clear on the sequence that had brought Madeleine back, or what she had been doing in the cathedral—probably running after Isabelle again—whatever her other faults, one had to grant her loyalty to her apprentices. "That's fine by me." Not that she was in a position to raise any objections. But still . . . "Asmodeus?"

"Yes?" he said, halfway to the door.

"I need to know where you stand."

"Why, where I have always stood."

"You know what I mean."

He turned then, his eyes unreadable behind his horn-rimmed glasses. "What do you want, Selene?"

"You know what I want. Space and time to rebuild, without having all the Houses at my throat."

Asmodeus smiled. "You lost a game, Selene, not the war. The days of destroying Houses are over. What would I gain by gutting Silverspires?"

"You seemed quite happy to help," Emmanuelle said, quite pointedly.

"To help you fall? Of course," Asmodeus said. He put on his white gloves again, taking an exaggeratedly long time; finger by finger, with the elegance of a pianist stretching before a concert. "As I said, my position hasn't changed."

"I'm sorry," Selene said, finally. "About Samariel."

His face didn't move. "We declared the matter closed, I should think. But thank you." He turned again toward the door. "I won't interfere, if that's what you're worried about."

"I see," Selene said. She didn't. She didn't understand him at all; never had.

Emmanuelle, as usual, was blunter. "Why?"

"Consider it . . . a whim," he said. "But should you rise too high, Selene, it will be my pleasure to help you fall again. Farewell, until next time." And he left, sidestepping roots as if they were mere inconveniences.

"Do you think we can trust him?" Emmanuelle asked.

Selene took her lover's hand, and squeezed it. "Probably not," she said. The future stretched out in front of her: sorting and clearing the rooms of the House, and rebuilding from scratch what needed to be rebuilt, with the presence of Morningstar always in the background, a mute reminder of what she had done, as head of the House; no better or no worse than what he had done. Perhaps Philippe was right, and perhaps all Houses were equally bad—perhaps they did, indeed, deserve to be wiped from the surface of the Earth.

But this was her House, her dominion, and she would fight tooth and claw for it until her dying day.

MADELEINE'S dreams were dark, and tormented—images flashed by, memories of lying in the darkness emptying herself of all blood; of Elphon's death; of Isabelle, stumbling backward with her eyes staring at nothing—falling, again and again, into the maw of darkness, and never managing to wake up.

There were footsteps in the distance; a warmth that enfolded her like a fire in winter; someone lifting her, the steady rhythm of their walking as they carried her.

"Where—" she whispered.

"Shh," Asmodeus's voice said. "We're going home, Madeleine."

And she ought to have been scared or angry or grieving—but all she felt, sinking back into darkness, was relief that she was no longer alone.

PHILIPPE buried Isabelle near the Grands Magasins. He waited until night had come, so that no one would see him. Then he moved *khi* currents of earth to create a makeshift grave beneath the cobblestones—into which he lowered her body, and the wings she had borne.

He closed the grave, and stood for a while, staring at the undisturbed earth that was her final resting place.

The curse was still within him; the pull of the darkness that had once doomed him. He had been a fool to think that he would ever be free of it: it was his burden to bear, just as her silence in his mind was his, forever and ever, through the ages of the world; a reminder of the task he had set for himself, walking away from the ruins of Silverspires.

He had seen Morningstar; not the phantom of his nightmares, not through Nightingale's bitter memories; but as a living, breathing soul.

Somewhere in this city—somewhere in this teeming mass of

Houses and gangs and other factions—was a way to resurrect the dead. And he could wait until Quan Am finally saw fit to grant Her mercy to a Fallen and give Isabelle the blessing of reincarnation—knowing that she wouldn't reincarnate here, or now, or any place that they would have in common—or he could go out and look for that way; and return to Isabelle what had been stolen from her.

"Fare you well, Isabelle. Wherever you are. I hope we meet again."

He knew they would.

ACKNOWLEDGMENTS

NOVELS, of course, do not happen in a vacuum; and this one went through a number of iterations!

I owe big thanks to Trish Sullivan and Steph Burgis, who have read multiple drafts of this, and supported me along the writing journey.

Many thanks as well to Alis Rasmussen, Kari Sperring, and Rhiannon Rasmussen-Silverstein, for convincing me not to set fire to the entire manuscript while we were in Brittany together. D. Franklin read the book (and other things) in record time and kindly discussed possible fixes with me. My writing group, Written in Blood (Genevieve Williams, Keyan Bowes, Traci Morganfield, Dario Ciriello, Doug Cohen, and Chris Cevasco), provided much-needed critiques right before I submitted the manuscript. Leticia Lara, in addition to being generally awesome, provided some much-needed feedback (and the much-needed feeling that this could be a real book!).

C. L. Holland came up with the awesome title during our brainstorming sessions on Twitter. Joe Monti very kindly gave me advice on publishing and promotional efforts.

I would also like to thank Elizabeth Bear, Mary Robinette Kowal, and Ken Liu for their advice and general support.

Many thanks to John Berlyne, John Wordsworth, and Stefan Fergus for making the right encouraging sounds on the first scenes of this; and the right comments on how best to revise this once I was done with the hard slog of writing it. My editors, Gillian Redfearn at Gollancz and Jessica Wade at Roc, are awesome, and their suggestions really helped put this book into (I hope) much better shape than the one I handed in. Many thanks as well to the Gollancz and Roc teams for their work on the book, and putting up with my newbie questions.

Finally, this book would not have happened if not for the support of Rochita Loenen-Ruiz, who listened to me vent about my inability to produce something I had faith in, and convinced me to put together an old idea of ground angel bones as magic and my abortive urban fantasy set in Paris—and who was beside me at every stage of the process. I could not have finished this without her.

And, as always, thanks to my husband, Matthieu; my son the snakelet (mainly for not crashing my laptop too much when I was revising the manuscript!); my sister for the general support, laughter and geeking over books; my parents and paternal grandparents for the love of reading—and a special thanks to my Ba Ngoai for the myths and legends that underpin the Seine.

Aliette de Bodard is a multi-award-winning author. She is a half-French, half-Vietnamese computer and history geek who lives in Paris and has a special interest in non-Western civilizations, particularly Ancient Vietnam, Ancient China, and Ancient Mesoamerica.

CONNECT ONLINE

aliettedebodard.com
twitter.com/aliettedb

Coming in April of 2017

THE HOUSE OF
BINDING THORNS

a Dominion of the Fallen Novel
by Aliette de Bodard
available from Roc wherever books are sold.